Darling, just go ahead and love your life. Take pictures of everything. Capture the moments big and small that make you feel alive. Tell people you love them. And mean it—truly mean it. Talk to random strangers. Learn their stories. Do all the things that excite you and stop playing small. Stop being worried about all the things that can wrong when the only thing that matters is all the magic that could go right. There is so much life to be lived. So much love to receive. Open yourself up. Bloom.

— ALYSHA WAGHORN

A LOVE LIKE *That*

jenna hartley

ISBN: 9798376843796

Editing: Lisa A. Hollett
Cover design by Indie Sage

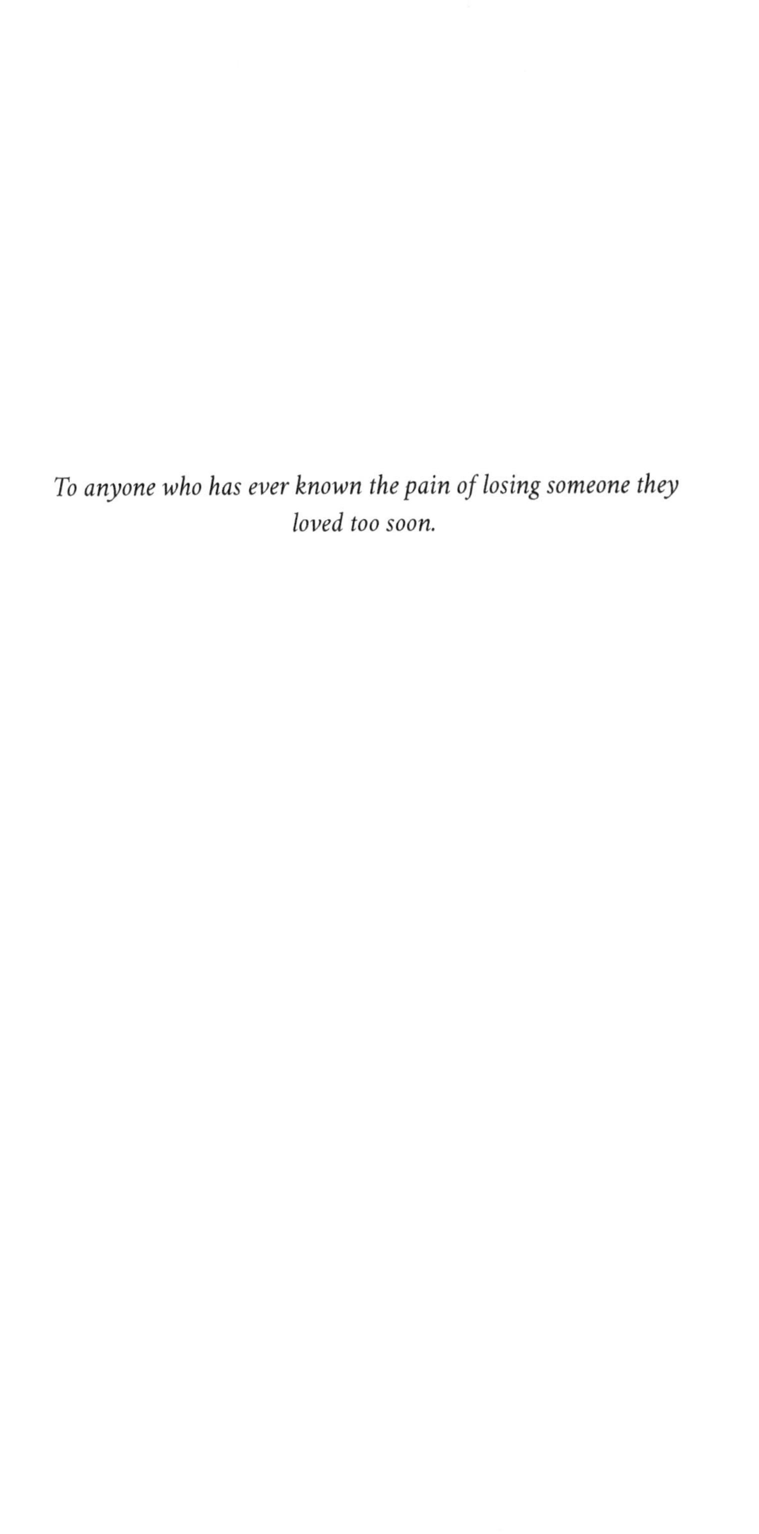

To anyone who has ever known the pain of losing someone they loved too soon.

PLAYLIST

"Ghost" by Justin Bieber
"Learn to Love Again" by Audien
"Fake A Smile" by Alan Walker, Salem Ilese
"Back to Life" (from Bumblebee) by Hailee Steinfeld
"Just as Much" by Delaney Jane, Virginia To Vegas
"I Don't Know Why" by NOTD, Astrid S
"Breathe" (feat. kaspara) by Syn Cole, Kaspara
"Lift Me From The Ground" by San Holo, Sofie Winterson
"There's No Way" by Lauv, Julia Michaels
"Trust" by Jonas Brothers
"One Night" by GUNNAR
"Tie Me Down" (with Elley Duhe) by Gryffin
"This Is Heaven" by Nick Jonas
"Lease On Life" by Andy Grammer
"Corners" by Shallou
"Stars Align" (with Jolin Tsai) by R3HAB
"Sideways" by ILLENIUM, Valerie Broussard, NURKO
"Save Me" (feat. Violet Days) by GATTUSO, Violet Days,
Tungevaag
"Broken" by William Black, Fairlane

"Want You Back" by 5 Seconds of Summer
"Breathe" by Lauv
"Nobody" by NOTD, Catello
"Do It All Over" (feat. Marc E. Bassy) by Cheat Codes
"Fuck, I'm lonely" (with Anne Marie) by Lauv
"Flyby" by Virginia To Vegas, Mokita
"Lost in Japan" (Remix) by Shawn Mendes, Zedd
"Missing You Today" by PUBLIC
"All 4 Nothing (I'm So In Love) by Lauv

You can find this playlist and more at
https://www.authorjennahartley.com/playlists

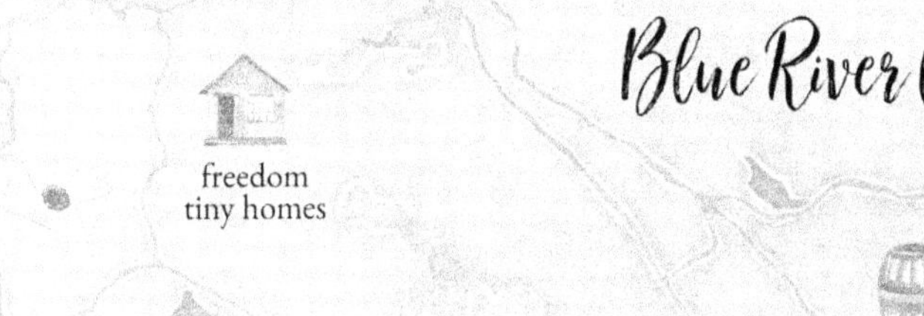

Blue River Creek
freedom tiny homes
pore over
little bird studios
alondra valley animal clinic
Fall River
Alondra
allen landscaping
fall river estates
bibliolater
wildflour bakery
lick
alpaca acres
Cortina
woodhouse spa
St. Cecilia
jenna hartley

CHAPTER ONE

Tristan

With my eyes closed, I inhaled deeply, pulling Tessa closer. The scent of her shampoo filled my lungs, grounding me. I shifted, the sun warming my back through the open curtain, the smell of pancakes wafting up the stairs to our room.

Pancakes?

My stomach growled, and I wondered how Tessa could be making pancakes while lying in my arms, but I didn't question it. Didn't want to. We deserved this moment. A lazy Sunday in bed, laughing around the breakfast table in our pajamas. No soccer practice. No errands to run. Nowhere to be, but together.

Someone jumped on the bed, and the panting alerted me that Rex had decided to join us. I laughed and shook my head, but then he was licking my face and reality was forcing its way in. I wasn't holding Tessa; I was clutching her pillow. And that wasn't an alarm. It was the smoke detector, and it was angry.

Fuck.

I jolted upright and bounded down the stairs in my

boxers, grabbing the fire extinguisher on the way. All the while, my heart was pounding, wondering what scene I was going to discover when I made it to the kitchen.

My only thought was of getting to the kids. But when I skidded into the doorway of the kitchen, I was met with a pan blackened with batter and two sheepish grins.

"Hey, Daddy." Savannah blinked up at me a few times, flour smeared across her forehead and dusting her princess nightgown.

I placed a hand to my chest. Stay calm. Stay calm. Stay— "What the *hell* were you guys thinking?" I roared as the smoke detector continued its annoying cadence.

Savannah hung her head, but Maddox stiffened. He clenched his little fists, anger coursing through his body.

I set down the fire extinguisher with a sigh. "Why didn't you wait for me?" When they said nothing, I added, "You know you're not supposed to turn on the stove without an adult. Right?"

"Yes, Daddy," they said in unison, wearing matching downcast expressions. They were three years apart, but they looked like mirror images of each other. Carbon copies of their mother. Curly blond hair like Tessa's. Curious bright-blue eyes.

I padded farther into the kitchen, grabbing a baking sheet as I surveyed the damage. "You scared the shit out of me."

"Dad!" Savannah chided as I dragged a stool over to the smoke detector. "You're not supposed to say that word. Or…" She scrunched up her nose. "The other one."

The other one?

Who knew what I'd said at that point. It didn't really matter.

"Right." I shook my head, rubbing the back of my neck. I was fucking this all up. I was fucking everything up.

Unable to say anything, I climbed on the stool and started fanning the smoke detector. I needed to do something.

Without being asked, Savannah and Maddox joined me in the cleanup, wiping batter from the counters and floor. How had they made such a huge mess? It looked more like the scene of a crime than pancakes on a Sunday morning.

"It was my idea," Savannah finally said, handing me a bowl. Her eyes were brimming with tears.

"What was your idea?" I asked, forcing myself to adopt a gentle tone as guilt gnawed at me. Why did I always have to lose it?

"The pancakes. We just wanted to do something special for you for your birthday, like Mommy always does. *D-did.*" She lowered her voice to a whisper and said, "She always made you a special breakfast."

My heart sank. My birthday? I glanced at the wall calendar with a photo from last year, my heart clutching painfully at the smile on Tessa's face as she cradled Maddox to her chest. I confirmed it was indeed January twelfth and then squeezed my eyes shut briefly.

"I'm sorry, Daddy." Savannah choked out the words, the tears already falling.

I felt her pain as if it were my own. It didn't matter that it had been nearly nine months since Tessa's death. Sometimes it felt more like nine minutes. And it was days like today— milestones I didn't want to face without Tessa—that made the passage of time more poignant. A wet, hot tear rolled down my cheek. But I quickly pulled Savannah and Maddox to me for a crushing hug to hide my sorrow.

I couldn't breathe. I couldn't…

My chest was so tight, and it was only when they were safe in my arms that I felt like I had oxygen in my lungs. The only reason I was alive and breathing was because of them. The only reason I was able to get out of bed every morning was because *they* needed me—Maddox and Savannah needed me because I was the only parent they had. I had to be both mom and dad now that Tessa was gone.

"You know what I'd love for my birthday?" I asked, reluctant to let them go.

Ever since Tessa died, Maddox rarely let me hold him, show him affection. It hurt, but I tried not to let him see that. I tried to be there for him in whatever way he needed, even if I wanted to hug him tightly and never let him go. He was too young to have lost his mom; they both were. Too young to have to bear so much pain and loss.

Fuck, I was thirty-three. Well, thirty-four now. And I couldn't make sense of what had happened. I couldn't imagine being four like Maddox, or eight like Savannah, and trying to understand.

"What's that?" Savannah asked, perking up.

Thinking fast, I said, "I'd love to try some donuts from Hole in One." It was a new donut shop in town that boasted donuts made from scratch and mini golf. I hadn't been, but the kids had been begging me to try it ever since their friend River had gone.

Maddox frowned. "Daddy hates donuts."

I did, or at least that was the story I told them. Mostly because I had zero self-control when it came to sweets. It was bad enough that one of my best friends was a world-famous pastry chef who loved using us as guinea pigs for new flavors. I didn't need the added temptation of a weekly trip to a gourmet donut shop.

Besides, since Tessa's death, I'd put a stop to all that. Sweets didn't taste good anymore anyway. And if I was Savannah and Maddox's only parent, I was determined to take better care of myself.

If something ever happened to me, I knew Maddox and Savannah would always be taken care of financially. Tessa and I had seen to that years ago. When I'd sold my first company and made millions, we'd put the remainder of the money into trusts for the kids that were untouchable. At least until they were older.

But as far as who I trusted to be their guardian, to raise them, well…it was something I preferred not to contemplate. Though after Tessa's unexpected death, I'd had to consider it more seriously.

My in-laws were a piece of work. My parents were loving and nurturing, and they helped out a ton when they could. But they lived forty-five minutes away, and they were busy taking care of their horses and their land. My siblings lived on the opposite side of the country. And Tessa's sister was still in college. I didn't think Ellie would want to be saddled with two young kids, even though she adored Maddox and Savannah.

"Yeah." Savannah nodded. "I thought we weren't supposed to eat donuts because they'll fog our arteries."

I chuckled despite myself. "Clog, not fog, honey." I ruffled her hair. "Today's a special occasion. I think we can have some donuts."

They glanced at each other as if afraid to get their hopes up. As if my body had been inhabited by aliens or something. Had I really become *that* dad? The controlling, depressing dad, who never smiled, never had fun, never allowed donuts?

Rex barked, pulling my attention from my thoughts. He was darting around, trying to stuff his nose beneath the couch. I frowned and hooked my thumb over my shoulder. "What's up with Rex?"

Savannah shrugged, but then Maddox's eyes went wide. "Oh no! Hedgie!" he whispered.

"Hedgie what?" I asked, scared to know the answer.

Savannah raced over to the cage where the newest member of our family, Hedgie the hedgehog, resided. At least, where Hedgie was supposed to reside. Savannah stilled, and I could sense the panic rolling off her from across the room.

The moment of calm was brief. And then she exploded, her face turning red before she started yelling. "Maddox, I told you not to open the door to the cage!"

"But I feel bad for him." Maddox pouted. "He's trapped in there."

"It's better than being eaten by Rex! Hedgie's not safe out here." Savannah started tossing pillows aside, ducking her head beneath the furniture as she searched high and low for the missing hedgehog. "And neither is Rex."

I sighed and stood. She was right.

"Rex," I called. His ears perked up, and then he ran off in a blur of gray-and-white fur. "Rex. Come back here!"

Maddox's and Savannah's voices echoed off the walls as I chased our mischievous husky up the stairs. I scrambled over some dirty laundry and then cursed when I stepped on a small plastic truck. I grimaced and reminded myself that it could be worse. I *could've* stepped on Hedgie.

Fuck.

What had I been thinking? I dragged a hand through my hair. A pet hedgehog?

"Rex!" I yelled again, hoping I found our dog before he found Hedgie.

I peeked in the guest room, but there was no sign of either of them. Rex was way too quiet. And while Bennett—one of my best friends and the local veterinarian—had assured me the two animals could get along, he'd been adamant about keeping a close eye on them. Especially now, while they were still getting acclimated to this new living situation.

The yelling downstairs turned to crying—Maddox wailing. But I huffed and continued on. I wanted to comfort my children, but first, I needed to find the stupid hedgehog.

Out of the corner of my eye, movement caught my attention. My eyes went wide as I realized that Hedgie was headed for an opening between the spindles of the staircase. Rex, of course, bounded out of my bedroom at that moment, tongue lolling. Hedgie curled up into a spiky ball that I feared would tip over the edge and not survive the landing.

"Rex," I said in a low, authoritative voice, angling my body to keep him away from Hedgie. "Sit."

Reluctantly, he did so.

With Rex's excitement barely contained, I said, "Rex, stay," in a commanding tone.

His tail thumped the floor, and I knew he might bolt at any minute. Somehow, I just needed to get a towel from the bathroom and then grab that ball of quills. All without Rex going batshit crazy.

"Now, Rex," I said. "I need you to stay right there. I'm going to grab a towel, and then I promise to give you a treat."

I could've sworn he licked his lips. I took a few steps to the bathroom, grabbed a towel, and then crouched down to scoop up Hedgie. The moment I stood, Rex was at my side, jumping at me as Hedgie twitched in the towel.

God, I did not want to be poked. *Please, no poking.*

"Down, boy. Down," I said to Rex, while holding the hedgehog above me. "Savannah!" I called downstairs.

"Yes, Daddy?"

"I found Hedgie. Can you please come get her from me, and I'll put Rex outside?"

She ran up the stairs. "Oh, I'm so glad you're okay." She cradled Hedgie to her chest in the towel, mindful of the hedgehog's quills. She was so gentle and nurturing. "I won't let that happen again."

It was in moments like this that I remembered why I'd let her have a hedgehog for Christmas. And for a second, she looked so much like Tessa when we were younger, I felt as if I'd traveled back in time. I wasn't a thirty-four-year-old widower and single dad, but a boy with his best friend. A boy who had no idea of the joy and sorrow that would lie ahead of him.

I shook my head and blinked a few times. What a morning.

Once Rex was outside and Hedgie safely returned to her crate, the kids went to get dressed, and I made myself a cup of coffee.

"Dad," Savannah called. "Have you seen my pink dress?"

I squeezed my eyes shut briefly. *Shit.*

I was supposed to do laundry last night, but I'd been too exhausted to care. We were all adjusting to being back in school after winter break. And between the kids and work and dealing with all the legal crap from Tessa's death, I was overwhelmed. Then, on top of it all, my company's biggest potential investor in the Series A funding round had fallen through.

I just didn't have the desire or energy to give a fuck about anything. But soon, I wouldn't have much of a choice. If I didn't find an investor, Lockwood Industries would fail. All my employees would be out of a job, and they were counting on me.

"Dad?" Savannah called, reminding me that she'd asked a question.

"I think it's in the laundry basket," I said.

I heard her sigh of disappointment from down the hall. "Okay."

"I'll wash it tonight," I said. "Promise."

"You said that yesterday."

I dropped my elbows to the counter and cradled my head in my hands. I'd let Savannah down. I'd promised something, and I hadn't followed through on it. I hated that feeling, and it had been happening more and more lately. And if I couldn't secure another investor, I'd be letting even more people down.

I let out a deep sigh and straightened. As difficult as work could be, I'd never understood the true meaning of failure until I'd become a parent.

I'd graduated from Stanford with honors, no problem. Started my own company. Sold that company, took a gamble, and started another. And yet, being a dad—especially a solo parent—was the most demanding job I'd ever held.

I went upstairs and pulled on some jeans and a T-shirt. Tessa's clothes still hung in the closet. Her toothbrush still on the counter. I'd only removed her shoes from by the door because Rex kept chewing on them. Otherwise, it was as if Tessa might walk in the door any moment and announce she was home. Foolishly, I held out hope that she would.

Even though the doctors had told me she was in a permanent vegetative state and would never recover. Even though I'd kissed her lifeless lips and held her limp hand as they ended life support. Even though I'd attended the funeral along with everyone else, it was still difficult to convince myself she would never come back.

I gripped the doorframe to the closet, taking a few breaths to steady myself. I was still grappling with the fact that I'd made the call to terminate life support. Those had been Tessa's wishes—both written and expressed to me. But her mother had fought me on it all the same.

"You guys ready?" I asked from the hall.

Maddox nodded but said nothing, and I wondered if this morning's incident had scarred him for life. I worried that pretty much everything I did would scar him for life. Him and Savannah.

Ever since Tessa's death, there'd been a noticeable shift.

My once cheerful children had become withdrawn. Maddox rarely allowed anyone to hold him, and Savannah often agonized over the smallest things. I hoped it would get better with time—and counseling—but I hated feeling so powerless.

"Let's go," I said, trying to infuse my voice with some enthusiasm.

I buckled Maddox in and turned up the radio. Despite the upbeat tune, everyone was silent as we drove to the donut shop.

"What's wrong, sweetie?" I asked Savannah when she got out of the car.

She grunted and ground her heel into her shoes. "I think my shoes are too—" another grunt "—small."

Great. Just one more thing I need to take care of.

I'd always appreciated all the things Tessa did for our family; I just hadn't realized the full extent of it until after she'd died. The kids' clothes. The bills. Summer camps and activities.

I didn't know what I was going to do when the kids were out of school, but winter break had shown me that having them home all summer wasn't a plan. I hadn't gotten any work done. It had only compounded the feeling that I was falling short in every aspect of my life.

I was drowning in parenthood, work, and paperwork, and it only seemed to get worse. There were documents to be filed since Tessa's death. Arrangements to be made. A local attorney, Audrey Monroe, had been helping me with all the legal issues.

Now, if only someone could help me navigate life.

CHAPTER TWO

Tristan

Six Weeks Later

I tugged at my collar, scanning the rows of guests for Maddox and Savannah. Harper and Enzo's vineyard was packed, everyone in town showing up for Bennett and Wren's wedding. I finally caught sight of my kids, and my heart softened. Savannah looked so grown-up in her dress and Maddox in his suit. And yet their smiles remained innocent, despite everything they'd been through.

If Tessa were here, she would've insisted on taking a family picture to capture the moment. It was something I needed to be better about—documenting the happy memories. But all I could focus on was the fact that the most important member of our family was missing. Tessa was literally out of the picture, and for the rest of their lives, my kids would have a finite number of images with their mom. No more memories made. No more photographs taken. At least not any that she'd be in.

My chest ached, and I stared up at the sky, wishing so fucking badly that Tessa were here. Since she'd died, it felt as if a part of me had gone missing. As if my heart had been surgically removed.

While things had slowly gotten better over time, I still had so many days I found it impossible to breathe. At times, the grief could be suffocating. Tessa had been my entire world for so long, I'd forgotten what it was like to live without her.

A breeze blew through the vineyard, bringing with it the scents of home. Of the land that Tessa loved and the community where we'd made a family. I watched as Bennett jogged back toward the altar, a huge smile on his face.

I was so happy for him. I knew what it was like to find your soul mate, and I believed Bennett had found that in Wren. But seeing them smile up at each other as they exchanged their vows was breaking me.

I could remember the day I married Tessa as if it were yesterday. She'd looked so beautiful, like an angel. And I'd been so proud to become her husband. To promise my life and my heart to her.

My entire life, not ten fucking years.

Asher nudged me, and I realized the ceremony was over. I'd missed my cue to walk with Wren's friend Sydney back down the aisle. An uneasy silence came from the guests as I forced myself to smile and headed toward Sydney, offering my arm as if there weren't a huge fucking hole in my heart.

"You look handsome," Sydney said, smiling at me.

"Thank you," I mumbled, not entirely sure what else to say. I was barely holding on, while the other guests were smiling and celebrating.

Because life moved on. Everyone else grieved for their friend, but then they went back to living. And I felt very much alone in my loss.

Liam was the only one who came close. Of all our friends, he'd been closest to Tessa. And since her death, he'd been there for me. He listened. But he didn't know what it was like to lose the love of your life.

Sydney and I joined the others for photos, everyone pressing in close. While the rest of the group smiled and laughed, I tucked my hair behind my ear. It was long, longer than I'd ever had it before. Tessa probably would've hated it, but I couldn't bring myself to get it cut.

"Here," Asher said, handing me his flask as we waited our turn for photos.

"Thank you." I gulped some down, grateful when he made small talk with Sydney so I didn't have to.

I took another swig and returned it to him before joining the wedding party for photos. I wasn't sure I could smile and hold it together much longer, but Bennett was one of my best friends and I wanted to show my support. When no one was looking, Asher passed me his flask again.

"Are you trying to get me drunk so you can have your way with me?" I joked, the whiskey warming my throat as the photographer gave us instructions.

Asher took a sip and then pocketed the flask. "You'd like that, wouldn't you?"

I laughed and shook my head. "Nah. You're not my type."

"Is Sydney?" he asked, careful to keep his voice low.

I shifted uncomfortably. "*Tessa* was my type."

He clapped a hand on my shoulder when the photographer dismissed us; the group dispersed. "Maybe you should think about it."

"Think about what?"

"Sex. With Sydney."

I stared at him. "You're joking, right?"

"If you're not interested, do you mind if…" He trailed off.

I scoffed. I wasn't sure whether to be relieved that he was letting me off the hook or pissed he'd suggested I sleep with someone other than my wife in the first place. Either way, it wasn't happening. "Be my guest."

"Thanks." He grinned and took off to follow Sydney, while I turned toward the bar.

My parents had offered to keep an eye on Savannah and Maddox, telling me to "have a good time." What a joke. I was under so much stress I thought I might crack.

I was *still* struggling to find a new investor for Lockwood Industries. I'd taken out a second mortgage on the house last year just to keep the company going. The business was viable, but we needed cash and *soon*. We needed investors who had faith that our good ideas could be turned into a successful, money-making enterprise.

And I needed another drink.

I headed for the bar and nearly turned around when I spotted my mother-in-law, Gloria Curran.

Gloria saw me before I could escape, calling my name as she waved. As always, she looked impeccable. Her blond hair twisted at the nape of her neck. Her dress perfectly tailored. Disdain dripping from her along with all the diamonds she wore.

"Tristan, dear." Gloria placed her hand on my shoulder, and I prepared myself for a lecture. She wasn't just my mother-in-law; she was the mayor.

I could practically see Tessa standing off to the side, just out of view. She'd always had this uncanny ability to mimic her mother's mannerisms and gestures. A smile ghosted my lips at the reminder of my beautiful wife who was nothing like her mother.

"I'm surprised you came."

I scanned the room, praying for an out. "Bennett's one of my best friends. I wouldn't miss his wedding."

"But it's okay to miss family dinner?" She tsked. "Allowing traditions to lapse is unacceptable. They're important. The children need family and continuity, perhaps now more than ever."

I just wanted to be done with this conversation. This evening. This life.

God, that was a terrible thing to think. Tessa would've done anything to live another day, and here I was squandering the gift I'd been given. Though it felt more like a curse at the moment.

"It's not just traditions," Gloria droned on. "There are other things we can't let…slide. I know you've been through a lot, but try a little harder. For the children."

I am *trying.*

I gnashed my teeth but said nothing. It wasn't worth it. Gloria wouldn't listen anyway. It was easier to let her speak her mind and then do what I thought was best. Tessa had always told me that. But Tessa wasn't here anymore, and I wasn't sure I cared what Gloria thought.

"Do you have a specific complaint, or is this a general critique?" If she noticed the snark in my tone, she ignored it. Maybe I needed to lay off the alcohol.

"Tristan," she sighed, as if I were a petulant child not a thirty-four-year-old man. "Your children look like street urchins."

Street urchins? I wanted to laugh at her phrasing. What was this, Aladdin's Agrabah?

But apparently, she wasn't done. "They need haircuts—you too, for that matter. How do you expect investors to take you seriously?"

I ignored her dig at me and glanced over to where the kids were playing, ready to refute her accusation. They seemed happy. And yeah…maybe Maddox's pants were a few inches too short. And—true—I didn't know the last time Savannah had gotten a haircut, but in the grand scheme of things, those seemed so trivial compared to losing their mom.

"I'll tell you what," Gloria said, clearly interpreting my silence as agreement. "I'll book them both in at Mane Street salon and take them shopping for some new clothes."

If it would get her off my back and was one less thing for me to do—great. "Thank you, Gloria. I'm sure they'd enjoy that."

"Excellent." She clapped her hands together and smiled, clearly pleased to have gotten her way. I was more than happy to let her believe that. Though her expression soon darkened. "If only Eleanor were so easy to persuade."

"Eleanor?" I asked, wondering what Tessa's younger sister had done to disappoint Gloria now.

As far as I knew, Ellie was attending college in Australia. Before I could ask about Ellie, Doc Allen and Linda joined us, along with Harper and Enzo. The conversation turned to other matters, but my mind was stuck on Ellie.

"Doc," Gloria said, shaking his hand. "How are you?"

"I'm good. Nice to see everyone for such a happy occasion." He gave me a kind smile, and I wondered if he was thinking about Tessa's funeral. All of Alondra Valley had shown up to pay their respects.

"Yes. Such a lovely couple," Gloria said, almost absent-mindedly. "My Teresa was such a beautiful bride." She sniffled and procured a handkerchief from her purse to dab at her nose.

"She was," Linda said, giving Gloria's shoulder a squeeze. "How's Ellie?"

Enzo drew me into a discussion about the latest improvements we'd made to his winery using the software developed by my company. He'd been an early investor, and I appreciated all his support during launch and as we continued to grow. He was business savvy and enthusiastic. More than that, he'd become both a great ally and a good friend, especially after Tessa's death.

He'd traveled his own path of grief after losing his father. Since Tessa's death, Enzo had shared his journey with me, and I valued his friendship. I appreciated his willingness to listen.

I knew him well enough to suspect he was trying to distract me. And as enthusiastic as I was about the winery's progress, I was more interested in the conversation between Linda and Gloria. They were speaking in hushed whispers, something about "screwed up" and "student visa." Along with the words, "so irresponsible."

Ellie had always been close to Tessa, but I hadn't talked to her in years. Not since she'd graduated high school and moved to Australia. It had always seemed so…sudden. Unexpected, even. I knew she'd been applying to colleges across the country. But to move across the world? I couldn't ever imagine doing it myself. The AV was home.

"As usual," Gloria sneered. "Eleanor screwed up, and now she expects me to fix it."

I frowned, my protective instincts kicking in. Tessa had always watched out for Ellie; so had I, by extension.

Perhaps it was the thirteen-year age difference. Or maybe it was the fact that Ellie had been adopted by Gloria and Dan. But no matter what else was going on, Tessa had always looked out for her sister. Now it was up to me.

Between two kids, a hedgehog, and one crazy dog, didn't I have enough to worry about?

Tessa's blue eyes swam in my vision, and I sighed and turned to Gloria. "What happened?"

"Eleanor's visa was revoked, and now she's being deported."

I jerked my head back. Holy shit. "Deported?"

"She's losing her nanny job, her place at the university,

and she won't be able to finish her degree." She shook her head. "On top of all that, she needs a place to live until she sorts herself out. Though who knows when—or *if*—that will ever happen," she added under her breath.

The way Gloria talked about Ellie grated on me. I didn't understand how she could be so callous and cruel to her own child. Ellie could never match up to Gloria's exacting standards, and she'd never attempted to hide her disappointment.

The more she talked, the angrier I grew. Until I found myself blurting, "She can live with us."

"Oh no, no, no." Gloria frowned, though the movement was barely perceptible thanks to all the work she'd had done over the years. "You have enough going on without adding Eleanor's circus."

"But she's been working as a nanny, right?" I asked, the idea taking shape in my mind. This was perfect—I would get some much-needed help with the kids, get Gloria off my back, and Maddox and Savannah would be thrilled. Win-win-win.

"Yes, but—"

"And you suggested I need help with the kids." And I did —at least when they were out of school for the summer.

"True, but—"

"Then it's settled."

Gloria's cheeks puffed out like a balloon before all the air leaked out of her in a slow, steady stream. I wasn't sure I'd ever seen her speechless. She was trapped, and she knew it.

She dropped her shoulders. "Fine. I'll give her the option."

An option I was almost positive she would take. Hell, I didn't blame Ellie. I wouldn't want to live with Gloria either. I shivered just thinking about it. The woman was like a dragon.

When Gloria got sucked into another conversation, I

continued on to the bar. Savannah waved to me from the dance floor where she was tearing it up with River, Aiden, and Maddox. I grabbed a drink and watched them from a high-top table, Asher coming to stand next to me.

"Gloria give you a little 'friendly advice'?" Asher asked, and I wondered what had happened with Sydney.

I chuckled. "Does she ever not?" The woman stuck her nose in everyone's business. Though I supposed as the mayor of Alondra Valley, it was her job. Sort of. "She always has an opinion to offer."

"Mm." He tipped his head back, downing the contents of his glass.

I sipped my drink before resting my arms on the table. "Ellie's moving home."

"Really?" Asher asked. "Since when?"

"There was a mix-up with her student visa." I had a feeling there was more to the story. Or at least, I wanted to give Ellie the benefit of the doubt.

His eyes went wide. "Oh shit. That sucks."

"Yeah." I nodded, smiling when Maddox spun so fast he nearly fell on his butt. I was glad he was having so much fun. "I offered to let her to stay with us in the meantime."

He started laughing, and I glanced over at him. "What's so funny?"

"Ellie? Stay with you?"

"Yeah. Why?" I lifted a shoulder. "She's been working as a nanny, so it'll be like having another kid around. One who's actually helpful."

He chuckled. "Right. Another kid."

"What? Ellie's practically a child. She's not even twenty-one."

"When was the last time you saw her?"

I had to think about it. She hadn't been able to make it home for the funeral, and before that, Tessa had visited Ellie with the kids while I'd been in the middle of a big launch. It was the Christmas before Tessa's diagnosis, and now I wished I'd gone too.

Otherwise, Ellie hadn't come home to the AV since moving to Melbourne. Flights were expensive, and Ellie wasn't exactly motivated to come home. Not that I could say I blamed her, considering who her mother was.

"Probably her high school graduation," I said. Maddox had just been born, and that time period was all a bit of a blur.

But Tessa had always kept me updated on Ellie's adventures and successes. And before Ellie had left for Australia, she'd been part of our lives.

"So, it's been a few years, then," Asher mused.

What was he so smug about?

"Clearly." I took a sip of my drink, ready to drop the matter.

Asher pulled out his phone and typed something on the screen before setting it on the table in front of me. My eyes widened, and I had to lean closer just to make sure I was seeing things correctly. Image after image of Ellie. At least...I thought it was her.

She was such a chameleon, changing her look in almost every photo. Ellie with pink hair in a matching hot-pink bikini on a beach. I tried to ignore the way my body reacted to the sight of hers. Ellie brushing her hair with a big smile and blue eye shadow that made her violet eyes pop. Ellie in a formfitting sequined dress that left little to the imagination, a mysterious smile playing at her full pink lips.

My mouth went dry, my cock stirring in my pants. Oh shit. She was hot.

And she's your wife's younger sister.

Asher patted me on the shoulder. "Still think it's a good idea?"

Ellie

I stood on the porch of Tristan and Tessa's house, my finger hovering over the doorbell. Cars zipped by on the road behind me. The scent of wisteria lingered in the air, heralding the beginning of spring. I tried to remind myself that this, too, could be a new beginning.

And yet, I hesitated.

I'd spent my whole life in Tessa's shadow. It was only in the last few years—since moving to Melbourne and focusing on my online persona—that I'd finally been able to break away from it. I'd gained followers, cultivated collaborations, made friends, *true* friends.

Like Piper. She had a popular vlogging channel on YouTube and was an Instagram content creator. And her best friend, Sumner. Sumner was a life coach who'd written several bestselling books. Her TED Talk had gone viral a few years ago.

And then there was me. A college student in Australia with a midsize following and a few collaborations under my belt. Well, at least I had been.

Now that I'd returned to the AV, I had to confront the

truth of my situation. Everything I'd worked so hard for the past few years was at risk. My degree. My ability to get into the Japan Exchange and Teaching Program. My entire future. I'd applied to teach English through the government-sponsored JET Program, and I didn't have a backup plan.

My fingers curled in on themselves, and I retracted my hand as I debated my options. I'd been kicked out of Australia. I couldn't live with my parents for the next few months, but did I really want to live in Tessa's house? Surrounded by all her things? Her family?

The thought of Maddox and Savannah's smiling faces erased all doubts from my mind, prompting me to ring the doorbell. Barks came from within, and I grinned when I heard Savannah yell, "I got it!"

A moment later, the door swung open, and Savannah smiled and quickly leaped into my arms. "Auntie Ellie! I love your purple hair! Ohmigod, you look just like a Disney princess."

She said it all in one breath, and it made me laugh. This was why I loved kids. They were always so enthusiastic.

A princess might be a slight exaggeration, though I did appreciate the comparison. I'd tried to apply enough makeup to make myself feel like my armor was in place but not so much that it seemed like I was trying too hard. It was a small town; of course I'd see someone I knew.

"Look at you, getting so big!" I held her tightly, breathing her in. I'd missed this kid. She was good for my confidence.

Her little body relaxed, and she said, "I'm so glad you're here."

Tessa's words floated back to me—life is too short. I'd already missed a lot of my niece's and nephew's milestones. I hoped to make up for lost time these next four months. I hoped to be there for them in the way Tessa had always been there for me.

"Me too, kiddo. Me too."

"Savannah," Tristan's voice boomed. The commanding tone was equal parts intimidating and sexy.

Tristan came into view, holding Rex back by the collar, Maddox peeking out from behind him. "What have I told you about answering the door?" His question was clearly directed at his daughter.

Savannah straightened, hands on her hips, chin jutting out. "I checked the camera, Daddy. I knew it was Auntie Ellie."

He let out a deep sigh, then said, "Okay. Fine."

Rex barked and tried to pull out of Tristan's hold, and that was when he finally seemed to notice me.

"Ellie, hey." Tristan smiled, but it didn't quite reach his eyes. "Give me a sec to put Rex in the backyard, and then I'll give you a hand with your bags."

"No worries," I said and pulled my luggage behind me.

"Hey, Mads." I smiled. He ducked behind Tristan, and Tristan's smile was apologetic.

I shrugged off his concern. I knew it might take the kids a while to warm up to me. I hadn't seen either of them in person in a year and a half, and they'd lost their mom.

I couldn't remember the last time I'd seen Tristan. Several years, at least.

I'd received Christmas cards, of course. But they didn't do the man justice. He was… Wow. Tessa had really lucked out in the husband department. Though that was no surprise. Tessa had always been the luckier of the two of us, at least until the brain tumor. No one had seen that coming. And for the first time in my life, I hadn't envied my elder sister.

"Come on, Auntie Ellie." Savannah grabbed my hand, pulling me from my thoughts of Tessa. "I'll give you a tour."

"Honey," Tristan said, heading for the back door, dog in tow. The muscles of his forearm flexed as Rex struggled to get free, his back straining against the material of his T-shirt. Had he always been so...fit?

He looked at me, and then I glanced away quickly. *Crap!*

"Ellie's probably tired after her flight. We should give her some time to settle in."

"Oh, it's fine." I waved away his concern and tried to ignore my body's reaction to him. "I'm sure I'll crash later, but I'm okay for now." I turned to Savannah. "And I'd love a tour."

She jumped up and down, and I rolled my bags out of the way. Shoes littered the space by the doorway, so I kicked off mine and added them to the pile. Several dog toys were strewn about the carpet, but the house seemed surprisingly clean for having two children living in it. I wondered if they'd picked up in anticipation of my arrival or if it was always this tidy.

Savannah took my hand and smiled up at me. "So, this is the living room."

"Mm-hmm. Very nice." I paused by a crate in the corner of the room with a spiny inhabitant. "And who's this?"

"This—" Savannah beamed "—is Hedgie. My hedgehog."

"So cute."

"Right?" She practically squealed.

I laughed, wondering if this was a recent acquisition. I couldn't imagine Tessa being in favor of a hedgehog, but what did I know? She would've done anything for her kids.

"Here's the kitchen," Savannah said. Like the rest of the house, it was cozy and inviting. The kids' artwork was displayed on the fridge, and a basket of craft supplies spilled over the table.

The backyard, though... I frowned, tears pricking my eyes. Tessa's once lush garden was full of wilting and dead plants.

All this time, I'd known she was gone, at least intellectually. But it was the first time I'd been hit with the realization that she wasn't coming back. Seeing her garden in such a state of disrepair tugged at my heart, and emotion lodged squarely in my throat.

"How's school going?" I asked, turning my back on the garden so I wouldn't cry.

Savannah shrugged. "It's fine."

I followed Savannah through the large laundry room that also doubled as a mud room and space for Rex's crate. A built-in bench had baskets beneath for shoes, and hooks were positioned above where backpacks hung. She pointed out her cubby and then Maddox's, as well as Rex's leashes and food.

"I'm in a class with one of my best friends," she said. "So, that's nice."

"River, right?" I asked, smiling at the thought of her free-spirited best friend.

She nodded. "Aiden ended up with a different teacher, but we all hang out after school. And we're going to spend a ton of time together over spring break, which will be awesome."

I smiled and let her lead me around the house, giving me a tour as if I'd never visited before. When we reached the top of the stairs, I stopped in the hallway, studying the photographs of Tessa and her family. Tessa and Tristan. His hair was a lot longer now, the skin near his eyes etched with concern, but he was a handsome man. They were a beautiful couple—the golden couple, as the town had dubbed them.

"Come on." Savannah tugged on my hand. "Come see my room. Well, mine and Maddox's now."

"Oh yeah?" I followed her down the hall to their bedroom. One side—Savannah's, I presumed—was covered in animal posters. The other—Maddox's—had a space theme. "This is awesome."

"Right? It used to be my room, but Maddox doesn't like sleeping alone. So now we share." She smiled brightly.

I joined Savannah on the floor where she showed me her dollhouse inhabited by small, plastic animals. She informed me that it was a clinic for orphaned animals just like on her favorite TV show, *Izzy's Koala World*.

"I wish your mom and I had been closer in age so we could've shared a room," I said.

"Yeah." Savannah's tone was filled with wistful longing, and I tried to gauge her reaction to talking about Tessa.

Despite a thirteen-year age gap and the fact that I was adopted, Tessa had never treated me with anything but kindness and love. She was the one person in my life who had ever truly believed in me. Had loved me. And now, she was gone.

Savannah's expression changed, and she popped up from the floor. "Your room's just down the hall. Want to see?"

"Of course." I grinned, taking the hint. She didn't want to talk about it. That was fine—neither did I.

"Here's Dad's room," Savannah said, pointing out the large bedroom at the end of the hall. It was tidy, though I did a double take when I saw the nightstand. It was as if Tessa were still alive. Her phone charger, a stack of books she'd been reading, her glasses—all of it was still sitting there, as if waiting for her to come back. Apparently I wasn't the only one who'd been living in denial.

It made me feel both better and worse. Better that I wasn't alone. But sad that Tristan was going through the same thing. He was a good man. He didn't deserve this.

"And here's your room," she said. I swallowed hard and forced myself to follow Savannah across the hall.

"Oh." I chewed on my lip.

"You don't like it?" She frowned.

"Oh no." I stepped farther inside, smoothing my hand

over the patterned comforter. "It's very nice. But, well, what if Maddox wants his room back?" I asked, remembering that this used to be his, though the décor was different.

The crib was gone, and in its place was an upholstered daybed. There was no mobile. No sign that it had ever been the nursery, apart from a few framed pictures of the kids as infants. Seeing it now, it was hard to believe that I'd helped paint it before he was born.

Savannah shook her head. "Trust me. He won't."

"A desk. Perfect," I said, trailing my finger along the top. I'd just need to get a mirror, and then I could set up my ring light and do my makeup there. Between the ring and the natural light, I had a feeling my tutorials and photos would turn out great.

There was a knock at the door, and I glanced up to find Tristan watching me curiously. "I see you found your room."

I nodded and leaned my hip against the desk. "I did. Thank you. I really appreciate you doing this, Tristan."

He leaned against the doorframe and crossed his arms over his chest. His wedding band flashed at me from his left hand, and a piece of me broke for him. For all of them. I'd been so lost in my own pain for too long. Tessa's family was hurting.

"You'll have to share a bathroom with the kids. There are towels in the hall closet."

"Perfect."

"Oh," Tristan said, tucking his hair behind his ear. "I almost forgot. Some mail already arrived for you."

"Great. Thanks."

I followed him back downstairs to the kitchen. Maddox and Savannah went out back to play in the yard with Rex, leaving me alone with Tristan.

"Can I get you some coffee or something to drink?" he asked.

"A glass of water would be great."

He handed me a few envelopes, and I riffled through them until I found the one I'd been hoping for. I grinned and tore it open, eagerly reading the contents.

He set the water on the counter in front of me. "Here you go."

"Thanks," I said, still focused on the letter.

I'd been selected as a finalist for JET. My placement was contingent on completing my degree. And fortunately—at the insistence of my adviser—I'd been able to convince Melbourne University to agree to let me finish my last few courses online.

Despite that major victory, my scholarship had been revoked. There was a clause requiring the student to reside in Australia while obtaining the degree. And so, I'd had to fork over all the money I'd been saving the past two years from various jobs and online gigs to cover the cost.

But I was still on track to achieve my goals. Assuming all other requirements were met, I'd move to Japan at the end of July.

"Good news?" he asked, resting his hip against the counter.

"Very."

I hesitated a moment, then slid the letter across the counter, taking the opportunity to study his face as he read. Tristan's eyelashes were dark, fanning out over his brown eyes. Scruff shadowed his jaw but did nothing to hide the hard angles and high cheekbones.

Gray lined his temples but didn't detract from his appearance. His hair was long, almost long enough to pull back into a small ponytail. Even so, he was handsome. He'd always been handsome. I'd just never allowed myself to appreciate my sister's husband before.

"Wow, Ellie." He grinned, looking up at me. "I had no idea you wanted to go to Japan."

I bit back a smile. "Yeah. Well, I want to be anywhere that's not here," I teased, though it really wasn't a joke.

Moving away from the Alondra Valley had been one of the best decisions I'd ever made. It had given me a chance to explore, to find myself, without always living in Tessa's shadow. Without having my mother constantly questioning my decisions or berating me for my life choices.

She still did it, of course. But it was much easier to ignore her from nearly 8,000 miles away.

"I get that," Tristan said, surprising me.

I jerked my head back. "Really? I thought you loved the AV."

"I did, but that was...*before*."

I nodded slowly, understanding dawning. *Right.* Before Tessa had died.

The moment the plane had touched down in the AV, I'd been flooded with memories of my sister. I could only imagine what it was like for Tristan. They'd been together my entire life. Everywhere he went, he was probably reminded of her and the life they'd shared.

"Why don't you move?" I asked.

He laughed, though the sound was mirthless. "Maybe someday."

I arched an eyebrow, wondering if he'd say more.

He dragged a hand through his hair, and I followed the movement. The dark strands seemed so silky. I envisioned what he'd look like after a trim and a good face mask and... "But I think it would be hard on the kids."

I lifted a shoulder. "You never know. It might be good for them. Moving to Australia was definitely good for me."

"I can tell." He seemed to appraise me, and I wondered if I'd imagined the way his eyes lingered on the bare skin of my stomach. "And now, Japan. Tessa would be really proud of you."

"Thanks." I forced a smile, my cheeks warming from his compliment. "It's nice to talk about her." Painful too.

He nodded, his smile sad but knowing. "It is."

"Anyway," I sighed. "I really appreciate you letting me stay here."

"If anything, you're doing me a favor." He crossed his arms over his chest. "I was just trying to get your mom off my back."

"Oh yeah?" I tilted my head, curiosity overriding my better sense. "Since when does Madame Mayor criticize you?"

He let out a sigh. "You're not the only one she critiques. You know that, right?"

I scoffed.

"You're not," he said again. "Though she's been more vocal about her opinion since Tessa died."

"Aren't you lucky to have such a compassionate mother-in-law."

He lifted a shoulder. "I knew what I was getting into when I married your sister. I'd like to think that Gloria's trying to help, even if her efforts can be a bit heavy-handed at times."

"A bit?" I choked on a laugh. Yeah. He definitely hadn't had the same experience with my mother that I had. But that was probably because he toed the line.

I'd lost count of how many times I'd heard how lucky Tessa was to have a husband like Tristan. What a good provider. An attentive partner and a doting father. If I didn't actually like the man so much, I probably would've hated him.

His expression soured. "She thinks I need help with the kids."

My heart softened. "Do you?"

He hesitated a long moment then nodded. "Honestly, yes. I can't keep up with everything, no matter how hard I try. I'm either letting them down or dropping the ball at work, and it's exhausting." He shook his head. "I don't even know why I'm telling you all this." He blew out a breath, flattening his palms on the counter. "Maybe because I want to make sure you understand what you're getting into by living here."

"What?" I grinned. "You mean it's not sunshine and rainbows all the time?"

He barked out a laugh, and it was good to see him smile, genuinely so. "Definitely not."

I hoped my expression came across as sympathetic and not pitying. "I'm sure you're doing better than you think."

"Even so, I know how much you love the kids, and they you. And since you have experience nannying, it seemed like an elegant solution."

"An elegant solution." I nodded, thinking it was, indeed. "I'm so happy I can help. Just tell me what you need from me." I reached out and touched his forearm.

His eyes darkened, and then the moment passed just as quickly as it had come. But my body was still ablaze from that simple look. I got the feeling that moving back to the AV was going to be challenging, but not for the reasons I'd expected.

CHAPTER FOUR

Tristan

I slid a check across the counter. "For the first week."

"What? No." Ellie ignored the check and pushed it back to me. "I don't expect you to pay me. Letting me live here and spend time with my niece and nephew is more than generous."

I shook my head. "I insist. Please."

"How are you envisioning this working?" she asked, clearly ignoring my offer.

"They're in school now, which is good since I know you have class yourself. If you could help me pick them up sometimes. Help them get ready in the morning, that kind of thing."

She leaned her hip against the counter. "Yeah. No problem."

"You'll have to let me know what your availability is for spring break since it's coming up, and I'm guessing you'll still have class."

"We'll figure it out," she said, and I felt myself relaxing at her confidence.

I dragged a hand through my hair. "And then in the

summer, I'll sign them up for some day camps. Savannah's been talking about an overnight camp, but I don't know if she's ready for it."

"Oh man, I loved overnight camp when I was her age. I know you didn't ask for my advice. But if she's excited, maybe you should let her go."

"Okay." I chuckled. "Maybe *I'm* not ready for it."

"What about Maddox?"

"I need to look into day camps for him—he loves space. And my parents want to take both of them to Disney at some point for a few days."

"Awesome!"

"Does all of that sound okay?"

"Yeah. Of course. I'd be happy to help research camps and sign them up for any you approve."

"Really?" It sounded too good to be true.

"Absolutely." She slid a hand through her purple tresses.

"You sound way too excited by the prospect."

She laughed. "Dorky, right?"

"Nah." It wasn't dorky; it was endearing. And incredibly helpful.

"And if you ever want to go out with your friends or *whatever*," she said, her eyes darting to the side. Cheeks pinkening. "I'm happy to stay with the kids."

Or whatever. Did she mean dating?

The back door swung open, saving me from a response. The kids came running inside, Rex trotting behind them. Ellie crouched down to pet Rex, and her sweatshirt gaped at the neck.

Was that a tattoo?

My eyes were drawn lower still. Her breasts strained against something hot pink and lacy, and I forced myself to look away. What the hell was wrong with me?

Yes, she was attractive.

And yes, obviously, I wasn't immune to it.

My body had been dormant for the past year. Did it really need to wake up now? For Ellie, of all people?

It was wrong. So, *so* wrong on so many levels.

Even so, my eyes kept drifting back to Ellie—her soft skin and easy smiles. She was somehow the same and yet different from what I remembered. She seemed more confident. More self-assured. Or maybe I'd never paid as much attention to her as I was now.

"So…what's on the schedule for the weekend?" she asked.

"Dinner with Mimi and Pops tonight! You're coming too, right?" Savannah asked.

"I, um—"

"Yeah!" Maddox jumped up and down. "Please. Please."

"You have to come," Savannah said. "It's family dinner, and you're family."

Ellie pulled Savannah into her side, but her wan expression told a different story. I had a feeling it had more to do with the prospect of dinner with her mother than exhaustion from all the travel she'd endured the past few days. I understood. An evening with Gloria was draining, even at the best of times.

"I can make an excuse about you being too tired if you want," I offered.

"It's fine," Ellie said, turning her attention to Maddox as he approached her with a picture. She beamed down at his drawing as if he'd presented her with an original Monet. "Thanks to *The Vine*, everyone knows I'm back in town. I might as well get it over with."

I groaned. "Don't tell me you read that trash."

"Oh please." She rolled her eyes. "Everyone reads *The Vine*. It's like the AV version of Gossip Girl. Besides, how else was I supposed to keep tabs on everything while I was in Australia?"

I laughed. "Whatever. I should never have asked."

"Do you know who's behind it?"

I shook my head and turned my attention to the fridge. "No. And I don't want to."

"Oh, come on." She hopped up on the counter, legs dangling. She was so different from the kid sister I remembered. "You're not even a little curious?"

"Nope."

Maddox walked between her legs, and she trapped him. He giggled and tried to break free, and they made a game of it. I wished I could be so carefree when it came to the kids. She'd been here barely an hour, and already, it seemed effortless.

"Want to play outside with me?" Maddox finally asked Ellie. "We can be astronauts!"

Savannah frowned. "Ellie was going to read a book about koalas with me."

The kids started arguing, their voices growing louder every second. I could feel my blood pressure rising. I was trying not to lose it. I didn't want to scare Ellie off when help had only just arrived.

"Kids." I held up my hands. "Let's give Ellie some time to settle in. In the meantime, you can help me take Rex for a walk." And distract him from digging that damn hole.

"Thanks." Ellie ruffled Maddox's hair, and he didn't recoil. He didn't scowl. He…let her. "We'll have tons of time to play, I promise. Right now, I should shower and put on something more 'suitable' for dinner."

I didn't see what was wrong with her outfit. Other than the fact that the sliver of her stomach was distracting. But knowing Gloria, Ellie was right.

I grabbed Rex's leash while Savannah gave Ellie a hug. Maddox and I put on our shoes then he surprised me by running back to Ellie for his own hug. She wrapped him up in her arms, and I swallowed hard before looking away. I just… I couldn't.

I was his father. I'd been here all this time. And yet…

Stop.

This was a good thing—Maddox letting someone in. Seeking comfort and affection. It shouldn't matter that it wasn't from me. Though it was easier to tell myself that than to accept it.

During the walk, the kids talked nonstop about Ellie and all the things they were going to do together. I hadn't seen them this excited in a long time, and I was even more glad I'd invited her to stay.

Even so, I worried—they were already growing attached. One day, months from now, she'd leave. And then I'd be left to pick up the pieces—again.

WHEN WE ARRIVED AT ELLIE'S PARENTS' HOUSE, I PARKED along the curb. The kids unbuckled themselves and headed up the path to the front door, knocking before Ellie and I had even finished getting out of the car.

At least someone's excited to be here.

Ellie was clearly dragging her feet, fidgeting with her top, dreading the encounter.

"Should we have a secret signal?" I asked as we headed up the walkway to the large two-story Craftsman-style bungalow with a red door.

"A secret signal?" she asked, tilting her head.

"Yeah. You know—like you tap your nose if you want to bail."

She tapped her nose.

I chuckled, hoping to make light of the situation. "We haven't even stepped inside."

"And yet—" She tapped her nose again. "I'm ready to bail."

"I'm sure your parents will be happy to see you."

She scoffed. "Doubtful."

"Hey." I placed my hand on her shoulder. "It's just a dinner. One meal. And then we'll go. It'll be okay. Yeah?"

Slowly, reluctantly, she nodded. "I hope you're right."

As we approached the house, I could hear the kids talking with Gloria through the open door.

"Don't you look nice?" Gloria said to Savannah.

"I wanted to look extra fancy because Auntie Ellie's here." Savannah's voice rang with excitement.

Gloria glanced up at Ellie as we joined them. "Oh. Hello." She almost sounded surprised that Ellie was joining us.

Ellie grasped the strap of her purse so tightly, I thought she might rip it. I glanced between the two women, trying to understand their dynamic.

Ellie nodded. "Hi, Mom."

It struck me as odd that Gloria didn't even move to hug her own daughter. She was always affectionate with Savannah and Maddox. Yet, a coldness stretched between Gloria and Ellie that seemed worse than ever before.

"Eleanor." Gloria inclined her head toward the dining room. "Your father is through there."

"Mm." Eleanor didn't make a move to head that direction or even step farther inside the house. For a minute, I wondered if she was going to leave.

"Glad you came, Tristan," Gloria said to me. Then she smiled down at Savannah. "Why don't you go see if Maddox and Pops need any help?"

"Okay!" Savannah said, skipping off.

"Aren't you going to come in?" Gloria said to Ellie.

Ellie hesitated a moment before finally crossing the

threshold. It was almost as if she had to physically push herself over the ledge and into the home.

"Thank you for taking the kids to get haircuts," I said to Gloria, trying to defuse some of the tension.

"Of course." She forced a smile.

"Savannah told me how much she enjoyed your shopping trip. And I appreciate it."

Ellie was looking at me with a mixture of gratitude and annoyance. I hoped she realized that I was kissing Gloria's ass for *her*.

"I'm always more than happy to help. You know that."

Ellie rolled her eyes then bypassed Gloria and headed for the kitchen. "I'll go check on the kids."

Gloria watched her go then turned to me. "Are you sure about this? What kind of example is she setting for the children?"

I frowned. What was that supposed to mean?

"She got kicked out of college," Gloria continued. "Doesn't have a job. And that purple hair is—" She shook her head. "So unprofessional. Who will want to hire her?"

"I would. I trust her with my children, and I think if you look past the purple hair and the tattoo—"

Gloria whirled on me. "Tattoo?"

My eyes widened. *Oh shit.* I probably should not have mentioned that.

"I-I—"

But Gloria was marching off in the direction of the kitchen before I could undo the damage I'd caused. I cringed then sped after her. I was going to owe Ellie big-time.

By the time I'd made it to the kitchen, the kids were outside with Dan. And Gloria had cornered Ellie. Their argument was growing heated, but then I realized it was one-sided.

Gloria was berating Ellie, but Ellie's face was frozen, as if she had no feelings. No expression. I'd seen it happen before when she was with Gloria, and I hated it. It was as if her body had gone into some sort of shock as a protective mechanism.

"A tattoo, seriously? Are you trying to ruin your life? Who will want to hire you now?" Gloria sneered.

Ellie dropped her head, her hands clenched at her sides.

I couldn't take it anymore, and a surge of protectiveness had me blurting, "Enough."

Ellie's eyes flashed to mine in shock. Hell, I'd surprised myself.

"Oh, come on," Gloria sighed as if I were the one being unreasonable when she was criticizing her daughter. "Eleanor has no degree. No experience."

"Even if that were true, it doesn't give you the right to speak to Ellie like that."

Shocked. Stunned. Silence.

I wasn't done. If Ellie wouldn't speak up for herself, I would. "Ellie's working on her degree, and she has a job. She's moving to Japan to teach English at the end of the summer."

Gloria's attention whipped from me back to Ellie. "Is this true?"

Ellie nodded. Why didn't she defend herself? And why did Gloria always assume the worst?

I gnashed my teeth. "Ellie's worked really hard to get into the JET Program." She'd told me about it earlier, her excitement growing the longer she spoke.

"I wish she'd apply herself more toward a master's program or something useful. Not this frivolous..." She sighed, completely belittling Ellie and her accomplishments yet again. "You know, Teresa—" She adopted a lofty tone that annoyed the shit out of me.

"Yes," I cut her off, not wanting to listen to her deify Tessa yet again. Yes, my wife had been a wonderful, smart, caring woman, but that didn't mean Ellie wasn't all those things as well. Both could be true. And the more Gloria talked, the more Ellie shrank into herself. "Tessa was wonderful. She achieved many things, just as Ellie has. And I'm sure she'll continue to do so. Regardless of her accomplishments, she's an incredible person."

I didn't wait for Gloria to respond. I placed my hand on Ellie's lower back and ushered her into the dining room. I kept my attention straight ahead, but out of the corner of my eye, I could see Ellie's mouth gaping open and closed like a fish.

Gloria had never been a particularly easy person to deal with, but our relationship had been strained since Tessa's death. Gloria was bitter. Angry. She blamed me for Tessa's death, when I'd merely been following Tessa's wishes, heartbreaking as they were.

It was as if Gloria had become a different person. Or maybe I'd finally seen her for who she really was—hypercritical. Negative. A perfectionist.

"You okay?" I asked Ellie after Gloria had gone outside to be with Dan and the kids.

"Yeah. I, uh—" Ellie blinked up at me in shock. "I can't believe you spoke to her like that. No one..." She blinked a few times, and I knew she wasn't used to anyone contradicting her mom. Because everyone in town was terrified of Gloria.

"She deserved it."

"Yeah, but—" Ellie placed her hand on my arm and swallowed. "No one's ever stood up for me. Not even..." She let the words trail off, but we both knew who she was referring to. Tessa.

I lifted a shoulder, not wanting to make a bigger deal out of it than it was. "Do you want to leave?"

"Yes, but I won't. I wouldn't do that to the kids."

She gave my arm a squeeze before sliding her hand slowly down my arm as she walked away. It felt as if my entire body had come alive from that touch. And I stood there, staring after her.

The back door opened, and the kids ran in ahead of Dan. He called out a greeting, his attention focused on the large tray of food he was carrying. Gloria shut the door behind him. Her smile was tight, her back straight. I braced myself for a "fun" evening.

We served up the food and then took our seats around the table. Maddox sat on one side of Ellie, and I took the other. Flanking her, protecting her.

The kids provided a good buffer, and Savannah was more than happy to tell us all about her recent field trip to Alpaca Acres. Gloria updated us on town news and gossip. The longer we stayed, the more everyone seemed to have relaxed. Everyone except Ellie.

I hated it. I hated seeing her clam up like this. Withdraw.

From everything I knew about the past few years from Tessa, and even what I'd seen on Ellie's social media profile, Ellie was a strong, vibrant woman. She should never feel belittled or small, especially not by her own mother. I leaned into her so our shoulders touched, wanting to show my support. She stilled briefly then relaxed, her body warm next to mine.

"So, we heard all about Eleanor's and Savannah's career plans," Gloria said over dessert. "What about you Maddox? What do you want to be when you grow up?"

"I want to be an astronaut so I can visit Mommy," he said without missing a beat.

Gloria's attention swiveled to me. I gave her a subtle shake of my head, hoping like hell that she wouldn't ask. But of course, she couldn't just leave it at that.

"Why do you think you'd get to see Mommy if you were an astronaut?" Gloria asked, and Ellie and I tensed.

Maddox played with the edge of his place mat then said, "Mommy lives with the stars. So, if I'm an astronaut, I can go see her any time I want." His little blue eyes were full of hope.

Unfortunately, it didn't quite work like that, but I didn't have the heart to tell him.

"I'm going to space camp this summer," he continued.

"Did you know that astronaut comes from the words 'star sailor'?" Savannah asked, chiming in.

"I didn't," Gloria said. "That's pretty neat."

"And I'm going to shadow Bennett," Savannah said. I was grateful for the change of topic.

"That's nice, honey," Gloria said, never taking her attention off Maddox. "But I'd like to circle back to this astronaut thing. You know that Mommy lives in heaven now, right?"

"Yeah." Maddox took another bite of his ice cream. "That's in the sky."

"It might be, but it doesn't have an address or what they call coordinates for space. We can't—"

"Mom," Ellie said around gritted teeth. It was a warning, and she'd uttered it before I could even fully process the situation.

She wouldn't stand up for herself, but she was protective of my kids. Despite cowering in front of her mother, she'd spoken up for my son.

"I'm just saying," Gloria continued, undeterred. "We can't fly to heaven. It's impossible."

Ellie stood, the feet of her chair scraping against the floor. "You need to stop. *Now.*"

Maddox's eyes welled up, and then he started crying. Ellie wrapped her arm around him, and he let her. He cried into her chest, and the helpless look in Savannah's eyes told me she might burst into tears at any moment.

"Look what you did *now*," Gloria sneered, her eyes on Ellie.

Perhaps I should've listened to Ellie when she'd said this was a bad idea. I just hadn't realized their relationship had become so explosive. I hated it for Ellie, and I hated it for all of us. Tessa would've hated it too.

"Now, Gloria—" Dan said.

She held up a hand. "No. You always make excuses for her, but I will not be treated this way in my own home." Gloria stood from the table, placing her palms on the surface.

"Thank you for dinner," I said to Dan. "It's time for us to go. Come on, kids." I stood and grabbed Savannah's hand, eager to leave before the situation could get any more out of hand.

"That's not necessary," Gloria said, then glared at Ellie. "If anyone should go, it's *her*."

Ellie picked up Maddox, carrying him toward the door. She spoke to him in hushed tones, and I watched them go.

"Daddy, I want to go," Savannah whispered, her voice carrying through the room.

I rubbed her shoulder, trying to remain calm. "Yep. We're going, sweetie." My voice was tight. "Can you grab your sweater? I'll be right out."

She nodded and snatched it from the chair before bolting for the door. As soon as I heard it close, I turned to Gloria.

"That was completely uncalled for." I was so angry, I was practically vibrating with the force of it. "And if you ever speak to Ellie or my kids like that again—" I shook my head, trying not to completely lose it. "Family dinner will be off the table."

CHAPTER FIVE

Ellie

I stared up at my parents' house, still fuming about the whole astronaut thing. I could not *believe* my mother had said that. I couldn't believe she'd crush her grandson's hopes, and his spirit, by telling Maddox that we couldn't fly to heaven, no matter how much we might want to.

I wanted to scream at her. Slap some sense into her. *Something.*

Maddox was four years old. *Four!*

He'd lost his mom and was just looking for a little comfort.

Tristan placed his hand on my thigh, perhaps sensing the murderous turn to my thoughts. "You okay?" he mouthed.

I glanced back at the kids, noting their downturned expressions. Then I faced the windshield and shook my head. No. I was *not* okay. Because those kids were hurting. Maddox and Savannah were hurting.

All evening, I'd held it in. For years, actually. When my mother belittled me and my choices. When she made snide remarks. I'd let so many things slide, but this time, she'd gone too far.

I clenched my fists, wishing I could go back in time and erase that entire conversation. It was irrational, I knew. But I would do anything to protect those kids, and I did mean anything.

Tristan gave my thigh a squeeze then released me, yet the feel of his touch remained. For a moment, I forgot about my mom and focused on his hands. It was as if he'd branded my skin.

During the drive home, I toyed with my necklace—the one Tessa had given me for my eighteenth birthday. It was a gold outline of a chrysanthemum with my name as the stem of the flower. She'd told me chrysanthemums were symbols of optimism, friendship, and joy. All the things she'd said I'd reminded her of.

She'd added a matching gold chrysanthemum charm to the bracelet she'd always worn. I peered out the window and wondered what had happened to it now that she was gone. I hoped Tristan had saved it for the kids. One of her most prized charms had been a disk with Tristan's, Savannah's, and Maddox's first initials.

As we drove through town, I admired the storefronts, studying the new arrivals in an effort to calm myself. Lick was still there, of course. I was going to have to pay the ice cream shop a visit soon. The bookstore, Bibliolater. I'd seen posts about a mystery event coming up, and I studied their window display for any clues. I was intrigued, and I knew the kids were too.

We passed by the restaurant Larkspur. A new yarn store —Get Knotty. And *The Vine* had posted about it and several other upcoming developments, as well as a new "Ask V" advice column. If I'd dared to write in, I wondered what pearls of wisdom V would've had about my mother, Mayor Gloria Curran.

When we got home, the kids asked me to put them to bed. I went upstairs to help them get ready, and Tristan took Rex out. While Savannah showered, I grabbed a pair of Maddox's pajamas from the drawer and set them on top of the dresser.

"I don't want those," he huffed.

He grabbed the space-themed pajamas and shoved them back into the drawer, before grabbing a pair of dinosaur ones. His movements were agitated, and he avoided my gaze.

"That's fine," I said in a calm tone.

"And I don't want to go to space camp."

I sat on his bed and gave him a minute to process his feelings. When he seemed a little calmer, I asked, "Is this about what Mimi said? About your mom?"

"No. I just—" He huffed. "I think it's dumb. Space is stupid."

"What?" I bugged out my eyes, trying to make him laugh with how ridiculous I looked. "You mean you don't want to know what it would be like to float?"

He lifted a shoulder but said nothing.

"What about pooping? Surely you want to see what it's like to poop in space."

"Ellie!" He giggled.

"What? I mean, I want to know. Does it float? Does it stay in the suit? What do they do?"

He laughed some more then said in a very serious tone, "We're not supposed to say 'poop' at school."

I covered my mouth, my eyes really wide. "Oops!" I lifted my hand, cupping the side of my mouth. "Can I say fart?"

"No!" He laughed some more, and I was trying not to laugh myself.

"Doo-doo?"

"*No!*" He jumped on the bed, laughing as he said, "No potty words."

"What about—"

He hopped down and covered my mouth with his hands. "I mean it, Ellie." He shook his head, his expression grave. "Don't do it. You'll have to go to the thinking spot."

"Oh no." I widened my eyes. "Not. The. Thinking. Spot!" I knew it was really just a chair where the kids had to go to calm down. But being a rule follower like his mom, Maddox probably thought it was the worst thing ever.

As a kid, I'd spent a fair amount of time in the thinking spot. It was honestly kind of nice. Quiet.

"I'm never going to see her again, am I?" He plopped down on the mattress next to me, the brief moment of levity gone.

"I don't know," I said, wishing I had a better answer. A more comforting answer. "I'm not sure anyone knows what happens after we die."

"But Mimi—"

I placed my arm around Maddox and pulled him into my side. "That's what Mimi thinks. What do you think?"

I was still fuming over the whole thing, but also...I couldn't believe I'd actually stood up to my mom. She'd picked on me—picked me apart—my entire life. And I'd taken it. Again and again, I'd taken her abuse. But I would not let her do that to Maddox and Savannah.

I only wished I'd said something more. Sooner, even.

He stared at the floor. "It's silly."

"You want to know what I think?" I asked, rubbing his arm.

He nodded, sniffling, so I said, "I like to imagine that your mom is in a big library with all the books she could ever want."

He smiled. "I like that."

"Yeah?" I asked. "Do you want to add to it? Maybe we can close our eyes and visit her together."

He considered it a moment then nodded. I watched him close his eyes and bow his head. "She'd like a fireplace."

"Yeah. Good one." I grinned, imagining it too. "And a big, cozy chair."

"Oh. Oh. Maybe it's like the Beast's library."

"From *Beauty and the Beast*? She'd love that!"

"And a garden." He was growing excited now, and it made me happy.

"Yes!" I gave him a squeeze. "Maybe she's in a castle with a beautiful garden and stone walls. Do you see her?"

When I glanced over at him, his eyes were still closed, a smile playing at his lips. Slowly, he nodded. And something in my heart eased. I couldn't bring back his mom, but I could be there for Maddox. Most importantly, I could remind him of all the things Tessa had loved. I could ensure that he knew how much she loved him.

"You can talk to her too," I said.

He furrowed his brow. "I can?"

I nodded. "Anytime you miss her, you can close your eyes and meet her in the castle library and talk to her. She may not say much, but she was always a good listener."

His shoulders slumped, and I hugged him to me as he cried. I wondered if I'd done something wrong. But then he said, "I'm afraid I'll forget her face."

"Then look at her picture," I said. "Or look in the mirror. You look a lot like her."

He straightened. "I do?"

I nodded. "You do. I see her smile and her eyes in yours."

"Savannah's nose looks like Mommy's."

I smiled. "See?"

"You look like her too sometimes," Savannah said, joining

us. She pushed off the doorframe, and I wondered how long she'd been standing there.

"Do I?" I asked.

She settled on her bed and crossed her legs. "Yep. Something about your face. Though your eyes are more purple. Do you wear colored contacts?"

"Sometimes." I laughed. "But the violet color is all me."

"It's really cool. I wish my eyes were that purple."

"Yeah, but yours are cool because they change color. Sometimes they're more greenish blue, and other times, they're more of a pure blue."

"What about me?" Maddox asked, bouncing on the mattress next to me. "Do me. Do me."

I laughed. "Your eyes are more like the sky. They don't change colors, but they remind me of a beautiful spring day. Of happiness and sunshine."

He ran over to the mirror and peered at himself. "You can see all that in my eyes? Cool!"

"All right," I said, glancing at my watch. "Time to get in bed."

"Aw, man," Maddox said, flopping down on the mattress.

"I thought you were excited to read *Ivy + Bean*?"

He curled up into a ball, knees clutched to his chest. "Scared." His teeth chattered, body shaking dramatically.

"Of what?" I asked.

He whispered, "Ghost," then quickly ducked his head beneath his arms.

I tried not to laugh as Savannah rolled her eyes. "It's not a ghost. There's no such thing."

I lifted a shoulder. "Let's find out."

We settled in to read, Savannah on her bed, Maddox and me on his. It was cozy. Nice. I'd never felt as loved and accepted as I did when I was with these two kids. Savannah and I took turns reading *Ivy + Bean*, and then I stood and turned out the lamp.

"Good night, Maddox." I leaned down to kiss his forehead, and he wrapped his arms around me and squeezed.

"I love you."

My heart melted. "I love you too, Mads."

I went over to Savannah and gave her a hug and a kiss, telling her that I loved her before closing the door behind me. I'd only been back a day, and those kids already had my heart.

I headed downstairs and found Tristan sitting on the couch, flicking through options until he landed on *Lost in Space*.

"Hey," I said, taking a seat at the opposite end from him.

"Hey." He set the remote on the coffee table. "You okay?"

I nodded, tucking my leg beneath me. "Yeah. I, um, I'm sorry if I upset the kids."

"Ellie." He rested his arm on the back of the sofa. "You have *nothing* to apologize for."

"I ruined dinner."

"No. Hey," he said, tapping my shoulder when I continued staring at the TV. "Your *mom* ruined dinner. I only wish I'd spoken up sooner."

"You defended me." The reminder of that brought a smile to my lips. I still couldn't believe it. No one had ever done that for me.

"And then I told her about your tattoo." He cringed. "I'm sorry. I thought she knew."

My lips curved into a sly smile. "How did *you* know about my tattoo?"

"I, uh—" He cleared his throat, the tips of his ears turning pink.

The only way he could've seen it was if he'd caught a glimpse down my shirt. *Had he been checking me out?*

"How was bedtime?" he asked after a beat, and I allowed him to change the subject. "I know they really wanted you to read them stories."

I pulled a pillow into my lap and smoothed my hand over the fabric. "We had a good time. They seemed okay when I left."

"Thank you," he sighed. "I can't tell you what a relief it is to have you here. They're really happy about it."

"So am I," I said. "Even if I wasn't happy about moving back to the AV at first."

"I'm curious," he said. "And you don't have to answer. But why did you move back? Are you okay?"

I tugged at the corners of my eyes. *Was I okay?*

No one had asked me that, apart from Piper and Sumner. My mom had blamed me, accused me of being irresponsible. And my professors had been sympathetic. But Tristan was the first person who really seemed to care about me and what had happened.

"My visa was canceled."

"That's pretty serious."

I nodded. "Yeah." I tucked my hair behind my ear. "I'd gone to Japan to interview for the JET Program, and when I returned, I'd received a letter from the immigration department."

He frowned. "Because you took a trip to Japan?"

"No." I laughed, though the sound was humorless. "It was because of something that had happened a few months before that. I nannied for a family, and one night, the parents were in a car accident on their way home."

He swallowed hard. "Were they okay?"

I nodded. "Yeah. Fortunately, it was all pretty minor. But they had to go to the hospital to get checked out. So, I volunteered to take care of the kids. I wouldn't let them pay me, and not because I'd been worried about my visa require-ments. I'd just wanted to help."

Especially after what had happened to my sister. I hadn't been there for her kids during her diagnosis and after, so in some strange way, helping another family had felt like a redemption of sorts.

"I'm sure they appreciated that."

"They did, but immigration viewed it as additional hours worked beyond what was permitted," I continued.

"Thus violating the terms of your visa," Tristan finished for me.

I nodded. "I spoke with my adviser and the deputy vice-chancellor of international students, and they advised me to seek legal counsel. So, I met with a solicitor who specialized in immigration, but he couldn't help."

In fact, he'd merely confirmed my worst fears. I was out of options. Well, except for one—admit failure and go home to the Alondra Valley.

An idea that had filled me with enough dread I could've drowned in it.

Moving across the world had been for the best. In Australia, I could start over. Start fresh. I could be whoever I wanted. I could be myself.

Not the mayor's daughter. Or Tessa's little sister. But me —Ellie.

"You couldn't appeal?"

"I could, but only after I'd come home to the US." I blew out a breath. "What would be the point?"

"Mm." He nodded. "Does your mom know all this?"

I scoffed. My mother had accused me of being careless. I hadn't been careless. In fact, it was *because* I cared about the family I nannied for that I was even in this mess in the first place.

But I couldn't reverse the immigration department's decision, just like I couldn't change my mother's mind. She'd always find a way to blame me.

"Let me guess," Tristan said. "She didn't let you explain."

I nodded, wishing I hadn't gone tonight. It was easier to ignore my parents than face the truth. My parents had been lying to me for my entire life, and yet my mom acted as if I could never do anything right.

If something similar had happened to Tessa, Mom would've been sympathetic. Patient. Understanding. She would've blamed it on everyone but my sister. They would've helped her.

But for me…never.

Nothing I did was ever good enough for Madame Mayor.

"She actually said, 'Teresa would've never allowed something like this to happen.'" I made my best attempt to mimic my mom's imperious tone.

Of course not. Because Tessa was perfect.

My mother wanted me to be someone I wasn't. Even now, she was comparing me to a ghost. I wasn't Tessa, and I never would be.

And in my mother's eyes, I'd always be a disappointment.

Tristan let out a heavy sigh. "No one's perfect, but it's easy to put someone on a pedestal after they die."

I wondered if he was speaking from experience. I still couldn't believe he'd cut off my mom earlier when she'd been talking about Tessa. While I hated being compared to my sister, I could empathize with the desire to remember only the good things about someone you loved after they were gone.

"I can appreciate that, but my mom is always so stuck in the past," I said, thinking more about her anger toward my dad and me.

I could understand why Gloria might dislike what I represented, yet it wasn't *my* fault that my dad had had an affair. Gloria had been holding on to this grudge for seventeen years. *Seventeen.* I was beginning to wonder if she'd ever let it go.

But Tristan didn't know the truth about my dad. No one did.

As far as everyone knew, Gloria and Dan had adopted me when I was three, after struggling with latent secondary fertility for years. That was all true, but they'd adopted me after my biological mom, Sicily, had died in a car crash and named Dan—my biological father—as my guardian.

I didn't have many memories of her, and that only made me more determined to help preserve Maddox's and Savannah's memories of their mom. It was only after I'd left for Australia that Dan had sent me any information on Sicily. And even that had been limited. A few pictures, some notes about the things she'd liked, about the college she'd attended.

Dan and I may have the same genes, but you wouldn't guess it based on our looks. I definitely favored Sicily. She had the same honey-colored locks—at least if I hadn't colored mine purple. The same striking violet eyes. She was beautiful.

I'd often wondered how my life might've been different if Sicily hadn't died. But then I remembered how pointless it was to think that way. Focusing on the past would only cause more grief than good.

CHAPTER SIX

Tristan

I blinked a few times, trying to clear the blurry image on the TV screen from my vision. There was a warm body next to me that smelled of sweetness and a hint of spice. *Ellie.*

Carefully as I could, I glanced down at her sleeping form. Her eyelashes fluttered against her skin. Her lips parted just slightly. Purple hair splayed over the cushions.

It was funny sometimes, to look at her now. To remember the girl she'd been and yet see the woman she was becoming. Sometimes it felt as if I'd known her forever, and then others like I didn't know anything about her at all.

"Ellie, hey." I nudged her. It had been so nice to spend another evening with someone instead of alone. "Time for bed."

She groaned and turned over, pulling the blanket higher.

"Hey, sleepy girl." I shook her gently. "Time for bed."

"Mm." She pushed me away. "I'll be up in a minute."

I chuckled and stood, tucking the blanket around her. I checked the doors then proceeded upstairs, peeking in on the children before heading down the hall. I switched on the lamp in my bedroom and paused to stare at Tessa's nightstand.

Ever since the disastrous dinner with her parents the other night, I kept asking myself one question. Was I like Gloria—stuck in the past?

Or was I just *stuck?* Afraid to move on, as if doing so would somehow erase all that had come before. Erase Tessa's importance in my life.

It was exhausting. Seeing her things there—waiting—every night was depressing. The morning was no better; I'd wake up, and the sight of her nightstand was jarring.

I'd been putting it off. Making excuses. As difficult as it was to move on, I didn't want to be stuck in the past either. And being confronted by these crushing reminders all the time wasn't helping.

I wondered if it was as difficult for Ellie to be in this house—surrounded by memories of Tessa—as it was for me. More and more, it felt as if the walls were closing in on me. Instead of honoring Tessa's memory, I'd made a shrine to the past. A prison of my own making.

But Tessa wasn't coming back. Not today. Not tomorrow. Not ever.

I removed Tessa's books, phone charger, and glasses from the nightstand and tucked them in a box in the closet. A glance at her clothes told me I had a lot more work to do. It was daunting, but even that small change felt like a step in the right direction.

When I checked the time on my phone, I knew Enzo would still be up. I texted him a picture of the empty nightstand, and he immediately responded.

Enzo: Bittersweet, I'm sure. Moving forward can be painful, but also liberating.

Yes. Can't believe how much money was
raised for the new library.

Enzo: It's a testament to the AV's love of
Meghan Hart and Tessa.

I smiled to myself, thinking about how touched I'd been by everything Liam had done to make the new branch of the library a reality. He'd given part of his land in St. Cecilia to the AV for the purpose of building a library that would be dedicated to Tessa. And he'd donated the proceeds from Meghan Hart Day to help stock it with new books.

Are we still on for Tuesday?

Enzo: Meet you at four.

I'd always loved taking long bike rides through the AV countryside, but I'd lost my riding partner when Asher had moved to New York. Then he'd moved to LA, but ever since he'd returned, he'd had absolutely no interest in cycling.

When Enzo had heard I was looking for a riding buddy, he'd offered to join me. He hadn't done much cycling in the past, but he was still incredibly fit from all his years of playing professional soccer. And he was always up for a challenge.

I brushed my teeth and stripped out of my clothes before slipping between the sheets. As I drifted off to sleep, I thought of the girl with the purple hair and violet eyes. I thought of the past and the present. And for the first time in a while, I allowed myself to wonder about the future.

The next morning, I woke to the sounds of music and laughter. I peeked in the kids' room, but it was empty, the beds already made. I blinked a few times then went to get ready for the day.

When I got downstairs, Ellie was dressed in yoga pants

and an oversized sweatshirt, her hair in a loose bun on top of her head. Her face was devoid of makeup, and she looked young. Pure. Innocent.

Beautiful. Absolutely beautiful.

I could just imagine her on her knees for me. Those big doe eyes peering up at me. Wanting to please me. My breath quickened, my pulse skittering.

Whoa. I jerked my head back. *Where did that thought come from?*

"Oh, hey." She smiled, and I forced myself to push those dark fantasies from my mind. "Want some coffee?"

"Um. Yeah." I accepted the mug of steaming coffee from her. "Thank you."

"Of course." She smiled, and my eyes were drawn to the curve of her lips. They were pouty and pink and luscious.

And...dangerous. This is dangerous.

I quickly refocused my attention on my coffee and took a few sips, my taste buds rejoicing. "Damn. That's really good." I peered down into the cup as if searching for answers. "How did you make that again?"

"My secret is freshly ground beans and a pour over." She gestured to the counter, where a variety of coffee paraphernalia was laid out. A white ceramic cup with a base. A travel-size coffee grinder.

"You really do love your coffee," I said, forcing myself to focus on a safe topic. An *appropriate* topic. Instead of how badly I wanted to see her lips wrapped around my cock.

She laughed. "Yeah. I blame the Aussies and their coffee culture."

I took another sip, still trying to wrap my head around this new norm. The kids were happy and helpful. I was being served fresh coffee. After the unending slog and loneliness of the past year, it felt as if I'd hit the jackpot. "I'll make the kids' lunches."

She returned to the stove and flipped the pancakes with ease. "Already done."

"Really?" This was too good to be true.

"Yep." She mussed Maddox's hair, and he smiled up at her. "Maddox and Savannah helped."

"Really?" I was beginning to sound like a broken record, but seriously?

I usually had to beg them to get dressed. Nagging them the entire morning as we barely made it out the door on time. Now they'd gotten ready without a fuss *and* had helped pack their lunches? I wondered how long this would last, but I'd take it for as long as it did.

"Yep. And I'll pick them up from school."

"And River," Savannah said from the table.

I pinched the bridge of my nose. I'd forgotten that I'd offered to pick up River so Bennett could take Wren to her doctor's appointment. They'd only recently told the guys and me that they were expecting, and Bennett was beyond ecstatic. I was so happy for him, for their family.

"I can pick them up," I said, not wanting Ellie to feel responsible for an additional child. She'd already done way more than I'd ever hoped for or expected.

"Don't be ridiculous. I've got it covered. We'll have fun. Right, kids?" She glanced over her shoulder at them.

"Right!" Maddox and Savannah cheered.

"Okay. If you're sure."

"Absolutely." She smiled, and something in my chest eased. "I'm here to help, and I'm happy to."

After all these months of doing it alone, of *being* alone, I hadn't realized how much Ellie's support would mean to me. I hadn't expected to trust her so easily or for the kids to latch on so quickly. She'd only just arrived, yet my relief was immense.

And my attraction to her was off the charts. *Fuck.*

"Thank you," I said, hoping she'd hear the sincerity in my tone.

"My pleasure. Now—" she turned to the kids "—who wants chocolate chips in their pancakes?"

Both their hands shot into the air. "Me! Me!"

"Awesome." She winked at me and then spun back to the stove.

I stared at her in awe. Ellie had no idea how much this meant to me. I'd been drowning, and she'd offered me a life preserver.

"You okay, Daddy?" Savannah asked, and I forced myself to drag my eyes away from Ellie's ass.

"Yeah. Of course." I finished off the rest of my coffee and placed my mug in the dishwasher. "If you're good here, I'm going to head to work."

With her back still turned to me, Ellie waved over her shoulder with the spatula. "Have a good day."

A week ago, I would've laughed at such a seemingly preposterous idea, but that actually seemed...possible. Despite Maddox's latest night terror, despite everything else, I actually felt somewhat hopeful. All thanks to Ellie.

She'd calmed Maddox down when he'd woken up screaming in the middle of the night. She'd restored some sense of order to our home. She'd made me feel less alone.

I kissed the top of Savannah's head. "Have a good day, sweetie." Then I moved over to Maddox and gave his shoulder a squeeze, which he shrugged off. "You too, Mad."

"Bye, Dad!" Savannah singsonged. "See ya."

I headed for the door, giving the top of Rex's head a pat. When I glanced back, everyone was smiling. I breathed a sigh of relief and shut the door.

When I arrived at the office, my assistant, Olen, jumped up from his chair. "You're early."

I grunted my acknowledgment. I was early or on time

for the first time in about a year. But since I was the boss, no one cared when I showed up. Add in the fact that my wife had died, and more often than not, I saw pity in their eyes.

"What's new?" I took a seat at my desk and switched on my computer.

Olen shoved a hand through his hair. It was a dark brown, the same color as his polo pony. I wondered if he'd lose his beloved horse if we lost the company.

"We have new data from Fall River Estates and Hummingbird," he said, and I forced myself to focus. "Two more Sonoma wineries signed up as well."

"Great."

Lockwood Industries used artificial intelligence to streamline the wine making process. After an initial investment from Enzo, we'd successfully developed systems to monitor and improve use of the equipment across the region. Now, we were looking to raise thirteen million dollars of additional backing so we'd be able to further optimize our user base and product offerings. Ideally, we hoped to scale the product across different markets.

"We got a call from a potential investor," Olen said, following me into my office.

We'd been talking with a few venture capital firms, but I was beginning to think our best bet might be an "anchor" investor. I was tired of dealing with all the politics.

With everything that had happened the past year, courting investors had been less of a priority. So my team had focused on building the software's capabilities instead.

"Stan?" I asked, hopeful.

Olen shook his head, and I tried not to let my disappointment show. Stan's good opinion was worth as much as his money. His investment would show confidence. Strength.

"Who?" I asked.

If I hadn't been watching, I wouldn't have seen him wince. "Celeste Duyk."

I frowned, knowing she wasn't our first choice. She had money, lots of it. But it often came with strings attached. She was a shrewd businesswoman, and I should've been relieved. I should've been, but I wasn't.

Even so, I needed to entertain every offer. I was getting desperate, though I couldn't let on. Not even to Olen. "What'd she say?"

"She invited you to her annual Fourth of July party on her yacht. I checked, and your calendar is open."

I frowned. Celeste and I had met a few times in the past, mostly for dinner or drinks. She'd never invited me to stay on her yacht, and I had a feeling she'd only done so because she was hoping to mix a little business with pleasure. My stomach churned.

"Her yacht?" I asked.

He nodded. "It's a good opportunity to network. Even if it doesn't pan out with Celeste, you might be able to secure someone else."

"Over the Fourth of July?" The AV always had a big event downtown. They blocked off the streets and had live music and events. The kids loved it. It was tradition.

"Yes. You'd be gone two nights and three days."

I let out a sigh. That long? *Fuck.*

"Try to change it to a lunch. And move up the date. July is too far away." I didn't want Celeste to get the wrong impression. This was business, nothing more.

"Lunch?" He shook his head. But when I said nothing, he added, "Tristan, most people would kill for this opportunity."

I groaned and turned my attention to my computer, wanting to be done with this conversation.

"She's our best shot at the moment. You can't..." He

smoothed his tie and forced a smile. "We shouldn't piss her off."

"I have an idea." I leaned back in my chair, steepling my fingers beneath my chin. "How about you go for me?" Olen knew the company and our technology inside and out.

He laughed, at least until he realized I wasn't joking. "Um, no. I have a feeling she'd be far from satisfied with that solution."

Yeah. So did I.

He was right, though. Lockwood Industries was my baby. I was the CEO. And if we were going to secure investors, I needed to be the one to make the pitch.

I tapped my pen to my chin, spinning so my back was to him. I stared out the window at the valley. Sunlight radiated off the vines the region was known for. The vines we were helping make more productive and sustainable. I really did not want to go, but I also didn't see a way out of it.

"I'm not sure I can leave the kids for that long," I said. Before Tessa's death, a business trip wouldn't have been a big deal. Before her death, a lot of things hadn't seemed like a big deal.

"It's a business meeting. You can't take them."

I stood. "Let's see what develops in the meantime."

"Regardless," Olen said in a patient tone that grated on me. "She'll expect an answer. Soon."

"Stall by playing to her sympathies," I said, softening. Olen was just trying to do his job. "Remind her that I'm a single dad, and it's during my children's summer break." I spun on him. "No. Not that. Do not mention the word 'single' in connection with me."

"Be honest. Do you have another potential investor?"

I sighed.

"That's what I thought." He nodded. "You can't afford to

upset Celeste. Not when she's our only real option at the moment."

"She's not—" I growled. I knew how important this was. I didn't need him to remind me.

Fuck. The mortgage statements in the mail were reminder enough. As were the loyal and smiling employees I had to walk by every day. Employees who would be out of a job if I couldn't seal the deal with Celeste or someone else.

"So, is that a yes to Celeste, then?" he asked.

Whatever face I made must have shown my displeasure because Olen said, "Tristan, please. You just need to play nice for a few days. At a party. On a superyacht. It's really not that awful. Besides, we're *so* close." He placed his palms together as if in prayer.

I knew he was right. Like it or not, we needed Celeste's financial backing even more than Olen realized. I had too much riding on this.

How far was I willing to go to save it all?

CHAPTER SEVEN

Ellie

I walked my bike around the path to the back of the house, pausing at the sound of Tristan's laughter. Several others joined in, and I hung back for a moment, watching. For the first time since I'd moved in a few weeks ago, Tristan seemed relaxed. Happy almost.

I pushed up on my tiptoes to try to figure out the identity of the others, but the leaves crunched under my feet, giving away my position. *Shoot.* I ducked down, trying to stay out of sight though I didn't know why. I wasn't doing anything wrong. Yet I still felt like the kid sister sneaking around.

"Hello?" Tristan called out.

"Hey!" I hopped up and waved, hoping the darkness might conceal my embarrassment. "It's me. I'll just go around front."

"No need," he said, ambling down the steps to the back-yard to help me with my bike. My eyes roamed his chest beneath the soft gray T-shirt, the jeans that tapered in at his waist. "Hey." His smile was relaxed, and something inside me lit up like fireworks.

"Hey." It was the best I could manage when his hand

grazed mine, taking my bike from me and wheeling it ahead. "Thanks." But then I frowned at the sight of him limping. "Are you okay?"

He sighed and parked my bike against the fence. "It's nothing."

"Tristan, it's not nothing. You're limping." I crouched down to peer at his leg, but I couldn't see anything visibly wrong with it. Unable to resist, I traced a finger over his scar. "Your old football injury?"

He sucked in a jagged breath. When I peered up at him, his eyes had darkened. Only then did I realize just how close my mouth was to the bulge in his pants. I caught myself staring then popped straight up.

"Oh. Um. Sorry." I dipped my head. "Are you okay?"

"I must have tweaked it on my ride with Enzo. It probably just needs some rest."

"Rest, ice, and elevation," I said.

He lifted a shoulder, taking his time as we made our way toward the back porch. "Guys," he said to the group, tucking his hair behind his ears as if he could force it to stay there if he pushed hard enough. "You remember Tessa's sister, Ellie."

I smiled and glanced around, recognizing Bennett Nash, of course—River's dad and the resident veterinarian.

"Hey, Bennett." I gave him a little wave, and he smiled in return.

"This is Asher," Tristan said, gingerly lowering himself into one of the chairs. The dark-haired man straightened, flashing me a wicked smile.

I knew *of* Asher, mostly from Instagram and his amazing pastries. Apart from his boss, winery owner and former pro soccer player, Lorenzo Mancini, Asher Hansley was one of the AV's biggest celebrities. Asher had worked for a three-star Michelin restaurant in New York for a few years before moving to LA and then finally back home.

"And I'm Liam." Liam lifted his beer toward me by way of greeting. "Want one?"

"Liam—" Tristan punched his shoulder playfully. "You know she isn't twenty-one."

Liam shrugged. "Maybe not, but I doubt this would be her first 'adult beverage.'"

"Hardly." I laughed. "We used to go out almost every weekend in Melbourne, but the drinking age in Australia is eighteen."

"See," Liam said, grabbing a beer from the cooler, as if that proved his point. He held it out to me, but Tristan tried to snatch it from his hand. "Lighten up, man."

"I'm responsible for her," Tristan growled, and my body tingled with awareness, while my head rejected his statement.

Responsible for me? Was that how Tristan viewed me? As if I were another child? Or that I somehow couldn't make appropriate decisions for myself?

Fuck that.

"Thanks." I snagged the bottle from Liam, then turned to Tristan. "I'm responsible for myself."

The other guys guffawed, clearly enjoying my show of defiance. I ignored them and held Tristan's gaze as I popped open the bottle and took a long, satisfying gulp. His eyes were dark as he tracked my movements, but he was silent as he took a drink from his own.

While beer wasn't usually my first choice of beverage, this one was good. Light and fruity and somehow rich too. I peered down at the label—Faulty Brewing. Local, then.

When Tristan winced, I went inside and grabbed a bag then scooped some ice into it. I sealed it and went over to Tristan. "Foot up." I indicated to the outdoor coffee table.

He grumbled but did as I asked. I gently placed the ice on his knee, and he finally said, "Thank you."

"You want some pastries?" Bennett asked, holding out the box to me.

"Really?" I peered down at them, appreciating the effort and design that had gone into making each mini work of art. "Oh my god, I've been dying to try one of these. Are you sure you're willing to part with one?"

He laughed. "It's fine. Asher brought me another box to take home for Wren and River."

I sucked my lip between my teeth. Gah. They all looked so good. Finally, I selected one—chocolate and caramel.

"Thanks!" I was totally taking a selfie with this and posting it online.

I turned and headed for the house again when Liam said, "Oh, so that's how it's going to be, huh?"

"What?" I asked, turning back to glance at him.

"Taking our beer and pastries and leaving."

I laughed. "Well, I didn't want to crash your party."

"You're not crashing," Bennett said. "Join us."

I glanced to Tristan, seeking confirmation. Approval. What, I didn't know. He sipped his beer and said, "Up to you. If you want to hang out with a bunch of old guys on a Friday night, be my guest."

His eyes danced with amusement, and I could tell he was goading me. So, I took a seat and decided to tease him back. "Not like there's much better to do in this town."

There really wasn't. Most shops closed at eight o'clock, if not before. There were a few restaurants downtown, but no nightlife. It actually reminded me a lot of Hampton, though downtown Melbourne was always just a short train ride away.

I missed having friends to hang out with. Apart from Lizzie, most of my friends from childhood were away at college. And between working at Bibliolater and taking care of her ailing mom, Lizzie had her hands full.

Piper had invited me to visit, and I hoped I'd get to see her again before I left for Japan. But we were both so busy, and LA was at least a five-hour drive. I didn't even have a car.

"Wow," Liam scoffed. He narrowed his eyes at me then turned to Tristan. "Speak for yourself. I'm not old."

"You're six months older than me," Tristan said.

I was amused by their banter, even as I took photos and added filters to get the perfect shot of my éclair. Finally satisfied, I took a bite, moaning around it. Oh god, that was good.

"Yeah, but you've always acted mature for your age. You were always the responsible one of the group. Besides, that beard you're rocking, and the shaggy hair?" He gestured at Tristan's head. "Definitely makes you look older than me."

Tristan frowned but said nothing.

"I tend to agree," Asher said. "Though maybe we should ask Ellie since she's the resident hair and beauty expert."

"Me?" I laughed.

"Yeah. I follow you on social media. You're really creative."

I smiled. Coming from Asher, that was high praise indeed. My cheeks flushed with heat at the unexpected compliment. "Thanks. I actually just tagged you in my new post."

"Awesome. I'll be sure to like it and comment."

"What the hell is even going on right now?" Bennett muttered into his beer.

"Ellie." Tristan turned to me, along with Liam, Bennett, and Asher. "Tell Liam he's wrong."

I laughed, oddly pleased that Tristan had sought my opinion.

I studied him, trying to push away any preconceived images I had from before or now. And I tried to imagine him as a blank slate for me to style. He had a chiseled jawline. Full lips. Intense eyes. And a lush mane of hair, even if it was a bit unkempt at the moment.

He definitely didn't look old. Even with the "shaggy hair," as Liam had called it, and the overgrown beard, Tristan was a handsome man.

"Well?" Bennett asked me. "What's your verdict?"

I glanced away from Tristan, my skin heating with the realization that the rest of the guys were watching us curiously. Studying our interaction. I needed to do a better job of hiding my attraction to my brother-in-law because he was firmly in the off-limits zone, no matter how much my body tried to say otherwise.

I considered my words carefully, then decided to turn the tables on Tristan. "How do you feel about your hair?"

He lifted a shoulder. "I haven't given it much thought. It's just hair."

"Just hair?" I held a hand to my chest. "*Just* hair?"

He chuckled, though there was a nervous undercurrent to it. "Yeah."

"No." I leaned forward. "It's not *just* hair. Good or bad, it makes a statement. It gives people information about you. It makes you feel a certain way. Hold yourself a certain way."

"That still doesn't answer the question," Liam said, elbows resting on his thighs.

"Well," I sighed, my attention still on Tristan. "I think you could choose a haircut and facial hair style that would highlight your attributes."

"Because he looks like an old man."

"Not old, but maybe…tired?" I winced a little, immediately wishing I could take it back. "A face mask could help or daily moisturizer."

When the guys started laughing, heckling Tristan, I turned to Liam. "If you don't moisturize daily with sunscreen, you should." I shifted my attention to Bennett. "You too."

"What? No suggestions for me?" Asher asked, a teasing tone to his voice.

"You could smile more."

The other guys chuckled, and I sipped my beer. I heard someone mutter "Ballbuster," and it made me smile.

"What were you up to tonight, Ellie?" Liam asked. "Before bumming beers and pastry off us."

"I had some assignments to catch up on, so I hung out at the library most of the afternoon."

"Sounds just like Tessa," Asher mused.

I frowned, and when I looked at Tristan, so was he. I didn't like being compared to my sister, and Tristan didn't like being reminded of his dead wife. It was too painful.

"If you get sick of the library, you should check out Pore Over," Bennett said. "Wren and Harper's studio is in the same building, and I'm sure they'd love to join you for coffee sometime."

"Thanks." I smiled, appreciating his efforts to make me feel welcome. "I'll do that."

Asher asked me about Australia, and the conversation turned to lighter matters. Local gossip. The kids. I hadn't enjoyed myself so thoroughly in a long time, except for when I'd visited Piper and Sumner before coming to the AV.

I glanced at my phone, surprised by all the missed notifications. I couldn't remember the last time I'd gone so long without checking my phone, apart from my flight back to the States.

"I should probably head out," Bennett said, standing. "I imagine Wren's getting impatient for her pastries."

"I bet that's not *all* she's impatient for." Asher emptied the last of his beer then tossed it into the recycling bin, where the bottle clinked against the others.

"Dude." Liam groaned. "We talked about this. Just because I'm okay with them being married doesn't mean I want to hear about my sister's sex life." He shuddered.

Asher cleared his throat. "Maybe it wouldn't bother you so much if you hadn't fucked things up with Penny."

I wanted to laugh, but both Liam and Tristan had gone rigid. Oh boy. I wondered what the story was there.

"Okay," Tristan said, rubbing his temples. "Time for bed before this gets even more inappropriate."

"Mr. Prim and Proper would never want to defile a lady," Asher said in a British accent that wasn't half bad. If Tristan was the responsible one of the group, Asher was certainly the shit-stirrer.

I leaned closer to Asher, laughing as I said, "Well then, it's a good thing I'm not a lady."

He chuckled, looping his arm over my shoulder. "I like you, little Curran. I think you're exactly what was needed to shake things up around here."

Tristan growled. When I glanced at him, he was watching us, fists clenched.

"Come on," Bennett said to Tristan. "Let's go inside. I'll help you clean up."

Tristan didn't blink. Didn't move a muscle. "Asher," he gritted out, eyes full of menace.

Asher stood there a moment, and I felt like I was a toy they were fighting over. I didn't understand. Was Tristan concerned that Asher would… What? Try to seduce me?

The idea was laughable. And besides, why did Tristan even care?

"Oh, come on, Tris." Asher didn't remove his arm. "I'm just being friendly."

Tristan took a step forward, before Bennett grabbed his shoulder and steered him toward the house. "Inside." Then I thought I heard him mutter, "Before you do something foolish."

Tristan finally, reluctantly, went inside with Bennett. I busied myself by fluffing the pillows on the outdoor sofa. Liam turned off the outdoor heater, while Asher hopped over the railing, landing in the grass with a fluid motion.

"I'm out," he called, throwing up his hand with a peace sign. "Good to see you, LC."

Liam nudged me. "He means you."

I scowled at Asher in the darkness. "LC?"

"Little Curran."

"Night." I shook my head with a laugh and returned my attention to the pillows, straightening everything.

"How do you like living here?" Liam asked once we were alone.

"It's, uh… Yeah. Good." I glanced up to find Liam watching me curiously. So I added, "I love spending so much time with the kids."

"And Tristan?"

I wasn't entirely sure what he was getting at, so I merely nodded.

"How's he doing?" he asked, careful to keep his voice low. "Be honest."

I was touched by Liam's concern for his friend. The guys may joke around, but it was obvious they cared for one another.

I blew out a breath and glanced up at the house. "He's…okay."

"Yet something's bothering you," he said.

"Just, um, it was kind of tense for a moment…" I dipped my head, embarrassed for even mentioning the disagreement between Tristan and Asher.

From everything I'd seen, Tristan always seemed very in control. Almost overly so.

Liam waved a hand through the air. "They'll be fine. If I were Tristan, I'd be more concerned about what revenge you'd enact on me in my sleep."

"*Moi?*" I placed my hand on my chest, though I was fighting a smile.

His expression softened, and he let out a heavy sigh. "I think he forgets sometimes that he's not responsible for the entire world."

I nodded, knowing how right Liam was. But Tristan's comments still rankled.

My entire life, my mother thought I was immature and foolish. I'd never gotten the impression that Tristan viewed me that way. Considering he trusted me to take care of his children, I thought, well… I thought it was different.

Liam placed his hand on my shoulder. "Tristan's protective of the people he cares about. And he cares about you."

I hesitated a moment then nodded. "Thanks, Liam. It was good to see you."

"You too, Ellie." He gave me a side hug.

I headed inside and intercepted Bennett on his way to the back door. I glanced around, wondering where Tristan was. "Did Maddox call out?" I asked, hoping he hadn't had another night terror. They were awful.

Bennett shook his head. "No. Tristan said he was going to take something for his knee and go to bed."

"Oh. Okay. Thanks."

"I'm glad you made him ice it."

I laughed. "Not sure he agrees."

"He will." Bennett took a step forward then paused. "It's nights like this, I really feel Tessa's absence," Bennett said, surprising me. "She often joined us after putting the kids to bed."

"I know this hasn't been easy on him. On any of them."

Bennett shook his head, and for a moment, it looked as if

he might cry. "I can only imagine the pain he's feeling. If anything ever happened to Wren…" Silence hung in the air, along with his unspoken sentiment. The strength of his love for his wife was clear.

"I know," I said, wishing I could comfort Bennett. "He misses her. We all do."

Bennett's expression was solemn as he placed his hand on my arm. "I'm not sure I ever told you this, but I'm sorry for your loss, Ellie. Tessa loved you very much."

I swallowed hard, appreciating his words. "Thank you."

"Well, I better head out. If you ever need anything, please don't hesitate to give Wren or me a call." He handed me a business card for the Alondra Valley Animal Clinic, where his name and contact information were printed. Then another for Little Bird photography studio with Wren's name.

I took both and thanked him before locking the back door. Rex was sleeping in his bed in the laundry room, Hedgie tucked safely in her cage. I checked the front door before heading upstairs.

The kids were both sound asleep in their room, their night-light casting colorful shapes on the walls and ceiling. I smiled, watching them sleep peacefully, then continued down the hall to my room. Tristan's door was ajar, the lights off.

I was tempted to peek inside, but I stopped myself. I was… Well, I didn't know what I was doing. He was my brother-in-law, and opening that door would only get me in trouble.

CHAPTER EIGHT

Ellie

E*llie,* a little voice whispered.

I rolled over in my sleep, hugging my pillow to me. It was warm beneath the covers, and I didn't want to get up.

"Ellie." The little voice called to me again. "Auntie Ellie."

I jolted awake, realizing it wasn't a dream.

"What's wrong?" I turned on the light and found Savannah standing beside my bed. Her eyes were rimmed red, and she worried her bottom lip.

"It's Rex." She sniffled. "Something's wrong. He's whining like he's in pain. And he threw up on the floor."

Ugh. Great.

I pushed back the covers and stood, rubbing my hands over my face.

"Where's your dad?" I asked, wondering why she hadn't gone to Tristan first. Half wishing she had so I wouldn't have to clean up this mess. I was *so* not good with vomit.

Savannah sucked her bottom lip between her teeth and shook her head quickly. "He's really out of it."

That concerned me. As a solo parent, Tristan had

mentioned he was often hyperalert to sounds. But if his knee had been bothering him… I frowned, wondering if I should check on him.

"Please." She tugged on my hand, urgency surging beneath her words. "Will you come? I'm really worried about Rex."

And now I was worried about Rex *and* Tristan.

"Okay. Okay." I followed her toward the stairs.

Downstairs, Rex was curled up in his bed, his whines persistent and painful to my ears. And yep…it definitely smelled like vomit. I tried to breathe through my mouth so as to avoid the stench.

"Hey, boy," I cooed and reached out to touch him. "It's okay," I said when he snarled at me. "I just want to help."

His belly looked bigger than normal, though that could've just been the way he was lying. But it was his eyes that were the most telling. They spoke of sadness and pain. Exhaustion. Something was *definitely* wrong.

I turned to Savannah. "Do you know if he's eaten anything unusual?"

She shook her head. "I don't. I'm not—" She started to cry, big, fat tears rolling down her cheeks. "I don't want him to die. I don't want him to—"

"I know." I gave her a squeeze, hoping to reassure her. I had to stay calm for her. "I don't either. We're going to do everything we can to help him. But we have to stay calm for Rex. As a veterinarian, you'd need to stay calm for your patients, right?"

She hesitated a moment then nodded. "Right."

"I need to take him to the emergency animal clinic. Do you think you can help me find some old towels?"

She sniffled. "Okay. But I'm going to the clinic too." She ran off and returned a minute later with some beach towels.

Rex's breathing was uneven, and I was starting to get really concerned.

Stay calm. Stay calm.

"Great. Thank you so much." I smiled. *Stay calm. Be the calm.* "Can you get your shoes and coat? I'll just let your dad know we're leaving."

"What about Rex? Who will stay with Rex while we do that?"

I glanced around. Right. Of course. "Um. Do you want to stay with Rex while I grab your jacket?"

She nodded and settled in by the dog, running her hand over his fur. I could hear her speaking softly to him, but I couldn't make out the exact words she said. It didn't really matter. Rex was in bad shape, and if I didn't get him help soon, I feared he would, indeed, die. I could not—would not—let that happen.

I ran up the stairs, intent on Tristan's room. I knocked gently on the door to his room, accidentally pushing it open in the process.

"Tristan," I called. When he didn't stir, I took a few tentative steps inside. "Tristan." I spoke a little louder this time, feeling as if I were doing something I shouldn't.

I shouldn't be in his room.

I shouldn't be studying the naked muscles of his back in the moonlight.

I shouldn't be…

He turned so he was on his back, the covers dipping low on his stomach. My mouth went dry at the sight of his toned abs and those lines that dipped into—

For god's sake, Ellie. Snap out of it!

I shifted back and forth next to his bed. "Tristan," I said quietly, knowing I needed to get out of here as quickly as possible. For *oh*-so many reasons. "I need your help."

"Mm." He seemed to rouse a little, his movements sluggish. Finally, he opened his eyes and surveyed me in a slow, sexy perusal. Then he grinned, tucking an arm behind his head. "What kind of help?"

My nipples pebbled in response to his suggestive tone, and I crossed my arms over my chest. Not *helping!*

"I, uh—" My eyes darted toward the door. I tried to focus on what needed to be done, but I remained frozen to the spot, my core flaring with heat. My body at war with my head.

When I still didn't move, he pushed himself to a seated position on the edge of the bed. My eyes darted to his crotch, and I tried to ignore the outline of his cock in his boxers.

He hung his head and sucked in a few deep breaths then paused. I realized his eyes were on my chest. "I was right."

I didn't have time for this, but I couldn't resist asking, "About what?"

"Your tattoo. I thought it was a flower." He traced the design with his finger, and I shivered from his touch.

He tugged on the neckline of my shirt, bringing it lower on my chest. He was barely touching me, and yet it felt as if his hands were branding my skin.

"Now, what can I help with?" he rasped.

When I still didn't answer—I couldn't. I'd somehow lost the ability to form words.

Tristan stood and grasped my chin. His pressure was firm as he brought my gaze to his.

This was wrong. So wrong. But damn, it felt good.

"I-I—"

"Elle." He leaned closer, and I could smell the sweetness from the hops on his breath, the scent mixing with mint. Mingling with the smell of him. "I asked you a question."

My core flooded with warmth from the tone of his voice, the sheer power he radiated. *Holy fuck, that was hot.*

I struggled to regain control of the situation, even as my body begged me to stay. To give in to this. Give in to *him*.

"Tristan," I panted. "I...*we*..."

"Ellie," Savannah hissed from downstairs. My eyes widened at both the prospect of being caught and the panic in her voice.

Tristan's entire demeanor changed as he bolted for the door. But I grabbed his arm to stop him. "Wait. Um—" I peered down at his crotch, and his gaze followed mine.

"Right. Shit." He turned away from me and adjusted himself.

"I'll handle it," I said.

"What's Savannah going to think if she sees you leaving my room?" he whispered.

"She knows I'm in here."

He froze, brow furrowed. "What?"

I had the insane urge to kiss his forehead to smooth away those lines.

"I, um... Just a sec." I backed away, trying to compose myself. To pretend as if I hadn't seen how thick his cock was through his boxers.

Stop thinking about your brother-in-law's cock!

I ran out to the banister and peered down at the living room.

"Rex threw up again," she whispered.

"I'll be right there." I crept into her room and grabbed a sweatshirt for her and tossed it over the side. "Put this on and stay with him. 'Kay?"

She nodded up at me with tears in her eyes. I darted back to Tristan's room with no time to lose. I found him sitting in the chair, struggling with a pair of jeans and cursing.

"Are you okay?" I asked, frowning. "I didn't think you had that many beers."

"I didn't." He groaned, bending forward and putting his

head between his thighs. "But I took something for my knee, and I don't think it mixes well with alcohol. It's making me dizzy. Now tell me what's going on with Savannah."

"Not Savannah," I said. "Rex. Something's wrong with Rex, and I need to take him to the animal hospital."

He stood but immediately steadied himself with the dresser. His hair was deliciously mussed, his skin bare. "Let's go."

"You're in no state to drive." I placed my hands on his shoulder then immediately regretted it. Smooth, hot skin. It was…distracting, to say the least. "Where are your keys?"

He grabbed them from a leather catchall and handed them to me. "Thanks. I'll text you later when I know more."

"I'm coming with you."

"Not unless you want me to take you to the doctor as well." I met his eyes to make sure he was listening. When he grunted, I asked, "Are you okay to stay here with Maddox? He's still asleep."

"I'm fine," he huffed, moving to stand again. "I'll help you with Rex."

I narrowed my eyes at him. "Tristan. Don't make me tie you to the bed."

As I left the room, I could've sworn I heard him mutter, "Princess, it'd be the other way around."

I swallowed hard and shook my head to clear it. *Off-limits.*

Lust was coursing through my body as I rushed down the stairs. But as soon as I found Savannah clinging to Rex, all thoughts of Tristan and his cock and what had just happened fled my mind. Barf was the furthest thing from sexy.

"Okay." I assessed the situation. "You grab the towels. I'll get Rex."

She nodded.

"Hey, Rexy," I said, searching for some fur that wasn't

covered in vomit. Oh god. This was disgusting. But I felt so bad for him that I finally caved and smoothed my hand over his head. "We're going to get you feeling better. Do you think you can come with me?"

If a dog could moan, I was pretty sure Rex just had. He let out a long howl unlike any I'd heard from him before.

Okay. Well, shit. I let out a sigh. "I guess I'm going to have to carry you."

I squeezed my eyes shut briefly. I had no idea how I was going to do this, but whatever happened, I planned to block out as many memories of this ordeal as possible. Well, the memories that didn't involve Tristan anyway.

When we finally got to the animal hospital, I rushed inside and explained the situation. One of the employees followed me back out to the car. But as I was helping unload Rex, he barfed all over me.

Oh god. I could feel the bile rising in my throat, my stomach revolting.

Think of something, anything, *else.*

"Ellie?" Savannah asked. "You okay?"

I held a hand to my mouth, trying to ignore the stench and the warm, wet feel of my clothes. "Yep. Yeah." I nodded, following them inside.

Rex was rushed down the hall, and a woman at the front desk offered me a clean pair of scrubs. She led us to an exam room where I stripped out of my clothes and threw them in the trash. As soon as they were in the bin, I shuddered.

Savannah sat in a chair and studied me while I washed my hands, my arms. I wondered what she was thinking, at least until she said, "Your body looks different than Mommy's."

"Yeah?" I asked, using some wet paper towels to clean my chest and dab at my bralette before pulling on the shirt.

"Yeah. Her boobs were smaller. And she had these weird

lines on her stomach. Grannie has really big boobs," she said, referring to Tristan's mom. "But they hang down low." I tried not to laugh. I knew she was merely making innocent observations.

"Isn't that cool?" I asked, tugging on the pants.

She tilted her head to the side. "What?"

"Well, I think it's really neat that bodies—like families—come in all shapes and sizes. And all bodies are good bodies."

From her quizzical expression, I knew she was processing my words. "Like River."

"What about River?"

"Well, his family has a mom, a dad, and a baby on the way. But Bennett wasn't always his dad."

I nodded. "That's right."

River's adoption made me think of my parents. I'd only seen them once since that explosive family dinner. I'd run into them at the grocery store, and it had been tense. My dad wanted to talk. My mom wanted to criticize. And I wanted nothing to do with either of them.

It was the same thing. It was *always* the same with them. I couldn't even bring myself to be disappointed by my dad's behavior because he was following the same script he always had.

"Do you think one day I'll get a new mom like River got a new dad?" Savannah asked.

Oof. How the heck was I supposed to respond to that?

I sat on the chair next to hers and wrapped my arm around her shoulder. "No one can ever replace your mom," I said. "She was one of a kind, and she loved you very much."

She nodded, lip quivering. "I really miss her."

"I know, sweetie. I miss her too." It had been the hardest part of coming home, knowing Tessa wasn't here. "And she'll always be with you in your heart and in your memories."

"But it's not the same!" she cried, surprising me with her sudden outburst.

"You're right." I rubbed her arm, hating that I couldn't do more to comfort her. "It's not."

She cried as I held her. And as her sniffles echoed off the cold tile, I wondered if I'd completely screwed up.

"You know, you're not like the other adults," she finally said.

I wasn't sure whether to take that as a compliment or not. So instead, I asked, "How so?"

"Usually when I cry, they try to tell me that I'm fine."

I frowned. I wasn't surprised, but I didn't like it. "No one has the power to tell you how you feel."

"See! That's what I mean." She sat up straighter. "You're, like, way cooler. And you're honest. I like that about you."

I smiled. "Thanks. I think you're pretty cool too."

She settled back against me. "Plus, Dad's a lot happier since you arrived."

I gnawed on my lip but said nothing. I mean… Had all of that really happened?

I rewound the evening in my head. Savannah had talked about my boobs. Tristan had *looked* at my boobs.

I shook my head. I still wasn't sure what to make of his actions, let alone his words. I'd been turned on; that much was certain. So had he.

I sighed and stared at the ceiling tiles, unable to forget the feel of his touch. The way his gaze heated. The timbre of his voice when he spoke in that commanding tone.

He'd been…so *different*. So hot.

Savannah sighed and laid her head in my lap, her limbs growing heavy. I knew she had to be tired. It was the middle of the night, and her little body had been filled with worry for Rex.

"Do you think Rex will be okay?" she finally asked, yawning.

"I hope so," I said, smoothing my hand over her hair. "I know we did everything we could for him. I'm really proud of you, Savannah."

She hugged my legs. "I love you, Auntie Ellie."

My heart melted, and I bent forward to hug her back. We were like a big pretzel. "I love you too."

Whatever had or hadn't happened tonight between Tristan and me, none of it mattered because I was here to help with the kids. Wanting anything more would be foolish.

CHAPTER NINE

Tristan

My head was ringing. Or was that my phone? It was too early. Too bright.

"Fuck," I muttered into the mattress.

I groaned and stood, catching myself on the dresser. I frowned when I noticed my keys were gone. And then everything came back to me in a rush.

Ellie standing by my bed. I could still remember the feel of her skin beneath my hands. The warmth and softness.

Savannah calling out…

Oh god. That got my heart pumping even faster.

Bennett's name flashed on the screen, and I assumed he was calling about Rex. I fumbled to answer it. "Hello?" I cleared my throat and tried once more. "Bennett?"

"Hey," Bennett said. "Were you sleeping?"

"I, uh—" I rubbed my eyes, still disoriented. "I took something for my knee last night, and I had a bad reaction."

"You okay?"

"I will be." My head was spinning, but at least my knee wasn't throbbing. "What's up with Rex?"

After Ellie had gone downstairs last night, I'd tried to get dressed so I could help them load Rex into the car. But I'd barely made it a few steps before I'd had to lie down so I wouldn't vomit.

I was never mixing beer and those pills again. Fucking terrible idea.

"Rex's surgery went well, and he's recovering. We'll keep him overnight, and you can pick him up from the clinic tomorrow."

"Surgery?"

"He swallowed a string, and it was blocking his intestines."

I winced. How had I not even noticed? And then to be completely useless when everyone needed me? To hit on Ellie and to…

"Don't beat yourself up," Bennett said, as if he'd read my thoughts. "These kinds of things happen all the time."

I let out a deep sigh and sank down on the edge of the bed. The things I'd said to Ellie. The things I'd done… *Fuck.*

And all the while, she'd just been trying to tell me that she needed help with Rex.

"Ellie was right to bring him in, and she was great with Savannah."

My eyes widened. Savannah? *Shit.* The kids should've been my first thought.

Bennett was still talking, explaining something about Rex's procedure and the recovery protocol. Ending on, "Rex really is going to be okay."

I scoffed. Yeah. That's what the doctors had said about Tessa after her surgery too. And she wasn't fine. Far from it.

Tessa. I squeezed my eyes shut as bile rose in my throat. "Gotta go." I ended the call and rushed to the bathroom, dry heaving over the toilet until I slid down the wall to sit on the floor.

What have I done?

Trusting that Ellie was downstairs with the kids, I switched on the shower and stepped inside. I replayed everything that had happened from the moment I'd seen her standing next to my bed to the moment she'd threatened to tie me to it.

We hadn't kissed. We'd barely touched. And yet it felt like so much more.

I couldn't stop thinking of Ellie's soft curves and smooth skin. Her tattoo. My cock stirred, and I pressed my hand against it.

What had I been thinking?

I hadn't been. That was the problem. I'd been acting on instinct. Finally giving in to my desires.

I angled my head against the tiles and closed my eyes. How had I so completely misread the situation?

Well, not entirely. I may have misunderstood her reasons for coming to my room, but I couldn't forget the desire in her eyes. The way her nipples hardened to tight peaks beneath her shirt.

My cock throbbed in my hand, and I gave it a tug. Nope. Stop. Do *not* go there.

She's Tessa's sister.

Tessa had been my first kiss. My first love. My first everything. And I'd always assumed she'd be my last.

But as Enzo liked to remind me *"Non tutte le ciambelle riescono col bucco,"* which roughly translated to "not all donuts have a hole." Or life didn't always work out the way you planned.

I sure as hell hadn't planned on this when I'd asked Ellie to stay with us.

I switched the faucet to cold, standing beneath the spray as if it could cool these unspeakable thoughts. As if it would extinguish this inferno raging inside me. Finally, I gave up and switched off the water completely before stepping out of the shower.

Nothing happened.

I straightened, but I couldn't meet my eyes in the mirror. I kept telling myself nothing had happened, but I knew that was a lie. Worse still, I'd wanted it to.

The way I'd spoken to her...

Commanding. Possessive.

And the way she'd responded...her lips parting. Thighs squeezed together... I shook my head and got dressed.

Before going downstairs, I removed my wedding ring, feeling the weight of it as I spun it around in my fingers. I stared at the engraving of "Always and Forever" on the inside with the date of our wedding, and I sighed before placing it inside my dresser drawer. Without it, I felt both naked and surprisingly free. It was an odd sensation, and one I didn't wish to dwell on.

The smell of bacon and the sound of laughter lured me to the kitchen, where Ellie and the kids sang and danced around the island. Ellie was just as enthusiastic as the kids, belting out the lyrics with a smile as she held a wooden spoon to her lips.

I couldn't help but watch her. Be captivated by her. The way her purple hair swirled around her. The sway of her hips and the jostling of her breasts. It was fucking hot.

"Daddy!" Savannah called, waving me over.

I jerked my attention away from Ellie.

"Good morning," I said, pulling my daughter in for a hug. "I hear you had quite the adventure last night." I peered down at her. "Sneaking out of the house with Ellie." I shook my head and tsked, trying to keep it light. I turned my attention to Ellie. "You're a bad influence."

Ellie smirked, but the dark circles beneath her eyes spoke

of a sleepless night filled with worry. I tried to read her expression for clues. Was she upset about what had happened between us? Did she feel uncomfortable around me? Did she want it to happen again?

Savannah laughed and rolled her eyes. "Yeah, Dad. *Such an adventure*. Rex threw up on Ellie."

I cringed and glanced at her. "Is that true?"

"Yep." Ellie crossed her arms over her chest, and I tried not to stare at her tits.

"And…" Savannah giggled. "And— Oh my gosh." She was laughing so hard she had to stop to catch her breath. "You should've seen Ellie try to carry Rex to the car."

"Try?" Ellie placed her hands on her hips. "I did not *try*. I did it. And that dog better love me forever. He's heavy."

Maddox started laughing as Savannah tried to reenact the scene, and then we all joined in.

Savannah was really sensitive, especially toward animals. The fact that she could already joke about the whole ordeal was a big relief. I had a feeling that was all thanks to Ellie.

After they finally stopped laughing, I gave them the update on Rex. Ellie sagged against the counter, quickly straightening when Savannah glanced her way. She had to be exhausted after last night. They probably both were. I couldn't imagine how frightened Savannah must have been, yet she seemed remarkably unfazed.

I gripped Savannah's shoulder. "I'm proud of you, kiddo. You were very brave—speaking up and getting help for Rex."

"Thanks, Dad."

"Is breakfast ready?" Maddox asked. "I'm hungry."

Ellie smoothed her hand over his hair, and it was completely natural for her. "Yes, baby."

For a moment, I was struck by the rightness of the situation. The kids. Me. Ellie.

I joined the others at the table, marveling at how…happy

the kids seemed. Despite what had happened with Rex, they were talking and having fun. And that was all because of the woman sitting across from me. The woman with the purple hair and the pouty pink lips. The woman who had turned our life upside down in the best possible way.

Ever since Tessa's death, I'd felt like I was spinning. Spinning. Spinning. Like taking a ride on those damn teacups the kids loved.

But then Ellie had come into our lives and promised order. Routine. Control.

More importantly, Ellie had brought joy and light back into the house. Back to my children. And last night, I'd nearly fucked it all up.

I'd been reckless. Irresponsible.

It didn't matter that I'd liked it. It didn't matter that she'd seemed to like it too. Her response was irrelevant; I had no right to behave the way I did. I owed her an apology.

After breakfast, the kids went to watch cartoons, and I started cleaning up. Ellie grabbed some dishes and brought them to the sink.

I moved closer to her, careful to keep my voice low despite the hum of the TV in the background. "Thank you for handling everything with Rex last night. I really appreciate it."

Her answering smile was tired. "No worries."

"Still. That was…irresponsible of me. And definitely more than should be expected of you."

She frowned. "*Expected* of me?" There was hurt in her tone, so I replayed my words.

"No." I placed my hand on her arm but quickly retracted it. "That's not what I meant. I just—" I huffed. "I appreciate all that you're doing, and I'd never want you to feel like I've taken advantage of the situation." *Or you.*

"Tristan, I said it's fine." Though she still seemed annoyed.

"I understand that you weren't exactly…" She hesitated as if searching for the right word then said, "Yourself last night."

I should've been relieved. Part of me *was* relieved. But then why did I feel somehow disappointed?

Like I'd shown her a part of me I hadn't even known existed. It was as if I craved dominance, especially when everything else in my life felt so out of control. And Ellie wanted nothing to do with it—me.

WHEN I GOT HOME FROM WORK A FEW DAYS LATER, THE HOUSE was noisy and full of life. It almost felt like old times. *Almost.*

I kicked off my shoes and loosened my tie before heading into the kitchen.

Savannah was at the table doing homework with River. Ellie watched on from the counter, where she was cutting apples for their snack. Maddox was wild, wilder than normal, which could only mean one thing.

"No nap," Ellie mouthed.

I shook my head. I'd figured as much. He was wired because he was so tired.

Despite the chaos, at least things between Ellie and me had returned to normal. She hadn't mentioned the night of Rex's surgery again, and neither had I. It was almost as if it had never happened. Or at least it would've been, if only I could stop thinking about it.

I took a seat at the table with Savannah and River. They were telling me about their day at school when there was a loud crash. Everything and everyone stilled, a tense moment of silence following.

I rushed over to Maddox, holding my breath as I tried to stay calm. The silence was the worst. Because I knew any minute… *Yep.* He started wailing. His face red, fists balled up. Rex howled as if to alert us, and Savannah hurried to my side.

"Maddox, what happened? Where does it hurt?" Tears welled up in her eyes as she looked up at me with fear. "Dad, do something! Call 9-1-1."

"Sweetheart," I said in a calm voice as I assessed Maddox. He was breathing. There was no blood. As far as I could tell, he'd tripped on the rug and was just a little shaken up. "Let's give him a minute. Can you get some ice?"

She nodded and ran to the kitchen to grab an ice pack. I moved closer, trying to assess the situation. Was he hurt or just scared? Both?

"Hey, buddy. Where does it hurt?"

He kept crying, paying me no attention. His face was red and blotchy, and his cries were ear-piercing in their intensity. I balled my fists at my sides, a knot forming in my throat. I was trying to stay calm, for everyone. But I didn't know how to help. I hated not knowing how to help.

"Hey," I said in a soft tone, scooting closer. Trying a different tactic, even though I had a feeling it wouldn't work. But I had to try.

"No!" He pushed out his hand, shoving me away just as I'd feared. "I don't want you!" he yelled, and I felt utterly helpless.

I pinched the bridge of my nose, crouched down to his level, and tried to get closer. I was his father, and I should be able to comfort him. But he turned away yet again, putting his back to me.

"I want—" He hiccupped around a sob. "I only want Mommy!"

"Hey." I placed my hand on his shoulder. He spun around and started kicking at me. I held up my hands to protect myself. "I can't let you hurt me."

When he wouldn't stop, I backed away. I took a few deep breaths, but he just kept chanting, "I want Mommy. I want Mommy," over and over again.

It was tearing me apart.

Finally, I couldn't take it anymore. The screams. The pleas for Tessa. I slammed my fist against the floor. "She's not here, damn it!"

Everyone froze, and then Maddox started wailing even louder. *Fuck.*

It was heartbreaking to know my son was hurting but not be able to help him. To know I'd made it worse.

At this point, I knew there was nothing more I could do. He didn't want me, and I was only upsetting him. So I retreated to the kitchen, shooting Ellie a helpless look, which she correctly interpreted as a plea for assistance.

"Hey." Ellie crouched down beside Maddox. She talked to him in a low voice, and I couldn't hear what she said, but he seemed to be calming down. I felt both powerless and grateful; it was frustrating.

Savannah grabbed an ice pack from the kitchen, but not before glaring at me. Because *clearly,* this was all my fault.

I mean, could I really blame her? I was the parent. Or at least, I was supposed to act like an adult.

Ellie said something about "tips the cows over." Then she started laughing, and Maddox did too. Why couldn't I have done that?

Eventually, Maddox calmed down. But I was still struggling to regulate my emotions. How could I have lost it like that?

"So…" Ellie said after it was clear Maddox was okay. "I don't know if this would be okay with your dad, but if it is, do you all want to help me with a makeup tutorial?"

River's eyes went wide, and he fist-pumped the air. "Yes! Yes! Yes!"

Savannah seemed to perk up at the idea, then turned to me, hands clasped before her. "Please, Dad?"

I turned to Ellie, and before the question was out of my mouth, she said, "I already talked to Wren about it, and she said absolutely."

I laughed. Well, okay then. "Go for it. As long as you don't post any pics of them online." What she did online was her business, even if I didn't understand the appeal. But my kids were my responsibility. And they were too young to decide about their online presence when they didn't fully understand the implications.

"Of course not," Ellie said to me then turned to the kids. "Eat your snack, then we'll go upstairs. Yeah?"

"Yeah!" They all ran over to the table and started eating their apples with peanut butter and marshmallows.

While the kids were distracted, I approached Ellie and placed my hand on the small of her back. "I'm sorry. I shouldn't have lost it like that. Thank you for stepping in."

She kept her attention on the dishes. "I know it's hard sometimes to keep your cool. Trust me, I do. Especially with little ones."

"Thanks," I sighed, grateful she wasn't judging me or my parenting skills.

She was the first person I'd confided in about the kids, apart from their trauma counselor. And while my parents saw some of our struggles, they tried to keep things light and fun for the kids. I was grateful for that, but sometimes it made me feel even more alone.

I dipped my head, careful to keep my voice low. "I just… Why does Maddox always have to push me away?"

It wasn't the first time this had happened since Ellie's arrival, but it was the most brutal.

She switched off the faucet and dried her hands before peering up at me. "Do you want to know what I think?"

I nodded. "Please." Ellie spent more time with Maddox than anyone. Even in the relatively short time she'd been here, he'd allowed her to comfort him more than he had me.

She crooked her finger, beckoning me to follow. Curious, I let her escort me into the laundry room, watching as she closed the door softly behind us.

"He's scared," she said, her scent filling the room, making it difficult to think straight. "I think he resists connecting to you because he lost his mom. And he's afraid if he gets close to you, he'll lose you too."

I dipped my head, feeling even more ashamed. Why could Ellie so easily read the situation and my children, and I couldn't? And was I doing the same thing to my kids—subconsciously pushing them away—because I was afraid of losing them?

"I, um… Sorry." She hunched her shoulders as if retreating into herself. "Maybe I said too much."

I shook my head. "You were right to say what you did." I respected her more for it. "Thank you. And I owe them an apology. It's just, I feel like I'm holding it all in all the time. I have to moderate my feelings when they're interrupting me a million times. I have to keep my cool when I want to explode. And, fuck—" I dragged a hand through my hair. "It's exhausting."

She placed her hand on my arm, her touch soothing. "I'm sure it is. And you probably don't hear this enough, but you're a good dad."

I rubbed the back of my neck. I wasn't so sure about that. Most of the time, it felt as if I was fumbling around in the dark, just trying to survive. "Thanks."

"The fact that you care so much proves you're a good parent. And it's normal to have doubts."

I smiled. "When did you become so wise?"

She lifted a shoulder. "Almost everything I know about parenting is because of Tessa or the internet." She pressed her lips together, and a tear snaked its way down her cheek before she quickly swiped it away.

Without thinking, I pulled her into my arms for a hug. She stiffened then sagged, allowing me to hold her. I was surprised by how well she fit in my arms. And I rested my chin on the top of her head, allowing myself a rare moment of solace.

All I'd wanted was to console her, but I found my body reacting to her nearness. To her scent—spicy and somehow sweet. It was mysterious and comforting. Somehow arousing and calming. Much like Ellie.

I squeezed my eyes shut and tried to force those thoughts away. She was family. We were both grieving. This was about supporting each other, nothing more. It could never be anything more.

But as I held Elle to my chest, I knew I wanted more. And I hadn't realized how much I'd missed this—connection, intimacy, touch—until now. Until Elle was in my arms. It was both terrifying and comforting. Just like everything with this woman.

"Thank you," she exhaled. "I needed that. I'm sorry."

"Why are you sorry?" I asked as I reluctantly released her.

"Because here you are comforting me, when you lost your wife."

I placed my finger beneath Ellie's chin and lifted so her gaze met mine. "You lost someone you loved too. She was your sister. Your best friend."

"God—" She huffed and stared at the ceiling, emotion building in her eyes. "Hearing Maddox cry for her was…"

She pulled her lips between her teeth, another tear trailing its way down her cheek.

"I know." I used my thumbs to wipe away her tears. Every time I was tempted to get lost in my own grief, I was reminded how difficult it must be for my kids. And for a moment—with Ellie—I didn't feel so alone.

CHAPTER TEN

Ellie

Stomp. Stomp. Stomp.

The light fixture jingled from the movement, and I sighed and stared at the ceiling again. What the heck was Tristan doing up there?

Rex and I glanced at each other, wearing matching looks of confusion. He was almost fully recovered from the surgery and back to his old self. I was glad, even if he could be a bit hyper at times.

The kids were at school, and Tristan had come home early from a meeting. Since then, it'd sounded as if an elephant were pacing upstairs. I could barely concentrate, and I was trying my best to stay busy and not think about the fact that we were alone in the house. Well, apart from Rex and Hedgie.

Being alone with Tristan was dangerous. It made me want things. Things I couldn't have.

But I cared too much about him and the kids to jeopardize everything for a little fun. And besides, what would be the point?

Was I curious how good it would be?

Yes.

Did I imagine it?

Often.

Especially after that night.

I'd often lie in bed thinking about the way he'd said my name. The commanding demeanor he'd adopted that was so different from his usual persona.

But I was on track to move to Japan at the end of July. And even if I weren't, the situation was too complicated.

So, I tried to ignore my attraction to Tristan by burying myself in my studies and preparing content. I used the kids as a distraction.

It was nice… Normal, even. At least when we didn't have to do the weekly dinner with my parents. After that first disastrous attempt, we'd taken some time off. More recently, we'd been meeting at Fall River Estates or Larkspur. Public places forced everyone to be on their best behavior, and my mom seemed to delight in showing off her family. Well, her family that wasn't me.

I sighed and tried to focus on my assignment, a seemingly impossible task. Despite my best efforts, it was as if I was attuned to Tristan's every movement. To his very presence.

I finally gave up and opened a new browser window on my phone and navigated to *The Vine.* V's new advice column was surprisingly thoughtful and well written. The ax throwing place was having a grand opening soon. Tristan was planning to meet Asher, Bennett, and Liam.

I kept scrolling but paused when I came to an image of the hardware store. The post was titled "Nailed It!"

Huh. Okay. I read on.

Tired of dating apps? Looking for love the old-fashioned way?

In some cities, Starbucks is the place to meet a new love interest. Here in the AV, we do things a little differently. If you're in the market for love, look no further than Screw This hardware supply.

Judging from this past weekend alone, it might be the best place for both finding a screwdriver and someone to...ahem. Well, you get the drift.

I wanted to laugh, but then Tristan's name caught my eye. And the more I read, the angrier I became.

Tristan Lockwood was seen helping several women with their needs. Who can resist a sexy single dad who's good with his hands? It's good to see him getting back out there.

Getting back out there?

V, *The Vine*, all of it was so dumb. She, whoever she was, clearly had it all wrong. He spent all his time with the kids and me. I would've known if he were dating, wouldn't I? I mean, the way he looked at me...

Watch out! I read, unable to stop myself. *It looks like the AV's hottest bachelor is back in the game.*

Hottest bachelor? I snorted. I mean, I didn't disagree, but still...I couldn't believe V would write something like that. Actually, considering this was *The Vine*, I could.

I'd been featured once—a story about my homecoming—but that was it. And I hoped it would stay that way. I worked hard to cultivate my image and build relationships with my followers online. *The Vine* was a loose cannon. And I could only imagine how Gloria would react if *gosh forbid* I did anything scandalous.

I snorted at the idea. My mere existence posed a threat to her image as the perfect mayor. The mayor's husband's secret love child? Ooh boy. That would turn some heads.

But the town's golden boy and widower with his late wife's younger sister? I shook my head. I could only imagine everyone's response. Shock. Disappointment. Disgust.

Even so, it was difficult to ignore the anger and jealousy coursing through me at the thought of Tristan "helping" all these other women with their "needs." I had no claim to him. No right to feel jealous, and yet, I did.

I was so distracted, I hadn't realized Tristan had come downstairs and was padding into the kitchen. "Hey, Ellie. I have a favor to ask. Two, actually."

I jabbed the power button on my phone. "Sure. What's up?" I asked, hoping he hadn't seen what had been on my screen.

"I, um—" He rubbed the back of his neck. "I wondered if you'd be willing to give me a haircut."

I blinked at him a few times, positive he was joking. When I realized he wasn't, I said, "Oh, you're serious." I laughed. "I'm flattered. But why not just go to Mane Street or wherever?"

"I just—" He rubbed the back of his neck. "I can't. *Don't* want to."

"Okay," I said, dragging out the word, hoping he'd elaborate.

"I have a meeting with a potential investor coming up."

"That's great."

"It is if it works out. If it doesn't, I'll be spending July Fourth on a superyacht." His expression was surprisingly glum for how fabulous that sounded.

I frowned. "You don't sound excited."

"It's just another dog and pony show. They both are. But now you understand why the haircut is both important and time-sensitive."

I nodded slowly. Yeah. Right? No pressure. "Um, you definitely should seek professional help. With your hair, I mean," I tacked on quickly. "Though there's nothing wrong with seeking help regarding grief or…whatever." *Shut up, Ellie!*

He tilted his head, his eyes questioning.

I knew the kids attended trauma counseling; I'd taken them to some of their appointments. But I wasn't sure if Tristan had someone to talk to. I hoped he did. I hoped he knew he could confide in me.

He let out a deep breath as he glanced toward the ceiling. "I wish I could wave a magic wand and know how to help Maddox. He was always closer to Tessa, and I hate not being able to comfort him. I thought it would improve with time, but…"

I placed my hand on his shoulder but quickly retracted it. "It'll get easier." When he peered up at me with skepticism, I nodded and said, "It will."

Over the time that I'd been living here, I'd seen a big improvement in the way Tristan interacted with the kids. He was more lighthearted. More carefree. He was trying.

"If it's gotten easier, it's only because you're here. You're the only person besides Savannah he'll allow to hold him. But I worry that when you leave—" He shook his head, and I could see the concern in his eyes. The gratitude too.

I didn't want to think about when I'd leave. I spent a lot of time actively *not* thinking about when I'd leave. I was going to miss those kids—and their dad—like crazy. But I didn't say that.

"I'm sorry if I made you uncomfortable by asking you to give me a haircut. It's just—" His attention was on the floor, lips downturned. "Tessa always cut my hair. It's part of the reason I haven't—"

"Ah." I angled my head back in understanding. I hadn't realized… "I wish I could help, but I have zero experience. Well, apart from a botched attempt at cutting my bangs last summer."

"I'm sure it wasn't *that* bad."

"Oh no." I shook my head with a laugh, remembering just how terrible it was. "I bet Maddox could've done a better job."

I pulled up a picture on my phone. He winced, but I knew it was all in jest.

"Hm. Maybe I shouldn't trust you with my hair." I could

tell from the way the corner of his mouth lifted that he was teasing.

I crossed my arms over my chest as he continued to stare at the screen. "Exactly."

"Oh please, Ellie. You look beautiful there. Even if you decided to shave your head, you'd be beautiful."

I pulled my lips between my teeth and tried not to read too much into his words. I needed to focus on my degree and Japan, not get distracted by Tristan.

My classes had been kicking my butt lately, and remote learning in a completely different time zone while watching my niece and nephew was harder than I'd anticipated. I loved them, and I was grateful for this time together. But I missed my sister; we all did.

Though I wondered what was up with Tristan lately. He'd stopped wearing his wedding ring. He touched me in small ways nearly any chance he got. And I was just as bad, making any excuse to be close to him. But we were friends. Friends who lived together. Who were raising his children together —temporarily.

Besides, even if we did pursue something more, what would happen if it didn't end well? That could get awkward really fast. I'd have to find somewhere else to live for a few months. Or worse still, stay here while pretending every-thing was fine for the kids. None of which sounded appealing.

"When someone gives you a compliment," he said, "you should say thank you."

"Thank you," I said in a flippant tone. I felt exposed. *Seen.*

He shook his head, stepping closer. Invading my space. "You're beautiful, Ellie."

I stared at the floor, but he grasped my chin, lifting my gaze to his. His expression was expectant, so I whispered, "Thank you."

He nodded, clearly pleased. And that did something to me. The idea that I'd pleased him by being nice to myself.

He cleared his throat and dropped his hand. But it was too late. My body was already pumping with desire.

"Right. Um. Where were we?" I asked, putting some distance between us. "How much are you wanting to cut?"

He leaned his hip against the counter. "I'm open to suggestions."

I wasn't opposed to the longer hair. It was actually kind of hot. But I got the impression this was about more than a haircut. He hadn't cut it since before Tessa's death. The hair was symbolic of his grief. And if he truly wanted a new beginning—and a confidence boost to woo those investors— he needed to feel more like his old self.

"I assume you have scissors and a trimmer?" I asked.

He nodded.

"*If* I'm going to cut your hair," I said. "Can I also give you a facial?"

He threw his hands in the air. "Why not?"

"Okay. You've got yourself a deal." I headed for the stairs, needing to grab some supplies. "But first, I need to watch a few tutorials."

"Well that's…confidence-inspiring."

I laughed. "If it turns out badly, don't say I didn't warn you."

"Fair enough. I'll take Rex for a walk, and then we can meet back here when you're ready."

"You mean Houdini," I said, petting Rex when he wandered over to us.

Tristan chuckled and grabbed the leash. "Bennett warned me about huskies, but I was not prepared."

I nodded, thinking of Rex's latest escape attempt. We'd gotten a call from one of the neighbors after she'd seen Rex's head poking out from beneath the fence, tongue lolling. The picture she'd sent Tristan would've been funny if I weren't so concerned with how close Rex had been to getting out.

I went upstairs and watched a few videos, hoping it wouldn't be too difficult. I took beauty risks all the time—on myself. My friends. But Tristan? Tristan was different.

I texted Piper about Tristan's request, and she immediately responded.

> Piper: He must really trust you.

> Not helping! I'm freaking out here. What if it looks terrible?

> Piper: Even if it does, he can always pay someone to fix it.

> Yeah, but…it feels like more than just a haircut.

She didn't know about what had happened the night of Rex's surgery. I was determined to forget about it and move on, and talking about it wouldn't change anything.

> Piper: How so?

I debated before typing and sending my next message.

> My sister used to cut it for him.

Three dots danced on the screen. Appearing and disappearing. I paced, anxiously awaiting her response.

> Piper: Interesting.

"Interesting? *Interesting?*" I huffed. What the heck was I supposed to do now?

Piper: Do you want to cut his hair?

Yes. No. I don't know!!

Piper: He clearly asked you for a reason. I
have to go pick up Dolly, but call me later. I
want to hear all about it.

"Oh, come on, Ellie." I finally straightened. *Piper's right.* "It'll grow back, or he can get it done professionally."

I smiled at my reflection, feeling more confident. I grabbed my supplies and carried them downstairs. While I laid everything out next to the trimmer, scissors, comb, and spray bottle, Tristan stood behind me to observe.

"You sure you have time for this?"

"It's fine." I smiled over my shoulder at him, sucking in a breath when I realized just how close he was standing. "I needed a break anyway."

I turned my attention back to the counter, hoping he didn't notice the way my hands shook. "Ooh. Should we take a before and after picture?"

He groaned. "What have I gotten myself into?"

"I promise not to post them online. Unless you'd be cool with that."

He took a seat on one of the barstools and ran a hand through his hair. I was already trying to envision what he'd look like once I was done. "I'm not sure I fit your aesthetic."

"What?" I jerked my head back, fighting a smile. Had he checked out my social media? "Are you kidding? My followers would go crazy for you."

Especially now. One bare foot was propped up on a rung of the stool, his body relaxed. He had one hand planted on his jean-clad thigh, the contours of his chest visible beneath his soft gray T-shirt.

He laughed. "I'm a bit old for your followers, don't you think?"

Was he asking if he was too old for them or me? I wanted to believe it was the latter.

"I don't think so." I wasn't talking about my followers. Age didn't matter, at least not to me. But I got the feeling it could be a sticking point for Tristan, especially considering his previous comments about my not even being twenty-one.

I went to the pantry and grabbed the honey and brown sugar. I put them in a little bowl and started mixing them up.

"Here," I said, handing it to him. "Wash your face with warm water and then spread this over your skin in gentle, circular motions."

He stared at my hands then me. "Are we baking cookies or doing a facial?"

"Ha-ha." I placed my hand on my hip and pointed at the sink.

He stared down at the bowl again. "You really want me to put this on my face?"

"It's all part of the experience. I'll do it too if it'll make you feel better." I went over to the sink and started the water, waiting for it to warm. "Trust me. It will taste *and* feel good. Your skin will thank you."

He stood and joined me at the sink. "If you say so."

I grinned. "I know so. Here—" I handed him a washcloth, and we both rinsed our faces then started to apply the home-made exfoliant. "A little gentler." I demonstrated. "And put some on your lips too."

He licked his lips and smiled. "Mm. That does taste good."

"See!" I rinsed my hands. "Who doesn't want soft, kissable lips?"

His eyes darted to my lips, then my eyes, then away. If he wasn't thinking about kissing before, I had a feeling we both were now.

"Okay," I said, trying to get us back on track. "Now, use the cloth to wash it off."

Once that was done, I mashed up some avocado with olive oil. Tristan watched me, his expression wary. "Don't tell me…"

"Yep! We're going to moisturize now." God, this was too fun. His reactions were so amusing.

"We'll let it sit for about twenty minutes."

He dipped his fingers into the bowl before smearing some onto his face. "That's cold!"

I laughed and applied some to my skin as well. "It's refreshing."

"Mm-hmm." Despite his skeptical tone, I could tell he was enjoying himself.

We rinsed our hands, then I led him over to one of the barstools. I draped a towel around his shoulders. "Now for your haircut, sir." I selected one of my essential oil bottles from the counter. "How do you like the smell of this?" I waved it in front of his nose.

"Mm." He inhaled slowly. "That's nice. What is it?"

"Bergamot." It smelled like oranges and sunshine. Like happiness.

I put a few drops in my hand and then spread it over my palms. I held them up and asked, "May I?"

He tilted his head to the side, curiosity lighting those gorgeous brown eyes. "May you…"

"Touch you?"

A muscle in his jaw tensed, and then he nodded. I stood behind him, and for once, I allowed myself to touch him without hesitation. Without reservations.

I massaged his scalp, reveling in the way he groaned with pleasure. I wondered what else I could do to elicit such a sexy sound. My brain conjured all sorts of ideas as I continued my ministrations.

It felt so nice to be able to do something for Tristan. To take care of him. Not just the kids, but this man.

He seemed stressed lately. And while I knew a big part of it was this investor meeting, I wondered if something more was going on.

"Wow. That feels…" He sighed, his shoulders visibly relaxing as I continued to massage his scalp and his neck. "So good."

I moved so I could massage his temples, which put my breasts right at his eye level. His breath caressed my skin, and my nipples pebbled in response. When I'd agreed to cut his hair, I'd been nervous about screwing it up. I hadn't considered how close we'd have to be. How intimate the experience would be.

His hands went to my hips as if to steady me, and I was grateful. Because our proximity and the way he'd been looking at me had me off-kilter. I was supposed to avoid distractions. Especially the man sitting in front of me.

I just needed to focus on Tristan and his needs and ignore my own. I'd already been doing it the past few weeks. How difficult could it be?

He moaned, and the sound went straight to my core. He leaned his head back, mouth opening, the skin around his eyes easing. I wanted to kiss him so damn bad.

So much for ignoring my attraction.

I didn't care that we were wearing matching avocado face masks. I didn't care that he was my sister's husband. I didn't care…

"This is… *Damn.* I was just expecting a haircut."

"Only the best." I winked. "For my VIP client. Well, my only client, really."

"Yeah. I should probably pay you extra, huh? This isn't part of the typical nanny job description."

"Oh, please. I certainly don't think of myself as the kids'

nanny. And you know I'm happy to help in any way I can. I appreciate your letting me live here."

It wasn't the first time we'd had this conversation. He was adamant about paying me, and I was determined not to let him.

His expression was stern. "Paying you is the right thing to do."

I didn't want him to pay me. I didn't want anything. Well, that wasn't entirely true, but he wasn't going to give me what I wanted.

"I told you, I'm not accepting your money."

"And *I* told you—" he glowered "—that I won't accept no for an answer."

Frustrated and annoyed, I lifted the spray bottle and aimed it at his face.

He narrowed his eyes at me. "You wouldn't."

Oh, I would. I grinned and pulled the trigger, spritzing his face with the water.

"Hey!" he sputtered, blinking rapidly. "You're messing up my face mask."

I sprayed him again, and he reached for me, but I was too fast. I moved to his side and returned to wetting his hair as if I'd never blasted his face with water.

"Ellie," he growled—low, deep. "Don't make me spank you."

"Don't make promises you don't intend to keep." I lifted the bottle as if to spray his face again.

He gripped my wrist, his pupils swallowing the brown iris. We watched each other for a weighted moment before he said, "You'd like that, wouldn't you?"

You have no idea.

I was so hot, I was tempted to spritz myself with the water bottle.

Instead, I cleared my throat. Tristan dropped my wrist,

and I turned away, busying myself with the supplies since I sensed responding would get me nowhere.

I grabbed the scissors from the counter and moved behind him. "Last chance," I said, reveling in the metallic snick of the scissors opening, preparing to make the first cut.

"Do it," he said with a smile in his voice.

CHAPTER ELEVEN

Tristan

Kiss My Ax.

I chuckled to myself as I peered up at the neon sign that hung over the newly renovated warehouse. I pulled open the steel door. I wasn't sure what I was getting into, but I hoped it wouldn't end in a trip to the hospital. Savannah would really freak out then.

I didn't want to alarm my daughter, but throwing axes in a controlled environment, under the guidance of a coach, seemed relatively low-risk, all things considered. And with all the pent-up tension I felt around Ellie *all* the *fucking* time, throwing anything sounded pretty damn appealing. Because nothing else seemed to take the edge off.

Not working out. Or coding. Not even jacking off, which I'd done a lot of lately.

"Tristan, hey," Mackenzie said, greeting me at the door. We'd been friends in school, though she and her husband Chase were a year ahead of us.

"Hey." I hugged her. "This place looks great!"

"Thanks!" She grinned, hand on her hip. "Annie and I are

really happy with how it turned out. Oh—" She glanced around. "I was hoping to introduce you to her."

A loud chorus of wolf whistles cut through the music and the din of conversation. My attention darted to one of the bays where Asher, Liam, and Bennett were standing near a high table. I rolled my eyes and shook my head, grateful for the out. I had a feeling I knew why Mackenzie wanted to introduce me to Annie, and I wasn't interested in dating her friend.

Not that I had anything against Annie. I just… *Ugh.* There was only one woman I was interested in, but Ellie was off-limits.

Mackenzie got sidetracked by another patron, so I promised to catch up with her later, before heading over to the table where my friends waited.

"Hey, axholes," I said, greeting each of the guys with a handshake or a pat on the back.

"No." Liam groaned. "You did not just go there."

I grinned. "You better believe it."

"Is this what I have to look forward to?" Bennett hooked his thumb at me. "Cheesy dad jokes?"

I draped my arm around his shoulder and pulled his head down so I could muss his hair. "What do you mean, look forward to?" Bennett might not be River's biological dad, but he'd always viewed River as his son. "You're worse than me with dad jokes. And you know you love it."

"I do." He pushed me off him then straightened his shirt before fixing his hair. "You're in a good mood tonight." He smiled, then turned to the others as if sharing a secret.

"What?" I asked, glancing around the table, challenging them. "What's that look about?"

Liam clapped a hand on my shoulder. "I think we're all just wondering what's going on? Last week, you had us meet at Faulty Brewing for a tour and tasting. And now you have this sexy new look." He smoothed his hand over my jawline. "Damn." He grabbed my chin, turning my head side to side. "Lookin' good, Lockwood."

I laughed and stepped out of his hold, accepting the beer Asher had slid toward me. Just thinking about Ellie giving me a haircut had my cock straining against my zipper. She'd been so caring and sexy. God, she was sexy. I'd had to keep my eyes closed when she was cutting my hair so I wouldn't stare at her tits. I'd had to force myself to mentally write lines of code so I wouldn't try to kiss her.

I kept telling myself to leave her alone. To let it be. But if anything, my need for Ellie was getting worse.

Yes, I was physically attracted to her, but it was more than that. It was the way she made me feel. Special. Cared for. Loved. Not just when she was cutting my hair, but all the time.

And then when I saw my reflection, I'd actually recognized myself in the mirror. Or at least, a glimmer of my old self. And it was all thanks to Ellie.

Bennett took a seat on one of the barstools across from me. "Looks like the AV's hottest bachelor is finally trying to live up to his name."

I nearly snorted at the moniker. I might have been labeled "AV's hottest bachelor" by *The Vine*, but I was definitely not back on the market. If I was being honest, all I really wanted to do was go home and watch Disney movies with Elle and the kids.

"So does this mean you're back in the game?" Liam asked. "Because according to *The Vine*, you've been helping the women of the AV with all sorts of 'needs.'"

I rolled my eyes. I was never going to live that post down. My friends could give me shit about it, but I was more concerned with what Ellie thought.

"Since when are you the AV's hottest bachelor?" Asher

griped, tossing one beer in the recycling bin before grabbing another. His sullen expression would've been comical were it not so surprising.

He had millions of followers on social media. People traveled to the AV from all over the world just to eat his pastries. He was famous. Me? Well, I preferred to fly under the radar.

I didn't do social media because I'd seen the dark side of tech. I didn't care about followers or fame. The mere idea of being featured in *The Vine* made me uncomfortable.

"Since when do you care?" Liam asked Asher.

"Seriously, though," Bennett said to me, sipping his beer. "I'm happy that you're putting yourself back out there and trying new things."

I lifted a shoulder, not wanting to make it into a bigger deal than it was. This was a night out with friends. Nothing more.

"How's Wren?" I asked, ready for a change of subject.

Bennett's expression softened, love filling his eyes. "She's doing great. She's so excited about the baby. We both are."

For once, I didn't feel a pang of jealousy. I didn't feel a crush of sadness. I felt nothing but happiness for my friend. It was...nice.

"Yeah. Ellie mentioned some of Wren's plans for the nursery. She's really been enjoying hanging out with Wren and Harper. I'm glad she has more friends in town."

She had her online friends—Piper and Sumner—but they lived in LA. And Lizzie, of course. But I was grateful that Harper and Wren had been so welcoming, not that I was surprised. They really seemed to appreciate Ellie's input, and I hoped that gave Ellie more confidence in herself and the value of what she had to offer.

"They adore Ellie." He smiled. "River too. He cannot stop talking about Ellie's makeup tutorials."

I laughed. "Yeah. She's talented."

I'd never admit this, but I'd watched way too many of them myself. Not for the makeup tips, no. I was fascinated by Ellie. By her creativity and artistry. By the incredible transformations she regularly accomplished.

While Ellie was naturally beautiful, I loved how she really went for it. How different she could look based on the colors she chose or the way she wore her hair. She was like a beautiful chameleon. But instead of blending into the background, she stood out.

Her online persona was so…different from the woman she presented in person. I'd catch glimmers of it, especially when she was alone with the kids and me. The confidence and strength, the playful and tenacious woman. But I wanted more of it. I wanted Ellie to feel confident enough to be as bold in person with everyone as she was online.

Liam smiled wistfully. "Sometimes I can see Tessa in Ellie's expressions."

Bennett nodded. "Which is crazy, right? Since Ellie was adopted. But I think it's their shared mannerisms."

"Their personalities are different, though. I can never imagine Tessa moving to Japan or getting a tattoo," Asher mused.

I clenched my jaw. I didn't like the idea of Asher—or anyone—looking at Ellie so closely. Or comparing her to Tessa. They were sisters, family, not competition.

Though I had to agree with him about the personality thing. They were both wonderful in their own way, but it was interesting to note the differences all the same. Where Tessa hated surprises, Ellie loved them. Tessa was calm and patient, a steady, nurturing presence. Ellie was fun and expressive, caring in her own unique way. She'd be a great mom someday.

"Hey, guys!" One of the Kiss My Ax employees came over. "I'm Annie, and I'll be your coach for the evening."

She went around the table, and her eyes lit up when I introduced myself. I tried not to let my smile slip, though I didn't want to seem overly friendly either.

After she'd explained the rules and safety procedures, she asked if there were any questions. Then she said, "We'll do a few practice rounds before we get into the competition. Who wants to go first?"

Bennett, Asher, and Liam all turned to me. This was beginning to feel like more and more of a setup. I lifted a shoulder and tried to avoid tugging at my collar. "Sure. Why not?"

I stepped into the arena with Annie. I could feel my friends' attention on us, and I had a hunch they were observing more than just my ax-throwing technique. In fact, I wondered if this was going to somehow end up in *The Vine* as well, and I cringed.

I'd never paid the local gossip blog much attention, but that was because it had mostly ignored me. Tessa and I were settled. Everyone respected our privacy. And I'd always told myself that whoever was behind the blog was smart enough to know that if they messed with me or my family, I had the tools to expose them.

Apparently, V either didn't realize that—or no longer cared.

But I wasn't going to waste my time on V's silly antics. Between the kids and finding an investor for my company, I had enough other—bigger—things to worry about.

Olen had pushed me to meet with Celeste, and I'd finally relented. The meeting was still a few months away, and I really needed to nail my pitch. But all I could think about was nailing Ellie.

Annie gave me a few tips before I picked up the ax, getting used to the feel of it in my hand. I stepped up to the block. My heart was pumping in my ears, and I was focused on the target. When I released the ax, it went sailing through the air and landed. Not a bull's-eye but not bad either.

"Nice!" Annie grinned and held up her hand for a high five.

I slapped her palm, listened to her suggestions, and then fired off another ax. Then it was Asher's turn. Then Bennett and Liam. Finally, after she was satisfied, she explained the scoring for a match. She remained at the table with us, offering pointers when necessary, but mostly just hanging out.

Annie was nice. Fun. And as much as I was enjoying my evening out with the guys, I couldn't wait to go home and tell Ellie all about the ax throwing. It seemed like something she'd enjoy—quirky, slightly dangerous, an adrenaline rush.

I decided to text her to see how things were going with the kids, though it was mostly an excuse to talk to her.

How's it going?

A moment later, a picture of the kids came through. They were dressed up and standing in front of the TV, dancing. Savannah and Maddox were bursting with joy, and I smiled.

Looks like they're having fun. What about you?

Ellie: Always.

Picture or it didn't happen. I teased, using her own words.

Ellie: OMG, you didn't.

But then an image came through of Ellie and the kids—a group selfie. The kids were making silly faces, but I was more focused on Ellie. Her cheeks were a beautiful shade of pink, her eyes dancing with laughter.

"Looks like one big happy family," Asher said from over my shoulder.

I slid my phone back into my pocket. Annie was helping Bennett while he threw against Liam.

"It's nice having her here," I admitted. "She's been a huge help with the kids."

"Mm," Asher mused then took another swig of his beer. His attention was on the targets when he said, "Is that *all* she's been helping with?"

I clenched my fists. "Fuck off, Asher."

His answering grin was smug. "Oh, so you *are* interested in her."

Was that a question? It felt more like a trap. So, I sipped my beer and didn't respond.

"I wouldn't blame you if you were. She's sweet. Sexy. Smart. The whole package, really."

"Are you guys talking about Annie?" Bennett asked, rejoining us along with Liam. Fortunately, Annie had gone to help another table and was out of earshot. "She's great, right?"

"Actually, we were talking about Ellie," Asher said, his eyes still locked on mine.

"Oh yeah. She's a sweetheart." Liam turned to Asher. "Definitely too nice for you."

While Asher scowled, I smirked and tipped my beer to Liam's. Damn straight.

"Too young for you too," I said, voicing my own objection, as if our age gap was the biggest obstacle.

They watched me curiously, so I blurted, "What? She's thirteen years younger than me. *Him*," I added quickly.

Asher lifted his shoulder, his expression smug. "So?"

"Wren's five years younger than me," Bennett chimed in. "Age is just a number."

Were they serious? I glanced around the table and realized none of my friends seemed to think this was an issue—the age difference. But Ellie was still in college. *College!*

Thirteen years might not sound like a lot, but our lives were in completely different places. Ellie's was just beginning and mine was…well, when I'd lost Tessa, it had felt like my life was over.

Lately though, something had shifted. I felt hopeful. I smiled more. And I knew it was all because of Ellie.

The guys didn't seem to think our age difference was an issue, so why did it matter so much to me? Was it because she was Tessa's younger sister? Or would I have always thought it was a big deal?

"What about the fact that she's only here for a little while?" I asked.

Earlier this week, she'd received her placement for JET. And while it was contingent on her graduating, I had faith that she would. Which meant that in a few months, she'd be moving to Naruto, Tokushima. It sounded as foreign and far as the moon.

Asher leaned back, stretching his arms above his head. "Even better."

My stomach soured, and it wasn't from the beer. Someone as unique and amazing as Ellie deserved to be spoiled. Loved. Not discarded after a temporary hookup.

"If it were anyone else," Liam said to me, "I'd tell you to go for it. A short-term fling could be exactly what you need to get back out there. But—" he frowned "—she's Tessa's sister."

I knew it was more difficult for Liam to imagine me moving on, especially with Ellie, because of his friendship with Tessa. He'd trusted Tessa with the secret of his pen name, and she'd been his beta reader for years. He might want to give his characters a happily ever after as Meghan Hart, but fiction was different from reality.

"Just be careful," Bennett said. "If you do decide to pursue something, make sure the feelings you have toward Ellie are about *Ellie*, not her relationship to Tessa. You don't want to use her just to fill a hole."

"I think he'd be the one filling a hole," Asher said. "If you know what I mean."

"I don't want to talk about this anymore." I pushed back from the table, my stool nearly toppling. I stomped over to the cage to throw my next round.

"Ellie's hot. And if you're not prepared to make a move, someone else will. Hell, I will," Asher said from behind me.

The fuck he would.

I embedded the ax in the stump that served as a stand and stalked back to the table. "No. You will not." My voice boomed out of my chest.

I told myself it was because I was looking out for her, but I knew that wasn't entirely true. I didn't like the idea of anyone else touching Ellie. Anyone who wasn't me.

Oh fuck.

He lifted his chin, defiance in his eyes. "You don't control Ellie."

My nostrils flared. I wished I could control Ellie. The things I'd do to her.

"She wouldn't go out with you anyway," I spat. "You're… Well, you're all wrong for her." *Great. And now I sound like a petulant child.*

He stood, stepping closer. Challenging me with a gleam in his eyes. "You wanna bet?"

My chest heaved, and I was so damn close to punching him. I was usually so calm, so in control, but hearing Asher speak about Ellie like that… I gnashed my teeth.

"Guys. *Guys.*" Bennett placed himself between us, a palm

pressed to each of our chests. "Don't you remember the last time Liam and Asher bet on a girl?"

Liam groaned. "Don't remind me."

Asher and I ignored them.

"Well, what do you say?" Asher asked me, his smug condescension annoying. "Care to make a little wager?"

I huffed and turned away. No way in fuck was I betting on Ellie. That was beyond wrong.

And what you want to do with Ellie isn't?

"Come on," Bennett said to Asher, tugging on his arm so he'd back down. "Drop it."

"It's getting late," I said, finally realizing that people had started to stare. "I should get home." I was done with Asher's attitude.

As I walked away from the table, I heard Liam say to Asher, "What the fuck was that about?"

Anger marked my course to the parking lot. Before I made it to my SUV, footsteps echoed off the pavement behind me. If it was Asher, he could save his breath. I didn't want to hear it.

"Tristan, hey! Wait." Not Asher. Bennett.

I turned, wondering if I'd forgotten my phone or something. I patted my pockets, but everything was where it was supposed to be.

He blew out a breath and glanced at the sky. "Look, I know we were giving you a hard time, but if you ever need to talk, I'm here."

"Thanks," I said.

Bennett had always been kind and compassionate. It was part of what made him such a great veterinarian and friend. It was part of what made me want to confide in him, even now.

"I appreciate it. I'm just—" I dragged a hand through my hair. "Fuck. I feel like I'm going fucking insane lately."

"Because of Ellie?" he asked.

I hesitated a moment then nodded. If anyone would get it, it was Bennett. He'd been living with Liam's sister when they'd fallen in love. She, like me, was a solo parent. Bennett understood what was at stake—and the importance of keeping a secret.

"Did something happen between the two of you?"

I lifted my shoulder, unwilling to offer more. Somehow, I couldn't bring myself to tell him about the night Rex got sick.

"Okay. So, either something happened, or you want it to," he mused. He shoved his hands into his pockets, rocking on his heels. "You didn't ask for my advice, but you seem really happy since Ellie arrived."

"Because she makes everything so…easy. It's effortless with her," I admitted.

"Then what's the problem?"

I started pacing, dragging a hand through my hair. "She's twenty. And fucking—" I slammed my palm against the hood of my car "—Tessa's sister."

He nodded. "If anyone understands falling for someone you shouldn't, it's me."

"Yeah, but Wren is your best friend's sister. I know that was *not* without its challenges," I said, not wanting to diminish what he'd gone through. "But it's really not the same as your late wife's younger sister."

I cringed. That sounded even worse when I said it out loud.

"No, but I know how hard it is to fight that attraction. You try to suppress it, even as you're consumed by guilt. When really, I shouldn't have felt guilty. I should've just been honest about what I wanted from the start."

I nodded, wishing I'd talked to Bennett sooner. He didn't judge me; he understood me. "Yeah, but I have the kids to think about."

He lifted a shoulder. "And they adore Ellie, and she's great with them."

Because she's their aunt!

"You can't live your life for others. Trust me." Bennett shook his head slowly. "I've been there. I was so concerned about what Liam would think about me dating his sister. How River would feel about me dating his mom. And I was miserable."

Yeah, I was definitely miserable.

CHAPTER TWELVE

Ellie

"Hey, Tess." I placed my hand on the headstone, using the flashlight on my phone to illuminate the words "Beloved Wife and Mother" carved beneath her name. "How are you?"

I laughed at my ridiculous question, though the tears had already started.

"Yeah. I know. God, I still can't believe you're gone. I can't believe it's been a whole year." *And now I'm talking to your headstone.*

I sat on the grass and crossed my legs. The ground was cold but dry, and I tried not to think of her buried beneath the earth.

"I got a tattoo."

I lowered my shirt to reveal the skin just beneath my collarbone where I had a delicate line drawing of a chrysanthemum. My mother hated it, but it was the perfect way to honor Tessa's memory. Tristan, on the other hand, had definitely seemed to like it.

I pushed away inappropriate thoughts of my sister's husband and slid my shirt back into place. "You're probably wondering why it took me so long to visit."

Instead of explaining, I launched into an update about what had been going on, talking to her as I had when she was still alive. As I did, I continuously ran my hand over some of the blades of grass, their tips tickling my palm.

I was so excited to tell her about my success as a content creator. About my new friends and my future plans.

"I just finished my final exams," I said. "If I score well enough, I'll graduate and move to Japan."

If I didn't, well… I wasn't sure what I'd do then.

Though staying here was becoming more and more appealing with every passing day.

At least, when I didn't have to see my parents. I shook my head, thinking of my run-in with Mom on the anniversary of Tessa's passing. It had been brutal, especially on that day of all days.

Ever since Tessa had died, it felt as if my mom blamed me for my sister's death. As if I were somehow responsible for the loss of her favorite child. Her biological daughter, not the one her husband had fathered with another woman.

At least that was one thing to look forward to about leaving—no more family dinners. Though I'd suffer through them if it meant more time with Tristan and the kids.

I smiled through my tears as I told Tessa about the kids. I couldn't imagine how devastating that had been for my sister —to worry that she'd never get to see them grow up. To realize that she'd miss so much of their lives if the surgery didn't go well, and they'd miss her being part of them.

I was going to miss Maddox and Savannah when I moved to Japan, assuming I moved to Japan. Even so, I knew I could come back if I wanted. But the thought of being gone at all, let alone for a year, made me indescribably sad. Life was lived in the small, quiet moments. And I'd be missing them.

I stopped myself before I could tell her about Tristan.

Because even though Tessa was gone, he was still very much hers.

And the closer we'd gotten to the anniversary of Tessa's death, the more guilt I'd felt surrounding my feelings toward Tristan. Which was why I'd kept my distance the past few days; I'd practically lived at Pore Over in the evenings, using the excuse of my finals to justify my absence.

The library had always been Tessa's place, and I couldn't handle the pity and sadness from her former coworkers. Pore Over had amazing coffee and a cool atmosphere. Something about the vibe reminded me of Mr. Tulk Café at the State Library in Melbourne. Maybe it was the wood floors or the wall-to-wall bookshelves with the coziest chairs, but it felt familiar and inviting.

Plus, I frequently popped in on Harper and Wren. I was enjoying their friendship. Wren was passionate about photography, and crazy about her boys and baked goods. Sometimes I went to hang out at their studio, just so I could love on her adorable French bulldog, Toodles.

I loved hearing about Harper's adventures. I'd been giving her content ideas for the vineyard she owned with her husband, Enzo. As well as working with Harper and Wren on some ways to best position the photography studio, especially the boudoir shoots. It felt good to use my skills, and they seemed to really appreciate my help.

I didn't know how Harper juggled everything she did—wife to a former soccer superstar, mom, photographer, winery owner. But she seemed happy. Actually, she and Enzo reminded me a lot of Tristan and Tessa. High-achieving. Loving. Community-minded.

I shivered, blaming it on the coolness from the ground seeping into my pants. "Anyway," I said, knowing it was getting late. "I just wanted to come say hi. And I'm sorry."

I wrapped my arms around my legs and pulled them to

my chest. I wasn't sure what I was apologizing for. Not being there when she needed me. Missing the funeral. Lusting after her husband. All of it.

I sighed and grabbed my bike, riding home. The house was dark when I wheeled my bike up the back path. Rex lifted his head but then went back to sleep.

I tiptoed toward the stairs but barely made it a few feet when a deep, authoritative voice said, "It's past curfew. Where were you?"

I held a hand to my chest, my heart pounding. "Crap on a cracker. You startled me."

I frowned into the darkness, my eyes needing a moment to adjust. A light flicked on, and I spotted Tristan sitting on the couch. Drink in hand. For a moment, I wondered if he'd been waiting for me. The idea sent a thrill through me, but I quickly pushed it aside.

He's mourning his wife, you idiot.

I'd avoided the cemetery on the anniversary of Tessa's death, wanting to give Tristan the space he needed to grieve. But seeing him now, I realized I didn't want to be alone. I dropped my bag at the foot of the stairs then took a seat on the couch.

"I'm sorry if I scared you," he said.

I waved a hand through the air. "No. It's not that."

He frowned. "What's wrong?" When I shook my head, he said, "Ellie, you know you can talk to me."

My bottom lip quivered. I felt so raw. Like someone had cracked me open and spilled my insides.

But I didn't want to talk about it. Instead, I held out my hand. "Can I have some? *Please.*"

His brown eyes were filled with concern. "If I say yes, will you talk to me?"

"Yes," I croaked.

With a deep sigh, he placed his glass in my hand. I took a

deep gulp, the whiskey burning as it slid down my throat. Making me feel more alive. He gave me a moment then I handed the glass back, our fingers brushing in the process. I knew he expected me to explain, and he wouldn't ask again.

Finally, I took a deep breath and said, "Sometimes, I think being in Australia allowed me to ignore reality. Allowed me to pretend she wasn't really gone."

Tristan ran a hand through his hair. "Sometimes I think about escaping. Leaving and going somewhere that we could pretend this never happened."

"But…"

"But I know that no matter where we go, we will always feel the loss. And I can't change it. And I hate that I can't fix that for them."

I knew what he meant. Sometimes it was so heartbreaking to watch the kids. To know how much they missed their mom. Tristan and I could love Maddox and Savannah—and we did—but we could never replace that bond between mother and child.

Instead of telling Tristan that, though, I blurted, "I should've come home sooner," regret forcing the words from my mouth. I didn't need pressure from my mom to feel guilty about missing the funeral. I already felt terrible.

Yet my mom couldn't seem to let it go. It wasn't *my* fault that the flight had been diverted to Hawaii after a mechanical issue had deemed the plane unsafe to continue flying. By the time I'd managed to get another flight, it was too late. The funeral had already taken place, and if I hadn't returned to Melbourne, I would've missed my finals. Then Mom would've blamed me for that too.

Even so, I could've come home sooner. Not just for the funeral.

But now, I wondered if I'd been avoiding it. Reality. The truth. The pain. "I hate that I didn't come one more time before—" My voice cracked on the last word, and I gave up trying to speak for the moment.

Tristan placed his hand on mine. "You're here now."

"Even so…"

"Liam punched Bennett," Tristan announced, leaning forward to place his glass on the coffee table. I missed his touch instantly. "Here at the house, after the funeral."

My eyes went wide. Liam punched one of his best friends at his other best friend's wife's funeral? Whoa. I couldn't even imagine it. I mean, it seemed out of character for Liam. "What? Why?"

"Because he found out Bennett had been sleeping with Wren and lying to him about it."

"Ooh." I winced. "Wow. *Escándalo.*"

Tristan laughed. "No joke."

"But Liam's cool with it now?" I could tell he was happy for his sister and his friend, even if he didn't want to hear about their sex life.

"It took some time, but yeah. He came around. Liam was also really close with Tessa, and he took her loss especially hard."

I nodded. Tessa had often spoken of Liam. And while she'd always been good friends with Asher and Bennett too, she and Liam had seemed closer than the others.

"Man, now I really wish I'd been there. I bet my mom was *pissed.*"

He sighed, running a hand through his hair. "Honestly, that day was such a blur. I have no idea if Gloria saw what happened or cared."

I wasn't sure what Gloria cared about at this point, apart from her image as mayor. But I was more focused on Tristan. So, I nodded, placing my hand on his arm, wanting to do something, *anything,* to comfort him. Or maybe I was seeking my own solace. At this point, I didn't know. It felt as if our feelings blurred together.

"You want some more?" he asked, grabbing his empty tumbler and giving it a shake. The remnants of the ice cubes rattled against the glass.

"What happened to *no drinking until you're twenty-one?*" I teased, doing a poor job of mimicking his deep voice.

He lifted a shoulder and stood. "You know your limits. Besides, as you said, life is short. You may as well enjoy it."

I studied him.

"What?" he asked from the kitchen as he refilled his glass with fresh ice and prepared a second one for me. I followed him, searching for a snack.

"Is this a do as I say and not as I do type thing?" I asked, rummaging through the pantry for something, anything, sweet.

"What do you mean?" He reached past me and grabbed a pack of peanut M&Ms from a basket on the top shelf then placed them on the counter.

"What?" I stared at him, mouth agape. "You've been holding out on me all this time?"

He rolled his eyes. "No. I don't often keep sweets in the house."

"I've noticed. I was beginning to think you didn't like them."

"The opposite, actually. They're fucking tempting." The way he was looking at me was like I was a sweet treat he wanted to devour. Yet I knew he wouldn't. The man had more self-control than anyone I'd ever met. It was both admirable and infuriating.

"You say life is short, and you may as well enjoy it. But you don't seem to heed your own advice."

He stepped closer, and I wondered if it was intentional. Or if his body kept gravitating toward me, like mine did to him. All this time, I'd worried he regretted that night in his room. And now, I was beginning to wonder if he'd been waiting for me to take the next step.

"I meant for you," he said, grabbing a few peanut M&Ms from the bag. "You're young, Ellie. You have your whole life ahead of you—hopefully a long, happy, healthy one."

"And you're *not*?"

"Not what?"

"Not young? Not presented with opportunities?"

He popped a peanut M&M into his mouth but said nothing. That was answer enough. His whole attitude was pissing me off. Or maybe it was all the pent-up frustration I felt around him.

"Fuck that," I said through gritted teeth. If Tessa's death had taught me anything, it was that, "Life is too short not to live the way you want."

He sighed. "I'm just—" He ran a hand through his hair, tugging on the ends. "I'm under a lot of pressure. More than you know."

My stomach churned, and I worried what he wasn't saying. He reached for the M&Ms, but I swiped the bag from the counter and hid them behind my back.

"Can I have some? *Please.*" He batted his eyes, mimicking my words from before.

So I told him the same thing he'd said to me. "If I say yes, will you talk to me?"

He chuckled and lifted his glass and took another drink. "Sometimes I wish I were more like you. You're so carefree. Most of the time, you don't give a fuck what anyone else thinks."

"That's not entirely true, but it's nice to know that I come across that way, I guess."

"I just—fuck." He leaned against the counter, gripping the edge. "I feel so out of control, and I'm sick of it."

"That's the problem. You're trying to control everything, when you need to let loose. Want me to help you be more wild?" I teased, eager for a lighter topic.

"I'm sure you could." He chuckled, eyeing me with something suspiciously like desire. "But my life is wild enough as it is between two kids, a crazy dog, and a hedgehog. I mean, what the hell was I thinking?"

"With the hedgehog?" I asked. "I've been wondering. I mean, Hedgie is cute and all but not the cuddliest of pets. She's literally a ball of spikes. And a nocturnal one at that."

"Savannah has been obsessed with hedgehogs for as long as I can remember. It was our first Christmas without Tessa, and well, I would've done anything to make it better for her."

He straightened as if telling himself to cut it out. And I was tired of seeing him try to hide his pain. Holding it together for the kids was tearing him apart.

"Tristan." I took his glass from his hand and set it on the counter, wanting to make sure I had his full attention. "You deserve to enjoy life and all it has to offer."

That belief was part of what had pushed me to get a tattoo. To make the most of my time in Melbourne. To apply for the JET Program. Because what was the point of this one wild and precious life if not to do something with it?

"I did. Before…"

"You still can," I said, brushing his hair away from his face.

That night in his room, I'd resisted touching him. But now that I had, I couldn't seem to stop.

"Can I?" His gaze met mine.

Brown eyes tinged with sadness but curiosity too. This close, I could see the way the chestnut blended with gold like the colors in my favorite eye shadow palette, and I held his gaze. I clung to the connection, even as it filled me with an ache so strong I didn't know how much more I could take.

If life was too short, I didn't want to waste this moment. I didn't want to hold back.

"Sometimes I think you're the only person who understands me," I whispered, as if we were sharing a secret.

He sighed and closed his eyes, our foreheads kissing. "I feel the same way."

I smiled, relief and anticipation blooming in my chest.

He let out a deep breath, gripping my hips as if restraining himself. It felt as if this thing between us could barely be contained.

Let go, I chanted. *Give in.*

He cupped my cheek, his eyes assessing mine as if asking a question. Whatever it was, he seemed to have found the answer. He slid his hand to the back of my neck, pulling me closer still. My core throbbed, the ache intensifying the longer he looked at me like that.

I held my breath, anticipating the moment he'd press his lips to mine. I could smell the whiskey on his breath. I could feel the warmth radiating from his skin.

I waited, wanting him to take that next step. Make that first move to ease this unbearable tension that seemed ever-present between us. But when the seconds stretched on, I couldn't take it anymore.

I pressed my lips to his. And when he finally took control of the kiss, my body came alive in a way unlike ever before. His tongue was teasing my seam, making me open for him. When he nipped at my bottom lip and lifted me onto the counter, I was breathless.

Holy fuck. There was kissing, and then there was *this*.

It was soft and hard. He was both tender and passionate. I wanted to take my time, kiss him slowly until I'd gotten my fill. And yet I craved *more*. More of his hands on my skin, exploring. More of his lips tasting, capturing.

I'd never felt anything like this all-consuming need. And I'd never expected to feel it with Tristan.

With our foreheads still touching, and my body still quaking, he groaned. I'd never heard a sound more tortured.

"What are we doing, Elle?"

Not Eleanor or Ellie, but Elle. Apart from Tristan, no one had ever called me Elle, and I liked it immediately.

I didn't know what we were doing, but I knew I wanted more of it. More Tristan. And judging from the way his cock was nudging me through my leggings, he wanted more of this too.

"Kissing," I said, toying with the ends of his hair. It was silky and smooth. "*Living*."

He shook his head slowly and backed away. Severing our touch and breaking the spell. "I'll only end up hurting you."

"I don't believe that."

"Believe what you want, princess." He glared at me. "It's the truth."

"Princess?" I crossed my arms over my chest, annoyed by the nickname. What did he think I was? A spoiled brat?

He growled and put his back to me, chin lifted to the ceiling. "Go to bed, Ellie."

Ellie. Not Elle. Seriously? I gnashed my teeth, stung by the sudden shift in his demeanor. "I'm not a child."

When I didn't move, he spun to me with anger in his eyes, and it felt as if he was chastising me. "Go. To. Bed," he said through gritted teeth. "Before I do or say something we'll both regret."

Too late for that.

CHAPTER THIRTEEN

Tristan

"What. The. Fuck?" The words were muttered under my breath as I stomped out to the backyard. If Ellie wouldn't go upstairs, then I would leave. Because I sure as hell couldn't stay inside after that kiss. Not with her there to tempt me.

I'd been asking what the fuck. But I should've been asking *what the fuck is wrong with me?*

I mean, my late wife's much younger sister? *Really?*

And yet, I was drawn to Ellie.

My body didn't seem to care that she wasn't even twenty-one. That it was a shitty thing to do—get her drunk and then kiss her. She'd said life was too short not to live the way you wanted, but what if what you wanted was wrong?

Light from the kitchen spilled onto the backyard. I stomped farther into the garden and stumbled over a shovel, the metal scraping against the stone path. "Goddammit."

I caught myself before I could fall and picked up the shovel, ready to toss it aside. Instead, I glanced around. It was as if I was seeing the backyard for the first time. And it was a mess.

The garden had always been Tessa's domain. But since her diagnosis, it had been neglected. Forgotten. Then she'd died, and I'd never had the time or inclination to do anything about it.

I could've hired someone like Enzo's mother-in-law, Linda Allen, to bring it back to life, but it felt wrong somehow. Allowing the plants to bloom and flourish even as my beautiful wife withered beneath the ground.

Anger burned through me. Some of it was rage that Tessa was gone. A bigger part of it was disappointment in myself.

Without thinking, I started hacking at the roots of the first dead plant I saw. I was *so* sick of death.

I attacked another bush. The kids were asleep upstairs. It was the middle of night, and someone would likely complain about this to *The Vine*. But I. Didn't. Fucking. Care.

For the first time in a year, I felt alive. Alive and angry and… I panted. I was reeling from that kiss.

Not just *a* kiss. A fucking *amazing* kiss.

I chopped down another bush, satisfaction humming through my veins. Every time the shovel hit dirt, I kept going.

All the while, her words kept playing through my mind. Tessa's words. *Life is too short.* I chanted it in my head like a mantra. Followed by Ellie's words. *Life's too short not to live the way you want.*

I stopped for a moment, wiping the sweat from my brow. I was covered in dirt. My skin tingled with awareness, and I stood and glanced at the house.

Ellie was standing in the doorway, and for a moment, we stared at each other, the tension stretching between us. I was so sick of doing everything right. Everything expected of me. For once, I wanted to say fuck it and do what I wanted.

I wanted to kiss her for standing her ground with me

when she let her mother walk all over her. I wanted to punish her for defying me. I wanted… I heaved in a shaky breath. So many things.

I stalked toward her until we stood chest to chest on the back porch, our breaths sawing in and out. I hated seeing the pain in her eyes when I'd told her to go to bed. I'd been trying to protect her, but she was right—I'd treated her like a child.

I didn't think of her as a child. She didn't deserve that.

"I'm sorry," I panted.

"For what?" She cocked her hip to the side, eyes blazing with anger and hurt. "Leading me on? Pushing me away?"

I should've said, *All of it.* But instead, I said, "I'm only trying to protect you."

She scoffed and took a few steps closer. "That's not your job." She jabbed my chest. "It's not *your* decision." She jabbed me again, anger lacing her words.

I clenched my fists, every bit of my being directed toward restraining myself. "Ellie…"

"Tell me," she demanded, planting her hands on her hips. "Is this because of my age? Or because you think I'm immature? Maybe both?"

"I—" I swallowed hard, knowing I needed to choose my words carefully. It had nothing to do with any of that. "I just…" I sighed. "Our lives are in different places. And pursuing something would be a bad idea."

"Even though you want to."

It wasn't a question of want. It was a matter of reason.

Finally, she huffed and said, "So, you want me, but you won't let yourself have me."

"Of course, I want you." I backed her against the side of the house, bracketing her in my arms. "Can't you feel how much I want you?" I ground against her.

Her eyes rolled backward, and she moaned. "Yes," she hissed.

"But we can't," I rasped, my control slipping away with every second. With every slide of my cock against her core. The friction from our clothes was maddening.

"Fuck," she said, rocking her hips against me, "*that.*"

I slid my hands onto her waist, up and over her ribs. This was… Oh god. I didn't know how much longer I could resist.

"*Please,*" she panted. "Please, Tristan. I need this."

I need you.

I growled, smashing my lips to hers, letting myself get carried away with the moment. She tasted like peanut M&Ms and hope. And it felt incredible to finally have her in my arms. To do what I'd wanted for so long. But then a car door slammed in the distance, and with it, some of the lust cleared.

I wanted this, her. But not like this. Not after she'd seemed so emotionally vulnerable. If we were going to do this, I wanted it to be for the right reasons.

"Not here," I panted, rubbing my thumb over her lips. "Not like this." I took a step back and shoved my hands into my pockets.

She swallowed hard, her eyes going wide as if realizing where we were. "Oh my god. You're right. What were we thinking? The kids."

I nodded. That was part of it, but part of it was selfish. I wanted to know that when we finally did this, I'd have her all to myself. There would be no distractions. I would get to take my time.

I was tempted to take her hand in mine, but I couldn't. Wouldn't. I knew I wouldn't be able to stop myself if I touched her again.

"Elle," I said, my chest still heaving.

"Hmm."

I leaned in, my lips nearly touching her ear. "Next time I touch you, I won't stop."

Her eyes darkened, and she bit back a smile. "I'm going to hold you to that."

I couldn't wait.

CHAPTER FOURTEEN

Ellie

The house was empty when I returned from dropping the kids off at school, and I found the quiet unnerving. Or maybe I just didn't want to be alone with my thoughts. I was waiting for my final exam results, waiting to find out if I'd graduate and proceed with the JET Program. But it was so much more than that.

I couldn't stop thinking about Tristan and what had happened last night. But I hadn't seen him since.

He'd left for an early bike ride with Enzo. And by the time he was back to get ready for work, I'd been at school with the kids. Now he was at work, and I couldn't stop thinking about him. About his promise…

Rex nudged my hand with his head, urging me to pet him.

"Okay, boy." I laughed when he licked my palm because I hadn't responded fast enough for his liking. "I know. *I know.*"

I crouched down to his level, scratching behind his ears. His tongue lolled out of his mouth, and it made me laugh. I hadn't realized how much I'd enjoy having a dog around, though I had a feeling a big part of it was Rex's playful personality. Sometimes I felt as if we were having a conversation. He was so expressive, and he often barked at just the right time.

We spent a lot of time together, especially since the night of his surgery. He'd always been attentive, but he'd followed me around like a furry shadow since then.

"Is somebody needing some attention?" I asked in a cutesy voice. "Huh?"

I smoothed my hand down his coat, patting his flanks. "I have to work on a tutorial, but you can hang out with me. As long as you can stay out of trouble." I narrowed my eyes at him.

A little whine in response.

"Yeah, that's what I thought," I muttered, knowing I was asking a lot.

Before I headed upstairs, I refilled Rex's water bowl and responded to a few comments on social media. I checked the university website again, but the exam results still hadn't been posted. I let out a sigh and navigated to *The Vine*, where the large banner with an image of a grapevine and the blog site name filled most of the screen. I scrolled down, searching for any new posts. Anything to distract me.

According to *The Vine*, Bennett was organizing a cookbook with Mrs. Marcus to raise funds for feline renal research. Maybe I'd submit a pavlova recipe. It was a classic Australian dessert with a crunchy exterior and a fluffy, marshmallow-like interior.

I tossed my phone aside and went to shower, so I could film the tutorial. Anything to keep my mind off my exam results and Tristan. Besides, assuming my alter ego was always a welcome distraction.

At times, I liked the online version of myself better than the real me. Online, I was flirty and sexy and fun. I was a badass who wasn't afraid to express herself. And I was sought out for my expertise and passion.

Last night, I'd felt closer to that version of me, of the woman I wanted to be. I'd been flirty with Tristan. Brazen. And I hadn't backed down, even when he'd tried to push me away. And my persistence had paid off.

I toweled off and slipped into my favorite silk robe—a splurge from my previous trip to Japan—turning up the music playing on my phone. I was applying my eye shadow base when my phone rang, and Piper's name flashed across the screen along with a request for FaceTime. I made sure my robe was closed before I pressed the button to connect the call.

She waved, a huge smile on her face. "Hey, beautiful!"

"Hey!" I grinned.

"What are you getting all dolled up for? A date?"

I barked out a laugh. "Um. No. I'm trying out a look for a new tutorial in an effort to distract myself so I don't refresh the exam results page every two seconds." *Not like you haven't already done that all morning.*

"Ooh. Love it! And you did great. I know it."

I hoped she was right. I'd given it my best. As Tessa always liked to remind me, that was all I could expect of myself.

"So…any new developments since the *haircut*?" she asked.

"*Maybe.*" I bit back my smile.

"Mm-hmm." When I continued to focus on my eye shadow, she said, "I knew you had the hots for him!"

I let out a deep sigh. What was I supposed to say? I couldn't lie to Piper. And if I didn't talk to someone, I was going to explode. And I really, *really* did not want to tell anyone in town about my complicated feelings for my brother-in-law.

As much as I liked and trusted Harper and Wren, they were his friends too. First, really. And Tessa's. I slumped.

"Come on. Spill," Piper said.

So, I did. I knew I could trust her. Plus, the idea of my feelings toward Tristan somehow ending up in *The Vine* was terrifying.

"What is up with my friends falling for forbidden men?" Piper joked when I'd finished.

"What are you talking about?" What could possibly be worse than falling for your sister's husband?

"Surely I've told you about Sumner and her husband, Wolfe?"

"No." I shook my head. "What about them?"

"Her husband is her dad's best friend."

I covered my gasp. "What? You never told me that." My mind was reeling. "Oh my god. Seriously?"

Piper nodded, but my mind was still stuck on the fact that he was *her dad's best friend*.

I set down my makeup brush. "Her dad must have hotter friends than mine."

Piper laughed, but I mean, how much older was Wolfe? Twenty years? More? Tristan seemed freaked out by our age gap, but I had a feeling it was nothing compared to the one between Sumner and her dad's best friend.

"Yes, Wolfe is hot. And did I mention that he was also her boss for the summer?"

"Holy—" I wasn't even sure what to say. "What about Sumner's dad?"

"Oh, he was pissed. Wouldn't speak to either of them for a long time."

"At least I don't have that to worry about, I guess." I frowned at my reflection, facing an onslaught of conflicting emotions. Sadness that my sister was gone. Yet a bittersweet knowledge that if she were here, well, Tristan and I wouldn't be...whatever we were.

"I'm sorry, Ellie." Piper's tone was gentle. One I could

imagine her using with her daughter. "I know you miss your sister."

I nodded, forcing back tears. My twenty-first birthday was coming up, and Tessa had always made my birthdays extra special by sending me flowers and a new book she just knew I'd love. And she was always right about the book. Last year, even though my birthday was after she'd died, I'd received a book. I'd been shocked and yet not at all surprised that she'd put something in place before her surgery. But this year, I was dreading my birthday.

It was hitting me really hard that she was gone. That I was still here, living life. And she'd stopped having birthdays. She would forever be thirty-three. It all seemed so unfair.

Life is too fucking short.

"I sometimes wonder if that's why I gravitate toward Tristan. Because he's the only person who truly understands." I hadn't realized it until I'd spoken the words aloud.

"Shared experience, especially shared grief, is powerful."

"Yeah, but—" I glanced at the ceiling and sighed. "It feels like more than that. There's this—I don't know. Pull. I can't explain it, but I feel it." I jabbed at my chest. "Here."

"Are you sure *that's* where you feel the pull?" she teased as I closed my makeup palette and set it aside.

"Ha-ha. Yes, I'm attracted to him. How could I not be? He's smart and witty and such a good dad."

"Uh-oh." She grinned. "Someone's got it bad."

I rolled my eyes but didn't even try to deny it. "It's not like I'm looking for something long-term." I continued, just... needing to voice my thoughts aloud. To try to make sense of everything. "I'll be leaving again in a few months."

"True, and it could get hella awkward if you guys sleep together. You do realize that, right?"

I scoffed and opened another makeup palette. Boy, did I

ever. But I was already too far in to stop, and I was tired of thinking of reasons why we shouldn't be together.

"Surely there are some hometown hotties *besides* Tristan that you'd be interested in."

I scrunched up my nose and shook my head. I'd hooked up with a few guys in Melbourne. Guys who were fun. The problem was, all the guys my age seemed so immature.

But it was more than that. The few guys I'd slept with were boring in bed. I'd always been told I had a vivid imagination, and compared to what I'd imagined, so far, sex was disappointing. So, I'd resigned myself to using my vibrator.

I heard a noise from down the hall and realized Rex was no longer in the bedroom with me. "Thanks for listening. I should probably get going. Rex is off doing god knows what."

"Uh-oh." She laughed. "Anytime. Have fun!"

"Thanks." I waved and disconnected the call then stood. "Rex? Where are you, buddy?"

I frowned down at the empty living room. Hedgie was sleeping peacefully, but the house was quiet. Too quiet. And as I glanced around, my sense of dread only grew.

I jogged to the kids' room, my robe fluttering about my thighs. Empty. No sign of Rex.

"Rex?" I called again.

He growled, and then it sounded like he was struggling with something. *Oh no, what's he into this time?* After the string incident, I was paranoid about leaving him alone. He was too curious for his own good. He couldn't be trusted.

He growled again, and I cringed. I'd already checked several places, and judging from the sounds, there was only one place he could be. I really did not want to go into Tristan's room, so I tried to lure Rex out with something I knew he couldn't resist.

"Rexy. You want a treat?"

When he didn't come, I knew whatever he'd found was

definitely something he shouldn't be messing with. I took a few steps closer to Tristan's room, still hesitant to cross the threshold.

"Rex," I chided, creeping farther into the room. "Come here."

Tessa's nightstand was bare apart from a lamp, though Tristan had cleared it weeks ago. But now, he'd removed any photos of her in the room. That was new—at least from the last time I'd peeked in here. He'd ditched the patterned duvet cover, leaving white sheets and a white down comforter.

I wondered what had prompted Tristan to make all those changes. I wondered if it had anything to do with me.

Rex snarled, and when I rounded the corner to Tessa's closet, my heart sank. He had her shoe in his mouth, and he was gnawing on it. A box with the word "Donate" written on it had been overturned. Shoes littered the floor, and several dresses as well. There were scraps of fabric and leather and...

"Rex. No!"

I tried to grab the shoe from his mouth, but he thought it was a game. I tugged, and he pulled, my hair falling in my face as I grunted and tried to wrest it from his mouth. I lost my grip and flew backward, landing on my butt. I could've sworn he smirked.

I glared at him. "Rex."

He barked in triumph as he darted past me, taking off with his treasure. *Great,* I sighed. *Just freaking great.*

I was tempted to go after him, but the damage was already done. At least the shoe might keep him busy while I cleaned up and tried to salvage what I could.

Ugh. What a mess.

I crouched down, grabbing everything that was still intact and returning it to the "Donate" box. Then I moved on to the clothes. Tessa's closet was nearly empty, and I assumed the few items Tristan had kept were for the kids or for sentimental reasons.

I spotted a dress Tessa had worn when she and the kids had visited me in Melbourne. It was white with a peasant chic sort of vibe to it. I smiled, though sadness followed quickly on its heels. I'd always loved this dress, probably because I associated it with exploring St. Kilda and taking the kids to Luna Park. It was the last time I'd seen my sister in person.

I held it to my nose, the scent of her lingering on the material along with the memories. I smiled and slowly opened my eyes, spying my reflection in the mirror. I held Tessa's dress up to my body, wondering if it would fit.

I glanced around the room as if to confirm I was alone, making my way toward the door. I crossed the hall to my room and untied my robe. I slipped into the dress, the feel of the material gliding over my skin decadent. Sensual.

The dress was tighter on me than it had been on my sister, my curves barely encased by the material. I wondered if Tristan would like how it looked on me. I wondered if he'd like the feel of my body.

And while I did, I closed my eyes and squeezed my breasts, letting out a small moan. Unable to stop, I let my hand drift lower, dipping beneath my panties.

I imagined his reaction. His hunger. I'd seen him look at me with desire, and I imagined him finally snapping and losing control. Giving in to this, to me.

"Oh god, Tristan," I whispered. "Yes."

I pretended my finger was his, his lips caressing my neck. His hand on my breast.

I heard a noise and figured it was just Rex, so I ignored it. I needed to talk to Bennett about obedience school for that dog. But first, I really, *really* needed to come.

The pressure was rising. My fingers sliding against my

clit, my arousal coating my skin. I could envision it all so clearly, it was as if Tristan were standing there with me. It felt so real.

And then his deep voice reverberated through me. "What are you doing?"

I opened my eyes and startled. He was standing at the door to my room, watching me. And this time, it wasn't in my imagination.

CHAPTER FIFTEEN

Ellie

I yelped and dropped the hem of the dress, my cheeks flaming with heat. "I, um. I—"

"Elle," he chided.

"I'm so sorry. I—" I knelt to the floor and picked up my robe, holding it in front of me as if to shield myself. How long had he been standing there? How had I not heard him come in? "I didn't know you were home. I should've closed the door."

"Yet you didn't." His eyes darkened, his hands braced on the doorframe. My core throbbed, reminding me of the orgasm I'd been on the cusp of. "Why?"

"Rex—"

Where was that freaking dog? I couldn't believe the mess he'd made, leaving me to clean it up and then explain to Tristan why I was wearing his wife's dress. Touching myself while thinking of him. *Fuck.*

"Rex is in the backyard." His reaction was measured, controlled. But a muscle in his jaw clenched.

Probably burying that damn shoe. *Traitor.*

Tristan's tone did nothing to put me at ease. And yet, beneath the surface, excitement thrummed through me.

"He got into some...trouble in your room while I was getting ready." I dipped my head, the air charged with emotion. I couldn't bring myself to speak my sister's name. "I'm sorry."

It was then he seemed to notice what I was wearing. My nipples were visible beneath the white material, my breasts straining against the fabric.

"Seems like he's not the only one." His voice was laced with danger, his eyes black with anger—or was that need?

Tristan backed away, his eyes on me the entire time as he went to sit in the chair at my desk. "Show me what you were doing."

"In your room?" I asked, my voice breathy.

It felt as if we were playing some sort of game. One where I didn't know the rules or what was expected of me.

He shook his head slowly. "In the mirror."

My nipples hardened beneath the dress, the gauzy material erotic when it rubbed against them. His eyes went there, his jaw clenching. *Oh god.*

Was he serious? Was this what he'd hinted at last night when he'd promised not to stop?

I wasn't going to question it. I was sick of denying myself what I wanted. And I wanted Tristan.

I glided my hands up my stomach, his eyes growing hooded the longer it took me to reach my breasts. I slid my hands over my breasts, cupping them and pinching my nipples. It sent a jolt of lightning to my core, and I wished it were his hands on me.

"That's it." His encouragement made me want to continue.

Slowly, I smoothed my hands up my neck and into my

hair, closing my eyes briefly as I imagined his lips on my neck, my breasts.

Tristan's sharp intake of breath was gratifying, as was the way he continued to stare at me, mouth slightly agape. His legs were spread wide, the outline of his thick cock becoming more evident in his pants. He hadn't even laid a finger on me, and yet, I was so turned on I thought I might combust.

"Were you thinking of me while you touched yourself?" When I didn't respond, he narrowed his eyes. "Answer me."

I gulped at the power and intensity radiating from him. I was both nervous and excited, eagerly anticipating what he'd do next. I wasn't sure I'd ever been more turned on. This was even better than my fantasies.

"Yes," I hissed, wishing he'd touch me now.

He jerked his head toward the mattress. "Get on the bed."

I shivered, excitement racing through me. "Why?"

"Because I told you to. Now be a good girl and do as I said."

Oh holy… My breath caught in my throat. A rush of intensity flooded me—desire, longing, surprise. In any other context, I would've hated being called a "good girl." But hearing those two words from Tristan was like flipping a switch. And I wanted to do nothing more than please him so he'd continue to praise me.

I crawled onto the bed and faced him. The material barely covered my thighs, and he swallowed thickly as he drank me in.

"Look at you." He shook his head as if in disbelief.

I liked the way he was looking at me. I liked the way he gripped the arms of the chair, as if he were about to lose control. And I wanted to see him unravel. Drive him as crazy as he made me.

"How do you like to touch yourself?" he asked, his gaze

intense. "I want to see." It was as if he were studying me so he could learn the secrets of what turned me on. And that made me even hotter.

I reached between my legs, rubbing myself over my thong. The material was so wet it was sticking to me, my need at an all-time high.

And even though he wasn't actually touching me, it was as if there were an invisible thread connecting us. I always felt that pull to him, but even more so now. I peeled my panties aside, needing more pressure. More *something*.

He pressed down on his cock then froze. "Is that a piercing?"

I bit my lip and nodded, my hair falling around my face.

"Show me," he said through gritted teeth.

I lifted my hips to remove my panties, but he shook his head. "No. Keep them on."

I frowned but quickly masked my disappointment. Instead, I did as he asked and pulled my panties aside. I'd continue doing whatever he asked so long as I got more of this, *him*.

I used my fingers to spread my folds, giving him a clear view of my vertical clit hood piercing. For a minute, I feared he hated it, but then he groaned, "So *fucking* hot."

His words spurred me on, and I started rubbing myself again. This time harder, faster. I moaned as the pleasure built once more. And I was getting so close. I was on the verge of coming when he said, "Stand."

"Wh-what?" I was breathless. "Now?"

"Yes, now," he commanded.

I liked seeing Tristan's confidence and strength as he took charge in the bedroom. It was hot. At least when he wasn't withholding my orgasm.

I shook my head. I didn't stop. Couldn't.

"Elle," he cautioned. "Stand."

He might be the one issuing the commands, but I knew I could say no at any time. I knew if I told him I wanted to stop, we would. And even though I was tempted to defy him again, I was more curious to discover what he had planned.

So, I forced myself to do as he said. I stood and wobbled on my feet, nearly collapsing to the floor.

He patted his lap. Did he want me to…?

"Come."

Oh god, yes.

I squeezed my thighs together. I was most definitely going to come. Just from the scene he'd painted alone. The image of him… I swallowed hard and willed my feet to move. Nerves and anticipation flooded my bloodstream, and I was dying to see what he'd do next.

He parted his legs, sliding his hands down his quads, fingers spread wide. He inhaled a shaky breath and let it out slowly.

"On your stomach." He patted his thigh.

I tilted my head. "Wh-what?"

"Don't make me repeat myself. If you're not interested, say so now."

Oh, I was *definitely* interested.

I scrambled onto his lap, putting myself at his mercy. His cock prodded me in the stomach, my breasts smashed against his thigh. I had no idea what he was going to do next, and that thrilled me. I loved surprises. I loved not knowing what to expect.

"Mm." He smoothed his hand over my ass. "Good girl."

I squeezed my thighs together, and he hummed with satisfaction.

"You like that, huh?" he asked.

I bit my lip and nodded. I liked everything about it. The tone of his voice. The feel of his hand on my skin. The words he used.

"You want my touch?" he asked, and I nodded again. "I need words, Elle."

"I—" I swallowed. "Yes. I want more."

"Good." He seemed pleased, and my chest vibrated from the compliment. He lifted the hem of the dress, the cool air hitting my bare skin. "Love this ass. You have no idea the things I've imagined doing to it."

I was dizzy. Delirious. Dreaming. I was positive of it. All the blood rushing to my head as I lay across his hip for him to do as he pleased.

He slid his hand beneath the strap of my thong, and it added pressure to my clit. If my panties hadn't been wet before, they were soaked now. He gave it a little tug, and I inhaled through my nose and let it out slowly.

His hand disappeared, and then I felt a smack. I jolted, but his other hand was on my lower back, holding me firmly in place. Assuring me that I was safe. Cherished.

He smoothed the burn with his hand, but I wanted more. Again. Harder. I wiggled my ass on his lap, needing…friction. *Something.*

"Mm. You *do* like being spanked." He gave my ass another slap. "Though I already suspected as much." He soothed the skin with his palm. "God, how you torture me. But you already knew that, didn't you?"

When I didn't answer, he spanked me again, this time a little harder, as if he were gently testing my limits. "When I ask you a question, I expect an answer."

"Ye-yes." My nipples brushed against the material of the dress, my breasts heavy and aching for his touch. "And no. I didn't know that." But I'd hoped.

"Good. Should I reward you?"

I whimpered. And when I tried to glance back at him, he applied pressure to my upper back, holding me in place. "Yes, please."

He spread my ass cheeks wide with his hands, tracing my thong with his finger. "You're dripping for me."

"Does that please you?" I dared to ask.

"Very much so," he nearly growled, and it made me wetter still.

I was completely at his mercy, and I absolutely loved it. I loved the way he touched me—possessively yet tenderly. I loved the way he spoke to me, his own desire barely restrained. And I wondered what it would take to push him over the edge.

He continued smoothing his hand over my ass, and I was breathless with anticipation for what would come next. He was barely touching me, and already he'd worked me into a frenzy. I moaned when he slid his finger down my slit. Jolted when he pulled back my thong and then let it go, allowing it to flick against my sensitive skin.

Again, I squeezed my thighs together. Squirming. Aching.

And again, he applied pressure to my back so I was pinned in place. "Patience," he chided. "If you're patient, you'll be rewarded. Do you understand?"

"Yes," I breathed, my thoughts hazy. As much as I wanted a reward, my patience was running low after being brought to the brink of orgasm twice now and having to wait.

Slowly, ever so slowly, he slid his hand down my ass. He teased my clit through my panties, my arousal perfuming the air. He took his time, building my pleasure until I thought I might burst. And then backing off again. Over and over, he brought me to the edge, until I was begging him for mercy.

"Please," I moaned. "Oh god, Tristan."

I squeezed my eyes shut. Imagining his face. Imagining what we must look like, my body draped over his strong legs. His hand disappearing beneath my dress. The words indecent and erotic came to mind.

And then he slid a finger inside me, and my body simultaneously tensed and relaxed. He crooked that finger, and my eyes rolled back in my head. When he pulled out of me, I whimpered. But when he thrust back in again, I sighed.

"Not yet," he said, the hard edge to his voice the only indication—besides his erection—that he was just as affected as I was.

He tightened his grip on my ass, his fingers digging into my skin. All the while, he continued to torture me with his other hand. I'd been so close to coming so many times, I'd lost count. Sweat beaded along my forehead, my skin hot with desire.

I was close. *So* close.

"I love the sounds you make while I fuck you with my finger."

"Oh. *Oh*," I chanted when he changed pace, heightening the intensity. His words and movements driving me higher and higher.

And then when I thought I couldn't take it anymore, he rasped, "Good girl. Now you can come."

And I did. Shaking and crying out as my orgasm tore through me.

In that moment, nothing existed but the two of us, where our bodies were connected. Energy coursed through us. Power and pleasure, and it was intoxicating.

He kept at it until my legs were shaking, my body limp with exhaustion. Finally, he removed his hand, and I immediately mourned the loss of his touch. Even as hypersensitive as my body felt, I wanted him there—everywhere.

I tried to get up but immediately collapsed on his lap. My muscles were weak, my body wrung out. I'd never come so hard.

Finally, after I'd caught my breath, I lowered myself to the floor so I was on my knees facing him. His cock was straining against his pants, and I marveled at his restraint. I reached for his belt, but he stopped me, placing his hand over mine.

I blinked a few times, confused. But he merely shook his head.

He stood and started unbuckling his belt. "You have to earn the right to suck my cock. For now, you can watch and learn."

His gaze swept over me, his eyes lingering on mine as if seeking my assent. I swallowed hard and nodded fervently, a fresh rush of desire sweeping through me at his words. At his arrogance. *What is wrong with me?*

But then he removed his cock from his boxers, and it was all I could focus on. My breath came in short pants as he took himself in hand and began to stroke up and down. He was… God, he was hot.

I was so turned on that I squeezed my thighs together as if to stem the ache.

"Elle," he rasped, his movements jerky. Uncoordinated.

And the way he said my name made me hot all over. As if my skin couldn't possibly contain me. As if my cells would explode and my body would return to the stars just from the sound of my name on his lips.

He took a few steps forward, his face screwed up in concentration, his eyes hooded. I wasn't sure I'd ever seen anything hotter.

"Lift your dress."

"What?" I asked, too distracted by the sheer sight of him. By the sounds he made. I wanted to capture this moment and remember it forever.

"Lift. Your. Dress," he said through gritted teeth. And then I realized just how close he was to coming.

I scrambled to follow his command, pulling up the dress to reveal my chest. He stepped forward, planting his feet outside mine.

"Good. Now stay still so I can drink you in as I cover you with my come." And then he was coming, ropes of desire painting my skin as he finally let go. As he finally gave in.

So fucking hot.

It was all so deliciously filthy.

Then he shuddered and slumped over me, planting his hand beside my head. He swallowed hard, his gaze hazy. Delirious.

I wanted to soak him in. Soak in this moment. His muscular body poised over mine. The way he was looking at me, with both surprise and wonder.

"Hey." His tone was tender and so at odds with his rugged commands from moments before.

"Hey," I said, just as breathless. *Wow.*

"Are you…okay?" Certainty was replaced by hesitancy. It was almost…sweet. His concern.

I laughed. Okay? Was I *okay*? I was more than okay. "I'm amazing."

He cupped my cheek, the corner of his mouth tilting ever so slightly. "Yes. You are. But I've always known that."

Was Tristan trying to turn me into a puddle of goo? I mean, seriously. Between his words and the way he was looking at me with such sincerity and adoration, well—I'd been a fool to think I could ever resist him.

CHAPTER SIXTEEN

Tristan

I stared at Elle a second, still in disbelief. Had we really just done that? Had I really just jacked off in front of my sister-in-law, spraying my come on her stomach? And was she truly okay with it?

She seemed to be, judging from her satisfied smile and languid limbs. But still...I should've been more careful with her—more gentle. Shouldn't I?

I pulled her dress back down then tugged on her hand. "Come on. Let's get you cleaned up."

"I'm not the only one who's dirty." She bit back a smile as I pulled up my pants and gripped them at the waist.

"Oh, I'll definitely be joining you." I gave her ass a playful swat as we neared the hall bathroom.

I switched on the shower. While we waited for the water to heat, I stepped closer and lightly grasped the hem of her dress. I met her eyes, silently asking if it was okay to undress her. And when she nodded, I pulled her dress up and over her head.

She stood before me in nothing but a thong, my come still smeared on her skin. I held her gaze a moment before drinking her in. From the top of her violet-colored hair to her pale pink toenails, she was magnificent.

"You are…" I shook my head. Her breasts spilled out of my hands when I cupped them. Her rounded stomach was soft to the touch. And her generous ass was perfect for spanking. Her skin was still red from earlier, and I rubbed it with my palm. "So incredible."

I lifted her chin with my finger, pressing a kiss to her lips. I loved kissing her. I loved the moment when she opened to me, softening in my arms.

She moved her hands to my waist, her movements shaky as she reached for my pants.

"Did I say you could undress me?" I asked.

She licked her lips and ducked her head, but I gripped the back of her neck, stopping her.

"So bossy," she muttered, rolling her eyes.

I kept my smile in check, but I loved her fire. I loved that Elle felt comfortable enough with me—that she trusted me—to assert herself.

When I slid my hand around to her throat, her eyes darkened, lips parting. Did she like that? Did she like being controlled? I wanted to make her feel as consumed by me as I was with her.

I guided her to me for a kiss, rational thought becoming increasingly difficult as she ground against me. "Fuck. You're exactly what I need."

And fuck, that felt good.

Good enough to forget.

About the stress. The bills. The fact that she was thirteen years younger than me, and my late wife's sister. Adopted sister, I reminded myself, though I knew it didn't make it any better.

I turned Elle so she was facing the mirror, pulling her hair back from her ear. It was so soft it felt like purple cotton candy. And I couldn't wait to see if she tasted just as sweet.

"Tristan," she moaned as I palmed her breasts, teased her nipples, explored every inch of her.

"Yes?" I smoothed my hand down her spine, crouching to the floor behind her.

I pulled her panties down her legs until she stepped out of them. And then I ran my hands up her calves, her thighs, until I was gripping her hips.

"You…" I pressed a kiss to one butt cheek. "Are so…" I dotted her skin with more kisses. "Gorgeous."

She gripped the edge of the counter, gently pushing her ass back toward me. "I want to see you naked."

"Not yet," I rasped, inhaling her scent as I pried her thighs apart. "First, I'm going to taste you."

Our eyes met in the mirror, hers hooded and wanting. The violet almost black. Magical. And I knew she wanted this just as badly as I did.

"Oh dear lor—" The word died on her lips as I licked her slit.

I kept searching for the spots that made her sigh the loudest or press her hips back for more. I kept exploring and devouring, until she was on the verge of another orgasm. I was so close to taking my cock in hand, to stroking myself. But I wanted to be inside her when I came this time.

And when she started chanting my name, the last of my restraint crumbled. I drew back and stood.

She sagged against the counter. "What? *Why?*" She pouted.

I straightened. "Undress me if you want your next orgasm."

"Mm." She glanced at me over her shoulder, a wicked smile on her lips. "I think I can do that."

I expected her to rip off my clothes. I expected her impatience to win out. So when she took her time, painstakingly releasing each button on my shirt from its hole, I thought I was going to lose my damn mind.

But I remained still, letting her do as she pleased. Temporarily giving her control, even when every cell in my body cried out for me to take charge. To bend her over and plunge inside her until she was crying out her release.

She slid her hands beneath my shirt, pushing the material down my arms. I shuddered from her touch and the way she was looking at me, my body aching for her touch. Aching for her.

When I said, "I love the way you look at me," she dipped her head. So I placed my finger beneath her chin and drew her gaze to mine. "What have I said about when someone gives you a compliment?"

"I'm supposed to say thank you." She hesitated a moment then said, "Thank you."

I nodded and released her. She tossed my shirt aside, as I tried to steady my heart. Pulled my pants and boxers down my hips until my cock sprang free once more. She didn't touch me, but I could feel her gaze on my skin as if it were a tangible thing. And then she licked her lips, and I thought I might explode.

She was so perfect. So good.

"Get in the shower," I rasped, barely able to form the words.

She climbed in and I joined her, her hair already turning a deeper shade of purple from the water.

It was clear from the excited gleam in her eyes that she wanted this. We both did. And I was done holding back.

When I was with Elle, I felt alive. I didn't agonize over the past or worry about the future. I was free.

I kissed her beneath the spray of the shower, warmth bathing our skin as I rubbed my hands all over her body. I'd waited so long for this. For her. "God, you feel so good."

She peered up at me. Her violet eyes were filled with such longing. Such trust. I would've given her anything she wanted in that moment. *Anything.*

I took her nipple in my mouth, teasing the bud with my teeth, my tongue. My cock jerked her direction, but I did my best to retain control. Even while I was hanging on by a thread.

"Need you inside me," she gasped as I circled her clit with my thumb, loving the feel of her piercing.

I kept at it until she was whimpering, begging for it. My cock was aching to be inside her, and I longed for that connection. But I waited. I waited until she called out, her release making her body quake with pleasure.

And then, when I couldn't take it anymore, I pulled her roughly to me, her skin warm and wet and soft against mine.

"Show me how you take my cock," I rasped against her neck.

I backed toward the shower seat and took her with me. And then she wrapped one hand around my neck, her eyes never leaving mine while she held me at the base, lowering herself so I eased inside her. Sliding home.

She was so wet. So tight.

"Fuck," I groaned, watching her lips part on a gasp. "You feel so good."

"So good," she echoed in a whisper, leaning her forehead against mine.

I froze, gripping her hips.

"Condoms," I gasped. Her pussy was gripping me so tightly it made it difficult to think. "I don't have any condoms."

What was I thinking? I didn't know if she was on birth control. We weren't using a condom. I couldn't derail her future, let alone my own, with an unwanted pregnancy. *Shit.*

"I have an IUD."

"But—" I gasped when she rose up and sank down on me again. Taking me in all the way. How the hell was I supposed to focus on anything else?

The feel of her body on mine was ecstasy. The way her eyes held my gaze consumed me.

"Wait. Just wait." I gripped her hips, holding her above me, but only just.

"I had a preliminary physical for the JET Program. I was given a clean bill of health."

"I, um—" I cleared my throat. "I've only ever been with one person, and yeah…" I shook my head. "Same."

For a moment, we paused. Our eyes met, the ghost in the room weighing heavy—*Tessa*.

"Should we stop?" Elle asked.

"Do you want to?" I held her close. Not wanting to let her go.

She shook her head, and I knew I needed to take back control. For both of us. We were too far gone already.

"Then ride my cock." I pressed my fingers into her hips. "Make yourself come."

She did as I asked, determination marking her features. She seemed intent to chase away the demons. And I let her.

I reached between us, rubbing her clit with my hand. It felt as if my entire world, my entire being was wrapped up in her. And this moment.

"Yeah. Just like that," I said.

I smashed my lips to hers, craving that connection. Knowing this wouldn't last, but needing it to all the same. Even as she gasped into my neck, my name on her lips when she started to shake. Her walls pulsating with her release. Even when I started to unravel.

"Elle, I'm gonna—"

"Yes," she hissed, her movements wild, skin flushed. "Let go."

White lightning shot up my spine. "Fuck. Yes." I grunted, digging my nails into her skin as my climax ripped through me. I convulsed, coming inside her.

And then she collapsed against my chest, our bodies intertwined. My cock still inside her, throbbing deep within her core.

"Wow," she panted.

I stared up at the ceiling, still trying to catch my breath as water streamed down on us. "Yeah."

I wasn't quite sure what had just happened, but I was pretty sure my world had shifted.

"EARTH TO TRISTAN," ENZO SAID FROM BESIDE ME. HIS ARMS were crossed over his chest, his tattoos on display.

I'd gone to Fall River Estates to check in on the equipment and talk to him about a few updates to the software. But my mind was on Elle, as it often was. My thoughts consumed with the purple-haired ray of sunshine that currently resided in my guest room.

I didn't know what had come over me yesterday. I'd never been like...*that* in the bedroom. It felt as if something had been unlocked inside me—or perhaps, unleashed.

Yet with Elle, it had felt natural. Hot.

Fuck, she was so hot. I dragged a hand through my hair, my balls aching for release again. "You have to earn the right..." I mouthed to myself with a shake of my head.

Who the fuck said things like that?

Me, apparently.

"Tristan?" Enzo placed his hand on my shoulder. "You're flushed. Are you unwell?"

"I'm fine." I returned my attention to the screen.

"Uh-oh. I know what 'fine' means." He chuckled. "You, *amico mio*, are far from fine. What's going on?"

I scoffed. Where to start? My company was at risk of collapsing. I'd met with the other investor, but they were looking for something different. Something in the medical industry. Such a waste of time.

Now, even more hinged on the meeting with Celeste. But all I could think about was Elle. She was going to drive me out of my fucking mind.

Yet when I was with her, I felt sane. Free. Yesterday was the first time in as long as I could remember that I was able to let go of all the stress and the worry.

How fucked up was that? That controlling her had liberated me. And why had I liked it so much?

"Do you ever look at yourself in the mirror and wonder who you've become?" I asked Enzo before I could talk myself out of it.

"All the fucking time." He nodded. "At least, before I met Harper."

I nodded, my thoughts on Elle. In the short time she'd been living with us, Elle had changed my life, changed me. And I was still grappling with that.

Enzo arched his eyebrow in question. "Tristan, did you meet someone?"

I rubbed the back of my neck. "Sort of."

"Want to talk about it?" He crossed his arms, leaning his hip against a nearby table.

Where to start...

I could've talked to the guys about this, but they were all in such different places from me. Bennett was a newlywed with a baby on the way. Asher was a bachelor through and through. And based on our recent interactions, he was the last person I wanted to talk to about

Elle. And Liam, well, Liam was so absorbed with Penny and their writing and their new dog. Besides, he'd always been one of Tessa's closest friends. And somehow, I didn't think he'd react favorably to the idea of Elle and me.

"I—" I glanced around, making sure no one was around to overhear. "Until now, I've only ever slept with Tessa."

"Mm." He tilted his head back in understanding. "You're nervous about being with someone new."

I shook my head. "No, um—" I ran a hand through my hair. "I, *we* slept together, and it was…different."

He smoothed a hand over his jaw, and I sensed his curiosity. Still, he waited patiently for me to speak.

"I guess, well—" I paused, trying to figure out the best way to word this. "Forgive me if I'm wrong, but I'm guessing you've had several partners."

He hadn't met Harper until they were both in their late thirties, so my suspicion about his having a few partners didn't seem farfetched. Though I didn't know much about his life before meeting her. We'd talked about his dad and his grief. He'd only touched on his life in Italy and what it had been like playing professional soccer.

His nod confirmed I was correct in my assumptions, though he said no more.

"And I wondered if your…style," I said, for lack of a better word, "changed based on who you were with."

He furrowed his brow, his dark brown eyes swirling with confusion. "Style?"

"Yeah, um—" I cleared my throat. God, I sucked at this. But I'd never really talked about sex with anyone but Tessa. I was thirty-four, yet in many ways, I felt almost laughably inexperienced.

"In my new…relationship, I'm trying new things. Things I've never done before."

He chuckled. "Sounds—what's the word?—kinky. I say roll with it."

Easier said than done. This was Elle we were talking about. "I'm just worried I'll push things too far. Or that I already have."

Not that she seemed upset. Far from it. Yet my inclination was to demand more. Push her even harder next time.

Enzo's expression darkened. His body suddenly tense. "Why would you say that?"

"Because it made me realize just how different I am since Tessa died."

He relaxed, and I wondered if I was making him uncomfortable by talking about my sex life. But then he asked, "Did you enjoy yourself?"

I nodded, trying not to let it show just how much I'd enjoyed myself. Watching Elle pleasure herself had been sexy as hell. Knowing that she was imagining *me*…that she wanted *me*? *Fuck.* I was getting hard just thinking about it.

"Do you think your partner enjoyed herself or himself?"

I jerked my head back. "Wait. What? You thought I was talking about sex with a guy?"

He lifted a shoulder. "I didn't want to assume since you never mentioned the person's gender. And you were talking about 'new things.' And not recognizing yourself."

I appreciated Enzo's open-minded approach, but still. "To answer your question, yes, I think she enjoyed herself."

If the goal was to make her come, I'd definitely done that. Multiple times.

He furrowed his brow. "Yet you're concerned about something."

"I just—" I sighed. "It's like I'm a completely different person with her."

"Do you like the person you become with her?"

I thought back on it. Elle had been surprised initially. Hell, so had I.

I'd returned early from the investor meeting, expecting her to be at Pore Over. So to hear her moaning my name… And then to find her standing in her room, touching herself in front of the mirror… Well, it was something I'd never forget.

And it had only gotten hotter from there…

"Tristan?"

I considered it a moment then nodded. "Yeah. She makes me feel alive."

He clapped a hand on my shoulder, his face splitting in a smile. "That's awesome news. I'm so happy for you. *Auguroni.*"

"Thanks, but it's nothing serious." Elle was the fun in my life. Being with her was easy, when everything else was hard.

"Ha!" He barked out a laugh. "Right. Good luck with that."

I frowned. "What? Why would you say that?"

"Because that's exactly what I told myself when I met Harper in Bali. We were supposed to be a vacation fling, nothing more."

"What happened?"

"Fate intervened."

I started to laugh but then realized he was serious. I should've known Enzo believed in things like fate and luck. I'd heard rumors of how superstitious pro athletes could be. Even though Enzo no longer played soccer for the LA Leatherbacks, I could imagine those beliefs would be deeply ingrained, especially after such a long, illustrious career like his.

"I'm just…" I blew out a breath, realizing that perhaps I was already in over my head. "I'm not sure I'm ready for this."

"The sex? Or your feelings toward her?"

"It's complicated," I said, sidestepping his question.

I worried that I was using Elle as an escape. I worried that my feelings for her were so strong because of her connection to Tessa. I worried…

"It's only as complicated as you make it. As long as you both know where you stand, I don't see the problem. Do you want to see her again?"

I didn't have much of a choice, considering she lived with me. But I didn't mention that. Besides, even if Elle didn't live with me, the truth was, I *did* want to see her again. And not just for sex.

Elle was right; life was too short not to live the way you wanted. And I wanted her. Even if I could only have her for a little while.

CHAPTER SEVENTEEN

Ellie

"Ellie?" Savannah asked from the living room.

"Hm?" My mind was stuck on the other day, and I kept playing it on repeat. Tristan watching me. The shower. The…

"Ellie!" Her tone was more insistent this time.

I jerked my head up from the cutting board. "Yes? What?"

She scrunched up her nose. "I think something's burning." She pointed at the stove.

"What?" I spun around and realized she was right. The water was boiling over the pot. "Sh—*oot*. Shoot."

She laughed, giving Rex's head a playful pat. "You were going to say something else, weren't you?"

"I, um—" I darted over to the stove to turn it off. "I really need to focus on dinner."

"Yeah. What's up with you tonight? You're in la-la land."

I smiled, thinking about Tessa. I'd always associated that phrase with my sister. But then I cringed. I was standing in her kitchen. Cooking for her kids. And fucking her husband.

Well, I had once. At least, if you didn't count my other orgasms. *Ugh. Ellie. What is wrong with you?*

There was no way to justify this. But I also felt powerless to stop it. I didn't *want* to stop it. And while part of me felt guilty, I couldn't say I regretted my actions either.

Did Tristan?

Thanks to Maddox's birthday and the kids' busy end-of-year stuff, we hadn't had any alone time the past few days. I knew we were both busy and tired, but he acted as if nothing between us had changed. Obviously, I wouldn't expect things to—not in front of the kids anyway. But I still wasn't sure where we stood.

I finished preparing dinner just as Tristan walked through the door with Maddox.

"Hey. Good timing." I smiled as Maddox ran to me for a hug.

"Hey." Tristan smiled back at me, though it still gave me zero insight into his thoughts.

We ate dinner as a family and talked about our day. All the while, I wondered what to expect after the kids were in bed. Would Tristan and I watch *Lost in Space* as usual—curled up on the couch but not touching? Would he want to talk about what had happened? Did he want to do it again?

Waiting felt like agony.

Tristan helped the kids with their baths, and then they asked me to read them stories. I loved having that special time with them. When they asked to visit Tessa in her imaginary castle library, it only made me feel worse about what I'd done with Tristan.

I kissed Maddox and Savannah goodnight before pausing at the top of the stairs. Tristan was nowhere to be seen, and I couldn't sit still. So I grabbed my laundry basket and then the kids', adding its contents to mine.

Downstairs, I started loading clothes into the washer, pausing when I came to Tessa's dress. I glanced down at the material, my mind going back to the other day. I'd been wearing my sister's dress when her husband had covered me in his come.

I took a steadying breath as another thought occurred to me. I'd been wearing her dress when... Was *that* what had turned him on?

The room spun, and I hated that I even had to wonder if that was the case.

Not wanting to give the idea more power than I already had, I quickly shoved the dress into the washer along with the rest of the items and started the cycle. I switched off the light to the laundry room and opened the door, only to nearly crash into Tristan.

"Holy shit!" I jumped back. "You startled me."

He chuckled, but then his expression softened. "Hey. You okay?"

"Yeah. Yep!" I chirped.

He narrowed his eyes at me. "Elle."

"It's been a busy week. I've been...distracted. That's all."

"Mm." He cupped my cheek, rubbing his thumb over my bottom lip. "I know the feeling. I can't stop thinking about the other day. About you."

My lips parted on a sigh, relief mingling with desire. "I know. It was...incredible."

"*You* are incredible." He kissed me gently, deeply.

It was the type of kiss that spoke of an endless reserve of passion. Of restraint and power, and yet it was filled with anticipation.

"What about—" I panted. "The kids?" I whispered as he backed me farther into the laundry room, a hungry look in his eyes.

"We'll just have to be quiet," he said. "And get creative." He smirked.

"I can be creative," I said, his words calming my nerves

and putting my earlier fears to rest. "I have a very active imagination."

"Mm." He stared at my lips, his hands gripping my hips. "I bet you do. But do you think you can keep from screaming my name when I'm buried deep inside you?"

I sucked in a sharp breath, my core overflowing with need. "I-I can try."

"Good," he rasped, lifting me onto the dryer. "Because I want you, Elle."

Tristan's words reverberated in my head as he kissed me. *Me.* He wanted *me.* Not anyone else. Not my sister. Though, she wasn't an option, was she?

The voice in my head sounded like my mother's, and she had no business being in this room. In this conversation. In this moment.

So I pushed away those thoughts and concentrated on Tristan. It wasn't difficult. Especially not when he tugged my dress down, baring my breasts to him. I rubbed him through his pants, his cock growing even harder. We were needy and desperate. Reckless.

His mouth was on my breast. His breath warm. My skin grew even hotter with every pass of his tongue on my nipple. I needed him to touch me. I wanted to come almost as badly as I wanted to make him lose control.

I grazed the shell of his ear with my teeth. And when he hissed, gripping my thighs, I did it again. Delighting in his reaction.

I rasped into his ear, "Imagine how good it would feel to have my mouth on your cock."

"Fuck, Elle." He gripped my thighs and hissed.

When I licked the shell of his ear, he groaned, pushing my dress over my hips. "Trust me. I *have.* But right now—" He crouched before me, pushing my panties aside. "I need to taste you."

He gently separated my folds, inspecting my pussy as if it were the most beautiful sight he'd ever beheld. His gaze was full of reverence and wonder, and I loved being the object of his focus. I loved the way he could make me feel. Worthy. Special.

He circled my clit, and my hips jerked in response. My body was like a live wire, attuned to even the lightest of touches.

"I love this piercing."

"You're the only one who's seen it," I blurted, desperate to please him.

I'd gotten my clit hood pierced soon after I'd gotten my tattoo. And I hadn't slept with anyone since then. I'd been dying to see if it enhanced my pleasure during sex, and I had not been disappointed. Though I had a feeling the heightened sensations I'd experienced had more to do with Tristan than my piercing. Not just Tristan but the things he said, the way he talked to me. Touched me.

His eyes darkened, liquid heat blocking out the brown like a lunar eclipse. He teased the sensitive bundle of nerves, sending sparks of pleasure jolting through me.

"You have no idea how pleased I am to hear that."

He pressed his nose to my clit and began licking and sucking, determined to bring me pleasure. I slid my fingers into his hair, gripping it with one hand while leaning back on the other. It felt as if he was the only thing tethering me to this world. All feeling and sensation tied to the spot where our bodies met.

"You're so wet for me. So sweet."

Yes. I moaned as he flicked my clit with his tongue.

I swallowed hard, staring down at his head between my thighs. His dark, thick hair in my hands. My feet resting on his shoulders. Why was everything with him so erotic?

He slid one finger inside me, then two. And my pleasure

built and built and…

There was a whine and then a scratch at the door. I stilled. *Rex.*

"Ignore it," Tristan said, only removing his mouth from me for the briefest of moments.

I'd always believed Tristan was good at everything—captain of the football team. Insanely smart. Good-looking. And I'd been right. Because he was certainly a master with his tongue. Determined to give me the most powerful orgasm and nothing would stand in his way.

But as Rex continued to whine, I found it difficult to concentrate. My orgasm started to slip away. As much as I wanted to ignore Rex, I knew we couldn't.

"Tristan," I whispered. "What if he wakes the kids?"

Tristan stood with a huff. He placed his finger to my lips, the scent of my arousal marking his skin. Coating my lips then my tongue as he pushed his fingers into my mouth. "Mm. Yes, Elle. Wait here." His gaze was intense.

I nodded, sucking his fingers harder. Hoping he wouldn't be gone long.

"I'm going to take Rex out," he said. "Then, if you're a good girl, maybe I'll let you suck my cock."

I moaned against his finger, wanting so desperately to please him. But then Rex became more insistent, and Tristan adjusted himself, muttering something about Rex being a cockblocker as he shut the door behind him.

I wasn't sure how long Tristan was gone, but time seemed to stretch in his absence. I pressed my palms to the dryer, my core throbbing for his attention. I clamped my thighs together, but if anything, it only made it worse. I squeezed my breasts, aching for his touch. And when I couldn't take it any longer, I slid my hand down to my clit and started rubbing.

Oh god. Oh yes. I went faster, chasing my release.

I heard a noise and jolted, quickly removing my hand and lowering my dress to cover myself. Tristan pushed open the door a moment later, and my shoulders relaxed.

He took one look at me and narrowed his eyes in accusation. "What were you doing?"

"I, um…" I glanced away, sensing he already knew the answer.

He leaned in, his voice hard when he asked, "Did I give you permission to touch yourself?"

"I—" I gulped, the sound seeming to echo in the relative darkness of the room.

"Elle." His voice was gravelly, commanding. He would not be denied.

"No." I shivered.

"Now, that wasn't so hard." He kissed his way down my neck, and I melted in his arms.

Until he pinched one of my nipples—hard. It felt incredible. Almost like…like getting my tattoo had. The pain followed by euphoria.

And the surprise. God, I loved not knowing what to expect. One moment he could be aggressive and controlling, the next possessive and gentle. I loved all of it.

"Do you not trust me to make you feel good?"

I nodded quickly. "I do. You know I do."

My answer seemed to please him, and desire pooled deep in my belly.

But then he gripped the back of my neck, forcing our noses together. "No more orgasms unless they come from me. Do you understand?"

I swallowed hard. Was he serious? And why was that idea such a turn-on?

"Do you—" He maintained his hold on me while he nipped at my collarbone, a slight sting of pain that he soon smoothed with his tongue. "Understand?"

I nodded, eager to answer him. "Yes."

"I mean it, Elle. Not from another man. Not by your hand."

"Only in a car. But not from afar." I giggled, playing off his rhyme.

"Elle," he growled.

The laughter that had bubbled up died on my lips, replaced by lust. Anticipation. And need.

"I don't share."

Why did that growl of possession make me so hot?

But then I thought about the women around town. About Tessa. And my expression turned hard. "Neither do I."

"Good." He captured my lips, his kiss both hungry and possessive. To the point that I was dizzy with desire.

He released his hold on my neck, smoothing his hand down my back. Where his touch had been rough, commanding, only moments before, it was nothing but a gentle caress now. I liked that shift. That unpredictability and element of play. I didn't know if Tristan realized he was doing it consciously or not, but he was giving me exactly what I needed.

"What about all of your 'admirers' in town?" I was going to have to pretend to be disinterested while every woman in the AV hit on him.

He lifted a shoulder. "There's only one woman I'm interested in, and she's standing before me."

"Technically, I'm sitting," I teased, the intensity of this moment, of the conversation, making me squirm.

He narrowed his eyes at me. "Don't make me spank you."

"Mm." I smirked, challenging him as I raised my eyebrows.

"Elle," he growled. "Stop distracting me."

Oh, I planned to do a hell of a lot more distracting if that was the reaction I got.

Ellie

"Maybe you need to work on your focus," I said, cupping Tristan through his pants.

"My focus—" He swallowed. Eyes narrowed. "Ever since you came back into my life, my focus has been shit."

"Oh yeah?" I asked, wanting to hear more.

"You drive me crazy," he said, running his hands over my body. "I can't think straight. All I want, all I see—is you."

I smiled, pleased by his words. By the emotion and need bleeding from his tone. If I'd had any remaining doubts about Tristan, he'd just dispelled them.

"But we have to keep this a secret," he continued. "Especially from the kids. I don't want to confuse them."

"Absolutely." I nodded. "I would never want to do anything that might confuse or hurt them." I thought of dinner tonight and how nice it had been. How much I'd been enjoying my stay, even before this *thing* with Tristan.

He brought my hand to his lips, kissing the tips of my fingers. My palm. It both tickled and aroused me, and I couldn't wait to see what he'd do next.

"And no matter what, I need you to promise that this won't affect your relationship with Maddox and Savannah."

I frowned. "Of course not. Whatever happens between us has nothing to do with them. I will always look out for and love Maddox and Savannah."

He linked our fingers, placing them over his heart. "I know this is unconventional. And I know I'm asking a lot."

I shook my head, placing my fingers to his lips to silence him. "Tristan, you're not asking for anything I'm not willing to give."

He held my gaze a moment as if seeking confirmation that this was really what I wanted. As if cementing the promises we'd made. And then, finally satisfied, he crouched down and pulled my panties aside.

"Good. Now, where was I?"

He didn't wait for my response, merely resumed licking my clit with slow, languid movements. Oh god. That felt so good. Light flicks followed by long, lingering licks. As if I were the most delicious ice cream. And then he got into a rhythm that was just right.

It didn't take long. All our banter had been foreplay. So when he peered up at me from between my legs and our eyes locked, my orgasm barreled into me.

I opened my mouth to cry out, when his hand clamped over my lips. My toes curled. My core clenched. And I moaned my release into his palm.

I'd barely come down from the high when he tugged me off the dryer. I nearly stumbled to the floor, but he caught me, only to bend me over his knee on the bench.

"Mm." He smoothed a hand over my butt. "Every time I spank you, I want you to say the words, 'I am incredible.'"

I squirmed a little both on his lap and inside at the idea. Perhaps sensing my resistance, Tristan said, "It would please me very much."

I nodded eagerly, desperate to please him. To prove myself to him.

"Good. We're going to do it five times. If you need to stop before then, just tell me."

"I won't need to stop."

"Count for me." That was the only warning I had before his palm hit my ass. My skin stung from his touch, just as I was flooded with desire.

"One." I whimpered, trying to hold back. Rein in my excitement and need.

"Now, what do you say?"

"I am incredible," I whispered, which earned me a gentle rub.

My hair fell around me so the only thing I could see was the square patterns on the stone floor. The only thing I could feel was his muscular thighs balancing me above it. The only thing I could hear was his shaky inhale.

"Next time, I want to hear you say it louder. With more confidence."

"I thought we were supposed to be quiet."

"Elle," he rasped. Then he spanked me again, sparks dancing along my skin and between my legs.

"Two," I breathed. Then, "I am incredible," I said, repeating the words, though saying them still felt awkward.

He rewarded me with a kiss to the spot he'd just slapped, then said, "Better. Again."

I tensed just before his palm connected with my skin.

"Three," I said as my limbs relaxed. My skin stung, but it was pleasant. Especially when he planted wet kisses there. "I am incredible."

"Good girl," he said, massaging more deeply. I could hear the pride mixed with delight in his voice, and I loved that he was showing me this side of himself. That he was giving in to me. "Can you handle more?"

"Yes," I practically begged.

He lashed into my butt, a deep ache blooming within me. "Four," I panted, clenching my fists. "I am. Incredible."

"That was more convincing." He smoothed his hand over my skin, my body a riot of sensations. Pain. Pleasure. Ache. Desire.

I squirmed on his lap, needing more friction. More *something*. I knew he didn't want me to say anything. He wanted me to obey.

"Now, make me believe it." And then he laid into me, issuing his most punishing blow yet.

I squeezed my eyes shut, finding it difficult to swallow let alone speak. "Five," I croaked as he rubbed my ass. I took a deep breath and stared at the stones on the floor and said, "I am incredible." And I started to believe it might be true.

"Yes, Elle. Such a good girl." He pulled me into his lap, holding me close. Making me feel safe as he rubbed my back, kissed my temple.

I snuggled into him. "Thank you."

"I'm torn between making you come again or letting you suck my cock." As if on cue, his cock jerked, poking my core.

I moaned at the idea of taking him in my mouth. I wanted to make him unravel. I wanted him to come undone.

"You like that idea, princess?"

I nodded.

"Words, Elle." He gripped my hips, his fingernails digging into my skin. It was the only sign that he was losing control.

I didn't recognize the sultry tone of my voice when I said, "I want to suck your cock."

He smoothed a hand down my back. "I think you've earned it."

He lowered me gently to the floor so I was on my knees facing him. He stood, and the hiss of his zipper ripped through the air. And then his cock bobbed toward me, everything about him thick and enticing.

The strength in his thighs. The light dusting of hair along the skin. The precome dotting the tip of his erection.

"Mm," I hummed, rubbing my hands up and down my legs. I wanted so badly to touch him, yet I waited for his instruction. His praise.

"Good girl," he said, taking himself in hand. "So patient. Waiting for my command." He shook his head with a scoff. "Only you."

I nodded, my body aching with need for him. Yet, I waited. I was coming to realize the anticipation was a big part of the fun. Part of the payoff.

He stroked himself as he peered down at me, his eyes glittering with danger and excitement, lust and longing. At least, that's how it felt. That's certainly what I was feeling as he stepped forward and dragged the tip of his cock over my lips.

I remained motionless, scanning his body from his clenched jaw to his toned abs.

"There's nothing I love more than the sight of a princess on her knees for me," he said, sweeping his cock over my mouth again, more slowly. Slightly more aggressively, so my lips parted.

Even though I was the one on my knees, Tristan made me feel like a goddess. I knew we could stop at any time, not that I wanted to. Far from it. I was having a hard time holding myself back.

His breath was shaky as he took a step back, stroking himself as he watched me. "Tell me if it's too much."

"It won't be."

"Open your mouth," he rasped, sliding his other hand into my hair.

With my eyes locked on his, I wrapped my lips around

him and sucked him in. I swirled my tongue around his length, and his eyes rolled back in his head on a groan.

"You have the most perfect *fucking* lips."

I writhed at the barely shackled need in his voice. At the words he'd used to describe me. He made me feel powerful. Sexy. Wanted.

"Good," he panted. "Now, faster." He tightened his grip on my hair, and I chuckled, the sound vibrating through his cock. It only seemed to drive him wilder, and his ensuing groan was full of such desperation that I felt my core surge with a fresh wave of need.

I gripped his ass, exploring his body with my hands all the while. But I wanted a better angle. Something *more*. It still felt as if he were holding back, and I wanted to make him lose control.

I released him with a pop, licking my lips as I reveled in the salty-sweet taste of his precome. "More," I said, licking him from root to tip. "I want you to use me. Fuck my face."

His dark smile twisted my insides. And even without his saying it, I knew he was enjoying himself. I was certainly enjoying myself, especially when he threaded his fingers through my hair, twisting it away from my neck in a ponytail. His grip was light, but I knew that could change at any moment. And that element of unpredictability excited me.

His eyes were focused on mine, and I couldn't have looked away even if I'd wanted to. And I didn't want to. I didn't want to miss a moment of this. Not when Tristan was finally beginning to unravel.

"Yes," he hissed, starting to thrust into my mouth. His dark eyes were hooded. His breath coming in pants. "Yes, Elle. That's it."

His movements were harder. Faster. He'd allowed me to take the lead, but now neither of us seemed to be in control. I suppressed my gag reflex, allowing him to fuck my mouth how he wanted. And when his grip on my hair tightened, the muscles of his stomach contracting, I knew he was close.

"God. You're so beautiful." He traced my jaw with his finger, his gaze full of adoration.

I dragged my nails down his ass, lower still, down the backs of his thighs. He jerked in response, and I fought the urge to touch myself. To make myself come.

"If you keep going, I'm going to fill your pretty mouth with my come," he said. "Would you like that?"

The image alone had me writhing with need. And the words he said…

He tugged on my hair, forcing my head back. "Yes," I panted. I wanted it. I wanted to please him more than anything. "I want you to fill me. I want to take you in all the way."

"Then do it."

As soon as I'd wrapped my mouth around him, he pulled me back closer, so that my nose was nearly pressed to his stomach. I took a deep breath and increased the suction, driving him wild with my tongue. I was completely focused on Tristan and his pleasure, his grunts making me realize he was close.

"Fuck, Elle. I love the way you suck my cock."

I gripped his ass, holding him in place. Letting him know I wanted this. And then he growled his release, his body convulsing as warm, salty desire shot down my throat.

I kept going, licking until he was clean. Until he stumbled back and collapsed onto the bench. "Holy shit."

I sank down, resting my butt on my heels, still recovering from the intensity of what we'd just shared. He leaned his head back against the wall, a euphoric expression on his face. I'd done that. I'd made him lose control.

"You okay?" he finally asked, scrubbing a hand over his face.

I smiled up at him, a bit dazed. "Yeah. That was…"

"Right?" He dragged a hand through his hair. "Fuck."

The washer chimed, and I stood and fixed my dress, smoothing a hand over my hair. "I better take care of that." I yawned. I had no idea what time it was, but considering the washer had completed its cycle, it had to be late.

He dressed then said, "Go to bed. I'll take care of it."

I smiled to myself as I started moving the clothes over from the washer to the dryer, setting some aside to hang. I spied Tessa's dress and shoved it farther into the washer. Judging by what we'd just done, I might have been wrong about the dress. But I didn't want to give Tristan any reasons to think of my sister when he was with me.

I felt the ghost of his hand on my back. Tracing the curve of my hip. My body lit up from his touch, and then it was gone.

"Thanks, but it won't take long," I said.

Tristan swept my hair away from my shoulder and kissed my neck. "Thank you."

"Of course. You know I don't mind doing the laundry." I spun to face him, wrapping my arms around his neck.

"Thanks for that too." He grinned.

"Oh." I laughed. "Were you thanking me for the blow job?"

He considered it a moment then said, "For helping me let go."

CHAPTER NINETEEN

Tristan

"Okay." I crouched down to the floor, glancing between Maddox and Savannah. "What do we do when Ellie opens the door?"

Maddox jumped up from our spot behind the couch and yelled, "Congratalations!"

Rex yowled as if trying to harmonize, then started running around.

"Congratulations," Savannah corrected. "*Congratulations,*" she said more slowly.

Maddox nodded, his expression solemn as he tried to soak in every syllable. Elle would be home any moment, and we'd been planning this surprise for a while. Well, Savannah and I had. We hadn't told Maddox until about thirty minutes ago because he was terrible at keeping secrets.

I glanced around the living room at the decorations. There were colorful streamers and matching balloons. Plus, a handmade sign colored by the kids. I hoped Elle would like it.

Rex trotted toward the back door, and I heard the click of

a key in a lock. "Everybody hide," I whispered, ushering the kids back into position.

The door opened and I heard the rustle of a paper bag, and then a moment later, I nodded and mouthed, "Go!"

"Congratulations!" we cheered, jumping out from behind the couch.

Elle took a step back and held a hand to her chest, her smile widening as the shock wore off. "What's all this?"

She kicked off her shoes, shoving her phone into the back pocket of her shorts. Denim. Distressed. Short. I imagined stripping her out of them. Tugging down the thin straps of her tank top much like I had last night.

And the night before. And every chance I got.

I was ravenous when it came to Elle. Reckless, even. Leaving work in the middle of the day to have sex with her while the kids were at camp. Sneaking around after they went to bed. Touching each other every chance we got.

Maddox hopped over to her. "We heard you gradumated."

I coughed to hide my laugh at Maddox's latest iteration of graduated. Elle glanced at me over his head, biting back her own laugh. Her purple hair was in two space buns, as I'd learned they were called. And her violet eyes sparkled along with her purple eye shadow.

Savannah sighed. "Gradu*ated*. And congratulations, Auntie Ellie!"

"Thanks!" Elle beamed. "I love the banner. Did you help with that?"

Savannah puffed up her chest, and then Maddox jumped up and down. "Me too. Me too."

I laughed at their antics, and Elle laughed alongside me. I ached to place my hand on her back. My lips on her cheek. It was hard to resist touching her when she was so close. Especially when I knew there would soon be 5,500 miles between us.

5,500 miles. Holy shit.

But that had been the plan all along. She'd live here while she finished her degree and got the final approval to join the JET Program.

And yet, now that she'd graduated, it was starting to feel more real. If anything, time seemed to be speeding up, not slowing down.

I was happy for Elle and so incredibly proud of her. I knew how much the JET Program meant to her. I'd seen how hard she'd worked to graduate and proceed with the program despite the obstacles she'd faced.

But I wasn't ready for her to go. I wasn't sure I'd ever be ready.

Since she'd been here, so much had changed. The house was filled with light and joy again. The children laughed. I was laughing more.

The garden was blooming. The kids were flourishing. And I was no longer surviving, but thriving. All thanks to Elle.

Maddox came over to me, whispering so loudly the neighbors two streets away probably heard. "Can Ellie open her present now?"

I grinned and nodded, and he ran over to the table to grab the package. "Here, Ellie," he said, handing it to her.

"What's this?" She smiled at the gift, excited just as I'd hoped. Elle loved surprises, and I delighted in surprising her —both in and out of the bedroom.

She removed the tissue paper and smiled when she discovered the small box.

"Aren't you so excited?" Savannah asked, bouncing on her toes.

"Totally!" Elle grinned and lifted the lid. Inside was a gold charm with a California poppy to match the chrysanthemum she wore. She smiled when she saw it, though I sensed an undercurrent of sadness too. "Oh my goodness. This is beautiful. Thank you." She removed it from the box and held it up, admiring the delicate design. "Did you help pick it out?" she asked the kids.

They both nodded eagerly, and I tried not to laugh because Maddox had known nothing about it. At least nothing of the contents.

"The California poppy is a symbol of imagination," Savannah said, as if reciting a school report. "And we hoped it would remind you of us."

"That's so sweet." Elle opened her arms for a hug. "Thank you."

They immediately went to Elle, never shying away from her affection. It filled me with gratitude and relief, but also… worry. I had no idea how they—or any of us—were going to survive without her. Elle was the first person they'd truly let in since losing their mom. I didn't know how they'd react when she left, but I knew it would be difficult for all of us.

Elle spoke to the children in a low voice while holding them close. She was so nurturing and loving with the kids. They adored her. They needed her. *I* needed her. I rubbed at the ache in my chest.

"Do you *have* to move to Japan?" Savannah asked, voicing my thoughts aloud.

Elle's smile was forced. "I do, but it's only for a year."

"A whole *year?*" Maddox whined. "That feels like *forever.* Will you come visit?"

Her expression fell. "I don't know. But we can FaceTime whenever you want."

"Can we visit you?" Savannah asked, then glanced back at me. "Can we, Dad?"

I shoved my hands into my pockets. "I, um—" All three of them looked to me for an answer. I cleared my throat.

Elle and I hadn't discussed the future, but I knew it would

be best for everyone not to make promises I may not be able to keep. Even just thinking about the logistics—it was too complicated to contemplate something like that in the future.

So I finally said, "I'm sure Ellie will be busy with her students and exploring Japan. Maybe we can talk about it more after she settles in."

"Your dad's right," Elle agreed. If she was disappointed, she didn't let it show. "Moving there will be a big adjustment. But I can't wait to tell you all about it, and I would love for you to visit. If it works out."

"Will you bring us something back?" Maddox asked.

"Maddox," I chided, as Elle said, "Of course," and ruffled his hair.

Though I wondered when—or even if—she'd be coming back. She always talked about leaving the AV. I knew she'd never end up here permanently, at least not by choice.

She gave each of them one last hug then stood. "Thank you for the sweet surprises."

Savannah bounced on her toes. "You're welcome, Ellie."

"Welcome," Maddox muttered, though he was staring at the floor. I knew he was sad that Elle would be leaving; we all were.

A glance at the clock told me it was getting late, so I said, "We should get ready to leave for River's birthday party."

"Woo-hoo!" The kids ran off to grab River's present and finish getting ready.

"One more surprise," I said, handing Elle another small box.

Her eyes lit up, and she eagerly tore into it. Inside was one of the charms from Tessa's bracelet, and I knew from Ellie's tearful expression that she remembered it.

"Are you sure…?" She glanced up from the charm.

"Yes. And Tessa would've wanted you to have it too."

She nodded then slid the disk with the kids' and my initials onto the chain before holding it up to her neck. "Thank you."

"Let me help," I said when Elle fumbled with her necklace, trying to put it back on now that she'd added the new charms.

She handed me the necklace and pulled her hair aside. I dragged the charms up her chest, grazing her shoulder with my hands. She shivered, and I closed the clasp then leaned in to whisper, "Do you want to know why I suggested the California poppy?"

She nodded, her hair still pulled aside. I'd been aching to touch Elle all day. It was odd sometimes—being so close to her yet being unable to touch her most of the time. Talk about torture.

"Because it can also mean 'I dream of you.'" I pressed my lips to her neck, goose bumps rising along her skin.

"Mm." She turned, glancing at the upstairs landing before grasping my belt loops and pulling me closer. "What kind of dreams do you have, Mr. Lockwood?" Her voice was breathy, eyes hooded.

"The kind where we can spend a weekend in bed."

She groaned. "That sounds like heaven."

Sneaking around was hot, but unlimited time together alone in bed sounded even better.

Fortunately, it didn't have to remain a dream. I'd been working on a plan. "Would you want to go away with me for a weekend?"

She blinked a few times, her skin warm against mine. "You're serious?"

I could hear the excitement in her voice, but hesitation too. Did she not want to go?

"Yes, princess." I kissed her cute little nose when she wrinkled it. "What?"

She laughed. "Why do you call me 'princess'?"

"Partly because the kids think you look like a Disney princess, which I tend to agree with. But also, because you deserve to be spoiled. Cherished. Treasured."

"But not rescued, right?" She narrowed her eyes, daring me to challenge her.

"Never. You're a modern princess. Like Elsa."

She gasped, slapping my chest playfully. "Are you calling me an ice queen?"

I chuckled. "Okay. Anna, then."

"Would that make you Sven?" she asked with a contemplative expression.

I scowled. "Sven?" The reindeer. "Seriously?"

She laughed then said, "Tell me more about this dream weekend. What about the kids?"

I loved that Maddox and Savannah were Elle's first concern. It reassured me that she would always put their needs first, regardless of what happened between us.

"My parents got some crazy last-minute deal for Disney, so I was thinking we could go then."

"Go?" She tilted her head. "Where are we going? I thought we were staying in bed all weekend?"

"It's a surprise," I rasped against the shell of her ear.

She lit up. "Oh, I do adore surprises. And the kids are going to love Disney. Have you told them yet?"

I shook my head, holding a finger to her lips. "It's a secret."

"Part of me wishes I could go with them."

I chuckled. "You'd rather go to Disney with the kids than spend a weekend alone with me?"

She screwed up her lips. "Hmm. That is a tough choice. I mean, it would help if I knew *where* you were taking me."

"I promise to take you to Disney someday. And I promise you'll love where we're going," I said, hoping Liam and Penny didn't have plans to visit their cabin in Bear Creek that weekend. If they did, I'd have to find something else.

"I'm sure I will." She smiled. "Since I'll get to be alone with you."

"Okay, Dad," Savannah huffed, and I forced myself to back away from Elle. "We're ready."

A short drive later, we pulled up to Liam's house. I kept having to remind myself it was Penny's home now too. After months of back-and-forth between New York and California, she'd moved to the AV for good. Liam seemed more at ease since he'd met Penny. As if her presence calmed him. She was good for him—and his writing. Tessa would've loved her.

I smiled, still surprised I could think of Tessa without pain. It was such a relief. It wasn't always the case, but it had happened more and more lately.

As soon as the car was in park, the kids unbuckled their seat belts and ran up the sidewalk to the old Victorian house. Asher, Bennett, and I had helped Liam with countless home renovation projects over the years, and I pointed some of them out to Elle as we approached.

She asked questions, and I wanted to linger in this space —alone with her. We made our way to the white picket fence at a much slower pace than Maddox and Savannah. My alone time with Elle was always limited, but now that school was out for the summer, the kids were home more during the day.

I couldn't wait to take Elle away for a long weekend, just the two of us. Nowhere to be. Nothing to do but each other.

A breeze ruffled her hair, and she turned and smiled at me over her shoulder, music floating to us from the back-yard. *Fuck me.*

I placed my hand on the small of her back, sliding it beneath her tank top. "Do have any idea how sexy you are?"

She dipped her head and whispered, "Tristan." Though I got the distinct impression she wanted me to continue, based on her tone.

"My cock is hard just thinking about later and all the ways I'm going to make you come." I made sure no one was around and then slid my hand down to her ass.

She grinned but kept her eyes trained ahead. "Were you always this dirty?"

"Only with you." I gave her a squeeze then released her completely, even though I was reluctant to do so.

We continued through the gate to the backyard. The kids were playing a game, and River's grandma, Debbie, was leading the fun. Elle was quickly pulled into a conversation with Penny and Wren.

"I think Enzo's inside with Asher and some of the others," Wren said to me, rubbing a hand over her stomach. Her dress really showed off her growing baby bump.

"Thanks. Can I get you anything?" When Wren shook her head, I placed my hand on Elle's lower back and leaned in. "Elle?"

"I'll grab something in a little bit." Elle smiled, and only then did I feel Penny's and Wren's curious gazes pinging between the two of us. "Thanks."

"Before you run off," Wren said, linking her arm through mine. "I want to introduce you to someone."

Out of the corner of my eye, I saw Elle frown. But she smiled as soon as Penny asked her about some makeup technique.

"That's Miranda," Wren said, and I followed her gaze to a tall redhead. "Isn't she gorgeous?"

I cleared my throat. What was I supposed to say? The woman was attractive, but I was only interested in Elle. Though I couldn't exactly tell Wren that.

"She's super sweet. Loves animals and kids." She waved Miranda over and made the introductions before leaving us.

"So, you're Tristan." Miranda grinned. "Wren didn't exaggerate when she told me about you." She gave me an appreciative glance.

First Annie, now Miranda. I loved that my friends wanted me to be happy, but we really needed to have a talk. I wasn't interested in being set up with someone, and I had a feeling that if I didn't say something, it was going to keep happening.

Miranda and I chatted about the kids and our pets, made polite conversation. Until she said, "I'd love to hang out sometime and get to know you better one-on-one."

Aw. Shit.

I couldn't exactly tell her the truth, so I settled for something that was true. "My wife passed away last year."

"I'm sorry." She placed her hand on my arm. "I lost my husband a few years ago, and it can take a while to feel ready to take that next step."

I nodded, grateful she understood. Grateful I didn't have to say more.

"I'm sorry for your loss," I said.

She smiled and removed her hand. "Thanks. And if you change your mind, or you want to grab coffee sometime just to talk, call me. I get it. We're in the same shitty club."

We talked a little longer, sharing notes about grief. I admired her resilience. Her desire to get back out there and find love. She was nice, but I wasn't interested. And I certainly wasn't looking for love.

But when I glanced over at Elle, I knew it didn't matter whether I'd been looking for love or not, it had found me. *She* had found me. Even broken and at my lowest, she'd been there for me. She'd trusted me.

If you'd told me a year ago that I'd be here, I would've never believed it. Losing Tessa had shaken me to my core.

Becoming a widower and solo parent had nearly done me in. And yet, I was happy again. I was falling in love again.

That realization nearly knocked me on my ass. *Holy shit, I need a drink.*

I made my way over to the cooler for a beer. No sooner had I opened the lid than Bennett and Liam descended on me like a pair of vultures. I popped the top off my beer and took a long gulp, trying to steady myself.

"Hey." Bennett tipped his beer to mine, a sheepish grin in place. "I see you met Miranda."

I grunted and lifted my beer for another sip. Was he in on this? We hadn't talked about Elle again after that night at Kiss My Ax, but Bennett was perceptive and generally not one to push. I had a feeling this was more at Wren's insistence.

"So—" Liam nudged me. "How'd it go?"

"Um, yeah. It…went."

"Oh no." He cringed. "You blew it. It's okay, big guy." He draped his arm over my shoulder. "You're out of practice. It'll get easier."

I rolled my eyes. I wasn't out of practice. And, "I didn't blow it. I'm just not…interested."

"In Miranda or in dating?" Liam asked.

How the heck was I supposed to answer that? Fortunately, Bennett saved me from responding, saying, "I told you guys to leave it. When Tristan's ready, he'll take that next step."

I nodded, silently thanking him for that. Both for respecting my boundaries and keeping his mouth shut about Elle and me.

Liam's expression fell, and he kicked at the grass. "Yeah. Sorry. You just seemed happier lately. And you were making changes that made us…" He shook his head. "Never mind," he added more softly.

"I appreciate that you want me to be happy, but life isn't like the romance novels you write."

"I believed that once too," Liam said. "But that was only because I was scared."

Jesus, Liam. Save me the bullshit.

"Yeah, well. I *had* my happily ever after."

I wasn't scared, was I? Even if I was falling for Elle, I already knew how our story would end. She was leaving.

"I know how much you loved Tessa," Liam continued. "We all do. But you're young. Surely you don't want to spend the rest of your life alone."

"Of course not," I snapped, my tone harsher than intended.

"Then you have to get back out there. You have to try. Right, Bennett?" He nudged Bennett.

Bennett lifted his hands in the air. "You know me. I'm not getting in the middle."

Liam rolled his eyes. "You're my best friend and my brother-in-law. You're supposed to back me up on these things."

I sighed, dragging a hand through my hair. "Can we *please* talk about something else?"

Liam decided to take pity on me, pivoting to talk about his latest book. He was writing a story about an Olympic skier who was trying to overcome a tragic accident while also avoiding love. It sounded interesting, and Liam was a skilled storyteller.

When there was a lull in the conversation, I turned to Liam. "Can I borrow your cabin for a long weekend next month?"

"Of course." He sipped on his beer. "Not the Fourth, though, right?"

I shook my head, knowing how big a deal the Fourth was

in the AV. I hated to miss it. "No. I'll be on a yacht for the Fourth."

"You want company when you go up to the cabin? We could make it a guys' weekend."

"I, uh—"

"Did I hear something about a guys' weekend?" Enzo clapped a hand on my shoulder. "*Salve.*" He greeted the group.

"*Ciao,* Enzo."

"Tristan wanted to use my cabin later this summer," Liam said. "So I suggested we make it a guys' weekend, if he wants company."

"I imagine Tristan had *other* company in mind." Enzo grinned.

Suddenly, all attention was zeroed in on me.

"But you just said…" Liam frowned and glanced at Bennett. "I thought he wasn't interested in dating."

"Who said anything about dating?" Enzo chuckled. "Can't the man have a little fun?"

Liam stared at me, mouth agape. "Is he for real?" He pointed at Enzo. "Are you—" He leaned in to me and whispered, "Sleeping with someone?"

"I, uh—" I tugged on my collar.

Enzo and I had talked about Elle on our bike rides, though he didn't know she was the woman I was sleeping with.

"*Scusami.* I must have misunderstood," Enzo said, his accent suddenly thicker as he apologized. "Sometimes my English and Italian…"

I wanted to elbow him to shut up. We all knew he was perfectly fluent in both languages. And the longer he talked, the more questions it provoked.

"Did you know about this?" Liam asked Bennett.

Bennett took a drink and shrugged. "I've had my suspicions." Then said nothing more.

Liam frowned. "Why am I always the last to know everything?"

"Maybe because there's nothing to tell," I said.

"Fine. Fine," he sighed. "You clearly don't want to talk about it, which makes me wonder…" He got that look in his eye, the one that meant he was plotting. Usually about a book. Though this time, I felt like he was scheming about me.

"Nope." I held up a hand. "Whatever you're thinking, just stop. I'm not one of your characters, and you can't psychoanalyze me."

"I'm not—"

Bennett snickered. "You totally were."

Liam rolled his eyes. "Whatever."

I might not get another happily ever after, but I could enjoy right now. I was falling for Elle, but she was leaving soon, and thoughts of this being anything more than sex were dangerous. I'd already lost someone I loved; I couldn't go through that again.

CHAPTER TWENTY

Tristan

"Are you sure you don't mind staying with the kids for the long weekend?" I asked, folding my swim trunks and tucking them into my suitcase.

Elle was sitting on the floor, sorting the kids' laundry while I packed for the July Fourth weekend on Celeste's superyacht. "Of course not. We'll have fun. Besides, it will be nice to have some alone time with them before I leave for Japan."

Leave. She's leaving soon.

"Maybe we should ask my parents to watch them," I said, trying to quell my rising sense of panic. "You could go with me."

She laughed and placed another shirt in the laundry basket.

"I'm serious," I said, joining her on the floor. Perhaps it was selfish on my part, but I wanted her to agree. "Come with me."

She shook her head. "I can't. You know I can't."

"Why not?" I asked. "No one would know us. We wouldn't have to hide."

"Could we hold hands?" She peeked up at me from beneath her lashes.

I chuckled and tucked a strand of hair behind her ear. "If that's what you want."

She frowned. "You don't?"

I hadn't really thought about it, but clearly Elle had. I wondered what else was going on in that brain of hers. "I've never really been the hand-holding type."

"Psh." She waved a hand through the air. "We'll see about that."

I grabbed her hand and pulled it to my lips for a kiss, bringing her to her knees. "There are many parts of your body I want to hold." I freed her hand and gripped her breast then gave her ass a squeeze.

"You're terrible."

"And you love it." I grinned.

She straddled me and wrapped her arms around my neck. "I do." She kissed me, and it felt as if she was saying she loved more than my teasing. That she loved *me*.

I pushed away the thought. Even if she did, it didn't matter. She was leaving soon, and she hadn't given any indication that she'd be coming back. Definitely not anytime soon. Which was why I was even more determined to soak up every second together.

"Say yes, then." I kissed my way down her neck, grazing her skin with my teeth. "Say you'll come with me."

She tilted her head back. "Tempting as that sounds, I know how important this meeting is. I don't want to be a distraction."

It *was* important. Perhaps even more than she realized. There was a lot riding on it—my company, the house, our entire future. But the idea of having Elle there calmed me. Instilled in me a sense of surety and confidence, just like having her in the house did.

"You won't be." I kissed lower—decorating her collar-bone, her chest. "Promise."

"Mm-hmm." She fell back on the floor, sighing as I lifted her shirt and placed my lips to the underside of her breast.

"So that's a yes, then?" I teased, working my way down to her shorts and removing them and her panties.

"We can't," she said, then moaned my name as I began to play with her clit. "You know we can't. How would we explain my sudden need to go out of town? And what about the kids?"

I knew she was right, but I didn't want to admit it. So, I decided to torture her a little more instead.

"You really want to go three days without this?" I pressed a finger inside her, determined to drive her wild. "Three days without my touch." The words were whispered roughly, and she shivered as I added a second finger. "Without my lips." I licked the shell of her ear, and she sighed. "Without my cock." I nipped her skin, and she cried out.

"No." She thrashed on the floor, clutching at the rug. "No. Oh god." Her tone and her body shifted. "Yes," she hissed, her walls clenching around my fingers, my own need coiling tighter like a spring.

I kept at it—determined to drive her as crazy with my touch as my words. And I whispered dark fantasies and praise into her ear until she exploded with a cry. But it wasn't enough. I wasn't done.

I kicked off my pants, and she tore at my shirt. I climbed up her body to meet her lips, my cock hard and aching as it slid against her supple body. "I want you, Elle."

"Then take me," she gasped as I increased the pressure. "Own me. Make me yours." She sounded as desperate as I felt.

Or maybe that was just what I wanted to hear.

I kissed her—deeply. The taste of her mingled on our tongues, and it only made me harder.

"Fuck. You feel good," I said, sliding my cock between her thighs. Her piercing rubbed against my skin, and I fucking loved the sensation.

"So do you." She let out a shaky breath.

I kept going, sliding against her but not pushing inside, until both of us were panting. Then I rolled us so she was on top. Her hair curtained us from the world, our lips inches from touching.

"Ride me, princess."

She hovered over me and used her hand to guide me to her entrance. And then we both watched as her pussy swallowed me, inch by glorious inch. When I was fully seated, I sighed with relief.

I gripped her hips but allowed her to take the lead. As much as I loved being in control, I loved watching Elle take over. She was confident and beautiful, and sexy as hell.

"Fuck, Elle. *So* good." I cupped the back of her neck, bringing her lips to mine for a kiss.

She rode me, her walls clenching around me as she slid up and down my cock. Her breasts brushed against my chest, and we stayed like that, our lips locked, bodies connected. It was so intense, and not just the physical sensations. Everything about being with Elle felt life-affirming. Like she was more than just the joy in my life, she was the air I breathed.

She kept going until she was crying out as well, her release a beautiful sight to behold. The trust that she placed in me was breathtaking. And as her eyes zeroed in on mine, I held on tighter.

I didn't want to let her go. Not now. Not at the end of the summer.

I tried to push away that thought and focus on her pleasure. I was being unrealistic. Elle had her entire future ahead of her. How many times had she said she didn't want to live in the AV?

I needed to remember that this was temporary.

But for now, she was mine.

For now, I'd claim her. Love her.

My strokes were harder, faster. Almost punishing. I rubbed her clit, determined to make her come again. Make her come with me.

I didn't want this to end, yet I craved the release all the same. She fell over the edge first, and then I felt it—that tug deep within. I emptied myself inside her, and for a brief moment, I imagined getting Elle pregnant. I imagined more children. And then—like a flash—it was over.

I lay there as she curled up in my arms and stared at the ceiling in shock. *This— I—* I swallowed thickly. This wasn't supposed to happen.

"You okay?" She smoothed her hand over my chest.

I took a deep breath and tried to center myself. "Yeah. Why?"

"Your skin is really pale."

I grunted, not entirely sure how to respond. How could I?

I'd already lost my childhood sweetheart, my wife, and the mother of my children. Now Elle was leaving. I loved her, and she was leaving. And the idea of being separated from her was unfathomable.

"Tristan," Elle said, her tone taking on a note of panic. "Do I need to call Doc Allen?"

I grabbed her hand and brought it to my heart. "Don't tell me you're turning into Savannah now?" I teased.

Though, Savannah had seemed a lot less anxious. Maddox too. It was the happiest and most relaxed they'd been since Tessa's diagnosis. And I had a feeling I knew why.

That reason frowned down at me, her violet eyes filled with concern. "I'm worried about you. You seem stressed lately."

I was dying to tell her I loved her. It was on the tip of my tongue. And yet...I knew I couldn't.

So I rolled on top of her, kissing her deeply instead. Hoping she could feel how much I loved her. Even if I knew it would mean letting her go.

IN THE END, ELLE STAYED HOME WITH THE KIDS WHILE I WENT to woo the investors. Even though I missed Elle—and Savannah and Maddox—I was also surprised by the freedom that came from being in a new social situation. Celeste knew my story, of course, but no one else did. Or if they did, they didn't treat me any differently.

I spent the weekend networking with the other guests. Swimming in the ocean. Drinking. And just having fun.

Away from the AV, I wasn't defined by my role as a father or a widower. I wasn't subjected to anyone's pity or their attempts to matchmake. I was just me—Tristan. Or at least, a new version of me.

It was funny how much had changed since losing Tessa. Things I used to love weren't as important. Even something as simple as my favorite beer—hell, my favorite color—was different. *I* was different.

And while a big part of that was due to losing Tessa, another part had come from finding Elle. From rediscovering myself in her.

By the time I arrived home late Sunday evening, I was

more relaxed than I had been in a long time. The weekend had been a success. I'd secured an investor's backing, and I wasn't going to lose my company or my house.

And it hadn't taken compromising my morals as I'd feared. Celeste had hit on me, as I'd expected. But I'd made it clear I wasn't interested.

Olen had been right; the weekend on her yacht had been an excellent opportunity to network. I'd connected with Knox Crawford, the owner of LA's pro soccer team, the LA Leatherbacks. We'd bonded over our love of the AV—he had a vacation home in Blue River. And he'd been excited about Lockwood Industries and our technology.

As quietly as I could, I unlocked the back door and set my bag just inside. Rex lifted his head from his bed then fell back asleep just as quickly.

I crept farther inside, the TV flickering from the living room. I peeked over the couch to discover Elle curled up beneath a blanket, asleep. I watched her a moment then sat down and kissed her softly.

"Hey." I brushed her hair away from her face, watching her expression change as she slowly came to and realized I was home.

"Mm. Hello." She stretched, smiling as she did so.

"Were you waiting up for me?" I asked, realizing just how much I hoped the answer was yes. How much I loved having someone to come home to. Not just someone—Elle.

"Trying to," she whispered. "How'd it go?"

I missed you.

"Great. I secured an investor."

"Oh my god, Tristan." She popped up from the couch and wrapped her arms around me. Her body was warm. Welcoming. Delicious. "That's fantastic."

"Thank you." It *was* fantastic, but I was still stressed.

I may have saved my company from ruin, and we wouldn't have to give up the house, but I couldn't keep the one thing that meant more to me than all that—Elle.

I held her close, continuing to stroke her hair. Mostly to reassure myself she was still here. Still with me. Spending even a few days apart had made me realize just how much I was going to miss her.

I sat back down on the couch, this time with her straddling me. She played with my hair, traced my features. Having her in my arms had my cock standing up and taking notice.

"Oh hello," she teased with a little wiggle.

That did *not* help. Nor did the way her breasts jiggled in her thin tank top, her sleep shorts having risen up her thighs.

"Hi." I snagged her lips for a kiss. "I missed you. Can you tell?"

She giggled and started rocking against me. "Oh, I can tell."

I gripped her hips, fighting for control even as she continued to rub her pussy against my erection. This was a bad idea. If the kids opened their door…

"Upstairs," I whispered, giving her ass a tap. "*Now.*"

She shook her head, her eyes rolling back. "I don't want to stop. I don't want to move."

I switched off the TV and grabbed the blanket and wrapped it around her before standing. She gave a little squeak of surprise, and then I carried her up the stairs.

As soon as we were in my room with the door locked, I set her down. "Shorts off."

"What about my underwear?" she asked as I unfastened my pants and shoved them and my boxers down my thighs.

"Keep them on."

I sat on the chair in the corner and flicked on the lamp so

I could see her. She turned her back to me and slid her shorts over her hips, bending at the waist to give me a good view of her ass.

"Damn, Elle." I pushed against my cock.

She sauntered over to me, unbuttoning my shirt and lifting it over my head. All while I gripped her hips and slid my hands over her ass, her thighs. I couldn't stop touching her. I couldn't get enough of her.

"Sit on my lap."

"Mm. I had something else in mind first." She dropped to her knees in front of me then glanced up from beneath her lashes, a coy smile playing at her lips.

My cock twitched from the way she was looking at it, desire and hunger written across her face.

"May I?" she asked.

"I—" I gripped the armrests.

"Please?" She batted her eyes.

"Oh god, Elle. I'm not going to last long if you keep looking at me like that."

"So?" She leaned forward and took my erection in hand, sucking the tip into her mouth. Swirling her tongue around me. She took her time, and it was a slow kind of torture.

"Look at you," I rasped, tangling my fingers in her hair.

Her eyes met mine, and I nearly came undone. Was this how she felt when I teased her? Delaying her orgasms. Finally, when I couldn't take it anymore, I tugged her onto my lap.

I gripped her ass with my hands, spreading her cheeks as she began to glide up and down my shaft with only a thin, wet layer of silk between us. Her tits swayed from the movement, and everything about her was fucking erotic. I didn't want to close my eyes, but I was having a hard time focusing on anything but the feel of her body grinding against mine.

I tugged her panties aside, and my cock slid between the material and her skin. It was slick. Smooth. And hot. "You feel incredible."

"Need you," she rasped.

I yanked her top over her head, tossing it across the room. I sucked on her nipple. Her eyes closed, her mouth opening to form an "o."

"Fuck." I gripped her hips. "You make me lose control."

She grinned, dragging her nails down my chest, leaving a trail of sparks in their wake. "*I* make you lose control?"

I chuckled darkly. "You definitely unleashed a beast or something in me."

"Mm," she hummed, draping her arms around my neck, pulling me into her. "I have to admit, I've always wondered what it would be like to be fucked by the Beast."

I couldn't help it, I laughed. Both at her words and at the relief that had accompanied them. I couldn't believe she'd imagined fucking an imaginary character like the beast from *Beauty and the Beast*. Actually, considering this was Elle we were talking about, I could. She knew all the words to all the songs in all the Disney movies.

"Hey!" She slapped my chest. "Don't laugh at me."

I gripped her wrist, her breath catching. "I don't want you to imagine being fucked by anyone else—fictional or not."

That was the truth, even if I had no right to say it.

"Mm. Possessive too?" she teased, but I wasn't joking. And judging from the seductive lilt to her voice, she liked it. *Damn.*

"I'm serious, Elle." I held her gaze. "You're mine."

Her eyes were hooded, but she was clearheaded enough to ask, "For how long?"

I almost said, "Until you leave me." But I didn't want to think about that. I didn't want to think of her leaving. So, I smashed my lips to hers in a kiss that was messy and chaotic, reckless and exhilarating.

And this time, I didn't hold back.

CHAPTER TWENTY-ONE

Ellie

When I reached the top of the stairs, Tristan glanced up from the couch. He swallowed hard as he drank me in and stood, smoothing a hand down his navy slacks. He wore a white button-down shirt that was open at the collar, a smile that was reserved just for me.

I couldn't imagine a better birthday. The kids had prepared me a special breakfast—with Tristan's help. And then he'd dropped Maddox and Savannah off at his parents to give us the day alone. Tristan had told me to dress up for a surprise, and I had no idea where we were going. I couldn't imagine him parading me around town, but was it wrong to get my hopes up?

"Hey," I said when I reached the bottom of the stairs.

"Happy birthday."

"Thank you." I smiled, thinking it was off to an amazing start.

He stepped closer, grabbing my ass and pulling me into him. Letting me feel his growing desire. "Fuck, Elle. You look amazing."

"Thank you." I toyed with his collar, smoothing my hands down his shirt. "You look very handsome yourself."

I pressed my lips to his, drinking him in. Wanting to drown in him.

The doorbell rang, and he sighed.

"Ignore it," I whispered. I pulled him closer to me, our lips nearly touching.

He shook his head. "I can't. It's part of the surprise."

I furrowed my brow as he adjusted himself. He took a deep breath then swung open the door.

"Surprise!" Piper and Sumner cheered from the front porch. "Happy birthday!"

I blinked a few times. *Wait. What?*

I glanced between my two friends and Tristan. What were they doing here? LA was five hours away by car. They would've had to have planned ahead.

Which meant…Tristan was in on this? I was both touched by the sweet gesture and disappointed that I wouldn't get to be alone with him as I'd anticipated.

"Happy birthday," Piper said, giving me a hug.

"I can't believe you're here." I hugged Sumner.

We'd grown even closer since I'd moved back to the AV. Being in the same time zone helped, but so did bonding over mom humor. I might not be Savannah and Maddox's parent, but I needed all the help I could get sometimes. And my relationship with Piper and Sumner had become fuller, richer because of it.

Piper nudged Tristan. "You did a good job keeping the surprise a secret. I'm Piper, by the way."

"Tristan." They shook hands. "Nice to finally meet you in person."

They spoke a moment longer, and Sumner introduced herself, all while I stood there. Gawking at them.

"Come in," Tristan said. "Unless you need to get going."

"Yeah," I said, finally snapping into action. I wasn't sure I wanted them coming into the house. Judging me for sleeping with my sister's husband. Not that I thought they would, but suddenly I felt incredibly self-conscious about my relationship with Tristan. "Maybe we should—"

"Oh no." Piper winked at me. "We have plenty of time."

I narrowed my eyes at her. God, this was awkward.

"It's so quiet," Sumner said. "Where are the kids?"

"At their grandparents' house," I said, eager to fill the silence. Determined to keep talking so we'd avoid any awkward topics, like Tessa.

"You have a beautiful family, Tristan," Piper said, her gaze focused on the images lining the fireplace mantel.

"Thank you." He shoved his hands into his pockets, and I wondered what he was thinking.

The past few months, I'd grown accustomed to avoiding the pictures of my sister. And while Tristan had slowly removed some of them, Tessa still had a very visible presence in the house. It was bittersweet, honestly. The pictures of Tessa and the kids. Tessa and Tristan.

But now that Piper had pointed them out, the doubts started creeping back in. If Tessa and Tristan had always been the golden couple, what did that make me?

The other woman, my mother's voice whispered. *A dirty little secret—guess that's genetic. You'll always be a secret.*

Piper placed her hand on my shoulder, and I startled. "You okay?"

I nodded, grateful that Tristan was too busy talking to Sumner to notice. Sumner was gushing over the family photos, the lighting and the setting.

"That's all Wren. A local photographer," he said.

"I can introduce you later," I said, wondering how long Piper and Sumner were in town. And were they *trying* to call

Tristan's attention to Tessa? "I did a shoot with them. Little Bird Studios on Instagram."

"That's right," Sumner said. "Those photos were gorgeous."

"Thanks." Out of the corner of my eye, I saw Tristan smile, and I knew he was pleased that I'd accepted the compliment instead of trying to downplay it as I might've in the past.

Sumner glanced at Piper. "You ready?"

"Ready for what?" I asked, trepidation marking my tone.

"To celebrate your twenty-first birthday! Now, come on." Sumner grabbed my hand, tugging me toward the door.

Tristan chuckled. "Be safe."

When we reached the front door, Piper wrapped her arm around my shoulder. "We'll take good care of the birthday girl, promise."

They headed for the car, but before I could follow, Tristan said, "Elle, you forgot something."

They grinned and continued on, while I returned to the house. "What?" I asked as he shut the front door behind me.

He grabbed my hips and pulled me to him roughly. "This." He claimed my lips, his touch grounding me while sending me soaring. "Have fun and be safe. Call if you need anything."

I panted, still reeling from his kiss. Still wanting more.

"Thank you for my surprise. Though I have to admit, I was really looking forward to being alone." I pouted.

"Soon." He grinned, referring to our upcoming trip to the cabin. "Have fun with your friends. They wanted to do this for you, and it might be your last chance to see them before you leave for Japan."

I nodded, knowing he was right but hating it all the same. It was difficult to give up alone time with Tristan, especially knowing how limited it was.

"Now, go have fun. You deserve it." When I dipped my

head in response, he immediately lifted my chin so our eyes met. "Tell me."

I hesitated a moment even though I knew what he wanted to hear. Then finally, I said, "I am amazing."

"I already know that," he said. "Now, make me believe *you* do."

I took a deep breath and closed my eyes briefly. The more I said it, the easier it became. Yet part of me still doubted it was the truth. "I am amazing, and I deserve this."

"Better." He leaned in to kiss the skin behind my ear.

I angled my head to grant him access, sparks dancing along my skin from his touch. He kissed his way down my neck, stopping just above my dress.

"Don't stop," I pleaded.

"Your friends are waiting. But oh, the things I want to do to you."

I squeezed my thighs together, but it did nothing to stem the growing ache. "Tonight?"

I had a feeling Tristan's parents were going to invite the kids to spend the night.

I still felt weird about sleeping in his bed. The bed he'd shared with my sister. It didn't matter that he'd changed the décor and removed her pictures, I'd always think of it as *their* room.

Tristan shook his head. "No, but soon. Just know that I'll be dreaming of you."

I frowned. "Why dream of me, when you can share my bed?"

He didn't answer. Did that mean…?

He turned me so I was facing the door, my back to his front, his lips to my ear. "Are you going to think about me tonight when you touch yourself?"

I swallowed hard, my eyes fluttering closed. "Is that allowed?"

"For your birthday, I'm willing to make an exception. As long as you imagine it's my hand on your pussy. My tongue stroking you."

I shivered, remembering how hard I'd come last night from his tongue and his touch. "Yes."

He slid his hand up my chest until it was circling my throat. His pressure was gentle, too gentle. I leaned into his touch, craving more. I could feel his erection digging into my back.

"I better go," I said. Even though all I wanted to do was stay.

He released me, and when I stepped outside, my body was flush with desire and heat. Oh god. Why was that so hot? Why did I love it when Tristan took control and told me what to do? Why did I crave his praise and desire his worship?

I tried to steady my heartbeat as I neared the car. Sumner waved from the driver's seat, and Piper was in the back, leaving the passenger seat open for me.

As soon as I was in the car, the two of them rounded on me. "OMG," Piper said. "Tristan is even hotter than I expected. I can see why you slept with him."

My eyes went wide. "Piper!"

"What?" She crossed her arms over her chest and leaned back with a smug grin.

"We can't—" I sputtered. "That's a secret."

She made a big show of glancing around the car. "It's just the three of us."

"I know, but—" I ducked down in the seat as if someone might overhear us, even from inside the car. "No one can know."

"Obviously," Piper said as Sumner pulled away from the curb and headed for the stop sign at the end of the street. "But do you really think it's much of a secret? I mean...the way you two look at each other." She fanned herself. "I thought I might combust."

"He does not—"

"Yeah, he does," Sumner chimed in. "He looks ready to rip your clothes off or kill any man for daring to look at you."

"It's fierce and sexy AF," Piper said. "And the way you look at him…"

"Okay. Okay," I glanced out the window and frowned, suddenly realizing I had no idea where we were headed. "Where are we going?"

"You'll see." Sumner grinned at Piper in the rearview mirror.

We reached the outskirts of town, and then we wound up a dirt road. Trees lined the path, and I couldn't see what was ahead. Until finally, it opened up to a glass-walled home that overlooked the valley.

"Holy—" I swallowed, taking it all in, from the modern design to the gorgeous view. "What is this place?" I asked, shutting the car door.

Sumner removed a bag from the trunk that looked brand-new. Perhaps sensing my confusion, she said, "Tristan packed for you."

"Whose suitcase is that?"

"Yours." She grinned. "He thought you might need a new one for Japan."

"Oh." How…thoughtful. And practical. I eyed the sized of it then asked, "How long are we staying here?"

"Till Sunday. We're having a girls' weekend!"

I shook my head with a laugh. "You really thought of everything."

"Just wait." She shared a grin with Piper. I followed them to the house, my excitement growing.

"Is this a vacation rental?" I asked as Sumner punched in a code to unlock the door then disabled the security system.

"Sort of," Piper said. "Sumner's husband, Jonathan, co-founded a charity with Alexis. Alexis's best friend Juliana and her husband, Harrison, own this house."

I furrowed my brow, putting the pieces together. "Wait. Harper's friend Juliana?"

"Yeah." Piper set her purse on the console in the entryway. "You know her?"

I shook my head. "I know *of* her. Party planner to the stars. Married to a retired NFL player."

"Yep! That's the one." Piper smiled.

I followed them into the kitchen and stopped at the threshold. Lavender balloons in various shades lined one wall of the kitchen, a beautiful table setting with the most gorgeous flower arrangement.

"This is beautiful," I said, stepping closer to take it all in.

"You only turn twenty-one once!" Sumner spread her arms wide.

"Happy birthday." Piper hugged me.

"This is incredible."

"You deserve it!" Piper said.

Thanks to Tristan, I now found that easier to believe.

"Juliana helped with the vision. We merely executed it," Sumner said. "We also thought you might want to film some tutorials or other content, so we set up a makeup table. But it's your weekend, so we can do whatever you want."

It was all so thoughtful. So beautiful.

"Is it too early for champagne?" I asked.

"Never too early," Sumner teased, filling three glasses with champagne.

Piper returned from the kitchen with a lavish charcuterie board. I still couldn't believe they'd done all this—for me.

"That looks amazing," I said, in awe of the roses made of prosciutto, all the various cheeses, olives, crackers. I didn't know where to start.

Sumner handed us each a glass of champagne, lifting hers as we followed suit. "Happy birthday, Ellie. May you continue to shine brightly as you chase your dreams."

I smiled and sipped my champagne as I thought about my dreams. As I contemplated my upcoming move to Japan and how hard I'd worked to achieve that goal. And now, how much I was dreading it.

I didn't realize I was crying until Sumner placed a hand on my shoulder. "Ellie, what's wrong?"

She steered me over to the sofa, and Piper joined us with the champagne and charcuterie.

"I think my dreams have changed," I admitted.

"What do you mean, babe?" Piper asked. "I thought you were excited about Japan."

"I thought I was too," I whispered.

"Was it your dreams that changed, or you?" Sumner asked, always perceptive. It was part of what made her such a successful life coach.

I sighed, sinking deeper into the sofa. "I don't know. Maybe a bit of both."

"Change is inevitable," Sumner said. "And it's part of life, but it can feel unsettling."

"Yes, but… I feel lost. I'm not even sure what I'm doing or what I want anymore."

"Generally, or with Tristan?" Piper asked.

I knew what I wanted—Tristan. But I couldn't have him. Not in any meaningful way. Not beyond this summer.

But the more time we spent together, the more I wanted. We touched every chance we got. We shared our deepest thoughts, and he was constantly on my mind. Yet I knew it wasn't forever.

It wasn't even a real relationship. We were sneaking around. And while I knew it was necessary, for the kids, part of me wondered if that was just an excuse. Wondered if I was accepting less than I deserved merely because I couldn't fathom the thought of being without him.

"Ellie?" Piper asked gently.

I gulped down some champagne. "With everything, but especially with him. This was supposed to be Tessa's life, not mine. I'm just pretending."

"Pretending?" Piper asked.

"You know…" I sighed. "Playing house with Tristan and the kids when I could never match up to my sister."

"Maybe you don't need to," Sumner said. "Maybe you can be yourself and that's enough."

I shook my head. "It's not. It never has been."

"Did Tristan say that?" Piper asked, her expression turning murderous. "Because I swear to god—"

"No. *No.*" I placed my hand on hers. Quite the opposite, in fact. He was always trying to get me to see the amazing woman he saw in me. "I just—ugh. Sometimes I can't help but wonder if he's comparing me to her. If he wishes I *was* her."

He never acted like it. When I was with Tristan, I felt like the version of myself I wanted to be—confident, powerful, sexy. And yet, when we were apart, the doubts crept back in.

Sumner and Piper frowned at me, their eyes swimming with pity.

"Oh, Ellie," Piper said, pulling me into a hug.

Finally, Sumner said, "I'm sure this summer has been a lot for you. Moving home so suddenly. Finishing school. Taking care of your niece and nephew. No one could blame you for seeking comfort from Tristan."

"Yeah, but now it feels like so much more than that."

Suddenly, everything was spilling out of me. My fears and worries about the kids, about Tristan. Even my concerns about what my sister would think of everything. It felt good to confess it all. And I kept talking, answering their questions, until my throat was scratchy and my tears had run dry.

"You love him," Piper said softly.

I nodded, but her words only prompted a fresh wave of tears. I'd barely owned up to that myself, but I did love Tristan. "I do. I'm in love with him, but we can never be together."

"Why not?" Sumner asked.

"I just can't see a way for us to be together." Admitting that aloud felt like taking my heart and putting it through a paper shredder.

After all, wasn't I the one who'd told Tristan this didn't have to be forever?

Piper smoothed a hand down my back while Sumner talked. "I once felt that way about my husband, Jonathan. He was my boss for the summer. My dad's best friend." She smirked. "Talk about obstacles."

"But love always finds a way," Piper said with a certainty I envied.

I wanted to believe it could be true, but… I shook my head. They didn't understand. Sumner's situation was different. "I don't think it's love. At least, not for Tristan."

"He may need time," Sumner said. "Grief can be unpredictable. I'm sure it was difficult for him to ever imagine a future without his wife. Let alone a future with someone else."

"You mean a future with *me*. His sister-in-law." Because clearly, that was the bigger issue.

"Yes." She nodded. "That could be an obstacle too."

I was pretty sure it still was. Tristan might be okay with our relationship when it was just the two of us, but I could never imagine him walking down the street holding my hand. And while I told myself I could accept that—at least for the summer—I was finding it more and more difficult to reconcile. Especially since he'd given me Tessa's charm.

I toyed with my necklace. As much as I loved having something she'd treasured, I felt weird about wearing it. Like it didn't belong to me. And, as with her dress, it made me wonder if he saw me for me. Or if I was merely a stand-in for my sister.

But this wasn't just about Tristan and me. "Plus, there's the kids to consider. Our families. Our friends."

"I'm guessing everyone just wants him to be happy. He's suffered a lot this past year. You all have."

I shook my head. "You don't know my mother. She would *never* support this." And while I didn't want to care, part of me did.

"I worried my dad would never come around," Sumner said. "It took him a while. And it was painful. But eventually, he realized how happy Jonathan and I were together."

I scoffed and downed the rest of my drink, the bubbles scratching my throat. "My mom isn't like that. And we certainly don't have the relationship that you and your dad do."

I hadn't realized how much I was holding in. How much I was holding back. It was nice to talk to them, even if it wouldn't change anything. Tristan and I both knew I was leaving at the end of the summer, and that would be the end of it. The end of us.

I sighed. "It doesn't matter. I'm leaving for Japan soon. Tristan's life is here. It always has been, and it always will be."

It was selfish of me to expect otherwise. I knew how much the Alondra Valley meant to him. Him and the kids. He was firmly rooted here—he had a dog, a hedgehog, a house. His company. And the kids should be close to family and friends. To the community that continued to love and support them through their struggles and successes.

"You never know," Sumner said, refilling our glasses. "Men do crazy things when they're in love." She got a wistful look in her eyes.

Pretty sure Tristan would have to be in love first to even consider doing something crazy. But he would only ever love one woman, and she was dead.

CHAPTER TWENTY-TWO

Tristan

"Are you ready for another 'fun' family dinner?" Elle asked with mock enthusiasm.

Elle was never excited about dinner with her parents, but she seemed to be dreading it even more than usual. I wondered if it had to do with her parents, or if something had happened during her birthday weekend with Piper and Sumner. Because ever since then, she'd seemed…different. Almost withdrawn.

"Oh, absolutely," I teased, rubbing up and down her arms. I couldn't wait for our weekend away in Bear Creek. But as eager as I was to be alone with Elle, I also wanted to slow down time. Because not long after our trip to Bear Creek, Elle would leave for Japan. "But at least they've behaved lately, right?"

"Yeah." She rolled her eyes. "For the most part."

"Trust me. I'm not looking forward to it either. Gloria's already pissy enough about the kids' Disney trip." But I also didn't want to listen to her nagging if we missed dinner.

"Ugh." Elle huffed and glanced toward the ceiling. "So

ridiculous. Why can't she just be happy that Maddox and Savannah are going to do something fun?"

"Because it wasn't her idea. And they aren't going with her."

"True. But I don't understand the need for comparison and jealousy. Shouldn't we just be thrilled that the kids get to do something wonderful and create special memories with people who love them?"

"Yes. But we both know that's not who Gloria is." I rubbed the space between her shoulder blades, hoping to ease the tension there. "Is something else going on?"

She laughed, though it lacked humor. "Let's just say my birthday has always been a sore spot for my family."

"Because you're adopted?" I asked, trying to understand.

"Something like that," Elle said.

"I'm sorry." I rubbed her arms. I hadn't considered that her birthday might bring up feelings around her biological parents. "I'm sure that's difficult."

She nodded. "Thanks, but it's fine. I'm just glad we already celebrated with the kids since I know my mom will try to ruin it for me like she always does."

My body tensed at her words. It didn't seem to matter how many times I told Elle she was amazing; her mom always found a way to tear her down. I didn't understand why Gloria was so nasty. After losing Tessa, I would've thought Gloria would be more determined to have a good relationship with her only surviving child. But the opposite seemed true.

"Why don't you say something to her? Tell her how you feel."

Elle shook her head, her lips drawn. "What would be the point? It won't change anything."

I hated the idea of someone as amazing as Elle being so… defeated. I wrapped my arms around her from behind. While

I could've tried to spank her into submission, I had a feeling that wasn't what she needed.

"You never seem to have any issue standing up to me."

She leaned her head against me, and I reveled in the feel of her. "That's because you're different. You make me feel safe."

I kissed the top of her head. I was glad she felt safe with me. And I understood what she meant because I felt safe to be myself with her in a way I hadn't in the past. I could embrace my darker desires. I could have fun with them because I knew we were both on the same page.

"We'll leave as soon as we can. And—" I pressed my lips to the skin behind her ear "—I promise I'll make you forget all about it later."

"Mm. I look forward to it." She turned in my arms so she was facing me.

She slid her hand down my chest, and I loved the easy familiarity of her touch. It was effortless, just like having her in our lives.

I leaned forward to kiss her, just as Savannah yelled, "Dad! Have you seen my silver glitter shoes?"

I backed away and mouthed, "Later," my heart pounding as the kids raced down the stairs. That was a little too close.

"I think they're in the laundry room," Elle said, her cheeks flushed.

"Oh yeah." Savannah darted in that direction. "Thanks."

"Ready?" I asked a minute later, and we all headed to the car.

When we arrived at Fall River Estates, the hostess led us to our usual table. Dan hugged the kids and Elle before shaking my hand. Gloria smiled and hugged the kids, kissing Ellie's cheeks with a cold, detached expression.

The waiter quickly took our order, and the kids started talking about Disneyland almost immediately. The longer they talked, the more the tension gathered at the table, like a storm picking up speed. Especially when they shifted to talking about our family outing to Bouncing Off the Walls to celebrate Elle's birthday.

"Mm. Yes," Gloria said, taking a sip of her wine. "You two caused quite the stir. Getting kicked out of the inflatable jump place. Really?" Gloria tsked and shook her head.

Elle and I glanced at each other and frowned. Sure, things had gotten a little out of hand. And yes, we'd been asked to leave the premises after an unfortunate incident with a large inflatable cactus. But how did Gloria know?

The answer dawned on me just as Gloria said, "It was in *The Vine.*"

"Oh lord." Elle rolled her eyes as she toyed absently with the charms on her necklace.

Gloria's eyes caught on the movement, but then the waiter returned to remove our plates and refill our drinks. Before he could ask about dessert, a chorus of waiters advanced on the table with Asher at the front. He carried a plate of éclairs topped with a candle as everyone sang "Happy Birthday" along with him.

I wasn't sure whether to be grateful for the interruption or annoyed with Asher as he winked at Elle. He set the plate in front of her, leaning in to whisper something in her ear. And it took everything in me to keep my cool. To stay calm and act as if I didn't care.

Elle blew out the candle, and then the waiters returned to the kitchen. Asher stayed behind.

"I can't even—" Elle shook her head, her eyes glued to the plate, admiring the purple-iced éclairs topped with edible purple and white flowers. "These are too pretty."

"They're lemon-lavender éclairs," Asher said. "It's a flavor I've been wanting to try. Unique, sweet, and a little tart. Just like you."

I gnashed my teeth but remained silent. *That fucker.*

"Would you mind taking a picture with me for my Instagram?" Elle asked Asher.

"I'd love to," he said as she handed me her phone.

Asher placed his arm on her lower back while Elle smiled and held up the plate of pastries. All the while, I wondered if this was what it would be like in the future. She was only mine for a little longer, but the idea of Elle with anyone else made me want to break something. She belonged with me.

"Auntie Ellie, they match your hair exactly!" Savannah said.

Elle grinned. "They do, don't they?"

"Only the best for LC." Asher winked as I handed Elle her phone. "I know it's your favorite color."

"LC?" Gloria frowned. Actually, I wasn't sure she'd stopped frowning the entire evening. Except when one of her constituents might be watching, of course.

Asher cleared his throat. "Good evening, Madame Mayor."

Oh jeez. What a suck-up.

"Good evening. Thank you for the pastries, Asher."

"You're welcome. I'll, uh, leave you to your celebration." He backed away from the table, clearly not wishing to be under the mayor's scrutiny any longer.

"Here," Gloria said, sliding a gift bag toward Elle. "Happy birthday."

"Happy birthday," Dan echoed.

"What is it?" Savannah asked at the same time Maddox bounded over to Elle's side and said, "Can I help you open it?"

"Of course." She smiled at Maddox and wrapped her arm around him.

He tugged out the tissue paper, casting the contents on the table.

"Um. Thanks," Elle said, her tone flat.

"What is it?" Maddox asked, frowning at the plastic card.

"A gift card to Bibliolater."

"I bought it on Meghan Hart Day," Gloria said. "So a portion of the sale went to fund Teresa's new library." She smiled expectantly, as if this comment deserved extra praise or gratitude.

All the while, I tried to focus on my breathing so I wouldn't make a bigger deal out of her comment than it warranted. I didn't understand why Gloria always took something that should be about Elle and turned it into something about Tessa. We all loved Tessa. We all missed her. But Elle deserved her moment to shine too.

A glance at Dan told me he was just as uncomfortable. He tugged on his collar and sipped his wine but said nothing. I wanted to roll my eyes.

"A gift card. Sweet," Maddox said. Despite Elle's smile, I could sense her disappointment.

I didn't blame her. It was such an impersonal gift. And while Elle enjoyed reading, she was about to move to Japan. She couldn't take many books with her even if she wanted to. Besides, a gift card to Bibliolater was the type of gift Tessa would've loved, not Elle.

"When Ellie graduated, we gave her a charm for her necklace," Savannah said. "Isn't it pretty?"

"Let's see," Gloria said.

Elle laughed, though I sensed it was out of discomfort more than anything else. She lifted her necklace and showed Gloria the new charm. I loved seeing it around her neck, knowing she was wearing something I'd given her. That a piece of me was constantly touching her skin.

Gloria smiled, but her shrewd gaze was on Elle and me. I wasn't sure what she was thinking, but I felt like she *knew*.

Like she could see what we'd done written on our faces as if we were wearing a neon sign.

"There's Aiden!" Savannah pointed to the far side of the room. "Can I go say hi?"

"Of course," I said, sensing Gloria was about to blow. And, as usual, Dan would stand by and do nothing. "Why don't you take Maddox with you?"

"Okay." She grabbed Maddox's hand, and they raced across the restaurant.

"Are you sure that's…appropriate?" Gloria asked me after the kids had left.

I frowned. "The charm?"

She nodded, and Elle tensed beside me. "It seems rather intimate for a brother-in-law to gift his wife's younger sister."

I wasn't sure a charm would qualify as intimate. And it definitely wasn't as intimate as the pearl necklace I really wanted to give Elle. I got hot just thinking about my come marking her skin.

"Intimate?" Elle laughed, dragging me away from my thoughts. "It's a charm for a necklace."

She was right, but I had a feeling we were no longer discussing the charm.

"Yes, but what message is it sending, especially to the children?" She stared at Elle as if trying to read her body for any cues. "I'm concerned that they're getting confused."

Were they confused? Had I grown too lax about my relationship with Elle around the children? If Gloria suspected something, did Maddox and Savannah? I didn't think so, but I hated that I even had to wonder.

Wanting to defuse the situation, I said, "Savannah and Maddox picked the poppy charm because it reminded them of Ellie. And they wanted to give her a piece of California to take with her."

"So, you're still intent on going, then?" Dan asked, his attention on Elle.

"Yes," Elle said. "I purchased my plane tickets, and I have a guaranteed spot."

Fuck. I rubbed a spot on my chest. I didn't want to think about it. Couldn't think about her leaving, even if I knew it was best for her.

"That's great, honey," he said. But Gloria merely shook her head, her disapproval clear.

"Is it?" Gloria asked in a snarky tone.

Elle ran a hand through her hair. "I would've thought you'd be happy that I'm leaving, considering your *concern* for the children."

Gloria paused, her eyes glued to Elle's necklace once more. The charms had shifted so the disk with the kids' and my initials was in front. "What is *that?*"

"What?" Elle glanced around.

"That disk." Her tone was sharp. Her features drawn. "That's *Teresa's* charm," Gloria seethed. "You shouldn't be wearing that. Take it off. *Now.*"

"Now, Gloria—" Dan placed his hand on her shoulder.

"No." She flung away his hand. "Don't touch me. You wouldn't understand. Your—" Her eyes flared with anger, and I wasn't sure I followed.

Dan huffed and stood, retreating to the bar.

I was determined to put an end to this. "I gave her the charm."

Gloria took a moment to compose herself then narrowed her eyes at me. "I don't know what is going on between you two, but whatever it is, it needs to stop."

Neither of us said anything. What could we say?

But Gloria wasn't done. "Eleanor, you're moving in with us until you leave for Japan."

"I will do no such thing," Elle said in a steely voice that

both surprised me and made me proud. "The only reason I'm still in the AV is because of Tristan and the kids. And I'm not moving out unless Tristan wants me to." She turned to me.

I shook my head, wanting desperately to hold her hand beneath the table. To remind her that we were a united front. To show her how much I valued and loved her.

"I want you to stay," I said, and I didn't just mean for the summer. "The kids want you to stay."

Elle softened, relaxing at my words. She gave a barely perceptible nod, but it put me at ease all the same.

Meanwhile, Gloria looked as if steam might shoot out of her ears at any moment. It was kind of funny, actually, watching her attempt to retain some composure even as she was about to fucking lose it. I was even more grateful the kids weren't around.

"Then you will at least remove that charm," Gloria said in an imperious tone, making demands she had no right to. "It's perverse. To wear the initials of your sister's husband and children? What will people think?"

"Who cares?" I asked. "I doubt anyone will realize it belonged to Tessa."

"And if they do?" Gloria asked.

"Well, then the 'T' could be for Tessa." Though I'd wanted it to be for me.

Gloria shook her head. "I don't like it. First, *The Vine* post and now this?"

"You've never liked anything I've done, so I'm not sure why this is any different," Elle said, standing abruptly. Her chair scraped along the floor, but she retained her poise. She turned to me. "I'm going to find the kids. Come get us when you're ready to leave."

I was proud of Elle for standing up to her mom. But with her departure and Dan still at the bar, I was left to endure the wrath of Gloria alone.

Gloria leaned across the table and lowered her voice. "Have *The Vine* post taken down," she commanded. "I know you can."

I waved a hand through the air, unwilling to confirm or deny her claim. "It's a silly gossip blog."

"Oh, it's so much more than that, and you know it."

I leaned back, draping my arm over the seat next to mine. "I imagine removing a post would only lead to more speculation. But I'm not as well versed in maintaining the perfect public image as you are."

She forced a smile. "It's not the post that concerns me, but the perception it creates."

"So what?" I asked, sick of her anger. Her accusations. "I've never cared what people think of me. Why should I start now?"

She leaned forward. "Perhaps not, but you do care about your children's opinion and reputation." I frowned, not liking where she was going with this. "And, as I mentioned before, I'm afraid that having Eleanor around is *confusing.*"

"What exactly are you insinuating?" I wanted to cut straight through the bullshit. If she had the gall to accuse me of something, she damn well better come out and say it.

"Perhaps *distracting* would be more apt. And considering other ill-advised decisions you've made..." she said, a scarcely concealed dig at me for terminating Tessa's life support. *Wow.* "It makes me question your ability to parent those children."

I rubbed my brow as if to ward off my oncoming headache. She had no idea how hard I'd been trying to keep it together and all for those kids. And yet, she was questioning me and my choices. *Unbelievable.*

"*Those* children?" I practically growled. "Savannah and Maddox are *my* children." I jabbed at my chest. "*Mine.* And as their father, I'm the best person to know what they need."

She lifted a shoulder, her expression unaffected. "I only want what's best for Maddox and Savannah."

"No." I scoffed. "You want what's best for you. You're so out of touch with reality that you don't realize how hurtful your comments and actions are. Your own daughters despised you. And if you're not careful, you'll alienate your grandchildren as well."

I stood, tossing my napkin on the table. But Gloria stood as well, smoothing down her dress and forcing a smile as she grabbed my elbow. "And if *you're* not careful, I'll petition for custody."

I straightened, though her threat had me off-kilter. Was there any basis to it? Could she take them away from me? Despite my fears, I refused to show any outward reaction.

I turned to her, my expression steely. "I'd like to see you try."

I tore myself out of her hold and marched off. How dare she…

"Whoa," Asher said, nearly colliding with me as I stomped down the hall toward the kitchen and restroom. "Uh-oh." His teasing tone only set me further on edge. "Did someone hit on Ellie?"

I shook my head, my fists clenched. "Shut up, Asher. You don't know what you're talking about."

He glanced toward the dining room. "I wonder how many tattoos she has."

"Asher—" I charged at him, grabbing his chef's jacket and hauling him against the wall. I'd had enough. Of Gloria's threats. Of Asher's taunts. "I'm warning you."

"Ooh." He smirked. "Looks like maybe you do still have that fire."

The kitchen door opened, and one of the staff peeked out. "Chef?"

"Be right there," Asher said, his eyes never leaving mine.

I held his coat a second longer, our gazes locked before I released him.

What the hell was wrong with me? Storming off from the table. Nearly coming to blows with one of my best friends. I planted my hands on my thighs, panting. If I kept acting like this, Gloria really might have grounds for challenging my custody of the kids.

"Tristan?" Asher placed his hand on my back. "Talk to me. I know I've been an ass, but I'm here for you. What's going on?"

I drew in a few more deep breaths then straightened. "Fucking Gloria," I spat her name like the curse she was. "Everything's out of control. And your comments about Elle aren't helping."

"You know I'm just messing with you, right? I was never going to pursue her. I was actually trying to give you a push to go for it."

I dragged a hand through my hair. Asher as a matchmaker? Who would've guessed. Though considering Asher had always loved to stir the pot, maybe I should've suspected as much. "Oh, I went for it, all right."

His eyes widened. "Oh shit. Seriously?"

I rubbed the back of my neck. "You cannot tell *anyone*."

"Of course I won't."

"I'm sorry I grabbed your coat." I brushed the white fabric as if that would somehow erase what I'd done.

He patted my shoulder. "Nah. I should know better than to rile you up. You always act like you're so calm and in control, but it can take a lot of restraint to mask the truth."

I furrowed my brow. "Sounds like you have something you need to unload too."

He shook his head. "Maybe another time."

I slumped against the wall. "What a fucking mess."

"Everything okay?" Enzo's voice called from down the

hall. "I was told I might have to break up a fight outside the kitchen."

I chuckled, clapping a hand on Asher's shoulder. "Nah. We're good. Right?"

Asher had been my friend since forever. I knew he only had my best interests at heart, even if his methods were a bit misguided. Still, I felt like I could be a better friend. Something was weighing on Asher, and I vowed not to let my own shit get in the way of helping him. *Soon.*

Asher nodded. "Right. Catch up with you later," he said and then returned to the kitchen.

"You look like you could use a drink, *amico mio*," Enzo said.

I scrubbed my face with my hands. "I could certainly use something."

"Come on." He wrapped his arm around my shoulder. "Elle and the kids are with Harper and Aiden. I have some new whiskey a brand wants me to endorse. Let's try it, and you can tell me of your troubles."

Oh, my troubles. Elle was leaving soon, and Gloria was threatening to take my kids.

I was going to disappoint everyone I loved, even Tessa. And I would only have myself to blame.

CHAPTER TWENTY-THREE

Ellie

"Ellie?" Harper asked, placing her hand over mine. "Are you okay? You're shaking."

I stared at the flames, watching them flicker in the firepit behind her house. The kids were playing flashlight tag among the vines, their laughter ringing out in the night air. It was a beautiful evening, peaceful. At least if I ignored everything that had happened at dinner.

"I'm—" I lifted my hand to drag it through my hair. "Yeah. No." I shook my head. "I had a big fight with my mom."

"Oh no." She winced. "Living near family can be a good and bad thing."

"It's never a good thing when it comes to my mom. She drives me crazy."

"She's a strong personality," Harper said, laughing.

I returned my attention to the flames. "Strong is an understatement."

"You want some wine?" She lifted a bottle from the ground.

"Yeah, actually. I would."

"Well, at least you won't have to deal with her much longer," Harper said, pouring me a glass.

"Thanks." I accepted it from her. "And yeah. You're right," I sighed. But that meant I wouldn't get to see Tristan and the kids every day either.

I kept thinking back on dinner and how he'd asked me to stay. How badly I wanted to stay, and not just for the summer. But I had a feeling he wasn't referring to more than that.

She lifted her glass for a toast. "To new adventures."

"To new adventures." I smiled and took a sip, though it tasted bittersweet. I was about to go on a big adventure, and yet I'd be leaving my heart behind.

"How was orientation?" she asked.

Harper had been the most interested in my progress with the JET Program, apart from Tristan. Considering her love of travel, it wasn't surprising. She'd been to Japan years ago, when she was still working as a film location scout. But never to Naruto, Tokushima. I couldn't imagine many people would willingly travel there. I was still trying to wrap my head around the fact that I'd be *living* there.

I'd asked to be placed in one of the northern locations, yet I'd gotten the exact opposite. So instead of my dreams of snowboarding and wearing hoodies, I'd be sweating on an island. A hot island that no one visited.

Even so, it had one thing going for it. It was far away from my mom. Unfortunately, that meant it was also far away from Tristan and the kids.

I wouldn't be here for their first day of school. Nor their birthdays or so many other moments. My chest ached at the realization of all that I would miss out on. At the idea of just how badly I would miss Tristan.

"Ellie?" Harper asked.

"Hmm?" I slid my gaze to her.

"I asked how orientation was."

"Oh." I cleared my throat and tucked my leg beneath me. "Yeah. It was good."

"I'm sure you're feeling both excited and nervous." Her smile was kind, understanding.

I laughed. "You can say that again."

Though lately, my nerves were winning out. I was second-guessing myself a lot. Was I doing the right thing? Would the kids be okay after I left? Would Tristan?

"I know you're going to be busy, but Enzo and I talked about it, and we'd love to hire you as a content creation consultant for Fall River Estates."

I jerked my head back. "Really?"

I was flattered. I'd never imagined that helping occasionally would turn into a more permanent, paying job.

"Yeah." She smiled. "You're really talented, and we've definitely seen an increase in sales since implementing your tips."

"That's great, but…"

She waved a hand through the air. "Just think about it for now, 'kay? I could upload photos to a shared drive each month, and you could create content from them."

I nodded. "Okay. I just…" I sighed. "Thank you for the offer, but I'm not sure when I'll be coming back to the AV."

"I know, though I hope you'll come back before too long. It's funny," she mused. "I never imagined I'd end up living in the AV. I mean, in the back of my mind, I always wanted to settle down one day and have a family here. But I spent so many years traveling and living in LA that I figured I was past that."

"And then you met Enzo," I said with a smile.

"And then I met Enzo." She grinned. "And that was…*whew*. That was a whole different adventure."

I laughed, knowing bits and pieces of their story. How they'd started as a vacation fling. How she'd had no idea he was an internationally famous soccer star until after she realized she was pregnant with Aiden.

"Funny how things work out sometimes," she said.

"True. I wouldn't be here now if Tessa hadn't…"

She placed a hand over mine. "I know. I can't imagine how difficult that's been for you."

I nodded, staring out at the vineyards where the flashlights flickered and danced among the vines.

"The AV feels so different without her," I said.

"Losing someone you love changes everything."

I nodded, though Harper had no idea just how much had changed.

One of the patio doors slid open, and Enzo came to join us. He placed his hand on Harper's shoulder, the firelight flickering along his tattoos. "Hey, Ellie."

"Hey." I gave him a little wave.

"Uccellina." He bent forward to kiss Harper deeply.

I glanced away, trying to ignore the pang of longing it inspired. Would I ever have a love like that? A love like Tristan and Tessa had shared?

He'd always adored Tessa. Sometimes when he looked at me, it felt as if he loved me. But then I reminded myself that it was probably just lust.

"Where's *mio figlio*?" Enzo asked Harper.

She gestured toward the fields. "Playing flashlight tag with the others."

He chuckled and grabbed a flashlight from a box. He yelled something in Italian that I assumed was "Here I come" as he disappeared between the dark rows of grapes.

The kids cheered and shouted, but Harper merely shook her head. "He's such a big kid."

"It's good," I said. "He's a good father."

"So is Tristan." Harper sipped her wine.

"The best," I said, raising my glass to my lips. Which was

why I had faith that he and the kids would ultimately be okay without me. If they could survive without Tessa, they would certainly be fine without me.

The door opened again, and Tristan joined us. He took one look at me and frowned. Harper, perhaps sensing the change in atmosphere, rose and smoothed her hands down her thighs. "I'm going to check on the kids and Enzo. See if they want s'mores, if that's okay."

"Absolutely," Tristan said. "Thank you."

As soon as she was gone, Tristan sank down into the chair next to me. "Are you okay?"

I scoffed and shook my head. "I *knew* tonight was a bad idea."

"Well, you were right. I'm proud of you for standing up for yourself." He gave my shoulder a squeeze then leaned forward and rested his head in his hands. "And I'm done with family dinners."

I turned to him, mouth agape. "What? What happened?"

Tristan shook his head. "I've had enough of Gloria and her bullshit. I warned her…" He stopped himself, then said, "I will *not* stand by and allow her to treat you like she has. And I sure as fuck don't want her around the kids."

I jerked my head back, surprised by his reaction. "As angry as I am, I don't want to alienate Maddox and Savannah from their grandparents. They've already lost so much."

"I agree, but that doesn't give Gloria an excuse to be abusive and toxic."

I frowned. I knew Tristan was protective of me, but this seemed like more than that. And while I appreciated his loyalty, I sensed there was something else going on.

"What aren't you telling me? What happened after I left?"

He leaned back in the chair, dragging a hand through his hair. "It doesn't matter."

"The hell it does. I want to know what was said."

He clenched his fists and stared at the flames, a fire raging inside him. Seeing how tormented he was, I softened and went to his side.

"Tristan?"

He ran a hand over his mouth. "It'll only make you madder."

My body tensed, and I could feel my blood pressure rising. The only reason I was able to stay calm was because I was focused on comforting him.

I reached out and touched his arm. "Hey," I said. "I'm on your side, yeah?"

He continued staring at the fire, a muscle in his neck twitching. "I don't want there to be sides. I don't want you to have to choose."

"I would always choose you." I held his gaze. "You and the kids. Over and over again and for always."

He was quiet for long enough that I finally glanced away, wondering if I'd said too much. Did Tristan realize how I felt about him?

"I know, Elle. It's a big reason why I—" He cleared his throat. "It's something that I love about you."

Wait. No. Back up. Was he going to say he loved me?

"I need to ask you something," he said while I was still reeling. "But I don't want you to feel like you have to say yes."

"O-okay," I said, the word catching in my throat.

Was this it? Was he going to ask me to stay?

"If anything ever happens to me, I want you to be their guardian."

I stilled. Was he… "You're serious?"

He nodded. "I know it's a lot to ask. And I hope it's never necessary, but I know how much you love Savannah and Maddox. I know you'll always take care of them. I trust you more than anyone to raise them—"

"Yes. Of course," I blurted. "I'm honored."

Maybe he hadn't professed his love, but this was...this meant so much. He wanted me to raise his children if something ever happened to him?

I was touched. That he believed in me. That he trusted me to place them in my care. Though I hoped it never came to that.

The idea of losing Tristan was... I shook my head. I couldn't think about it. It was too painful.

"Thank you." He sighed, some of the fight going out of him. "That puts my mind at ease, especially after my conversation with Gloria."

The hairs on the back of my neck stood on end. "What conversation?"

"Apparently, she's concerned about the children and my ability to parent them."

How dare she. I stood. "Oh, *hell* no."

I headed for the door, but Tristan grabbed my arm. "Elle, stop. It's not going to help anything. If anything, it'll make the situation worse. We don't want to give her any ammunition to take them away."

"Take them..." I gasped, a sharp pang in my chest stealing my breath. "Away? What?"

"She's not going to. I won't allow it. But her threat rattled me. I'm going to talk to Audrey to find out what basis, if any, Gloria's claim would have."

"After all that you and the kids have been through..." I seethed. "I cannot even *believe* she would suggest such a thing."

"She's angry."

I dipped my head, my voice barely above a whisper when I said, "She's doing this to punish me."

"What?" He jerked his head back. "Why?"

"Because I'm not Tessa." I slumped.

"Huh?"

"She's mad that Tessa died and I'm still here. If she thinks there's something between us, well…"

He blinked a few times as if stunned. "Damn. Gloria's even more fucked up than I thought."

"Why do you think I wanted to move to Australia?"

"I thought it was for the cute koalas," he teased.

"That was part of it, but mostly, I wanted to get as far away from my parents and the AV as possible. Plus, as much as I adored my sister, I was tired of living in her shadow."

He tilted his head, his expression full of sadness. Regret. "I'm sorry, Elle. I had no idea."

"You have nothing to apologize for."

"I do, actually." He took my hand in his. "I have a lot to apologize for."

I frowned.

"I'm sorry for insisting that we come tonight," he said, rubbing his thumb over the back of my hand. "I'm sorry for asking you to keep our relationship a secret."

I waved my free hand through the air. I appreciated his acknowledgment, but it didn't change anything. "Tristan, we both know this has to be a secret. The kids…"

He nodded. "I know, but I'd never want to make you feel like…well, like you were somehow…"

"Less than?" I supplied.

He rubbed the back of his neck. "Yeah. Something like that."

I gnawed on the inside of my cheek, my eyes focused on the ground. "Thanks, but that's pretty much how I've felt my entire life."

He frowned. "What?"

"Oh, come on. You know how much everyone adored Tessa. I was *always* compared to her. I still am. I'm sure you do it too sometimes, even if it's unintentional."

I hadn't meant to say it, but now that I had, I wouldn't

take it back. Maybe I was being rash or unreasonable, but after the events of the evening, my heart was raw.

"What?" He sank into his chair.

I crossed my arms over my chest. "The dress?"

"Dress?" He furrowed his brow. "What dress?"

I stared at the sky then glanced around to confirm everyone was well out of earshot. "You know, the day you walked in on me…touching myself?"

"Yeah," he said slowly, brow furrowing. "What about it?"

"I was wearing Tessa's dress."

He tilted his head. "You were?"

I chewed on my cheek. "You didn't…realize?"

He chuckled. "I noticed *you*, not the dress, Elle. I wanted *you*."

"But—"

He placed his finger to my lips. "Wanting you has nothing to do with her. *Nothing*," he said again.

I hated this conversation. I hated my doubts. I hated that Tessa was gone. And yet, selfishly, I knew I wouldn't be with Tristan if she were still here. Which only made me feel worse.

He cupped my cheeks, wiping away my tears. I was a tangled-up mess of emotions when it came to this man. Guilt warred with desire. Longing clashed with obligation.

"Elle," Tristan sighed gently. "Why would I compare the moon to the sun? They both shine at their own time and in their own way."

"And when do I shine?" I sniffled. "Only when the sun goes down?"

"You—" he brought his finger beneath my chin, lifting my gaze to his "—my lovely moon, shine all the time. Even when the sun is out, you're still in the sky, ever-present yet ever-changing. Watching over us."

He drew in a shaky breath and continued. "You are the

moon, guiding me out of darkness. Giving me light and hope. You brought me back to life, Elle."

I...*wow*. I didn't know what to say. My body flooded with warmth at his words, at the way he was looking at me.

Again, I almost got the impression that he loved me. But if he did, wouldn't he have said it?

"Do you ever wonder what she'd think of this, us?" I asked. At this point, what did I have to lose? If I hadn't already planned to move to Japan, my mother's threats were proof that I should leave.

"I used to, sometimes."

"And now?"

He let out a heavy sigh. "Part of me will always love Tessa. I can honor her memory, but I'll never have those answers. So it doesn't really matter."

I rubbed my arms, surprised by how easy it was to listen to him talk about her in the past tense. To reconcile the idea of honoring her without being chained to her memory. I wasn't sure when it had happened. And it certainly hadn't been overnight, but we were both in a much better place than we'd been even months ago.

"I'm... Yeah. I feel that. I will always love my sister, and I will always talk about her with the kids. But there have been so many more days when the grief doesn't feel as...I don't know. Heavy."

He nodded.

"I hate to admit this—" I dropped my head. "But I think my mom was right about one thing." I took off my necklace and removed Tessa's disk. I opened Tristan's hand and placed it in his palm before closing his fingers around it. "This doesn't belong to me."

"But I gave it to you. I wanted you to have it."

I shook my head. I'd given it a lot of thought—both since

he'd given it to me and tonight. And it didn't feel right to wear Tessa's jewelry.

It wasn't about what my mom had said; it was about how the charm made me feel. And while I might be living in Tessa's house and sleeping with her husband, the disk felt like overstepping somehow.

"You should keep it for Savannah," I said.

"El—"

I smiled but stood firm, refusing to take it back. Instead, I asked, "Are you worried that the kids are confused about us?" I hadn't been until my mom had mentioned it tonight.

"Are you?" he asked. "You spend even more time with them than I do. Have they said anything to you?"

"No. Just that they wish I could stay. Though Maddox did mention hearing strange noises one night." I bit back a smile, thinking of all the nights Tristan and I snuck around the house, trying to be quiet even as we drove each other wild.

"Hm." He grinned. "Perhaps we should be more careful."

"Do you think we should stop?" I asked, thinking about how I'd almost blurted out the truth to my mom just to spite her. Now I was glad I hadn't. I'd never forgive myself if I jeopardized Tristan's relationship with the kids.

He rubbed the back of his neck. "Is that what you want?"

Fuck no. "I don't want to hurt the kids."

"You're going to hurt them much more by leaving." His voice was so low I barely heard it.

My shoulders deflated, and I started crying, finally letting my anger and frustration and sadness flow freely. He was right, but hearing him say it made me feel even worse. "You don't think I know that? I lie awake at night worrying about it."

"Fuck." He ran a hand through his hair, tugging on the ends. "I'm sorry, Elle." He sighed. "What I should've said was that they'll miss you."

I wanted to ask if *he'd* miss me, but I was scared.

"I'll miss them," I said. "I'm just—" I sighed. "I worry about them." *And you.*

"I know," he said, rubbing my shoulders. "But it's going to be okay. You'll see."

I hoped so because I couldn't stay here. Not when I was a liability to Tristan and the kids. And based on my mom's threats, I had a feeling she wouldn't relent until I was out of the picture.

CHAPTER TWENTY-FOUR

Tristan

I studied Elle as she slept. The rise and fall of her chest. The subtle flutter of her eyelids. Her purple hair splayed across the pillow. She was a goddess, and I could've watched her all day.

Eventually, she cracked open one eye and said, "Are you watching me sleep?"

"Maybe."

She stretched, the sheet drifting lower on her chest to reveal more of her delectable breasts. My mouth watered at the sight.

"What time is it?" She let out a sigh of contentment, which quickly turned to a moan when I nuzzled her chest.

"Don't know," I muttered between kisses. "Don't care."

She laughed but shifted so her leg was draped over my hip. My cock jutted toward her, seeking her heat. "I thought you were going to take me into town and show me off. Hold my hand as we walked down the street."

She was right. I'd promised. And I *did* want that.

But I also wanted her naked and all to myself.

We'd arrived at Liam and Penny's Bear Creek cabin

yesterday evening and hadn't left the bed since. We'd have to go to town soon, whether I liked it or not. There was nothing in the fridge and no delivery services. But I was too drunk on lust, on Elle, to care.

"There's plenty of time for that."

"Mm," she hummed, stroking my cock, clearly not interested in leaving any time soon either. "Can I ask you a question?"

"Of course," I said, kissing my way down her stomach. "As long as I don't need my mouth to answer."

I ducked beneath the covers, eager to put my mouth on her pussy. And then I didn't stop until her question was long forgotten and she was screaming my name.

After a not-so-quick shower, we finally headed into town. Our first stop was the coffee shop and bakery for breakfast. Well, lunch by that point. We held hands, as promised. And I reveled in the fact that I could kiss her whenever I wanted. Touch her anytime.

As we strolled down Main Street, laughing and kissing, I felt free. Freer than I had in a long time, except maybe when I'd gone to Celeste's yacht for the Fourth of July. But that hadn't been nearly as fun because Elle wasn't there.

In Bear Creek, Elle and I were a normal couple enjoying each other's company. No one gawked at us. No one cared about the difference in our ages or the fact that she was my late wife's sister. We were free to be ourselves without concern for what people might say or think.

I knew I was living in a fantasy, but it made me wonder… Was this what life would be like if Elle and I were together? *Truly* together?

Without the secrets or the sneaking around. But living as a couple. A family.

What would the kids think? Maddox was too young to

fully understand, but Savannah was older. Would she be upset? Feel somehow betrayed?

"You're awfully contemplative," Elle said.

I hugged her to me, grateful for this time together. Grateful that Liam hadn't asked any more questions or pushed for a guys' weekend when he'd given me the keys to the cabin. "I'm glad we were able to get away."

"Me too," she said.

We spent the afternoon hiking. Took our time shopping at the grocery store. Ate dinner at one of the nicest restaurants in town. The food was incredible, and the view was gorgeous. I couldn't imagine a more perfect day.

Now, the sun was setting, and we'd decided to enjoy the hot tub. Elle was upstairs changing, while I prepared the chocolate-covered strawberries and champagne.

I called the kids to say goodnight, eager to see their faces. They gushed about their day at Disneyland and all the rides they'd gone on. My parents had completely spoiled them, and I was glad. The kids deserved to have fun. They deserved an escape, and so did I.

When my dad called them to brush their teeth, my mom's face filled the screen. "How are you?"

"I'm good. Everything going okay with the kids?"

"We're having a wonderful time." Her tired smile spoke of all the fun they'd had. "What about you? Are you enjoying Liam's cabin?"

"It's gorgeous here," I said, moving aside so she could see the sunset through the large windows that lined the front of the A-frame.

"I'll be down in a minute," Elle called, and I froze, hoping maybe Mom hadn't heard her.

Mom furrowed her brow. "I didn't realize you..." She leaned her head back as her expression morphed into one of understanding. "Ahh. I see." Her grin was both knowing and content.

"Mom," I sighed, grabbing the champagne flutes and heading for the door that led to the front deck. Mom hadn't mentioned Elle's name, but I wondered if she'd recognized her voice. "I can ex—"

"Honey." She held up her free hand. "You're an adult. You don't need to explain anything to me."

"I—" I let out a deep sigh filled with gratitude and relief. "Thank you."

"Oh, before I go, I meant to ask you about the castle library." She furrowed her brow. "Maddox keeps asking to visit it, but I don't remember seeing that as an attraction at the park."

I smiled. "Ellie and the kids have this thing where they meet Tessa at the castle library every night. They imagine it and go there to talk to Tessa."

"Ahh." She tilted her head back. "That's sweet. I'm sure they enjoy having that ritual as a way to connect with their mom."

I nodded, hit with a pang of bittersweet longing. "Yes."

I kept waiting for Mom to ask me more about who I was with, but she didn't. She merely smiled and said, "I've gotta go. The kids want me to read bedtime stories. Be safe and have fun." She winked.

"Thanks, Mom. You too."

"I love you, sweetheart."

"Love you too," I said and then disconnected the call.

I rested my arms on the railing and let out a deep sigh. Well, fuck. So much for keeping Elle's and my relationship a secret. My mom may not have put two and two together, but even if she had, I trusted Mom would never tell anyone. More than anything, I was struck by how happy she'd been for me.

I returned inside to grab the strawberries and champagne then went back out to the hot tub and stripped out of my clothes. When Elle joined me, the sky was awash with pinkish hues and brilliant oranges as the sun dipped below the granite mountains. I rested my arms on the side of the hot tub, enjoying the sounds of the forest as the sun sank deeper into the horizon.

Elle's hair was twisted up on top of her head, her floral silk robe encasing her curves. I crooked my finger, inviting her to join me.

She untied her robe and let the material fall from her shoulders until it pooled at her feet. I studied the way the light hit her skin, casting her in a golden hue. My god, she was breathtaking. And she was mine.

Not for much longer.

"Spin," I said, my voice rough. "I want to see you."

She spun slowly, letting me drink her in. She wasn't modest. She didn't try to cover herself. And I reveled in her confidence and beauty.

"Come," I said, holding out my hand. "Join me."

She'd looked beautiful at dinner in her dress and heels, but I preferred her like this. Barefoot and fresh-faced. Comfortable in her own skin.

She stepped into the water, the jets bubbling around us, the sky slowly deepening to a darkish purple. I pulled her into my arms, our bodies sliding against each other in the most delicious way. I kissed her fully, deeply, until we were both panting. And then I rested my forehead against hers.

"Champagne?" I asked.

"What are we celebrating?"

"Life." I grabbed the glasses and handed one to her.

"To life." We clinked our glasses together and then each took a sip. It was fruity and effervescent, refreshing after a long day of exploring Bear Creek and each other.

We ate strawberries and drank champagne and stared at the stars as we chatted about everything and nothing. I lost track of time, just enjoying where I was and who I was with.

When Elle winced, I placed my hand on her shoulder. "Hey. Are you okay?"

She waved away my concern and forced a smile. "Just a headache. I probably should've had more water today."

Just a headache?

That simple phrase only caused more alarm. I stilled, my mind racing with thoughts. Memories. Fears. How many times had Tessa complained of a headache?

Before her death, she'd experienced intense headaches for months. When the doctors had finally determined the cause, it had been too late.

"A headache?" I whispered, my voice shaky like my hands. I set my glass on the deck, nearly knocking it over in the process. *Not again. I can't go through this again.*

I could remember it all so clearly. Months of Tessa not feeling well. Watching my once-vibrant wife fade away, until we discovered the truth. She had a brain tumor, and there was no guarantee the operation would be a success. Then, we'd made it through the stress of the surgery without knowing how it would impact her.

And just when we thought we'd overcome the biggest hurdle, her body had gone into shock. She'd slipped into a coma with no chance of recovery. Everything had happened so suddenly, and I hadn't known what or how to tell the children. Whether to have them come say goodbye before we terminated life support.

I dropped my head in my hands, my breath coming in pants.

It had been the most difficult thing I'd ever gone through. I'd had to face difficult and heartbreaking decisions. And Gloria had…

I was barely conscious of Elle shifting closer, placing her hand on my back. Her touch was soothing. "Tristan," she said. "Tristan." Again. More firmly.

"I…can't." I swallowed.

"You can't what?" she asked, her tone patient yet filled with concern.

Breathe.

Lose you.

I didn't say anything, merely crushed her to my chest. Needing to reassure myself that she was okay. Suddenly, everything else seemed silly and superficial in comparison to how awful things could be. How awful they had been.

"Hey," she said in a quiet voice, understanding softening her tone. "I'm okay. It's just a headache. Promise."

She couldn't know. She couldn't guarantee that.

"It wasn't just a headache for Tessa. It—"

"Shh." She held me close, and her touch was soothing. "I know. I know." She rubbed my back, waiting for my breathing to return to normal. I focused on her scent—sweet and spicy. And tried to listen to what she was saying. "The chance of brain tumors being hereditary is extremely rare."

Rare, but not impossible.

The chances of getting one *period* was rare. And yet Tessa had gotten one.

But then it dawned on me. "Hereditary?" I glanced up at her. "But you're adopted."

She gave me a lopsided smile. "Sort of."

I furrowed my brow, and she used her finger to smooth it. "What does 'sort of' mean?"

She let out a deep sigh, then said, "Dan is my biological father. My biological mom, Sicily, died in a car crash when I was three."

"What?" I shook my head. "Wait." I tried to piece it together. To understand.

"Yeah. I know, right?" she smiled, stroking her hand over my skin. "Dan had an affair, and he didn't know about me until my birth mom died. Sicily had named Dan as my guardian, and I was sent to live with him."

My eyes widened. "Holy shit. Did Tessa know?"

She shook her head. "Gloria and Dan told me when I turned eighteen but made me promise to tell no one. As far as I know, Tessa never knew."

I gnashed my teeth. I didn't like it. I didn't like it one bit.

How the hell was that supposed to make Elle feel? Like *she'd* somehow done something wrong? Like she was a shameful secret to be kept from everyone, even her own sister?

Yet here I was, asking the same thing of her. Asking for silence and secrecy. It made me feel even shittier.

Elle and I both understood the reasons for it. And I'd even apologized. But I could only imagine how it made her feel.

Less than, as she'd said the night of her disastrous birthday dinner.

That phrase had haunted me ever since. Someone as incredible and loving as Elle should never feel less than. It made my heart sick to think I was responsible for compounding her feelings of being inadequate or unworthy.

She massaged my temples, her focus always on helping others. "What are you thinking about in that big, beautiful brain of yours? Hmm?"

"Just...wow," I said, still reeling from everything. "How did you feel about that?"

She frowned. "Surprised. Hurt. Angry. So many things."

"I'll bet. Still, I'm surprised you didn't tell your sister."

She lifted a shoulder. "Sometimes I wish I had, but it doesn't really matter now."

I gave her a squeeze. "I'm glad you told me."

She kissed my forehead. "Me too. Sicily is actually part of the reason I applied for the JET Program?"

"Really?" I asked. "Why's that?"

"She spent a semester abroad in Japan. And I guess, I don't know…" Her smile was both sad and wistful. "It probably sounds silly, but I hoped it would help me feel somehow closer to her."

I rested my chin on her shoulder. "I don't think it's silly at all."

We were quiet a moment then she said, "I'm sorry if I wasn't as sensitive as I could've been about the headache thing. I didn't even—"

"I know you didn't mean anything by it," I said, but I still felt off-kilter.

After losing Tessa, I'd never expected to fall in love again. And I certainly wasn't supposed to fall in love with Elle. To know they were sisters…to realize there was even a remote chance of her being afflicted like Tessa was…

"Tristan?" She kissed my temple, her breasts pressed against me. Distracting me.

"Hm?" I asked, sliding my hands up her hips. Wanting nothing more than to get lost in the feel of her.

"I'm sorry."

"I know," I said, smoothing my hands over her ass.

"Not just about my comment but about…not being there when you guys needed me."

I took a deep breath and peered up at the sky. "There was nothing you—or anyone—could've done. Not even a team of highly qualified medical professionals could save her."

She settled into my arms. "I'm a good listener," she said. "If you ever want to talk about it."

I couldn't do that to Elle. It was my burden. My decision.

I also secretly feared that she'd look at me differently if she discovered the truth. Would she have sided with Gloria?

Would she have fought to keep Tessa on life support, despite her wishes to the contrary? It was so much easier to judge the situation after the fact.

"Thanks," I said, and I meant it. I might not intend to take her up on that offer, but I appreciated it more than she could know.

I held Elle close and peered at the sky, an endless blanket of stars. I kept telling myself life was too short, but when it came down to it, I was scared. Scared of letting someone in, only to lose them again.

CHAPTER TWENTY-FIVE

Ellie

"Ellie." Maddox tapped on my shoulder. "Will you come play with me?"

"I'll be there in a minute," I said, my attention focused on the computer screen.

Tristan and I had returned from the cabin earlier in the week, and since then, life had been busy. The kids weren't in camp this week, and I was leaving for Japan in three days.

As much as I'd rather spend time with Maddox and Savannah, I had to finish some paperwork for the JET Program. I'd waited until the last minute, procrastinating so it would seem less real. As if that would somehow make my departure less imminent.

All along, I'd known it was coming. But I'd wanted to soak up every second with Tristan and the kids that I could.

"Please?" Maddox begged, his pleas tugging on my guilt.

"I have to finish this, baby. Otherwise, I won't be able to go to Japan. As soon as I'm done, I'll come play. Promise."

His shoulders sagged, and he shuffled out of the room. I felt bad, but this really couldn't wait.

As soon as he was gone, I slumped forward, resting my

arms on the desk and cradling my head in my hands. I kept telling myself this was what I wanted. But all I really wanted was to stay with Tristan. To spend more time with him and the kids.

But that wasn't an option. And the sooner I finished this, the sooner I could enjoy what little remained of our time together.

I lost track of time, eventually completing the paperwork and shutting my computer with a sigh. I stood and headed downstairs as if in a daze. I needed something to eat; maybe the kids did too.

"Maddox? Savannah? You guys want a snack?"

No one responded, and I frowned at how quiet it was. I went back upstairs and checked their room, but it was empty.

"If you're hiding—" I called after I'd checked everywhere I could think of upstairs "—I give up."

Silence.

My pulse started rising, even as I told myself to stay calm. They couldn't have gone far. This was probably all just a game to them.

I checked the downstairs. Under the cabinets. In every hiding space I could think of, calling their names all the while. But there was no sign of them, and no sign of Rex either.

Exasperated and sweating, I wiped a hand across my forehead. I huffed out a breath and gave up my search, figuring they were out back.

Please be out back. Please be out back.

But when I glanced through the kitchen window, I didn't see them. I opened the door and called out, but Rex didn't come bounding up to me. And Maddox and Savannah were nowhere to be seen.

Okay. Don't panic. Maybe they went out front.

I rolled my eyes. They knew better than to go out front without an adult. But clearly, they weren't in the backyard or the house like they were supposed to be either. I jogged back inside, heart pounding, and grabbed my phone, nearly dropping it on the floor in my haste. I shoved my keys in my pocket, fumbling with my shoes. Rex's leash was still on the hook, so I grabbed that too.

I ran out the back door, calling their names again as I gripped the leash tightly in my hand. I whipped my head from side to side, images flashing through my mind of the worst-case scenarios. My voice sounded hysterical to my ears as I continued to call their names, but it was nothing compared to the sheer terror I felt at the idea of Maddox and Savannah going missing.

My chest grew tighter and tighter. Was this what it felt like to have a heart attack? *Oh god.*

"Maddox!" I yelled. By this point, I was growing hoarse. "Savannah!"

At the end of the block, one of the neighbors was gardening in her front yard. "Hey," I panted, jogging up the sidewalk. "Have you seen Maddox or Savannah?"

She stood and dusted off her hands. "No. Sorry. Is everything okay?"

I shook my head, sweat dripping down my back. "I can't find them." I couldn't breathe. "I need to find them."

"Have you called Tristan?" she asked.

I squeezed my eyes shut. I really did not want to do that, but I wasn't sure I had a choice. He needed to know what was going on, and I needed his help.

"I'm going to call him and keep looking. Please call us if you see them."

"Of course." She pulled out her phone and started typing. "I'll let the other neighbors know. We'll help search for them."

"Thank you so much." I jogged down the street, listening to Tristan's phone ring and ring.

Finally, he answered. "Hey, Elle. What's up?"

"I-I—" I spun around. *Where are they?* "Rex and the kids are missing."

"Are you sure they're not hiding? You know how they love to play games."

I wiped some sweat from my brow. "No. I'm sure. I checked everywhere. Rex is gone too."

"What?" he barked.

"I'm sorry. I was working on some paperwork…" I started crying, my words blurring like my vision.

"How long have they been gone?"

I wasn't sure. It could've been minutes, but it felt like a lifetime. If anything had happened…

"I don't know." I glanced at the clock on my phone. "Maybe thirty minutes? Longer?"

"Jesus, Ellie." He sighed, and I could feel his disappointment through the phone. "I'm on my way."

I curled into myself. This was all my fault.

"The neighbors are out searching as well," I said, wanting him to know that I was doing everything to find Maddox and Savannah.

"I'll call the police, but I doubt they'll do much at this point," he said in a frustrated tone. "Call me if anything changes. I'll be there soon."

"Okay," I said, and then the line went silent.

Fuck.

I glanced around. Where could they be? I closed my eyes and thought about it for a moment. Where would they have gone? The fact that Rex's leash was still at home led me to believe they were hunting for Rex. Which meant they could be anywhere. That dog was fast and agile.

I kept searching, until Tristan pulled up next to the sidewalk. "Get in."

I climbed in the passenger seat, and he barely waited until I was buckled in to drive off. As we wound through the neighborhood, we did so in a tense silence. So far, no one had seen the kids, and it was getting late. And hot. I worried that they were thirsty. That they were scared or hurt. My mind spun with possible scenarios.

Finally, Tristan's phone rang, Bennett's name flashing on the car's display.

"Savannah and Maddox are with us," Bennett said in a rush.

"Oh, thank god," Tristan said, loosening the grip on the wheel. "Are they okay?"

"They're a little dirty. And have a few scratches, but they're okay." His calm tone was reassuring.

"Is Rex with them?"

"No, but I emailed *The Vine,* and they already posted about it."

"Thank you." Tristan slowed at the stop sign, turning on his indicator. "We're on our way."

"See you soon," Bennett said before Tristan ended the call.

Tristan was silent on the drive over, breaking several traffic laws to get there more quickly.

"It's all my fault," I said, sobbing into my hands. "I'm *so* sorry."

He gripped the wheel tighter and clenched his jaw but said nothing. Which only made me feel worse.

As soon as he pulled up to the curb, he threw the car in park and jumped out. He jogged up to the house, and I followed, eager to see the kids safe and whole.

He pounded on the door, and it swung open.

"Hey," Bennett said. "They're just through here."

Tristan followed him inside, and I quickly dried my tears.

"Dad!" Savannah called, flinging herself into his arms as Maddox barreled toward me. "Ellie."

I caught him, and we nearly toppled over. "Hey, Mads," I whispered, trying not to cry as I glanced over his face, searching for any injuries. "I'm so glad you're okay."

"Thank you for taking care of them," Tristan said to Bennett, Savannah still clinging to him. "Where did you find them?"

"Down by the creek," Bennett said. "They'd followed it for quite a way."

"I can't thank you enough," Tristan said, heading for the door. "We should get home."

Maddox let out a deep sigh and rested his cheek on my shoulder. I carried him to the door, thanking Bennett for his help.

The drive home stretched in silence. I tried to get a read on Tristan while attempting to keep my emotions in check. I couldn't fathom how he was possibly keeping it together. But that was Tristan—calm, steady, in control. Sometimes it was sexy and reassuring. But other times—like this—it was confusing and infuriating.

"Daddy," Savannah said when we got home. "Are you mad at us?"

"Oh, sweetheart." He sat on the couch and patted his lap. "I'm not mad at you. I was scared. I'm so glad you're both okay," he said, hugging them both. "You're more important to me than anything."

"We're sorry we scared you," Savannah said. "But Rex got out, and we knew Ellie had to finish her paperwork, and…" She started crying, big fat tears. Maddox took one look at her and joined in.

"Hey," Tristan said in a soothing voice, rubbing circles on her back. "You're safe. We're here."

"But Ellie's leaving," Maddox wailed. "I don't want her to leave." He clung even tighter to me.

In that moment, my heart was breaking. I glanced to Tristan for assistance, but he lifted his shoulder. He was just as helpless as I was.

"I know it's going to be a change, and I will miss you like crazy. You and Savannah." I hugged Maddox closer while placing a hand on Savannah's back. "But I'm always just a phone call away."

"But I thought—"

When Savannah shushed Maddox, I frowned. "You thought what?"

"Savannah?" Tristan prompted.

She closed her eyes and took a breath. When she reopened them, she focused her attention on me. "Maddox thought you wouldn't leave if you couldn't find him. He was going to hide until after your flight was supposed to leave."

My heart ached at her admission. Both the idea that they were so desperate for me to stay. And that Maddox would vanish so I couldn't leave.

I was so tempted to tell her I wouldn't go, but I couldn't. I'd come too far to give up now. Besides, what would I even do if I stayed? Offer to keep living with them? Get a job in town? Take classes online?

For so long, my future plans had included the JET Program and moving to Japan that it was difficult to imagine anything else. I wanted to stay, but my relationship with Tristan was still a secret. And I didn't have much of a future in this town. As I'd told my mom, if it weren't for Tristan and the kids, I'd already have figured out a way to leave.

But I couldn't tell Savannah all that, so I said, "I love you both so much, you know that?"

Savannah nodded. "Love you too."

"And I'm not the only one. Mimi, Pops, Grannie and Grandpa, your dad."

"But it's not the same," Savannah cried. "They're not you."

Her words ripped me apart. What remained of my heart was shredded.

"Come here," I said, opening my arms for her to join Maddox. "Come on." I beckoned her in.

"Please don't go, Auntie Ellie," Savannah pleaded. "Please. Dad's happier now that you're here, and so are we. We don't want to…" She swallowed hard. "I don't want it to be like after Mommy died."

"Sweetheart," I said, lifting her chin. "It won't be like that. And you know how I know?"

She shook her head.

"Because you and Maddox and your dad are strong. You're the strongest people I know. I may have helped you, and I will always be here for you. But you're going to be just fine. I know it."

"Well, I don't." She pouted.

"Yeah." Maddox sulked.

Tristan's phone rang, and he went to the kitchen to take the call.

"I need you guys to promise me a few things," I said in a solemn tone.

"What?" Maddox asked.

"I need you to promise that you won't scare your dad like that again. And that you'll always listen to what he says because he loves you and wants the best for you."

They nodded in unison and said, "We promise."

"And I need you to take care of him after I'm gone," I said. "And yourselves."

They nodded again, and then I pulled both of them to me for a hug. I kept thinking of Tessa. Of how terrifying it must have been to go into surgery knowing how grim the outcomes were, and the very real possibility that she'd never see Maddox and Savannah again.

Tristan returned to the living room and took a seat on the couch. He shared a look with me but said nothing.

"Any news about Rex?" Savannah asked him.

He shook his head, his expression solemn. "*The Vine* posted about it, and everyone in town is looking for him."

"But—" Savannah's lip quivered again, and a tear slid down her cheek. "I'm worried about him."

"We *will* find Rex," Tristan said with more confidence than I felt. This was all my fault. "He's a smart dog, and he'll be okay."

He had to be. I knew how much the kids loved Rex. How much we all did. And I was worried about him.

"Can we search for him in the morning?" Savannah asked.

"Of course," Tristan said. "Bennett and River already volunteered to come help."

She seemed to relax a little at that.

For the rest of the evening, Tristan and I were focused on comforting the kids. I didn't know if he blamed me, but I certainly blamed myself. I simultaneously dreaded alone time with him and longed for it.

We ordered pizza for dinner and watched *Trolls*. Savannah sat next to me, and Maddox sat on Tristan's lap. He'd come a long way over the summer. They both had. It made me feel better about leaving them, but also…incredibly sad.

When the credits started to roll, Tristan said, "It's time to get ready for bed," and herded them upstairs.

There was no question of who was doing bedtime; Tristan took over. I wondered if he was trying to punish me for what had happened. Or—more likely—trying to reassure himself that they were both okay.

While he read the kids stories, I took a shower to rinse off the stress of the day. My mother had left me a scathing voice mail, but I'd deleted it after the first few seconds. She didn't have to tell me that I'd failed the kids; I knew.

When I returned downstairs, Tristan was sitting on the back patio. I wondered if he was waiting for me or if he wanted to be alone.

"Hey." I pushed open the door.

"Hey." He rubbed his face, and I could see the exhaustion in his features. I took one look at him and burst into tears.

"C'mere." He scooted back in the chair and patted the space in front of him. "Come on."

I tugged at the corners of my eyes and glanced around. "What if someone sees us?"

He reached behind him and flipped a switch. The lights went out, plunging us into darkness. "Better?"

He crooked his finger, beckoning me over, though my eyes were still adjusting to the darkness. I sighed and settled on the chair in front of him, his body molded to my back. He wrapped his arms around me and pressed his lips to my temple.

"I'm so—" I hiccupped around a sob. "Sorry."

"I know. I *know*." He held me even closer. "Shh."

"I was distracted, and I should've been paying better attention. And..." I was rambling, my words nearly incoherent.

"Elle, these things happen. I know you would never do anything to endanger Maddox and Savannah."

I shook my head. As much as I appreciated his understanding, I couldn't forgive myself so easily.

"I'm serious, Elle. Everyone fucks up now and then."

"You don't," I blurted.

"You're kidding, right?" he asked. "I've fucked up plenty of things, especially this past year." He smoothed his hands down my arms. "I've let Maddox and Savannah down more times than I care to admit. And I dropped the ball at work."

I turned back to peer up at the sky. "I'm sure that's understandable, given the circumstances. Plus, you've always been the AV's golden boy."

"I've made a lot of mistakes in my life. And I'm pretty sure I wouldn't be the 'golden boy' or whatever if people knew the truth." His lips grazed my cheek, his scruff tickling my skin.

My breath caught in my throat. "You mean the truth about us?"

"That and…" He paused, the air filled with tension. Did he regret us? If he didn't now, would he come to with time? I wasn't sure I wanted to know the answer.

"And what?" I asked.

He blew out a breath. "You know how I needed to secure an investor for Lockwood Industries?"

"Yeah." I knew he'd been stressed about it, but he rarely talked about work. When he did, he was filled with excitement for all the technology. But he seldom mentioned the business side.

"If I hadn't, the company would've folded. And I was this close to losing the house." He held up his thumb and forefinger.

I gasped. "Why didn't you tell me?"

"I was too ashamed. Besides, I've already burdened you enough this summer."

"Tristan," I sighed. "You could never be a burden."

He was silent, and I wondered if he believed me. I wanted him to.

Then another thought occurred to me. "Is that why you've been cleaning out…some things?" I asked, carefully avoiding Tessa's name. I'd thought he'd been cleaning out her stuff because he was moving on. Not because he was going to move.

"No." His voice rumbled through me like thunder. Powerful yet comforting. "It was time for some changes. Time to let go of the past."

I nodded, relieved by his answer.

"I didn't intend to tell anyone about this, but I wanted you to understand that you're not alone. And you're not a failure."

"Neither are you," I said, filling my voice with as much sincerity as I could.

I rubbed my hands up and down his thighs. They were strong, warm, holding me in. We were quiet for a moment, staring at the sky. At the vast and infinite universe. There were so many unknowns—about life, about my future, about everything. But right here, right now, I felt safe with Tristan.

"Maybe I shouldn't go," I said, finally voicing my fears aloud. "Maybe I should stay."

It was the closest we'd come to talking about the future. We'd always carefully avoided the topic. We'd both been clear about what this was, and I'd been too afraid to ask for more.

He was quiet, and I wondered what he was thinking. I held my breath, silently begging him to ask me to stay. To want me to stay.

"Elle." His tone was measured when he finally spoke, and suddenly I wished I could take it all back. "This was always meant to be a temporary detour. You were never mine to keep."

But what if I wanted to be?

CHAPTER TWENTY-SIX

Ellie

"I can't believe you're leaving tomorrow," Tristan said.

We'd spent the morning looking for Rex and the afternoon at Bennett and Wren's baby shower. It had been a long, emotional day. I was disappointed about Rex's continued absence. Saying tearful goodbyes to all my friends had been exhausting. And now, saying goodbye to Tristan…

The kids were in bed, and Tristan and I were out on the back deck. This was the last night we'd spend together. Perhaps ever. At least like this.

This might be the last time he held me. The last… I tried not to cry, grateful Tristan couldn't see my face. I didn't want to cry. I didn't want to be sad anymore. I just wanted one last night together. I wanted him.

All we have is now.

I'd known that all along, but I hadn't realized how hard it would be to say goodbye when the time came. But I didn't want to spend our last night together crying.

"Thanks for letting me spend so much time with the kids."

"Come now," he said, my stomach tightening from the deep timbre of his voice. He took my hand in his, bringing my palm to his lips for a kiss. "Surely it's not just the children whose company you enjoyed."

I smiled, trying to hold back the tears even as my skin tingled from his touch. "I did enjoy getting to know Harper." And I'd decided to take her up on the offer to continue managing the social media accounts for Fall River Estates.

"Mm." The sound rumbled from his chest into mine. "No one else?"

"Oh, and Wren and Penny," I teased, guiding his hands up and over my breasts.

I moaned when he squeezed my nipples through my dress. His cock dug into my back, and I wiggled in response. His lips were on my ear, his breath warm.

"Then I guess you won't miss my mouth on your pussy." He slid his hand down my stomach, cupping me over my panties. "Or my cock buried deep inside you."

His words sent heat racing to my core. I squeezed my thighs together, even as I pushed away the emotions that swirled inside me.

"And I suppose you won't miss me," I whispered, afraid to hear his answer. Afraid to know if this was just about sex for him.

"Of course I will," he said. "I can't tell you how much I appreciate everything you've done for me and the kids."

I nodded, holding back tears. It was nice to know I was appreciated, but I wanted to be missed for more than my help around the house or with the kids.

"I'm going to miss your breathless sighs and hushed moans," he continued, eliciting one of them from me as he dipped his finger beneath my panties.

My heart sank. But I forced myself to shove away my

emotions and focus instead on the sensations flitting through my body.

"What if someone sees us?" I asked, a gush of desire spreading through my limbs.

"Mm." He nipped at my ear as he started rubbing my clit. "I have a feeling you'd like that. Wouldn't you?"

I spread my legs a little wider, squirming on the chair. I told myself it was wrong, but the idea of someone watching us made it all that much hotter. I moaned, and he clamped his free hand over my mouth.

"Quiet, Elle. Unless you want me to stop."

My eyes went wide, and I shook my head quickly. I absolutely did *not* want him to stop. Not when he was making figure eights on my clit in the way that drove me crazy.

With one hand still on my clit, he pushed a finger from the other hand into my mouth. I sucked on it like I would his cock—eagerly, hungrily. He groaned. Fuck, the man was hot.

I closed my eyes and leaned my head back against his shoulder. He pushed another finger into my mouth at the same time he found the entrance to my pussy and pushed two fingers inside me. I gasped at the invasion. At the intensity.

"I need you," he rasped, and I swirled my tongue around his fingers. "I want to feel your tight little pussy wrapped around my cock."

I nodded, eager for that too. Eager to cement this connection. Desperate to know that I meant something to him. That I was just as much a part of him as he was of me.

"Yes," I hissed as he dragged his hand down my throat, his touch light. "Yes," I said again as he continued to strum my body.

My orgasm soon barreled toward me. And then I fell apart in his arms, my entire world bursting with color as waves of pleasure washed over me.

After I'd come down from that high, I slumped in his arms. He held me for a while, finally rubbing my arms. "Come on," he said. "Let's go upstairs."

Apart from the night he'd come back from the Fourth of July celebration, we typically slept in our separate rooms. It was too big a risk to take when the kids were home.

But I didn't want to be apart. Not tonight. Not ever, if I was being completely honest.

When we reached the top of the stairs, I grabbed his hand and pulled him toward my room. I tugged him inside and closed the door softly behind us. "Stay with me. Please?"

He glanced toward the door, smoothing his hands down my arms. "There's no lock."

So I asked, "What if I promise to be quiet?"

"Perhaps." He pulled my shirt over my head. "But I have to go back to my room before the children wake up."

"Yes. Agreed." I tugged on the hem of his shirt, taking my time to undress him. What if I never did this again?

He kissed his way down my neck, distracting me from my task. From my emotions. For the moment, we were the only ones that existed. Us and this room. And our bodies. And the way we felt about each other.

There was no past. There was no future. There was now.

He undressed me, taking his time with me as I had with his shirt. We both knew what this was—goodbye.

Everything he'd said was hot, but it was a reminder of everything he hadn't said. That he'd miss *me*. And as much as I'd wanted to believe this was about more than sex, I was beginning to realize just how wrong I'd been.

He sat on the chair and patted his thigh. I was taken back to that day all those months ago, when he'd caught me touching myself in the mirror. So much had changed, and yet the truth remained. He wasn't mine, and he never would be.

"What happened to my good girl?" he asked when I remained frozen to the spot, absorbed by my thoughts.

Maybe she doesn't want to obey.

I avoided looking at him, afraid what I'd see in his eyes.

"Elle," he rasped, mindful of his volume level. "Come." He crooked a finger, and I did. Because I always would. Even when I knew it would be to my own detriment, I always did as Tristan asked. And as always, he rewarded me with the most intense pleasure I'd ever known.

After, we crawled into bed, sated and boneless. As I lay in his arms, I listened to his breathing even out. My chest felt heavy. I wished I could slow down time. I wished I could relive this summer, so I replayed every moment of our time together. From that first day when I'd moved in, to his haircut, to our first kiss. And everything else in between.

I studied Tristan in the moonlight. The dark lashes that fanned over his face. His cheekbones. The rise and fall of his chest. I didn't want to fall asleep. I didn't want to say goodbye.

I wiped away a tear, inhaling a shaky breath and dragging in his scent. My heart was heavy, aching. And I felt physically ill at the idea of leaving Tristan and the kids.

Despite fighting sleep, at some point, I must have succumbed to the spell of being in his arms. But when I woke up alone, day was breaking, and it was time to face reality.

I showered and got dressed with a heavy heart. Then I headed downstairs, where I tried to smile and remain upbeat for the kids. Tristan was quiet, and I could feel the wall he was erecting between us. Putting the last bricks in place.

The drive to the airport was silent apart from a few sniffles from Maddox in the back seat. Savannah was quiet, her expression downturned. And Tristan was impassive. I peered out the window and tried to hold it together even as my world crumbled.

When we arrived at the airport, Tristan parked and carried my bag in. The kids each took one of my hands, and I kept squeezing them in mine. Trying to memorize the feel of them. Trying to reassure them that I loved them, and that I would see them again.

My flight was on time, and my bag had already been loaded onto the conveyor belt that would take it to the plane. I delayed as long as I could, but I couldn't wait much longer to go through security. I rechecked my stuff. I had my backpack, my purse, my ticket, and my passport, yet I felt so unprepared.

In some ways, I almost felt as if I was leaving Tristan and the children in a worse place than when I'd moved in. My mom had threatened to challenge Tristan's custody of the kids because I'd provoked her. Rex still hadn't returned. Considering how small the AV was and how determined everyone was to find him, I was beginning to worry we never would.

All I kept thinking was, how had my sister done this? How had she said goodbye, knowing there was a good chance she'd *never* see them again. And then I thought about the kids and how I was putting them through that same pain all over again. And for what?

Did I even *want* to go anymore? Was the JET Program what I really wanted to do? Or was it just something I'd chosen because it was far from the AV? Because doing something to bring me closer to Sicily would piss off my mom?

"I'm going to miss you, Ellie," Savannah said, hugging me.

"I—" I cleared my throat, my voice breaking. "I'm going to miss you too. So, *so* much." I squeezed her tight, trying not to completely fall apart. "And you, Mads." I opened my arms, inviting him to join us.

"Do you really have to go?" Maddox asked, his eyes red from crying.

I pulled in a deep breath then released it slowly, wiping a tear away from his cheek. "I do. But you know what, we can FaceTime."

Savannah sniffled. "It won't be the same."

I smoothed my hand over her hair. "I'm with you always." I moved my hand to her chest, placing it over her heart. And she nodded. "Just like your mom."

"Will you still meet us in the castle library?" Maddox asked.

"Of course. You can always find me there." I held them tightly to my chest, trying not to cry. I had to be strong—for them. Even if I was doing it with a gaping wound in my chest.

It was only when they made an announcement over the PA system for my flight that I finally released Maddox and Savannah. I stood and faced Tristan, his expression unreadable. His hands were in his pockets, and he kept glancing around. Looking anywhere but at me.

God, this sucks.

"Thank you for…well," I sighed. "For everything."

I shifted on my feet, debating whether to hug him or not. I wanted to, but I didn't know what he wanted. I didn't know if I could handle it. And the longer we stood here, the more awkward it was.

"Thank *you*," he said. His brown eyes swirled with gratitude and regret, and I wondered if he regretted us. Regretted *me*.

"Give her a hug, Dad," Savannah said, pushing Tristan toward me.

"Okay. Okay." He chuckled, though the tension remained.

He wrapped his arm around me, but the hug was short. Appropriate. I told myself it was for the best as I turned away and busied myself with my bag, swiping away a tear.

"Family hug!" Savannah said.

I forced myself to laugh, to pretend that everything was okay as I picked up Maddox. Savannah huddled between us, everyone squeezing hard. I closed my eyes and focused on the smell of Tristan's cologne. On the feeling of being surrounded by love.

"You should get going," Tristan finally said, releasing us.

His fingers brushed against mine. He locked his pinkie with mine, and his brown eyes held an unspoken universe of emotions. And then he nodded and released me, forcing a smile.

I nodded back, a knot growing in my stomach. This was it. It was time to say goodbye.

We walked to the security checkpoint, dread filling my steps and making it difficult to move.

"Let us know you made it safely," Tristan said, shoving his hands into his pockets.

"I will," I said, trying like crazy not to cry as I entered the line.

"Bye, Ellie." Savannah waved at me as I neared the TSA agent.

"Please don't go," Maddox cried. "I don't want her to go, Daddy. Please." Tristan picked Maddox up and held him in his arms. "Please don't let her go."

A tear slipped out, and I was so tempted to run back to them. To tell them that I wouldn't go. That I'd never leave.

"Next," the TSA agent called. *That's me.*

By that point, Maddox was full on sobbing. Savannah had started crying too. And Tristan's jaw was locked tight.

I can't do this. I can't leave.

As if reading my mind, Tristan shook his head. So I forced a breath through my lungs. I handed the TSA agent my ticket and ID.

And then I was through. I glanced back one more time. It took everything in me to smile and hold it together. I waved and blew kisses and made silly faces, but it didn't matter. My heart was breaking as I realized the enormity of everything I was leaving behind.

CHAPTER TWENTY-SEVEN

Tristan

"I don't want her to go," Maddox wailed. I picked him up, but he was flailing in my arms.

Beside me, Savannah was barely holding it together. And I wasn't faring much better.

"Shh." I held him close. "Shh. It's going to be okay. We will see Ellie again." *We had to.*

"But I don't want her to go," he said, though it was difficult to make out the words with how upset he was.

"Neither do I, buddy." I watched the other passengers go through security and wondered how Elle was doing.

"Then do something, Dad!" Savannah said.

I shook my head and peered down at her. "I can't."

"Why?" she pleaded, her eyes watery.

"Because…" I sighed. *Because this is what Elle wants,* I thought but didn't say that. "Because Ellie worked really hard for this."

"Yeah, but…what about us?"

I frowned. It was something I was trying to wrap my head around as well. But now that Elle was gone, there was no us. At least, not in the sense I wanted.

I draped my arm around Savannah, grateful when Maddox quieted and leaned his head against my shoulder. "Ellie still loves you. Ellie will always love you. And you can talk to her on FaceTime whenever you want."

"But it's not the same," she wailed, and I tried to steer us toward the exit before we could make an even bigger scene than we already had.

"I know, sweetheart. I do. But this is how it has to be for now."

"Why?" She stomped her feet, arms crossed over her chest. I was used to emotional outbursts from Maddox, not Savannah.

I unlocked the car and helped Maddox buckle in. Savannah stood with her feet rooted to the ground.

"Get in the car, Savannah."

"No." She scowled.

"Savannah." I softened, knowing how much she was struggling. How much we all were. "Please."

"No." She dug in her heels. "I'm not going. Not without Ellie."

I'd always known it would be difficult on the kids when Elle left, but I hadn't prepared myself for quite this reaction.

"Sweetheart," I said, my heart breaking for her—for all of us. "Ellie wanted to stay, but we have to let her go."

I was telling my daughter that as much as myself.

I thought about what Elle would do, how she'd handle this situation. I stepped closer, crouching down to Savannah's level. "You know that show you love—the one with the cute koalas?"

She sniffled. "*Izzy's Koala World*?"

I nodded. "Yeah. That's the one." She and Maddox had been obsessed with the adventures of eleven-year-old Izzy and the koalas she and her family rescued on Magnetic Island in Australia.

"Yeah." She sniffled.

"You know how Izzy and her parents rescue the koalas and take care of them and love them?"

"Mm-hmm."

"But ultimately, they have to let the koalas go. They have to let them live their lives."

Her shoulders slumped, the fight going out of her. She finally understood.

"The good news," I continued, "is that we can call Ellie. And we didn't have to paint her butt pink to find her in the future."

Savannah snorted through her tears. "Very funny, Dad."

From inside the car, Maddox started laughing. "You said 'butt.'"

And then we all started laughing, and I tried to tell myself it would all be okay.

As soon as we got home from the airport, I checked my phone, hoping for a text from Elle. I tried to imagine what she was doing. *How* she was doing.

For hours, I contemplated texting her to check in. But every time I picked up my phone or typed out a message, I talked myself out of it.

This was what she wanted.

I needed to let her go.

I fixed lunch for the kids and myself and tried to remain upbeat. But finally, I couldn't take it anymore. The silence was breaking me. The house felt so empty without Rex and Elle, and I felt myself going back to that dark place. To how out of control and lost I'd felt after Tessa died.

I pressed my palms to the counter and inhaled slowly, deeply. I reminded myself that Ellie was alive. I tried to visualize her arriving in Japan safely, but my mind kept conjuring images of a plane crash. Of wreckage in the ocean. Of…

"Dad?" Savannah asked.

"Yeah, honey?" I lifted my head, hoping my fears weren't written across my face.

"Can I go to Aiden's?"

"I, um—" Selfishly, I wanted to say no. I wanted to keep the kids close. I wanted the distraction. But I realized maybe that wasn't what Savannah needed, so I said, "Sure. Let me check in with Enzo and see if that's okay."

"Thanks, Daddy."

After I dropped the kids off at Aiden's, I went upstairs to do laundry and get the house back in order for the week. But when I reached the guest room, I paused. The bed had been stripped of the sheets. All of Elle's stuff was gone. *She* was gone.

I sank down on the mattress and dropped my head in my hands. Eventually, I lay on my back and stared at the ceiling. I stayed there until the sunlight started to dim, darkness creeping in. When I glanced at the time, it was late, later than I expected. So I texted Enzo that I was on my way and drove to the vineyard to pick up the kids.

When we returned to the house, it was as if their good moods suddenly vanished. They trudged toward the house, but then a dog yowled, and we all stopped.

The three of us looked at one another just before Rex rounded the corner to the garage and sprinted toward us.

"Rex!" Savannah called, opening her arms for him.

"Rex!" Maddox yelled, running in circles.

I didn't know where he'd been, and I didn't care. I was just glad he was home.

My first thought was to run inside and tell Elle. But then I remembered that she was gone. And unlike Rex, she wasn't going to magically return.

CHAPTER TWENTY-EIGHT

Ellie

Three flights. A million regrets. And endless tears.

I splashed some water on my face, scarcely able to look at myself in the mirror. I was exhausted and dirty, but I'd made it to Japan. Though I still wasn't quite sure how.

I was still haunted by the sound of Maddox's cries as I'd forced myself to walk through security. I remembered locking myself in the bathroom and crying so hard I couldn't breathe. I remembered quietly sobbing the entire flight to LA, grateful for the window seat and the oversized sunglasses to hide my face.

The flight from LA to Tokyo was no better. And I'd spent most of it wondering if I could still change my mind. But then I reminded myself it didn't matter.

Tristan didn't want me to stay.

My mind kept circling back to that. To our conversation where I'd offered to stay and he'd shut me down.

I sighed and forced myself to wash my face and brush my teeth. I smoothed my hair back into a ponytail and changed into a suit. And yet, I still felt no more ready to accept this as my new reality. I'd stopped crying but only because I was so dehydrated, my body could no longer produce tears.

The entire time, I wondered if I'd made a huge mistake. A fear that didn't improve when my third and final flight landed in Naruto. Nor after I'd collected my luggage and met my new supervisor and the others I'd be spending the next year with.

One year.

Twelve months.

So much could happen. It was a long time to be away from the AV. Away from the kids and Tristan.

I tried to smile and pay attention to what everyone was saying, but I couldn't. My head, my heart, were back in the AV. And the farther we got from the airport, the more I panicked.

It was hot and cramped in the van, and I was surrounded by unfamiliar faces. By unfamiliar terrain. All the research I'd done about the program, about where I'd be living, had done nothing to prepare me for the reality of it.

I desperately tried to angle myself toward the AC vent then went back to staring out the window so I wouldn't have to talk. It didn't look like Japan. It looked like a random small town, though all the signs were in Japanese.

I was sweating through my suit, wondering what the hell I'd gotten myself into, when my supervisor started asking about foods we didn't eat. I'd barely eaten since leaving the AV, and the thought of putting anything in my stomach was sickening. My breath started coming in pants, and I was really, really trying hard not to cry. Talk about making a great first impression.

As soon as we arrived at our new apartment building, I rushed inside. I flopped down on the bed, closing my eyes and wishing I could wake up from this nightmare. When I finally admitted that wasn't going to happen, I grabbed my phone and checked for any missed calls or texts, but there were none. I'd promised to text to let Tristan know I'd arrived safely, so I typed out a message before hitting send.

> Made it to Japan.

It took a few minutes, but then his response came through.

> Tristan: Thanks for letting me know.

That's it?

I waited and waited, but nothing more came. I dropped my head on the mattress, eventually drifting in and out of sleep.

My phone rang, jolting me awake. I immediately jumped to answer it, hoping it was Tristan or the kids. Wishing so badly that I could go back. That I'd never left.

But it was Piper's name that flashed on the screen, along with a request to FaceTime. I briefly contemplated not answering, but I *really* needed to hear a friendly voice.

"Hey!" She waved, her smile bright.

I immediately burst into tears, not that many came.

"Oh no. What's wrong?" Piper frowned.

"It's awful," I blurted. "I made a huge mistake." I was so freaking tempted to get a cab and go back to the airport.

"Whoa. Whoa. Slow down," Piper said. "Did something happen?"

"I just—" I sighed. "I don't want to be here. I thought this was what I wanted, but I don't."

"Because of the program or because of Tristan?"

"Tristan." I sniffled. "The kids. Oh god," I wailed. "You should've seen them at the airport. It nearly killed me."

"Oh, Ellie." Her expression was sympathetic.

"I can't do this." I clawed at my shirt. It felt as if it were suffocating me. "I can't."

"You just got there. You've had a lot going on the past few days. I'm hopeful that if you give it some time, you'll realize it's not that bad."

"Not that bad?" I shook my head and buried my face in my hands. "It's awful."

"Are you talking to Ellie?" Sumner said in the background. She waved, then frowned when she saw my face.

She sat next to Piper, and they turned the screen so I could see both of them, when all I wanted to do was hide. Piper gave her a quick overview, and Sumner listened patiently, finally saying, "I'm sorry, Ellie. I'm sure that was incredibly difficult for so many reasons."

I nodded, grateful she understood. That she didn't judge me or try to offer solutions. She listened.

"Did you and Tristan talk about the future at all?" Piper asked. "About staying in touch or what would happen after your time in Japan is up?"

I scoffed. "No."

"But he loves you," Piper said. "You know that, right?"

I wasn't sure I believed that. If anything, I was beginning to think he loved the idea of me. The escape I provided.

I'd had a lot of time to consider it on the plane, and I'd come to several realizations.

I was convenient.

I lived in his house. Cared for his children. And he knew I was only there for a short time.

He didn't love me.

"If he loved me, he wouldn't have let me go."

"Maybe he let you go *because* he loved you," Sumner said.

I buried my head in my hands. My head ached. My heart hurt. I couldn't keep second-guessing Tristan and his decisions and what it all meant. I was going to drive myself insane.

"It doesn't matter now," I finally said, ignoring them. "We're over."

I was exhausted. Physically and emotionally drained to a level I hadn't been since Tessa's death. And now I was heartbroken over my late sister's husband. I was pining for a man—and a life—that didn't belong to me. Would never belong to me.

My phone rang, Tristan's name appearing on the screen. For a moment, my heart stilled, but then I told myself it was probably just one of the kids calling. Even so, I checked my reflection in the mirror, smoothing my hair and swiping on some lip gloss before answering.

Apart from texting to let him know I'd arrived safely a week ago, I hadn't talked to Tristan—or the kids—since. I'd been busy with training and adjusting to my new life while battling jet lag. But I also hadn't wanted to upset the kids or their routine by calling. So, I'd waited to hear from them.

I connected the call, and Savannah's face appeared on the screen. "Ellie!"

"I wanna see her," Maddox whined, trying to push Savannah aside.

"Hey, hey," Tristan intoned from the background, and my insides quivered with excitement and anticipation. But I quickly shut it down.

Over the past week, I'd realized that I had to focus on myself. I had to focus on my future. A future that didn't include Tristan.

Maddox huffed, and then Savannah shared the screen with him. But Tristan was still out of view. I sensed he was still listening, or maybe I was just hoping that was the case.

"Guess what?" Savannah said.

I smiled, trying to emulate some of her enthusiasm and hoping it was good news. "What?"

"Rex came home!" She panned the phone over to Rex's bed, where he was chewing on a toy.

"Oh, I'm so glad!" I said, filled with relief.

We talked for a little while longer. About Rex's return. The kids told me about their new teachers and showed me the outfits they planned to wear for the first day of school. When Maddox's attention waned, he went to get a snack. Savannah talked a little longer but then handed the phone over to Tristan.

I kept blinking at the screen, unable to believe it was really him. That I was talking to him instead of staring at one of the pictures on my phone during a moment of weakness. For a minute, I didn't speak. Didn't breathe.

"Hey," he said, the creases around his eyes more prominent. He was still as handsome as ever, and I craved his touch.

"Hey," I whispered. I took a breath and steered the conversation to safe territory. "How are they? Really."

"Good," Tristan said, and I scrutinized his expression for clues. "We're all happy that Rex came home."

I nodded. God, why was this so awkward? I'd slept with the man. He'd been inside me. And now I could barely form words around him?

"How are you?" he asked.

I bit my lip and glanced around my apartment. "I'm... Yeah. I'm good." I returned my attention to the screen. "I have air conditioning, which is a pretty big deal."

He chuckled, though his smile didn't meet his eyes. "I'm glad."

He walked to another room, and I heard the door close. "How are you really?"

I lifted my shoulders, trying to play it cool, even though I suspected he'd see right through me as always. "Good. Yeah."

He furrowed his brow. "You look tired."

"I'm—" I paused. I couldn't tell him how I was really feeling, so I settled on, "Jet-lagged."

Which was only a portion of the truth. I was exhausted—physically and emotionally wrung out. I was still trying to adjust to my new life and job, while also keeping up with the demands of my clients. In addition to Fall River Estates, I was also creating content for a few other small businesses. And struggling with culture shock. But mostly, missing Tristan and the kids.

"Elle…" His unspoken words hung in the air. "The kids miss you. *I* miss you."

I'd longed to hear those words, but they were just that—words. If I was going to survive the next year, if I was going to accomplish the goals I'd set out for myself and actually move forward with my life in a meaningful way, I couldn't continue trying to straddle two worlds. I couldn't be living in Japan with my heart back in the AV.

I loved Tristan. And even if he'd loved me back, it wasn't that simple. I worried how the kids would feel if they knew about us. And how Gloria might retaliate if Tristan's and my relationship was no longer a secret.

God, I was so sick of secrets.

I deserved more.

But if Tristan had wanted me to stay, if he'd wanted a future together, he would've said something. And he hadn't.

Probably because we both knew it was pointless. Just like it would be pointless to tell him that I missed him. We both knew it couldn't be anything more. Trying to pretend other-wise would only tarnish the memories of what we'd had.

"Tristan," I sighed. "What we had was fun. But we agreed it was temporary."

"That's all it was to you? Fun?"

I took a deep breath, forcing myself to say the words I knew I had to. "That's all it can be."

"Why?"

"You said it yourself—our lives are in different places." In every sense of the word. "I came to Japan, and I need to focus on myself."

He glanced away briefly, returning his gaze to me with a hard expression. "If that's what you want."

I wanted to scream that was absolutely *not* what I wanted. But this wasn't just about me. So, I nodded.

"Daddy!" Maddox yelled.

Tristan sighed. "I have to go."

"I know." I forced myself to smile, wishing things were different. Wishing he'd fought me harder on it. "Tell the kids I love them."

And then I ended the call feeling as if I'd severed more than the phone connection.

CHAPTER TWENTY-NINE

Tristan

Four months later

I pulled to a stop at the light, glancing over at the empty passenger seat Elle had once occupied. A memory flashed through my mind. The streetlights cast a warm glow on her skin, skin I'd touched every inch of.

I'd leaned over to kiss her as a car pulled up behind us, but I hadn't cared who saw us. "You're beautiful."

"You're going to get us caught," she'd whispered, even as she'd nipped at my lips.

"Would that really be so terrible?" I'd asked, feeling reckless. Restless.

Instead of answering, she'd murmured, "Green," and I could still feel the ghost of a smile on her lips.

But this time, it was Savannah's voice instead of Elle's that I heard.

"Dad!" Savannah said from the back seat. "It's green."

"Oh. Right." I shook my head and pressed on the gas. "Thanks, honey."

"You're in la-la land today," Savannah said.

"I've got a lot on my mind."

Lockwood Industries was fully funded, thanks to Knox Crawford. But I couldn't stop thinking about Elle. She'd gone from offering to stay to telling me she needed space.

Ever since that conversation months ago, she'd really only talked to the kids. She'd rarely posted on social media. And when she had, the content was…different.

Some landscapes and updates on her time in Japan. But hardly any pictures of her. I alternated between thinking something was wrong and worrying she'd met someone new.

"Do you want to talk about it?" Savannah asked in a caring tone. The type of tone Elle used when she'd ask the kids the same question. Even in the short time she'd been here, Elle had made a lasting impact on the kids, on me.

And yet it felt as if she were slipping further away every day.

"I'm okay, but thanks. I could probably use something to eat."

"Me too," Maddox said. "I can't wait for pie."

It was Friendsgiving, the annual tradition Harper and Enzo had started a few years ago as a way to celebrate family, friends, and community. Everyone was welcome to attend and invited to bring a dish. Tessa had always loved the event, and it was hard to believe this was our second year attending without her.

So much had changed. And for a while—with Elle— things had been better. But then she'd left. And for a long time after, I'd been excited about nothing. Interested in nothing. I'd gone through my days on repeat.

The kids and I were in a much better place than we'd been when she first left, but I knew they missed her too. We all did, even Rex. He moped around the house like the rest of us, still wondering where she'd gone. Still hoping she'd come back.

"You have to eat—"

"We know. We know," Savannah interrupted as I pulled off the main road and headed for Fall River Estates. "Some vegetables and protein first."

I nodded, still trying to find that balance myself. "I'm definitely excited about pie, but I'm also looking forward to seeing all our friends and family."

"Even Mimi?" Maddox asked, referring to Gloria.

I furrowed my brow. "Of course." I unbuckled and stepped out of the car before opening the door to the back seat. "What makes you think I'm not happy to see Mimi?"

"We haven't had family dinner in a long time," Savannah said. "And we hardly ever see Mimi and Pops anymore."

"Do you guys miss them?" I asked, guilt gnawing at my gut. I wasn't trying to punish the kids, but Gloria's threats and her toxic behavior had forced me to limit our interactions.

My lawyer, Audrey, had assured me that it would be difficult for Gloria to challenge my custody of the kids. But the fact that Gloria had the gall to even mention it put me on my guard. I questioned whether she really had their best interests at heart.

Audrey and I had also used the meeting to finalize the rest of Tessa's estate. There had only been one matter outstanding, and it was a life insurance policy.

"Sometimes," Savannah said. "It's just..." She sighed, peering up at the sky as a flock of ducks flew overhead. "I think Mimi could use our help."

"How so?" I asked, grabbing the vegetable platter from the front seat.

"Mommy always said that if someone was mean, it was often because they were hurting."

I nodded, remembering it well. Tessa's kind heart was one of the things I'd loved most about her. About Elle too.

"Why do you think Mimi's hurting?"

"For the same reason you are and I am and Maddox is and Pops is. Because Mommy's gone, and Ellie left."

Her words cut me to the quick. Because it didn't matter how much I'd loved Tessa or Elle, they were both gone.

"I'm sure that's definitely part of it," I said as we headed for the entrance to the winery.

"I just think we should try to be extra nice to her," Savannah said. "And maybe that will cheer her up."

"That's a very sweet idea," I said, though I didn't know if it would make much of a difference. Gloria hadn't pursued a custody challenge. But she was who she was, and I was done making excuses for her.

My therapist and I had talked about it a lot the past few months. Gloria. Tessa. Elle. All of it.

After Tessa's death, I'd immediately enrolled Maddox and Savannah in trauma counseling. Yet I'd never gone for myself. I'd made excuses, but the truth was that I'd been resistant to therapy. That had changed when Elle left.

After she'd gone to Japan, after she'd told me she needed to focus on herself, I'd started to spiral out of control again. I couldn't go back to that place. I *couldn't*—for the kids, for myself.

It had made me realize that I'd never worked through my grief about Tessa's death. Nor had I processed my complicated feelings surrounding Elle and our relationship. My heart felt raw, ripped wide open. And yet, in a way, I felt healed. Stronger than I had even a few months ago.

I was a different person since Tessa's death. In some ways, I was better than before because I'd gained a new perspective. On life, on love, on loss. And while I sometimes wished Tessa could be here to see it, I was learning to appreciate how far I'd come.

I was finally feeling more centered again, and I was

beginning to realize that I had choices. I could *choose* to spend my life alone. I could *choose* to feel stuck or out of control. Or I could accept that my decisions and my mind-set were the only things I could control.

"There's River," Savannah said as soon as we stepped inside. "Can I go say hi?"

"Of course."

"Oh my gosh. I can't wait to hold baby Hazel!" she squealed before running off in River's direction.

I smiled. Savannah loved babies—human or animals. She'd always watched out for Maddox, and she adored River's sister, Hazel. She'd spent most of Thanksgiving break at their house, helping out.

"Grannie!" Maddox said, launching himself into my mom's arms.

I went over to greet my parents. My mom had hinted at my bringing "cabin girl" to Friendsgiving, but I'd brushed away her comments. How could I tell her that "cabin girl" was Elle?

I carried the vegetable platter over to the long table where the feast was laid out. I was surveying the offerings when Liam clapped a hand on my shoulder.

"Happy Friendsgiving."

"Happy Friendsgiving." I gave him a hug.

"Come. Come." He ushered me down the hall toward one of the private rooms. As we neared the door, I realized it was the same room where we'd gotten ready for Bennett's wedding.

It had been less than a year since that day, and yet it felt like a lifetime ago.

"Hey!" Bennett grinned when I stepped through the door.

"Hey." I glanced between Enzo, Asher, and Liam as Bennett shut the door behind me. All my closest friends. And they were all watching me curiously. "What's going on?"

Enzo poured a glass of wine for each of us then passed them around.

"To friendship," he said, raising his glass for a toast. "Thank you all for welcoming *un vecchietto*—" He cleared his throat and smiled. "An old man like me into your circle."

"You're not *that* old," Asher said.

"Hell," Liam chimed in. "Before Tristan's makeover, he could've passed for *your* older brother."

Everyone laughed, even as I narrowed my eyes at Liam in jest. Still, it felt good to laugh again. To live again, even if it felt as if half my heart was missing.

"LC did quite a number on you," Asher said.

I squeezed my eyes shut. *Damn it, Asher.*

"Wait, LC as in Ellie?" Liam glanced around as if seeking confirmation. "That's— She's—" He paused. "I knew it! She's why you were so happy. And now that she's gone, you've been a mopey bastard again."

"I have not—"

"He's right," Enzo cut in. "You have."

When I glanced around the circle, everyone was in agreement. *Jeez.* "Careful," I muttered into my glass. "This is beginning to feel like an intervention."

"Good." Bennett placed a hand on my back.

I nearly choked on my sip of wine. When I finally caught my breath, I realized they were serious.

"For the record," Liam said. "I voted to call it an 'intercession.'"

I wanted to laugh, but I didn't think he was joking. None of them was. All their expressions were stern yet compassionate, their concern directed at me. *Shit.*

"So, what's up with you and Ellie? Give us a recap since *some* of us are a bit out of the loop," Liam said, eyeing the others.

I dragged a hand down my face. "Do I have to?"

The answer was a resounding yes from all four of them.

I took a deep breath and then gave them a quick rundown. From the time Elle moved in, to sneaking around. How I'd fallen for her, only to let her go.

"She offered to stay?" Liam asked, his eyes lighting up. "Damn. This is romance novel gold."

I half expected him to whip out his phone and start taking notes. But Bennett elbowed him in the side, and Liam adopted a contrite expression.

"What did you say when she offered to stay?" That was from Bennett.

I lifted a shoulder. "She wasn't thinking clearly. The kids had just run away. Rex was missing. And neither of us wanted to say goodbye."

Besides, I wasn't willing to let her give up on her dreams. I knew how important the JET Program was to her, especially after she'd told me about her birth mom's semester abroad in Japan. I couldn't hold Elle back. I couldn't keep her from that. And her request for space months ago had only reinforced that I'd made the right decision.

"Have you talked to her since?" Enzo asked.

I shook my head. "Once briefly." And it had gutted me. "Otherwise, it's just been a quick hello here or there, mostly so the kids can FaceTime with her." But it wasn't enough.

Even from our brief interactions, Elle seemed happier lately, lighter. The spark was back in her eyes. And I knew from a recent conversation with Savannah that they'd offered to renew her contract for another year.

"How much longer will she be there?" Asher asked.

I rubbed a hand over my face. "I don't know." And that was the problem. If I didn't do something soon, I was afraid I'd lose her forever. "She could renew her contract for another year, maybe two." *Fuck.*

"What?" Liam set down his glass, staring at me intently. "Fuck no. You can't let that happen."

"I know, but what am I supposed to do?" I started pacing, dragging a hand through my hair. "I can't ask her to sacrifice her dreams for me. Our lives are just in different places." My own words continued to haunt me.

"So you follow her like I did Harper," Enzo said.

"You're joking, right?" I scoffed. He made it sound so simple when my life was anything but. "I have two kids, two pets, a house. A company. My whole life is here."

"Except Ellie," Bennett said softly.

Right. Except that—my heart.

"How would I even do that?" I asked, thinking the idea had to be as fantastical as it seemed. "I can't."

Asher chuckled. "Tristan, you graduated from Stanford with honors. You developed the LoveBirds dating app for fun."

I sliced a hand through the air. So what? That didn't solve my current problem.

"If you can figure out how to do all the incredible things you have, from raising two children single-handedly after your wife died to starting and selling a company for millions, I have faith that you can figure this out too," Liam said.

"That's because, now that you're in love with Penny, you refuse to accept anything less than a happily ever after."

"Damn right." Liam nodded, his expression firm. "And neither should you."

"But she… She told me she needed space. She said she needs to focus on herself."

"Maybe she told you that like you told her she should go to Japan," Liam said.

"No." I shook my head. "I can hear something's different in her voice. Something's changed."

"Tristan," Enzo said, placing a hand on my shoulder. "Do you love her?"

I nodded. There was no doubt in my mind—I loved Elle.

"Does she know that?" he asked, shaking me a bit.

I dropped my head. I'd tried to show her, but I'd never actually said the words.

"Then go to her," he said.

"I'm scared," I finally admitted, feeling fucking vulnerable.

"Understandably so." Enzo squeezed my shoulder before releasing me. "But life's short. You don't want to live with regrets."

How many times had Tessa told me that? How many times had Elle said those words? Had I repeated them to myself?

And yet here I was, wasting time. Letting fear get the better of me.

"You're right," I said, realizing the answer had been staring at me all along. I just hadn't been ready to accept it. And thanks to my hesitation and fear, I'd wasted *months*. "I have to go to Japan."

"Attaboy." Liam grinned. "Now, what do you need from us?" he asked, springing into action. He'd always been the leader of the group.

"I-I need someone to watch the kids for a week while I go to Japan. I don't want to get their hopes up, so we'll have to tell them it's a business trip or something."

"Done," Liam said. "Penny and I will take care of them. We can stay at your house if they'd be more comfortable there."

"Thank you," I said, my shoulders relaxing now that I knew the kids would be taken care of.

"Plane tickets." My mind was spinning. I needed to pack. *God, I hope my passport isn't expired.*

"On it." Enzo pulled out his phone. "I'm sure Crew would

be more than happy to let you use his private jet to get to LA."

Crew Dixon was the owner of the LA pro football team, the Hollywood Heatwaves. He was good friends with Enzo and Harrison Hayes, both retired pro athletes. And Crew was a local—he grew up in Blue River.

Still, Crew and I were more acquaintances than friends. And while he was a nice guy, asking to borrow his private jet seemed outlandish.

"It's done," Enzo said before I could protest. "Then you need flights from LA to…where is it?"

"Naruto, Tokushima."

"When do you want to leave?"

"End of next week." I sighed, wishing I could go immediately but thinking of all the preparations that needed to be made.

"I'll give you a ride to the airport." Bennett spoke up.

I shook my head. "You've got enough on your plate with a newborn."

"It'll be fine."

"I can help with meals for the kids and anything else that comes up," Asher offered.

I glanced at my friends, filled with gratitude. They weren't judging me for moving on after Tessa or even falling for her sister. They were happy for me, supportive. So much so that they were trying to help me make it happen. "Fuck. You guys are the best."

"Obviously." Liam smirked, and we all started laughing.

"What are you going to do about Gloria?" Asher asked.

I scoffed. "I have to win over Elle first. Then we'll deal with Gloria."

"Win her over?" Asher chuckled. "Ellie's crazy about you. Even if it took a little nudge for you to see it."

A little nudge? Ha! He'd flirted with her to push us together.

And while it was a relief to hear him say that, I still worried. What if Elle had gained some perspective during our time apart and didn't want to be together anymore? What if she'd moved on? That question haunted me—a lot.

"Do you think the kids will be okay with this? With Elle and me?" I asked, trying to convince myself it would all work out.

"I'm sure it will be an adjustment," Bennett said. "But they adore her."

I nodded. I knew he was right, but still…asking them to accept Elle as more than just their aunt… Well, I hoped they'd be okay with it. I hoped they wouldn't think I was trying to replace their mom. I could never replace Tessa, but I could make our family whole again.

There was a knock at the door, and Aiden peeked his head in, his eyes intent on Enzo. "Mom's looking for you."

Enzo and the others filed out, leaving me alone with Liam. "I'm surprised you're okay with this. Elle and me."

He furrowed his brow. "Why wouldn't I be?"

"Of all the guys, I know you were closest to Tessa. I just…" I rubbed the back of my neck. "I'm sorry for keeping this a secret from you, but I was worried how you'd react."

"Really?" Liam jerked his head back. "You're one of my best friends. I just want you to be happy."

"I know, but, well—" I shoved my hands into my pockets. "You knew Tessa really well. And I guess I wonder if you think she'd be okay with this."

"Ahh." He tilted his head back in understanding. "Do you know what her favorite book of mine was?"

I shook my head. "I'm not sure she ever told me. Actually, she acted like they were all her favorites, and she wouldn't pick one."

He laughed. "Ever the diplomat."

"So, which was her favorite?" I asked, curiosity marking my words with impatience.

"A manuscript I never published because it didn't fit my pen name. But I let her read it."

"And…?" *Jeez, Liam. Talk about a flair for the dramatic.*

"And it was a borderline erotic romance about a stepdad and his nineteen-year-old stepdaughter after the mom died."

That sounded…kinda wrong. But who was I to judge?

"Just because Tessa enjoyed reading something doesn't mean she'd be okay with it in real life."

"No, but when we talked about the story, she always said she loved the forbidden aspect of it. That she could really feel the emotions and see how they fell for each other."

I scoffed. "And you think that somehow means she'd approve of my relationship with her sister?"

"Honestly, I don't know. None of us can. But she was very open-minded. And I'm certain she'd want you to be happy. She told me that, you know?"

I shook my head. I hadn't known, but it also didn't surprise me. Still, it was reassuring.

"The book I was working on when—" He cleared his throat. "The last book she helped me with was about a widow."

I frowned. "I don't remember you publishing a story about a widow."

"I didn't. I haven't been able to finish it. Tessa would know how to fix it." He sliced a hand through the air. "The point is, she insisted on working on it. She told me it was a good distraction. And it was, but I could tell it was also more than that."

"What do you mean?" I asked.

"After her diagnosis, she talked a lot about what she would want if you were the main character." He took a deep breath. "She wanted you to be happy. She wanted you to find love. Find someone who loved you and the kids."

I swallowed hard, feeling as if he were delivering a message from beyond the grave. Knowing he was right. Tessa had tried to tell me the same, but I'd never wanted to hear those words from her when she was still alive.

But that's what it came down to. What it always came down to. Tessa was gone, but her wish was for me to live. To love. And I loved Elle.

"I never told you this," I said. "But thank you for all your support when we were going through everything. You really helped keep her calm. You helped her stay positive."

While everyone else had helped with the kids or meals, Liam had been Tessa's support. My support.

"It was my honor." His eyes were watery as he placed his hand over his heart. "And I would do it again in a heartbeat."

I hugged him tight, patting his back.

"Also—" He cleared his throat after I released him. "While we're, um, clearing the air. I'm not sure I ever apologized for my behavior at the funeral. I'm really sorry for my outburst. It was completely inappropriate."

I chuckled. "You know what? I'm sure she was looking down on us and laughing."

He smiled. "I'd like to think so."

"And she would've loved the new library." I'd recently seen the blueprints for the new branch of the library honoring Tessa, and they were perfect.

"I know." He smiled wistfully. "Though she would've hated the attention."

I laughed. "Very true."

"I wish she were here to see it," he said.

I wished she could see it too. Except then I wouldn't be with Elle.

Sometimes it was such a mindfuck—to wonder if this was

how it was always supposed to be. When I thought of Tessa's death and everything I'd lost, it made zero sense. But when I focused on Elle and everything I'd gained, it seemed more bearable. Like maybe something good could come from it all in the end.

CHAPTER THIRTY

Ellie

The last of my students had left for the day, and I was tidying my classroom before a few days off. I wasn't quite sure what I was going to do with myself. It certainly didn't feel like Christmas was a few weeks away. It was hot. And even though I no longer felt as lost as I had when I'd first moved here, Japan still didn't feel like home either.

I was nearly caught up on the work for my content creation clients. Maybe I'd go to the beach. Read a book.

I'd made some friends, but I'd spent a lot of time alone with myself and my thoughts. I was getting better at it—the silence. The stillness. But it was still uncomfortable at times, especially when confronted with difficult truths about myself and my choices.

I'd realized that the past few years, I'd posted online because I told myself I was helping others. But now, it was as if the spell had broken. I'd been lying to myself about the reason for my social media presence. I wasn't helping people. I was trying to somehow fill the vacuum of my parents' love and approval by seeking the validation of strangers online.

For a while, Tessa had filled that role. At least when I wasn't comparing myself to her.

And then I'd done the same thing with Tristan.

Now, I was learning to love myself, even if it felt as if part of my heart was missing.

Every day, I wondered what Tristan and the kids were doing. *How* they were doing. I'd checked in with Maddox and Savannah earlier in the week, but I hadn't talked to Tristan. I hadn't talked to him at all the past few months, apart from the occasional quick hello. And even that was painful.

I'd also avoided reading *The Vine* since I'd been gone. I was too afraid of what I'd find. Scared I'd discover a story that Tristan was dating. He was the AV's hottest bachelor after all. And he was too young, too incredible, to remain alone for long. Though it killed me to think of him with someone else.

It didn't matter. It *shouldn't* matter, I reminded myself.

I grabbed an eraser, wishing I could wipe him from my heart like I could the letters on the board. But it was as if he were written in permanent ink. As if he'd tattooed himself on my very soul.

I started wiping down the board when the door to the classroom opened. "Did you forget something?" I called over my shoulder, assuming it was one of my students.

"Yes." A deep, familiar voice vibrated through my entire being, but it couldn't possibly…

I stilled with my back to him, afraid to turn. Afraid if I did, it would ruin whatever crazy dream my mind had conjured. A dream where Tristan was standing in my class-room in Japan. Where…

Finally, unable to take it any longer, I made myself turn. And when I faced him, I had to grip the edge of my desk to steady myself. "Tristan?" I whispered. "Tristan?" I inched closer then stopped myself.

I couldn't possibly imagine a reason he'd travel across the world unless… I gasped, holding a hand to my mouth. "Are Maddox and Savannah okay?"

"Everyone's fine." He stepped farther into the classroom. "I came here for you. For us. The past few months, I've tried to give you the space you asked for, but I don't want to spend another second apart from you. I can't." His voice was gravelly with emotion.

I wobbled and sank down on the edge of my desk. "You—" I opened my mouth, closed it again. Smoothed my hands over my lap. "What? I mean—" I shook my head. "Seriously?"

"Yes, Elle." He smiled, taking my hands in his. "I love you. I'm *in* love with you."

"You—" I swallowed hard. "You love me."

"Yes," he chuckled. "I love you."

"But, but—" I sputtered. I didn't even know what to say. Was this real? Was *he* for real?

He tucked my hair behind my ear, my body arcing with electricity from that brief point of contact. "You changed your hair."

"Do you hate it?" I asked.

Even though I didn't want to care what anyone else thought, Tristan's opinion still mattered to me. Not because I needed his approval; I knew he'd love me no matter what.

But for so long, my bright hair color had been a badge of honor. An outward sign of rebellion. I loved the purple, but I'd loved pissing off my mom just as much.

But I was letting go of that. I was choosing things that brought me joy, regardless of what anyone else thought. I was finally becoming the confident, sexy, self-assured woman who'd been inside me all along. But it was no longer an act. And I no longer performed it for my followers. It was for myself. Because I was more than enough.

I could have purple hair or a honeyed blond like now. I

could cover my face in makeup or wear none at all. I didn't need to be anything other than myself.

Tristan's gaze lingered on mine, intense and all-consuming. "You're always beautiful to me."

I thought back to the time I'd cut his hair. When I'd shown him pictures of my own botched haircut and he'd told me I was beautiful. He'd told me I'd be beautiful even if I'd shaved my head. I'd believed him then. And thanks to him, I'd started to believe in myself. I'd begun to see myself as the woman he saw. One who was incredible and beautiful and worthy of love.

"I've missed you so much." My voice caught on a sob, and I held a hand to my mouth. "But I don't understand. What's changed? How can we be together? I have seven months left here."

I wanted to touch him, but I was afraid to get my hopes up.

"You're not going to renew your contract?" he asked.

"I hadn't—" I shook my head and swallowed. "No."

"Have you decided where you'll go next?"

I shook my head again, realizing that he was deferring to me. Seeking my input before offering his suggestions. "I have a few ideas, but no concrete plans."

I'd enjoyed my time in Naruto, but I was ready to move on. To experience something new. My supervisor and colleagues were awesome, but I was homesick and lonely. Not that I'd planned to return to the AV. I might not be living in my sister's shadow anymore, but it had been too painful to even contemplate being so close to Tristan if we weren't together.

He rubbed a hand over his mouth. "That could work."

I frowned. "I'm sorry. You're not making any sense. Work for what?"

"It gives the kids time to finish school. And me to sell the house."

"What?" I shrieked. *Sell. The. House?*

"I already talked to my Realtor, Vanessa, about it. And I've been looking into world schooling."

"Whoa. Whoa." I held up my hands. "Slow down. Sell the house? World school? You're going to leave the AV?"

He smiled and looped his arms around my waist, pulling me close. "We both know that life is short. And no matter how much time we do or don't have, I want to spend it with you."

If I hadn't already melted at his words, I would've then. He wanted to be with me. Tristan wanted *me*, and I wanted him. Maybe it wasn't so complicated after all.

"I want to be with you and the kids," I said through my tears. Tears of joy and relief. Of release. I knew we'd figure out a solution—together. That was all that mattered.

He pressed his lips to mine, a solemn promise. A vow to cherish each other and our time together, however long or short it may be.

It felt so incredible to be in his arms, I almost forgot where we were. And then the bell rang, bringing me back to reality.

With our foreheads still touching, I said, "I love you, Tristan."

"I love hearing you say that." He cupped the back of my neck. "And I love you." He kissed me again, this time more passionately. More deeply, until we were both panting.

"What about Lockwood Industries?" I asked, leaning against my desk. Putting some space between us. My mind was spinning. I had so many questions. "What about the kids? Are they here too?" I tried to peer past him, as if I might find Maddox and Savannah waiting in the hallway.

He shook his head, running his thumb over my bottom

lip. It was distracting to say the least. "They're staying with Penny and Liam."

I was sure they were enjoying that. Though I wondered what Tristan had told them. Did they know he was in Japan? Seeing me?

"Have you told them about your plan? About us? Are they in favor of it?"

I wouldn't do anything without the kids' agreement. I loved them, and I'd never want to hurt them.

He took a deep breath and smiled. "I haven't talked to Maddox and Savannah yet because I didn't want to get their hopes up."

I nodded slowly, my heart pumping at a fast clip. "Are you... What do you think they'll say?"

"Elle." He held me close. "They miss you like crazy. Surely you know that."

"I miss them too, but it feels like too much. I mean, to ask them to move from their home. To uproot their lives." I bit my lip, thinking about what world school would mean for them. "After everything they've been through..."

Was this really the best plan? Maddox and Savannah shouldn't have to sacrifice everything so their dad could be with me.

"I would never do anything that isn't in their best interest."

"No. Of course not. I wasn't suggesting—"

"I know." He placed a finger to my lips. "I know you weren't. But honestly, I think it would be good for them. For all of us. We could all use a fresh start."

As much as I loved what he was proposing, I still had reservations. Was he running? Was he worried that it would be too awkward to live in the AV, considering he'd been married to my sister?

"Is this because you worry about being openly together if we lived in the AV?"

"What?" He frowned, shaking his head slowly. "No. The guys already know, and they were super supportive. And while it might be awkward at first with…others," he said, and we both knew he was referring to my mom, "they'd have to get over it."

"Really?" I jerked my head back, shocked that he'd already been paving the way for us to be a couple.

I wasn't surprised that his friends were supportive, but I was grateful. I knew he valued their opinions, and so did I.

"Yeah. Really. I've been seeing a therapist, and she agrees that my feelings for you had nothing to do with Tessa. They never did. You were an escape, but I wasn't using you to avoid my grief."

"Nor was I," I said. "Your relationship to my sister complicated things, but that wasn't why I was attracted to you."

"Mm." He hummed, stepping closer. "Why *were* you attracted to me?"

I grinned. "That big brain of yours."

"Right. My big *brain*." He pulled me into him, letting me feel his erection. "That's not all that's big."

"You're very…distracting right now." I laughed.

"I'm willing to do whatever it takes," he whispered, nuzzling my neck, "to convince you to be with me."

"Is that so?" I asked as he kissed my cheek. My neck.

"Yes." He leaned back, eyes scanning mine. "So, what do you say? The kids are young, and this is a perfect time to travel. For years, I've wanted to do something like this, but I always made excuses."

"I would live in the AV if it meant being with you and the kids," I said, and I meant it. It wasn't that I disliked the region or small-town life. Quite the opposite, in fact.

I'd come to realize that I loved the AV and the people of

the community. And the only person who'd worried about how I compared to my sister was me. Well, and my mother. But I wasn't going to let her dictate my decisions anymore.

For so long, I'd made choices based on the opposite of what Tessa might do or what my mom might want me to do. But now, I'd released myself from that mind-set. Any choices I made were for myself.

"We can always go back at some point if that's what *we* decide. But for now, I want to take an adventure with you." He tucked my hair behind my ear, putting a little space between us.

"But your company…"

Now it sounded like I was the one making excuses. I wasn't. I was just…trying to wrap my head around everything. It seemed too good to be true.

"I talked to the Blue River Billionaires about it."

"The who what?" I joked.

He chuckled. "There's a new group of billionaires in Blue River. Knox Crawford is one of them."

"And…?"

"Based on what I told them, they suggested stepping down as CEO and consulting remotely."

"You can do that?" I asked.

He nodded, smiling. "We have options, Elle. Even if we don't sell the house right away, Tessa left a life insurance policy. I only found out about it recently, and well—" He dragged a hand through his hair. "This might sound crazy, but it felt like a sign."

"A sign?" I asked, not wanting to misinterpret his meaning.

"That Tessa would want us to use it to travel. To live."

I wiped away a tear and nodded, knowing he was right. This was absolutely what Tessa would've wanted.

"Yeah, but you would do that?" I asked, rephrasing my

question slightly. "You'd want to step down from the business you've worked so hard to build?"

"It will take a while to make the transition, but it's time for a fresh vision for Lockwood Industries. And a new challenge for me."

I considered it a moment. Though, really, what was there to think about? He'd assuaged every concern. As long as the kids were on board, I was game.

"I see those wheels turning," he finally said with a crooked smile. "Tell me what you're thinking."

"I'm thinking—" I wrapped my arms around his neck "—that as long as this is what Maddox and Savannah want, then yes."

"And if it's not?" he asked, hesitancy in his tone.

"What happened to your confidence?" I teased.

He chuckled. "I'm pretty sure they'd already be living with you in Japan if I would've let them. But still, I want to make sure we're on the same page before talking with them."

"Okay." I took a shaky breath. "Here's the deal. I don't have enough leave time to go back to the AV until my contract ends. You and the kids are always welcome to come visit during spring break or over the summer." Though it felt like an eternity until then.

He nodded. "That was my thought. We could use the summer as a trial run. It gives me enough time to make arrangements back home and secure passports and visas."

"What about Rex and Hedgie?" I asked, wishing we could bring them along but realizing how impractical it would be.

"Bennett agreed to keep them until we come back. However long that may be."

I shook my head, still amazed. He'd thought through everything and made a plan for us to be together. For us to be a family.

"What?" he asked.

"I can't believe we're really doing this." I practically squealed.

"Believe it, Elle." He cupped my cheek. "I plan to give you everything you've ever wanted for the rest of your life."

"You just did." I smiled through my tears. "All I ever wanted was you. There's nothing I need besides you and the kids."

He kissed me quickly and with passion. "That's all I want too."

"So, what now?" I asked, brimming with excitement.

"How about a trip to Tokyo?"

"Tokyo?" I furrowed my brow, and then the answer dawned on me. And my eyes went wide. "Don't tell me…" I was so excited I held my breath. There was a Disneyland in Tokyo. Did he really… Were we…

He grinned. "I once promised to take you to Disney, though I didn't specify which one. We're going to Disneyland Tokyo for their Christmas celebration." He glanced at the clock on the wall. "In two hours, in fact."

"Oh my god." I jumped into his arms, covering his face with kisses. "Yes. Yes. Yes."

He kissed me back, our bodies melding together as our hearts became indistinguishable from each other. "If this was your reaction, maybe I should've told you that first," he teased.

I laughed, smoothing my hand over his face. "God, I love you."

"I love you, Elle." Slowly, he set me back down on the floor. "And I'm sorry I wasted so much time that we could've been together."

"It wasn't a waste," I said, knowing we'd both needed the time apart to grow. "No more regrets, okay?" I held my hand to his cheek.

"No more regrets," he agreed, tilting his forehead to mine.

"From now on, we honor the past but we live in the present as we look toward the future."

"Wow." He chuckled. "That was... Have you been taking classes on mindfulness?"

"No." I rolled my eyes, but I was smiling the entire time. "But I have been working on loving and accepting myself more."

"I'm glad to hear my lessons have been sinking in." He gave my butt a gentle pat followed by a squeeze. "You're amazing, Elle. I've always known it, and I'm glad you're finally realizing it."

"Thank you." Unable to resist, I gave him another quick peck. "Now, we should probably focus on the future, or we're going to miss our flight to Tokyo."

He grinned, pulling me toward the door. "Well then, let's go. The future is waiting."

Tristan

"Can we go to Lick now?" Maddox asked. "*Please?*"

"Soon. I actually want to talk to you guys about something first," I said to Maddox and Savannah. "And then we'll go get ice cream."

I'd returned from Japan a week ago, and I'd been rehearsing what I'd say ever since. Navigating this conversation with my kids was more nerve-racking than any investor pitch I'd made, even when everything had been on the line. I saw now that I could've handled losing the house, losing the company. But I couldn't lose Elle.

Elle and I had talked about it during my visit, and we'd decided I should tell the kids on my own. Mostly at her insistence. She didn't want Maddox and Savannah to feel pressured to make a decision while she was listening in.

It spoke to her love for my children that she was so determined to consider their feelings and heed their wishes. Even if I had a feeling it was completely unnecessary. At least, I hoped so. Hence, my nerves.

I smoothed my hands down my thighs.

How would they feel about my relationship with Elle?

What if they didn't want to move?

What if they thought I was trying to replace their mom?

When I'd talked to my mom about it, she'd assured me she thought the kids would be happy. She was definitely happy for me, and it was a relief to no longer keep this huge secret.

Maddox furrowed his brow. "Are we in trouble?"

"No, buddy." I patted the couch cushion beside me. While I'd considered taking them for a walk to have this conversation, I wanted to be able to see their expressions.

Savannah plopped down on the other side of me then stilled. "Is everyone okay?" she asked, her sweet voice rising with panic. "Is someone dying?"

Oh god. I should've thought about that. The last time we'd sat down to have a serious conversation, it had been to tell them about Tessa's surgery. And while Savannah had been making progress with her anxiety—thanks in large part to her trauma counseling—she still worried more than most kids her age. It was understandable, but I should've considered that this might have triggered some of those fears.

"Actually, I have good news," I said, infusing my voice with enthusiasm while hoping to allay her concerns. I grabbed both her and Maddox's hands. "Good news and some decisions for you to make. Well, for us to make, as a family."

"What kind of decisions?" Maddox asked, a hint of hesitancy to his tone. *I get it, bud. I don't like change either.*

"Well, we need to figure out our plans for the summer. What would you guys think about going to Japan?"

"Really?" Savannah asked, grinning. "We'd get to see Ellie?"

"She'd be teaching still, but yes. We'd get to see her for the whole summer."

Savannah gaped at me. "The *whole* summer?"

"If that's okay," I said, worried she'd be disappointed about missing camp. Missing her friends.

"That's awesome!" she squealed, bouncing on the couch.

"Will we stay with her?" Maddox asked.

"If that's okay with both of you. Though I'd need to find a place that's big enough."

"Yes! Yes! Yes!" Maddox chanted as he punched his little fists in the air.

"We're going to Japan," Savannah singsonged before climbing on the coffee table to dance. I laughed, relieved by their acceptance and enthusiasm.

I wasn't going to tell them about world school yet. I didn't want to put that kind of pressure on them. But their reaction thus far was definitely encouraging.

Elle and I had decided to focus on the summer and see how that went. We'd agreed that if the kids were game for a summer in Japan, we'd rent out the house for the time being. Tourists flocked to the AV during the summer months, eager to explore the wine region's best-kept secret.

I was sure we'd have no problem renting out the house, and it was an elegant solution, as she'd suggested. I'd laughed at that, reminded of how well our last "elegant solution" had worked out. She'd come to live with me after being deported from Australia. And it had completely changed both our lives.

"There's more," I said once they'd calmed down a little.

"More?" Maddox asked, tilting his head. "Like what?"

"I, um—" I cleared my throat. "I want to talk to you about my relationship with Ellie."

Savannah frowned, and I held my breath. "Wait. What are we going to do with Rex and Hedgie when we go to Japan? Can they go with us?"

I shook my head slowly. "No. I wish they could, but Bennett and Wren offered to take care of them while we're gone. Or they can stay with Susan and Larry, Willa, and Daisy at Alpaca Acres."

"Oh. Okay." She considered it a moment. "I'll miss them, but I know they'll be in good hands. And I'm excited about our trip."

Well, okay. That had gone surprisingly well. I'd anticipated that Hedgie and Rex might be a sticking point for Savannah.

"But what about Ellie?" Savannah asked.

And here came the hard part. If the kids couldn't accept my relationship with Elle, we were doomed.

"You know that I love Mommy, and I will always love Mommy."

Savannah and Maddox glanced at each other. I wondered what they were thinking.

"And she will always be part of our lives. We will always talk about her and meet her in the castle library and honor her memory."

"Daddy, you're really scaring me," Savannah said, fidgeting with her hands.

I just needed to do it. I needed to say it.

"I love Ellie."

"I know. So do we," Savannah said.

I shook my head. They weren't getting it. "I love her, and I want her to be part of our family."

Maddox furrowed his brow. "She *is* part of our family."

I was fucking this all up.

"Yes, but I want her to be my girlfriend," I said, thinking it sounded odd to call Elle that when she was so much more to me. "My partner."

They were both quiet a moment. It was agony waiting for them to respond, but I wanted to give them space to process this news. I'd spoken to their grief counselor about it, and she thought it was a great thing. But I had no idea how the kids would react.

Finally, Savannah said, "So, you would kiss Ellie?"

I nodded.

"And do things like go on dates with her?"

"Yes. Exactly."

"Would she be our new mom?" Maddox asked.

"No, bud." I reached out and took his hand in mine, giving it a gentle squeeze. "No one can ever replace your mom. She'll always be part of our lives too."

"Would you have a baby?" Savannah asked. And if I wasn't mistaken, she sounded excited. Or maybe that was just me being hopeful.

"I, uh—" I tugged at the collar of my shirt. Jeez. My kids were grilling me. "Maybe in the future. I don't know. If we did, how would you feel about that?"

She started crying, and I pulled her onto my lap, rubbing my hand up and down her back. "It's okay to cry. I'm sure you both have a lot of big feelings about this. It's a huge change."

"I'm not crying because I'm sad," Savannah said, swiping away her tears. "I'm crying because I'm happy, Daddy."

The relief—and shock—hit me instantly, and I worked to keep my jaw from dropping. "Really?"

"Yeah. I love Ellie. And now we'll always get to be with her. And if you get married, I could be a flower girl. And if you have a baby, I could be a big sister." Her smile was radiant.

"Hey! What about me?" Maddox asked.

"A big sister *again*," Savannah said, rolling her eyes.

I laughed. She was definitely getting ahead of herself. But one day, *one day,* I did want to marry Elle. I wanted to have more children with her. I wanted it all.

"What about you, Mads?" I turned to him, surprised by how quiet he was. "How are you feeling?"

He lifted a shoulder but didn't say anything.

"Talk to me, bud," I pleaded.

"Yeah." Savannah nudged him. "What's up? You love Ellie."

"I know, but—" He heaved a great shuddering breath then started to cry. "I don't want to lose her too."

I immediately pulled him and Savannah to me. "I don't ever want us to go through that kind of pain again. But it comes with loving someone. You both give me so much strength—more than you will ever know. I need to know you're in this with me. Will you be brave with me?"

Savannah nodded, and then so did Maddox. I wiped their tears, and we talked some more about Ellie and Japan and their mom. It was one of the best conversations we'd had in a long time. And it was so nice to be in a place where we could talk with less pain and more love.

"Can we call Ellie?" Savannah asked.

I glanced at the world clock on my phone and shook my head. "It's the middle of the night, and I'm sure she's asleep. But we can definitely check in later."

"And you'll be on the phone too, right?"

I tilted my head. "Yeah. Why?"

"Just curious."

"Can we *please* go get ice cream now?" Maddox asked, to which I laughed.

"Absolutely. Grab your shoes and jackets. We're going to Lick!"

"Yes!" They both cheered.

We drove downtown, the streets lined with lights and decorations for the holidays. It was beautiful and charming, and I knew I would miss it. But I could always return. As I'd told Elle, it was time for a new adventure. A fresh start.

The kids bounced into the ice cream store ahead of me. When I entered, they were already sitting at the counter, chatting with the owner, Sandra. She waved to me, but her attention was glued to them.

"What can I get you?" she asked me when I took the stool next to Maddox. "Perhaps some mochi?" She winked.

I paused then laughed. The kids *must* be excited about visiting Japan—they'd clearly already spilled the beans to Sandra. I only wondered what else they'd told her.

I ordered the current special—peppermint ice cream served taco-style in a chocolate waffle cone with chocolate sauce and sprinkled with crushed peppermints. For what was life without a little indulgence now and then.

After we finished our treats, we stopped in Bibliolater to complete our holiday shopping. Savannah wanted to get a book on tree houses for Aiden, and she picked some funky socks for River. We chatted with the owner—and Liam's mom—Debbie, for a little bit before heading back out into the chilly air.

We were walking down the sidewalk when I saw Gloria approaching from the direction of Larkspur. *Aw. Shit.*

I wasn't prepared to have this conversation with her, especially not so soon after having it with the children. I mean, I hadn't even had the chance to tell Elle the good news, for chrissakes. But perhaps the universe was giving me the push I needed. Because I'd known all along that I'd have to deal with Gloria sooner or later.

"Hello," she said to me, her expression cold.

"Mimi!" Maddox cheered, hugging her legs.

"Hi there." She smiled down at him, softening as Savannah joined them for a hug. "I've missed you two."

"We've missed you, Mimi," Maddox said. "Will we get to come over for Christmas?"

"I hope so. It's something your dad and I need to discuss." She glanced at me, and for once, she seemed...defeated. Broken.

I crouched down to the kids' level. "If I give you some

money, can you be responsible and go shopping without me to get Rex's and Hedgie's presents?"

"Um, yeah." Savannah practically squealed. She held out her hand for some cash, then pocketed it before grabbing Maddox's hand. "Come on, Mads." They ran down the sidewalk toward the pet shop.

Oh boy. I waited until the kids had entered the store to turn and face my mother-in-law.

"I want to apologize," Gloria said.

Huh. Was this a trick? Gloria—apologize?

"I was out of line to suggest what I did."

"And what was that?" I crossed my arms over my chest. I wasn't willing to let her be intentionally vague, not after what she'd done. After what she'd put me—and Elle —through.

"Insinuating that you had an inappropriate relationship with Eleanor. That you were unfit to care for the children. You're a good father, Tristan. I never should've said what I did."

Wow. Okay. That was big. Definitely a start. At least, if she was being genuine, which I honestly thought she was. Still, it was Gloria. Which meant she likely had an ulterior motive.

I didn't want to be petty. I wanted the children to know, and spend time with, their grandparents. Family was important, even if it wasn't always easy. Tessa would've wanted the kids to have a good relationship with her parents; I wanted that too. So long as Gloria could respect Elle, and my relationship with her.

"I appreciate your saying that. Though you were right about one thing."

"Was I?" she asked, tucking her scarf tighter around her neck.

"Elle and I *are* together, but there's nothing inappropriate about our relationship."

She stilled, her expression going cold. "What about Teresa? What would she think of you moving on so quickly?"

It wasn't said with malice, but it was still a low blow. And in the past, her question might have derailed me. But now, I wouldn't let anything stand in my way.

"Grief, love, moving on, none of it has a timeline. But even if it did, it's been a year and a half. I love Elle. She makes me happy, happier than I've been in a long time, and I want to be with her."

"Your wife's younger sister…" She shook her head.

I lifted a shoulder. I wasn't going to apologize for who I loved. "Trust me, I fought it. But in the end, we're happy together."

"What will the children think?" she asked in a sharp tone. If she was trying to intimidate me, it wasn't working.

"I've talked to them about it, and they're thrilled. They'll always love Tessa, just like I will always love and honor Tessa. But we can make room for more love too."

"So that's it, then? Eleanor's moving home, and you're going to be one big happy family."

"Actually—" I shoved my hands into my pockets. "We're going to Japan for the summer to be with her. After that…" I shrugged. "We'll see."

She was quiet for a moment, considering. So I said, "Look. I want you and Dan to be part of their lives. The children want that too. But only if you can be respectful of Elle. If you can at least…" I sighed. "I don't know. Remain neutral about our relationship."

She was silent. Contemplative. I braced myself for her refusal. For another list of reasons why I shouldn't be with Elle.

But then Gloria inclined her head. "I will try."

I tried to keep my jaw shut. Had she really…relented?

It wasn't nearly enough, but it was a start. We'd be leaving for Japan next summer; maybe that would give Gloria time to work through her feelings on the matter.

"I shouldn't have to tell you this," I said. "But at the very least, Elle deserves to be treated with respect. It's not her fault that—" I stopped myself and sighed, noting the way Gloria's expression had changed. "You don't have to love her, but I wish you'd apologize to her. For both your sakes."

She seemed to consider my words, to consider me, finally saying, "Perhaps you're right. I've been blaming her for something that isn't her fault."

I nodded, hoping she would take what I'd said to heart.

"I should get going. Dan will be waiting for me."

"We'll see you soon."

She smiled. "I'm looking forward to it. Thank you. Family is important." She wiped away a tear. "And I need to do a better job of showing that."

Her emotion surprised me, but I nodded. I hoped she'd do a better job of showing Elle that too. Because Elle deserved nothing less than unconditional love and acceptance. And I fully intended to spend the rest of my life showing her that.

CHAPTER THIRTY-TWO

Ellie

A year and a half later

"Holy shit," I said, lingering on each and every syllable as I entered the main suite. I scanned the wall-to-wall, floor-to-ceiling windows overlooking Clifton Beach. And our home for the next week.

We'd only just arrived in Cape Town, South Africa. After spending that first summer in Japan, the kids had been eager to continue traveling. We'd spent the next few months exploring China and Southeast Asia. We'd celebrated Christmas in Sydney, and we'd traveled around various cities in Australia and New Zealand after that. It had been an adventure, for sure—full of mishaps and mistakes but also fun. And more love than I could've ever hoped.

I usually booked the accommodations, but Tristan had insisted on taking care of it this time. He'd said he wanted to splurge a little to celebrate the sale of Lockwood Industries. And wow had he ever.

I wondered how much a place like this went for a night.

The unobstructed ocean view alone was priceless. Plus, there a private pool. And five huge bedrooms. It was…amazing.

The kids were downstairs with the cook, discussing local cuisine. One of the best things about the trip was the sense of responsibility and confidence it had instilled in them. Maddox was now six, and he would regularly pack his day bag without being asked. He was learning to read and write, but this trip had taught us all so much more about one another and ourselves.

Savannah had really come into her own, shedding more and more of her anxiety. And she loved seeing so many different animals across the world. She'd helped us plan special stops where we could help local environmental conservationists or learn about various animals. I loved learning alongside her. I loved watching her blossom.

"This place is incredible," I said, unable to tear my eyes away from the view.

I heard Tristan's footsteps approaching. He wrapped his arms around my waist, pulling my back to his front. "It does have a nice view."

"Nice?" I sputtered. "You call this *nice?*"

He chuckled. "The house, the view, are nice. But the only thing I want is you."

I melted in his arms at his words. "You have me." *Always.*

He brushed my hair over my shoulder, and I shivered when his breath hit the skin of my neck. "Now that Lockwood Industries sold, this *could* be our life."

I swallowed hard. I hadn't asked how much the company had sold for but judging from this vacation rental and his promises about the future…a lot.

Was this the kind of house he'd want in the future? The kind of life?

We'd spent the last year and a half living well but also within our means. Despite having Tessa's life insurance to fund the trip, Tristan had continued working as a consultant for Lockwood until the sale of the company. And I'd built my business, creating content for my clients, even taking on new ones.

Six months into our adventure, he'd sold the house in the AV. The kids had been surprisingly okay with it, though they'd certainly gotten used to adapting to change on this trip. We'd gone home once, to finalize the sale and spend time with friends and family, including my parents.

They'd been happy to see us. Mom had apologized—genuinely apologized—and said she was working on her issues. She told me she was committed to having a better relationship, and she was sorry for how she'd treated me. I was encouraged, but wary. I wanted a better relationship, but it was hard to ignore all the pain she'd caused.

My dad had also apologized. For not standing up for me. For not loving me like he should've.

There were many years of hurt between the three of us, but for the first time maybe ever, I was hopeful that the future would be filled with more understanding.

It had been a surprisingly good visit, and we'd loved seeing Rex and Hedgie, but we hadn't been back. Since then, Mom and Dad would comment on the private Instagram profile where I logged our adventures. We'd also exchanged some emails. They seemed to accept my relationship with Tristan.

Savannah regularly FaceTimed with Aiden and River, often sending them postcards about our adventures. We chatted often with Tristan's parents. And I knew Piper and Liam and so many of our friends followed along with our trip online. Harper had been instrumental in planning our trip, offering ongoing insights and advice for many of our destinations.

"You know I don't care about money," I said. "As long as we're together. That's what matters."

"Agreed." He kissed my cheek and moved for the door. "It's a nice night." He slid open one of the large glass doors. "Let's go outside."

"What about the kids?" I asked, glancing back toward the bedroom door.

"They're fine. Besides, they're having too much fun helping the cook with dinner."

The cook. I wanted to laugh. This house really did have it all. A state-of-the-art security system, luxury SUV, cook, and housekeeper. And those were just a few of the amenities.

"Plus, they're dying to watch a movie in the theater room."

I laughed. "Sounds like they'll be busy."

"Mm." He hummed. "You know who else will be busy…"

He smoothed his hands down my arms, and goose bumps dotted my skin. I was so attuned to him, so turned on by him, and I was eager for some alone time. That was one of the hardest parts about traveling as a family; Tristan and I were rarely ever alone except after the kids went to bed.

But now that we were in a swanky house with some help, well, things were definitely different.

"Are you hungry?" he rasped. "Would you like something to drink?"

I shook my head, arching back into him. "I only want you."

He groaned and turned me to face him, sliding his hands up to cup my cheeks. The way he looked at me…I'd never felt more cherished or adored. "You're so beautiful, Elle."

Every day, he made sure I knew how much he loved me. And it was moments like this that I treasured. Small, quiet moments when it was just the two of us.

He claimed my mouth, kissing me with such passion and all-consuming need. And I felt that familiar ache building, urging me on. My body begging me for more. Now. Fast. All at once.

"Off." I fumbled with the buttons on his shirt. "Want this off."

"Not just yet," he said, still panting.

I frowned. "Why not? As you pointed out, the kids will be busy until dinner at least."

"Come here." He grabbed my hand. "Come on."

He led me farther onto the back deck overlooking the ocean. The waves crashed in the distance, the sun casting a pinkish hue over the sky. It was breathtaking.

Tristan stood behind me, caging my body against the railing with his. His hard-on dug into my back, and I wondered if he was prolonging the anticipation, as he often did. Driving us both wild.

"I could have all the money in the world, and yet it wouldn't mean anything without you," he said. "Nothing is worth more than these moments. Than this time we've had together and with the kids."

"I agree." I burrowed deeper into his arms. "I love you."

"I love you." He kissed my cheek then turned me to face him. "I've been waiting for Lockwood Industries to sell. I've been waiting to release that last piece of my old life so that we can start a new one—together."

"Pretty sure this adventure qualifies as starting a new life together," I joked.

"It does, but it's more than that. Elle—" He pulled back and knelt down, opening a box to reveal a stunning pearl ring set in a band of diamonds.

"Oh my god," I gasped, holding a hand to my mouth. Was this for real?

"Pearls are said to symbolize wisdom gained through

experience. And you have made me a wiser man, a better man."

"Tristan." I smiled down at him, knowing exactly how he felt. Because every day, he encouraged me to be myself. He loved me just as I was. And we were both stronger because of it. It was one of the things I loved most about us.

Our relationship had been forged in tragedy, but we'd turned it into something positive. We loved harder and more deeply. Because we both knew that nothing was guaranteed, and we didn't take our health or happiness for granted.

"A pearl also seemed fitting," he continued. "Since they're reminiscent of the moon, as well as a sign of new beginnings."

"You clearly put a lot of thought into this," I said, both impressed and touched.

"You deserve nothing less than the absolute best," he said. "And I promise I will spend every day of the rest of my life giving you my everything. I love you so much, Elle. Will you marry me?"

"Tristan—" I tugged on his hand, bringing him to a standing position. "I already have everything I could ever want."

He furrowed his brow. "Are you… Do you not want to get married?"

"Are you kidding?" I laughed through tears of joy. "Of course I want to marry you. I'm just saying—I'm perfectly content with our life. We don't need an expensive house or fancy cars or a big wedding. All I need is you."

"And all I need is *you*." He slid the ring on my finger. It was a perfect fit. And I loved the unique style. The pearl had a slight purple sheen to it and was set in a band of diamonds that glittered like stars.

He cupped my cheeks, claiming my lips in a kiss that spoke of passion, reverence, and love. I reveled in the moment and this man, but then another thought occurred to me. "What about the kids?"

He chuckled. "I have a feeling they're going to be thrilled."

"Still…" I hesitated, peering down at my engagement ring. "Do you think I should wait to wear it until we've had a chance to talk to them?"

"Nah." He draped his arm over my shoulder, and I marveled at how relaxed he was. This was *huge*. "They'll want to see the ring when we tell them. Come on."

"Now?" I froze.

What if this was too much? What if they were upset? I couldn't imagine that being the case, but still…getting married was a big step.

"Why wait?" He grinned, walking backward and pulling me inside with him. "Unless you're having second thoughts."

"Never." I pressed up on my toes and kissed him.

"Mm. Good. Because I can't wait to see my fiancée wearing nothing but her ring." He held up my hand and admired the pearl before kissing my palm.

I sucked in a jagged breath, taking the lead. "Mm. Are you going to give me a pearl necklace to match my ring?"

"Elle," he growled as I opened the door to the hallway.

I smiled at him over my shoulder, feigning innocence.

He grabbed me and spun me so my back was to the wall, and his body was bracketing me against it. When we came together, it was feverish and explosive, each of us determined to drive the other crazy with want. I loved it. And I loved us.

The kiss, our touch, was clumsy and rushed, and I craved it. I loved that we were both so desperate that the air felt charged with electricity ready to spark.

"Fuck, Elle. I love seeing my ring on your finger." He intertwined our fingers, using his other hand to pull me closer. "Now everyone will know you're mine when you wear it."

I loved that too. I wanted everyone to know that I belonged to him.

Though I didn't think it would take a ring to prove that. His eyes rarely left me. He was almost always touching me.

He might want me to belong to him, but he belonged to me just as completely. He was utterly devoted. Always doting on me and the kids.

"Speaking of new beginnings," I said. "I have a proposal as well." It was something I'd been contemplating for a while.

"Oh yeah?" He tucked my hair behind my ear. He often said it was the color of honey. "What's that?"

"I think we should move back to the AV."

He smoothed his hand down my side, over my curves. "Really?"

"Our trip has been incredible. But the kids are getting older now. I want them to have their friends and that wonderful sense of community that I did growing up. I want them to have that connection to their mom."

He considered it a moment then nodded. "I think you're right."

"You do?"

"Yeah. We can shorten our route and use the remaining time to start looking at houses in the AV. I'll have to see if Vanessa has anything with five bedrooms, or if we're going to need to build."

"Five bedrooms?" I furrowed my brow. It wasn't like we needed a guest room since most of our friends and family lived in the AV.

"One for us. Maddox and Savannah will each need a room—they're probably getting too old to share."

"What are the other two for?" I asked. "An office?"

He shook his head, smiling. "Our future children."

My heart softened. We'd talked about having more children in the past, but always in abstract terms. Now he was proposing marriage and talking about having babies, and my core heated with arousal. I wanted everything he'd described. Big family. A home. *Him.*

I smiled and grabbed his shirt and pulled him to me for a kiss. "Yeah?"

"Yeah." He kissed me again, this time more deeply.

"When?" I asked, breathless both from his touch and what he was suggesting.

"Whenever you're ready." He rocked his hips against mine, and I gasped as pleasure sparked deep within me. "I can't wait to see how sexy you'll look pregnant with my child." He ran his hands down my sides to my hips, over my ass, pulling me to him.

I moaned. "Tristan."

"Is that a yes?" He teased the shell of my ear with his teeth.

"Yes," I sighed. "Yes to everything."

"Dad! Ellie!" Savannah yelled. "Dinner's almost ready."

"Be right there," Tristan called, barely breaking the kiss. "Fuck," he panted. "I need you, Elle."

"Need you too." I pressed my forehead to his, wishing we could skip dinner. Or at the very least, delay it.

"Come on," Tristan said, stepping back and adjusting himself. He smoothed down the front of his shirt. "We should get down there."

"Okay." I took a deep breath, trying to steady myself. My heart was still racing, blood pumping so hard it was throbbing between my thighs. "Okay," I said again.

He chuckled then headed for the stairs but not before pressing a chaste kiss to my forehead. "I'll give you a minute."

When I'd finally composed myself enough to go downstairs, I headed straight for the dining room and stopped short.

"Congratulations!" Savannah and Maddox cheered,

tossing gold confetti into the air. The table was topped with flowers, and a champagne bottle was chilling on ice.

I glanced between them, mouth agape. "Wait. You guys knew about this?" I asked, holding up my left hand, the pearl glistening on my ring finger.

"Of course." Savannah smirked, hand on hip. "We helped Dad pick the ring when we were in Australia."

My jaw dropped. He'd been planning this since before we'd left Australia? "But you're terrible at keeping secrets," I said to Maddox.

He lifted a shoulder. "I'm six now."

I laughed and opened my arms for him. "Come here."

I shouldn't have worried that the kids wouldn't be happy about our engagement. They'd been in on this from the start. Even so, I wanted to make sure. "I guess this means you guys are okay with this?"

"Are you kidding?" Savannah asked. "I don't know why he waited so long." She hooked her thumb at Tristan, and we all laughed.

We talked about the ring, and the kids asked questions about the wedding. All the while, I was still wrapping my head around the fact that we were engaged.

Savannah's tablet chimed, and she carried it over to us with a big grin. "Now, it's official."

I furrowed my brow, and Tristan and I peered down at the screen. The internet browser was open to *The Vine*, and the newest post had a picture of the four of us on the beach. The title was "She said yes!"

I laughed. "Did you do this?" I asked Savannah.

She shook her head, and I looked to Maddox, then Tristan. My jaw dropped. "You did?" Tristan had never been a huge fan of *The Vine*, and he'd always hated being featured in it.

He chuckled. "Yep. Figured it was easier to announce it to everyone at once."

"I can't believe you emailed *V*," I said. "How did she…" I tilted my head. "You just assumed I'd say yes," I teased.

He smirked, holding out his arms. "I mean, really. Have you ever been able to resist me?"

I rolled my eyes, but we both knew I was joking. Resisting Tristan had been impossible—then and now. But I'd stopped feeling guilty or conflicted about our relationship long ago.

My eyes widened. Oh my god. My parents.

They were more supportive than they'd been in the past. I'd forgiven them for lying about the circumstances of my birth. And they'd been more accepting and loving. Even so, I didn't want them to be blindsided by this news.

Tristan placed his hand over mine. "Your parents knew I was going to propose," he said, as if he'd read my thoughts.

"They did?" I was afraid to ask what they'd said, though his smile was encouraging.

"They're really happy for us. Everyone is."

I smiled, filled with love and peace and hope for the future. We were a family, and I didn't need a ring or a proposal or a post on *The Vine* to make it official. But it was nice to recognize how far we'd come and how much had changed. To feel like we didn't have to hide who we were.

Life was short, but I fully intended to make the most of it. On my terms. With the people who loved and accepted me exactly as I was.

"I'm really happy, Ellie," Maddox said, giving me a hug.

"You know what? So am I." I smiled, hugging him back.

We were a family, and I'd never felt more at home than when I was with Maddox, Savannah, and Tristan. It didn't matter whether we were dining in a luxurious beach house in South Africa or eating pizza on the couch in the AV, because they were my home.

EVERYTHING'S COMING UP ROSIE

Ellie

Four Years Later

"Are you ready?" Maddox called to me down the hall.

"I'll be done in a minute," I said through the crack in the bathroom door. "Please keep an eye on your sister."

And please stay away from the bathroom.

I finished washing my hands and stared at the test on the counter, waiting for the timer on my phone to go off. I'd been feeling out of sorts the past few weeks—tired, cranky, nauseated. And I had a feeling I knew why. I hadn't told Tristan or the kids about my suspicions, hadn't wanted to get their hopes up.

"It's nearly four o'clock," Maddox said, exasperated. "Dad will be home soon, and then we have to leave to get Savannah."

"I know," I called. *"I know,"* I sighed, repeating the words more quietly to myself.

I was rushing around, trying to finish my makeup and not stress over the results. In my haste, I nearly knocked the test into the trash can, catching it at the last minute. And as I did, I saw it: two pink lines.

Pregnant.

"Holy shit," I whispered, peering at myself in the mirror. I didn't know why I was so surprised. I'd suspected this for weeks, but seeing the answer staring me in the face made it feel a lot more real.

Another kid. We were going to have four kids. *Four.*

Four kids. A dog. A new hedgehog. A kitten. And a chicken coop.

Have I lost my mind?

But when my gaze went to the wall behind me, I smiled when I saw the picture of the five of us. *Soon to be six.* I cupped my stomach, my pearl and diamond ring flashing at me from my finger. Reminding me of the man—and the family—who loved me unconditionally.

Six, I repeated to myself again.

It was a good thing Tristan had insisted on such a big house when we'd moved back to the Alondra Valley. Six bedrooms, four bathrooms, a beautiful garden that Tessa would've loved. My favorite part was the enormous couch where we piled together and watched movies. It was my happy place.

It wasn't as cozy as the old house. Nor as close to town. But I loved the wide-open spaces. I loved that Penny and Liam's property backed up to ours. And the kids loved it too, especially Rosemary, though everyone called her "Rosie."

My youngest wobbled into the bathroom, giggling as Maddox chased behind her. "Ma. Ma. Ma. Ma," she babbled.

I smiled at her and stepped in front of the counter to

shield the test from Maddox's view. I didn't know if he'd realize what it meant, but I wasn't ready to explain it to him.

"Sorry," Maddox said to me before picking Rosie up and bouncing her into his arms. "Come on, Rosie. Let's get you a snack."

I smiled, loving the way he doted on her. Despite their nine-year age gap, they were close. Their relationship often reminded me of Tessa and me.

I toyed with my necklace. I still couldn't believe she'd been gone seven years. It was difficult to believe how much had changed.

I'd graduated college. Fallen in love. Lived in Japan for a year and completed the JET Program. Started a successful content creation business. Traveled the world. Moved back to the Alondra Valley and built a home. Gotten married. Had a child. And now I was pregnant with another. It was enough to make my head spin, at least it would've been if I'd had much time to think about it.

Between three kids, two successful businesses, and our growing menagerie, Tristan and I barely had alone time together. Now we were going to add another kid to the mix?

I started crying, overwhelmed with emotions. I'd just secured a big new client, and now I was pregnant. I was elated and scared and excited and freaked out and...

"Elle?" Tristan's voice echoed against the tile, and I startled. I hadn't even heard him come in. "What's wrong?"

My eyes darted to the counter and the test. This wasn't how I'd wanted him to find out. But of course, he followed my gaze and then froze.

"Elle?" he whispered, kneeling before me. He cupped my cheeks, staring up at me with complete adoration as he wiped away my tears. "Are you...?"

"I—we're going to be late to the library."

"Savannah will understand," he said. "Talk to me. What's going through that beautiful head of yours?"

"I'm pregnant." I finally said the words aloud on a rush of air. It was both a relief and a reality check.

"How do you feel about that?" he asked in a measured tone. I appreciated that he wasn't trying to push me to feel a certain way. He was checking in.

"I'm…" I was so many things in that moment, so I settled on, "Overwhelmed."

"We'll figure this out. Together," he said, his tone taking on more of that command that was equal parts sexy and reassuring.

He was right. I knew he was right. But in this moment, I was spinning.

"I just signed Parris," I said, referring to the singer I'd been courting. In the past few years, I'd added several celebrity clients to my roster, including Meghan Hart. Though I now knew that was Liam's pen name.

Tristan's eyes went wide, a slow smile spreading across his face. "That's fantastic, Elle."

"Yeah, but I don't know how I can do it all. We're already crazy busy."

"What can I do to help?" he asked. "I can cut back on my hours. I can take the kids to school. We can hire a chef. You can bring on another intern to help with your workload."

He was so thoughtful and attentive, and it only made me cry more.

He furrowed his brow. "Did I say something wrong?"

"No." I laughed through my tears. "You always know just what to say. I love you so much."

He cupped the back of my neck, pressing his lips to mine. "I love you, Elle. And I want you to be able to enjoy this pregnancy. Whatever you need to make it less overwhelming, just tell me. Okay?"

I let out a slow exhale, feeling a little calmer. He was right. We were in this together. "Okay. Thank you."

He held my gaze a moment longer then stood. I allowed myself a few seconds to scan him from head to toe. Dark brown hair with flecks of gray at the temples. Smile lines that spoke of a life well lived. A white button-up shirt open at the collar. Charcoal slacks that showed off his muscular ass.

As soon as we'd moved back to the AV, he'd resumed his weekly rides with Enzo. And he'd started lifting weights with Bennett and Liam as well. Asher joined them when he could, but between his intense work schedule and three kids, he didn't have much free time.

Tristan offered me his hand, pulling me to a standing position. He stood behind me in the mirror, placing his hands on my stomach. I loved the sight of his platinum wedding band. I loved knowing he was mine, and I was his.

"Keep looking at me like that, and I'll get you pregnant again," he teased, smoothing his hands over my curves. His erection prodded my back.

"Really?" I asked.

"Fuck, Elle," he rasped in my ear. "I love your body always, but especially when you're carrying my child."

"Mm." I closed my eyes and leaned my head back against his shoulder, reveling in the feel of him. He was solid. Safe. Loving.

He roamed my body with his hands, his touch both comforting and arousing. His hands on my breasts, my hips, caressing my belly.

"And this is exactly why I'm pregnant again so soon," I teased. Rosemary was barely one.

"Do you regret it?" he asked.

We hadn't been using birth control for months, so we'd known this was a possibility. We'd been hoping for another child. And yet, I'd freaked out.

"No," I said, turning to face him, smoothing my hands over his chest. "I'm happy. Truly." I gave him a watery smile.

"So am I," he said, dipping his head and capturing my lips in a tender kiss.

It didn't stay tender long, quickly turning heated and frantic. He smoothed his hands down my back to cup my ass, bringing my body flush with his. Letting me feel his desire, while my own built and built and…

"Ma. Ma. Ma." Was our only warning before the door opened again, and Rosie waddled through.

Tristan's lips curved into a smile, and he broke the kiss to peer down at our daughter. "There's my sunshine." He scooped her into his arms, and she giggled as he peppered her face and neck with kisses.

My heart was full of love for this man and the family we'd built. The life we'd created.

"Da. Da. Da," Tristan said to Rosie, enunciating each syllable. "Da. Da. Da."

For weeks, he'd been trying to get her to say Dada. He was determined that it would be her first word.

I laughed and placed my hand on his back. "Come on. Savannah will be waiting for us."

He stepped back so I could go ahead, wrapping his arm around my shoulder. "You sure you're okay?"

I nodded. "Yeah. I just…wish we could have more alone time together. It already feels scarce, and now we're adding a baby?"

He held me to him, pressing a kiss to my forehead as Rosie squirmed and wiggled between us. "I already talked to your mom about taking the kids tonight."

"You did?" I asked.

Ever since we'd returned to the AV, my parents spent as much time as possible with the kids. My mom was no longer mayor, and she delighted in her grandchildren. I'd worried that she'd treat Rosie differently, but she doted on our youngest.

"Yeah," he said. "I've been craving alone time with you too. So, I asked her if she and Dan could help with a weekly date night for us. She said they'd be more than happy to."

My shoulders sagged with relief. "That sounds like heaven."

In the years since we'd moved home, my relationship with my parents had improved. It wasn't perfect by any means. We still had our disagreements, but we now operated on a basis of love and understanding. If only Tessa could've been here to see it.

"Good." Tristan rubbed my shoulder as we continued down the hall toward the kitchen. "And my parents have offered to do a sleepover once a month."

"Seriously?" I couldn't believe he'd already put all this in place. I pressed up on my toes to kiss him, and Rosie reached out for me.

"Yes. And on those weekends, we can stay at the cabin."

I furrowed my brow. "Penny and Liam's cabin?"

We'd used it a few times over the years, but I didn't want to impose.

He shook his head, a sly smile curving his lips. "*Our* cabin." He held out a key with a vintage-style keychain. It was emerald with a gold flower embossed on it. "Happy anniversary, Elle."

My jaw dropped. "Wow. How did you—"

"I love the kids, and I love you. But I miss *us*."

Yes. Exactly.

But how had he known? How could he have realized exactly what I was feeling? And he'd already put a plan in motion. One that involved purchasing a cabin.

While part of me was upset that he'd made such a big decision without me, a bigger part of me was overwhelmed with gratitude. Excitement. An escape all to ourselves. I couldn't even imagine. It sounded so luxurious.

"Elle, you act surprised, but I feel the same way. And I *know* you. I listen to you, and I want you to be happy."

"Of course I'm happy," I said, taking Rosie and settling her on my hip. I smiled down at her, making silly faces and cooing. "I have everything I ever wanted and more."

The love and acceptance of my family. A career that was fulfilling. A home. A man who absolutely adored me and our kids.

"So do I." He cupped my cheek, his gaze filled with devotion and longing.

I kissed him again, eager for our promised alone time. "I love you."

"I love you." He intertwined our hands. "Our relationship is important to me. *You* are important to me."

"There you are," Maddox huffed. "I already packed the diaper bag."

"Wow." Tristan and I looked at each other and smiled. "Thanks."

"I'll get Rosie buckled in," Tristan said, taking her from me. "Take your time. We'll be outside when you're ready." He kissed my temple.

I glanced around the house, doing a quick sweep of anything that we might need. I checked Rex's and Poppy's food and water bowls then headed out to the garage. On the way, Maddox played with Rosie in the back seat and told us about his day at school.

Tristan held my hand, toying with my ring as we passed through downtown and headed for St. Cecilia. The new branch of the library dedicated to Tessa had finally opened earlier this year, and Savannah had immediately signed up to volunteer. I was proud of her, and I knew Tessa would be too.

Tristan drove over the stone bridge that led to a winding path in the woods. The trees finally opened to a castle. The stone walls were covered in climbing vines and set in a beautiful garden. It was as if the architect had taken the version in our imagination—where we visited Tessa—and made it a reality.

It was perfect, thanks to Liam, Tristan, and my mom. Liam had donated the land and helped fund the book purchases through the annual Meghan Hart Day hosted by his mom and Bibliolater. And after Tristan had sold Lockwood Industries, he'd made a huge contribution that enabled the city to hire a renowned architect who could bring the vision to life. During her tenure as mayor, my mom had been more than happy to help see the project to fruition.

We unbuckled, and I carried Rosie through the garden filled with birdsong and volunteers. We passed Linda Allen, Harper's mom, pruning some rosebushes. She and her landscape design firm had donated their services. And a large crew of volunteers helped maintain the beautiful outdoor space.

Rosie reached out for one of the butterflies that flitted among the California poppies. I smiled at her and headed inside, the sliding doors opening onto an interior that was just as magical as the exterior promised. It was filled with books and cozy chairs, and even a fake fireplace where they hosted story time.

Even though Tessa had never been here, I could feel her spirit. As if she were a friendly presence watching over the space. Or perhaps it was because her photo always greeted us at the door, her kind smile and sparkling blue eyes hinting at a love of reading and a natural curiosity.

"There's your auntie," I said to Rosie, pointing to Tessa's portrait. "We named you after her."

I no longer felt as if I were living in my sister's—or

anyone's—shadow. But instead, that I could shine on my own.

We were all part of a larger constellation of family. My parents, Tristan's, the kids, Tessa, me. And we all had a role to play. We all had our time to shine.

"That's right." Maddox took her from me, carrying Rosie inside as he told her all about his mom and how Teresa's middle name had been Rosemary. And then he started singing "You Are My Sunshine," and I started crying again.

As I glanced back up at the picture of my sister, I thought about her legacy of service. But mostly the enduring power of her unconditional love and acceptance. Her time on earth may have been short, but her impact had been immense.

I silently thanked her and the universe for this beautiful family and this amazing life. For what was the point of life if not to love?

Yes, there was loss and pain and grief and sadness. But through tragedy could come great beauty, like the garden Tessa had always loved to tend. It could take time to cultivate the beauty, but all you had to do was keep growing.

BOOKS BY JENNA HARTLEY

<u>Love in LA Series</u>

Inevitable

Unexpected

Irresistible

Unpredictable

Irreplaceable

<u>Love in LA Series novellas</u>

Perspective

Unwritten

<u>Alondra Valley Series</u>

<u>Feels Like Love</u>

<u>Love Like No Other</u>

<u>A Love Like That</u>

For the most current list of Jenna's titles, please visit her website www.authorjennahartley.com.

Or scan the QR code on the following page to be taken to her author page on Amazon.com

SCAN ME

Acknowledgments

I've been wanting to write this story for over a year!!

I'd even started it a while back. Originally it was going to be the first book in the Alondra Valley series. But then I realized Tristan needed to come later. He needed more time to grieve the loss of his wife.

Some of you were very upset with me for killing Tessa in *Feels Like Love*, understandably so. That said, I hope you enjoyed Tristan's happily ever after in *A Love Like That.*

You may be wondering why I wanted to write a story like this?

When I was a kid, one of my first major memories regarding death was about a girl at my school. She was a grade younger than me, and she was at the mall with her mom and sister when their mom collapsed on the floor. The mom died almost instantly of a brain aneurism, and that really shocked and terrified me.

I often thought about the girl and her family and what that might be like for them. And so, I wanted to explore those feelings when writing Tristan's book. It was certainly heart breaking, but also heart warming to give him and the kids another chance at a happily ever after. Allowing them to honor the past—and Tessa—while finding a way to live in the present. I think it's a powerful lesson for all of us.

I also want to give a shout out to @spilledmilkmama on Instagram. Julie is a widower with two young kids, and I started reading her story while I was writing Tristan. I gained a lot of insight on the struggles of solo parenting and grief, and I find myself continually inspired and in awe of her.

It was fun to revisit other characters from the Alondra Valley. Bennett and Wren and River (and baby Hazel!), to peek in on Liam and Asher as well. I'm excited about Asher's story, and I can't wait to share it with you!

Thank you for reading *A Love Like That.* I love writing for the pure pleasure of it, but seeing all your reactions is definitely a highlight. I have to thank so many wonderful people for helping me get to "The End" of this story. I couldn't have done it without some AMAZING people cheering me on.

To all the bloggers, bookstagrammers, booktokers, and readers who get excited, who post about my books, and who have shown me a sense of genuine community and support —thank you!

To all the authors who have been so kind and generous. Who have been so supportive.

A big thank you to the Hartley's Hustlers and my Girl Gang (not just for girls!). You rock! I cannot possibly tell you how much your support means to me! I appreciate everything you do to promote my books and to encourage me throughout my writing journey.

To Angela. I appreciate your attention to detail. Your encouragement and support. And your willingness to dive in on this adventure with me. Thank you for always being so on top of everything so that I can focus on the things and people I love.

To my editor, Lisa with Silently Correcting Your Grammar. I so appreciate your attention to detail, and your patience with my questions. My books wouldn't be the same without your eye. I value your insight and your friendship.

Thank you to Najla Qamber for designing such a gorgeous cover that really captures the feel of the story and characters. You always exceed all my expectations.

Thank you to Ellen, as always. Thank you for being so supportive and positive, for being a friend. Your comments are always priceless, and this book was no exception! You always help add the small details that provide a richer experience.

A huge thank you to Kristen for being such an amazing friend. I value your judgment and honesty, and I so appreciate your support. We've been through so much together, and I treasure your friendship and advice. Seriously, I cannot thank you enough for all that you do. You're always willing to read "just one more time," and I so appreciate it.

Thank you, Jade. You're always so helpful with pacing, both big picture and within the scenes. Thank you for helping me see where I can—and should—draw something out more.

Thank you to Brit! I love writing strong, badass female main characters, and you help ensure that they live up to their potential. And that the men who dare to love them do too.

Thank you to JudyAnnLovesBooks for all your insight. I'm sure you're as sick of saying "timeline" as I am of thinking about it. LOL But I appreciate you being honest. I know this book is stronger because of your suggestions.

And an extra special shoutout to JudyAnnLovesBooks for helping me brainstorm names for the hardware store mentioned in *A Love Like That*. I'm glad to know you appreciate punny names as much as I do.

Here are just a few of the ones we considered:
- Not Your Daddy's Hammer
- Laying Pipe
- Nailed It
- Getting Hammered

A huge thank you to all my beta readers. Thank you for making me a stronger writer, for offering your unique insight and advice. You each bring something different to the table, and I'm always amazed and impressed by your suggestions. I'm so incredibly honored to have you on my team!

Thank you to my husband for always encouraging me. For always supporting my dreams. You are better than any book boyfriend I could ever imagine.

And to my daughter, for always putting a smile on my face. For always asking about my stories and showing genuine excitement when I talk about them. You are spirited and independent, and I wouldn't have it any other way. Dream big, my darling.

Thank you to my parents for always being so encouraging. For reading my books. For being my biggest fans!

And to my in-laws for their continuing support!

Dear reader, if this list of people shows you anything, it's that dreams are often the effort of many. I'm grateful to have such an awesome team. And I'm honored that you've taken the time to read my words.

About the Author

Jenna Hartley is USA Today bestselling author who writes feel-good forbidden romance, much like her own real-life love story. She's known for writing strong women and swoon-worthy men, as well as blending panty-melting and heart-warming moments.

When she's not reading or writing romance, Jenna can be found tending to her growing indoor plant collection (pun intended), organizing, and hiking. She lives in Texas with her family and loves nothing more than a good book and good chocolate, except a dance party with her daughter.

www.authorjennahartley.com